SUPER EDITION
WARRIORS

TALLSTAR'S
REVENGE

WARRIORS

THE NEW PROPHECY

POWER OF THREE

OMEN OF THE STARS

DAWN OF THE CLANS

EXPLORE THE
WARRIORS WORLD

SUPER EDITION
WARRIORS
TALLSTAR'S REVENGE

ERIN HUNTER

HARPER

An Imprint of HarperCollinsPublishers

ISBN 978-0-06-221804-9 (trade bdg.)
ISBN 978-0-06-221805-6 (lib. bdg.)

Typography by Megan Stitt
13 14 15 16 17   LP/CG/RRDH   10 9 8 7 6 5 4 3 2 1
❖
First Edition

Special thanks to Kate Cary

ALLEGIANCES

WINDCLAN

LEADER HEATHERSTAR—pinkish-gray she-cat with blue eyes

DEPUTY REEDFEATHER—light brown tabby tom

MEDICINE CAT HAWKHEART—mottled gray-and-brown tom with yellow eyes

WARRIORS (toms and she-cats without kits)

MOOR RUNNERS (cats responsible for aboveground hunting and border patrols)

REDCLAW—dark ginger tom

HAREFLIGHT—light brown tom

ASPENFALL—gray-and-white tom
APPRENTICE, DOEPAW

CLOUDRUNNER—pale gray tom
APPRENTICE, STAGPAW

DAWNSTRIPE—pale gold tabby she-cat with creamy stripes

LARKSPLASH—tortoiseshell-and-white she-cat
APPRENTICE, RYEPAW

APPLEDAWN—rose-cream she-cat

TUNNELERS (cats specializing in hunting and digging tunnels belowground)

SANDGORSE—pale ginger tom

WOOLLYTAIL—gray-and-white tom

HICKORYNOSE—brown tom

MISTMOUSE—light brown tabby she-cat

PLUMCLAW—dark gray she-cat

APPRENTICES (more than six moons old, in training to become warriors)

DOEPAW—light brown she-cat

STAGPAW—dark brown tom

RYEPAW—gray tabby she-cat

QUEENS (she-cats expecting or nursing kits)

PALEBIRD—black-and-white she-cat

BRACKENWING—pale ginger she-cat

MEADOWSLIP—gray she-cat

ELDERS (former warriors and queens, now retired)

WHITEBERRY—small pure white tom

FLAMEPELT—dark ginger tom

LILYWHISKER—light brown she-cat

FLAILFOOT—black tom

SHADOWCLAN

LEADER **CEDARSTAR**—very dark gray tom with a white belly

DEPUTY **STONETOOTH**—gray tabby tom with long teeth

MEDICINE CAT **SAGEWHISKER**—white she-cat with long whiskers

WARRIORS

CROWTAIL—black tabby she-cat

BRACKENFOOT—pale ginger tom with dark ginger legs

ARCHEYE—gray tabby tom with black stripes and thick stripe over eye
APPRENTICE, FROGPAW

HOLLYFLOWER—dark-gray-and-white she-cat
APPRENTICE, NEWTPAW

MUDCLAW—gray tom with brown legs

TOADSKIP—dark brown tabby tom with white splashes and white legs
APPRENTICE, ASHPAW

NETTLESPOT—white she-cat with ginger flecks

MOUSEWING—thick-furred black tom

DEERLEAP—gray tabby she-cat with white legs

AMBERLEAF—dark orange she-cat with brown legs and ears

FINCHFLIGHT—black-and-white tom

BLIZZARDWING—mottled white tom

LIZARDSTRIPE—pale brown tabby she-cat with white belly

QUEENS

FEATHERSTORM—dark brown tabby

BRIGHTFLOWER—orange tabby

POOLCLOUD—gray-and-white she-cat

ELDERS

LITTLEBIRD—small ginger tabby she-cat

LIZARDFANG—light brown tabby tom with one hooked tooth

SILVERFLAME—orange-and-gray she-cat

THUNDERCLAN

LEADER   PINESTAR—red-brown tom with green eyes

DEPUTY   SUNFALL—bright ginger tom with yellow eyes

MEDICINE CAT   GOOSEFEATHER—speckled gray tom with pale blue eyes
APPRENTICE, FEATHERPAW

WARRIORS   STORMTAIL—blue-gray tom, blue eyes

DAPPLETAIL—tortoiseshell she-cat

ADDERFANG—mottled brown tabby tom with yellow eyes

TAWNYSPOTS—light gray tabby tom

HALFTAIL—big dark brown tabby tom with part of his tail missing and yellow eyes

SMALLEAR—gray tom with very small ears and amber eyes

ROBINWING—small, energetic brown she-cat with ginger patch on her chest and amber eyes
APPRENTICE, LEOPARDPAW

FUZZYPELT—black tom with fur that perpetually stands on end and yellow eyes
APPRENTICE, PATCHPAW

WINDFLIGHT—gray tabby tom with pale green eyes

QUEENS   **MOONFLOWER**—silver-gray she-cat with pale yellow eyes

POPPYDAWN—long-haired dark brown she-cat

ELDERS   **WEEDWHISKER**—pale orange tom with yellow eyes

MUMBLEFOOT—brown tom with amber eyes

LARKSONG—tortoiseshell she-cat with pale green eyes

RIVERCLAN

LEADER   **HAILSTAR**—thick-pelted gray tom

DEPUTY   **SHELLHEART**—dappled gray tom

MEDICINE CAT   **BRAMBLEBERRY**—white she-cat with black spotted fur, blue eyes, and a pink nose

WARRIORS   **RIPPLECLAW**—black-and-silver tabby tom

TIMBERFUR—brown tom
APPRENTICE, WHITEPAW

MUDFUR—long-haired light brown tom

OWLFUR—brown-and-white tom

OTTERSPLASH—pale ginger-and-white she-cat

MARSHCLOUD—brown tabby tom, stout and short-tailed

MUDTHORN—brown tom with black ears

BRIGHTSKY—nimble ginger-and-white she-cat

PIKETOOTH—skinny brown tabby tom with narrow face and protruding canine teeth

LAKESHINE—long-haired gray-and-white she-cat

SHIMMERPELT—night-black she-cat with glossy pelt

FALLOWTAIL—light brown she-cat with blue eyes
APPRENTICE, SOFTPAW

QUEENS   **ECHOMIST**—long-haired gray she-cat

LILYSTEM—pale gray she-cat

ELDERS   **TROUTCLAW**—gray tabby tom

TANGLEFUR—long-haired tabby with thick knotted pelt

BIRDSONG—tabby-and-white she-cat with ginger patches around her muzzle, flecked with gray

CATS OUTSIDE THE CLANS

SPARROW—dark brown tom

BESS—black she-cat with white paws

MOLE—dark gray tom

ALGERNON—creamy-brown tom

REENA—ginger she-cat

JAKE—ginger tom

QUINCE—gray she-cat

JAY—black-and-white she-cat

PIXIE—fluffy white she-cat

MARMALADE—large ginger tom

RED—orange she-cat

NUTMEG—tortoiseshell-and-white she-cat

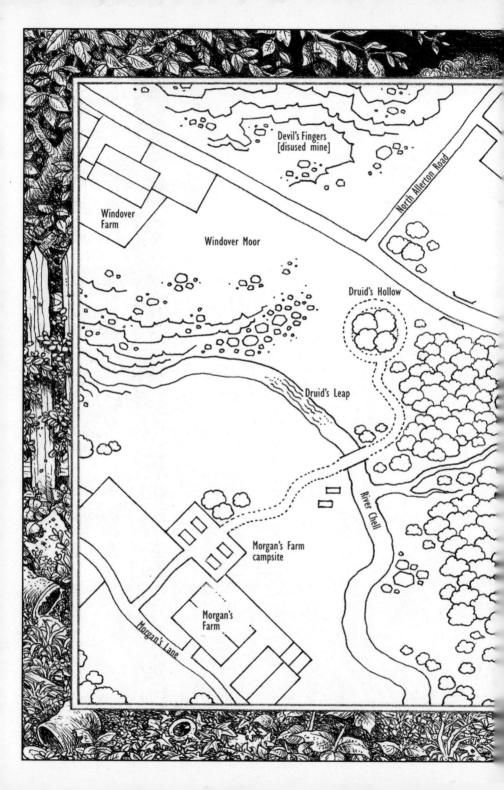

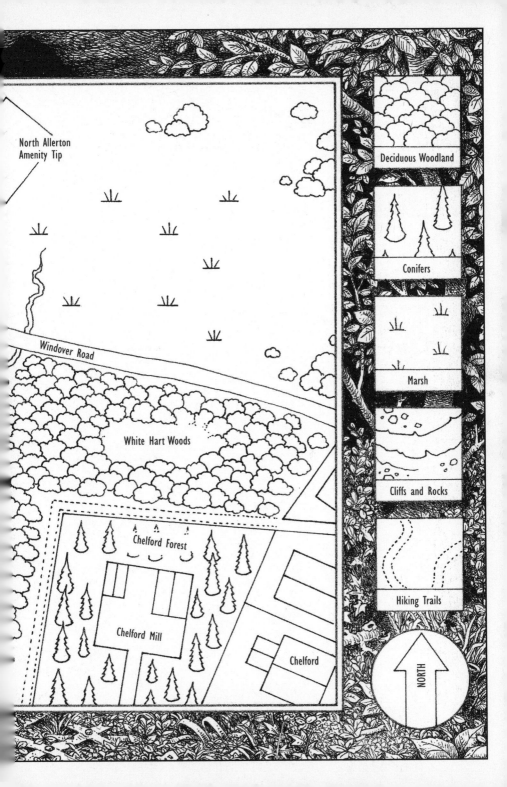

PROLOGUE

❧

The dark moor rose to meet the night-black sky. Starry pelts sparked like flint against the trembling heather. Grass streamed around the paws of WindClan's former warriors as they sat, whiskers stiff, unbowed by the wind.

"Welcome to StarClan, Heatherstar." A sleek tom with starshine glowing in his pelt faced the young WindClan leader. "I have watched you serve your Clanmates with bravery and loyalty as their deputy, and now I am honored to give you a life as their leader."

Heatherstar dipped her head. "Thank you, Thrushpelt."

"I died a medicine cat," the tom reminded her. "But before that, I was a warrior. I never hesitated to fight for what I knew to be right, however hard that seemed. I give you your eighth life and, with it, the courage to trust your instincts. When your heart speaks, *listen.*" Leaning forward, he touched his nose to Heatherstar's head.

As the new life pulsed through her, the gray cat groaned through clenched jaws.

Thrushpelt stepped back and glanced over his shoulder. "Daisytail?"

A light brown she-cat with ginger patches padded from

among her Clanmates, her fur blazing with silver light. "Do you know me?" she gently asked Heatherstar.

Heatherstar lifted her head and drew in a shuddering breath. "Yes! I have heard your name many times. You refused to let your kits fight against ShadowClan, and your insistence was so strong, it became part of the Clan code."

Daisytail nodded. "From then on, no kit was allowed to train for battle before they were six moons old. I would have taken on each of those ShadowClan warriors myself before I let my little ones suffer a single blow. Even though you do not have kits of your own, Heatherstar, I want you to share the strength of my conviction. For your ninth life I give you the force of a mother's love. Use it to protect your Clan." She pressed her muzzle to Heatherstar's head. "It is stronger than the wind and outlasts life itself."

Heatherstar rocked as a spasm gripped her. She lurched forward and stumbled onto her knees.

A mottled gray-brown tom stepped forward. "Heatherstar?" He leaned down to the new WindClan leader. "Are you okay?"

Daisytail flicked her tail. "She is strong, Hawkheart. I can feel it."

Heatherstar straightened up. "I'm fine," she told the tom. Trembling, she faced StarClan. "I promise that I will make WindClan a force to be respected among all the Clans of the forest. I will lead them well through my nine lives. And when I join you, I hope you will welcome me with pride at what I have achieved."

Murmurs of approval rose among the ranks of starry pelts.

"Remember," Daisytail called, "there is no power stronger than love!" As she spoke, StarClan blurred and began to spiral upward like a comet's tail, into the midnight sky.

"We should return to the Moonstone," Hawkheart murmured in Heatherstar's ear.

Heatherstar shook her head. "I'm not ready to leave StarClan."

Hawkheart watched the glimmering pelts fade. "But they've gone."

"Their scent remains." Heatherstar swished her tail stubbornly.

"Then I'll meet you at Mothermouth when you wake." Turning, Hawkheart padded down the slope, his pelt melting into the shadows until he was hardly visible against the heather. "The Clan will be waiting for us at home."

"I won't be long." Heatherstar watched the medicine cat vanish. Still unsteady, she climbed the moor, moving slowly at first but growing stronger with each step as the new lives throbbed beneath her fur. She broke into a run, charging across the windswept grass, her whiskers flattened against her face. She stopped suddenly as the moor dropped away. Balancing at the edge of the sandy precipice, Heatherstar gazed across woods and meadows stretching into darkness.

Paw steps sounded behind her. "Why do you linger here?" The mew was soft.

Heatherstar turned, blinking. The fading pelt of an ancient warrior shimmered in front of her. "I wanted to breathe the scents of StarClan for a while longer," she confessed. "Who . . . who are you?"

"I am Mothflight." The she-cat's green eyes shone. Behind her, the heather showed through her coat. Her pelt, once white, now glowed dimly, more starlight than fur.

"Mothflight?" Heatherstar's eyes widened. "You were WindClan's first medicine cat!"

Mothflight nodded.

"You discovered the Moonstone," Heatherstar whispered. "And now you've come to see *me*?"

"I watched your naming ceremony," Mothflight told her. "And waited for the others to leave so that I could speak with you alone."

"Do you have a prophecy for me?" Heatherstar curled her claws excitedly into the peaty soil.

"Not a prophecy, no. A warning, perhaps." Mothflight's voice was hardly more than a breath on the wind.

Heatherstar leaned closer, ears pricking.

"Listen carefully, Heatherstar," Mothflight insisted. "Whatever happens, do not demand the loyalty of your Clan."

Heatherstar lifted her head in surprise. "Of *course* I'll demand it! I've earned it."

"Warriors must decide for themselves where their loyalty lies."

"It should lie with the Clan and with me," Heatherstar hissed.

"But *you* cannot test it."

Heatherstar bristled. "I'm their *leader*."

Mothflight's tail twitched. "You are young. Wisdom will come with experience. Until then, let my words guide you."

Heatherstar snorted. "*I* will make the decisions for my Clan."

"Of course," Mothflight soothed. "But you don't yet realize that sometimes warriors must leave what they love before they understand what they truly value."

"Leave what they *love*?" Heatherstar echoed. "Do you mean their Clan?"

Mothflight stared back silently.

"Warriors who leave their Clan *betray* their Clan," Heatherstar spat. "*My* Clan will be loyal."

"There will be a warrior whose loyalty to WindClan will waver," Mothflight told her. "A cat who will have to seek far beyond the confines of your territory to discover where his heart truly lies."

Heatherstar curled her lip. "Are you telling me that one of my Clan will turn *rogue*?"

Mothflight blinked, her eyes like green stars. "He will stray, and you must let him, even if you fear he will never return. It is the only way he will discover where he truly belongs."

CHAPTER 1

Be careful, Tallkit!

Tallkit paused when he heard Palebird's anxious call. "I'll be okay!" he mewed. He glanced back at the nursery. The warm, milky scent of his mother drifted from the entrance.

Inside the thick gorse den, Brackenwing soothed her. "Barkkit and Shrewkit will watch out for him, I promise."

Tallkit shivered. This was only his second sunrise outside the nursery, and his paws pricked with excitement. A light dusting of snow had turned the camp white, frosting the tussocky grass and thick heather walls. The freezing air stung his nose. He fluffed up his fur.

Barkkit pawed at the white tip of Tallkit's black tail. "You look like you're turning to ice as well."

Tallkit flicked his tail away, purring with amusement. His white muzzle and white paws would just make it easier for him to hide in the snow!

Shrewkit bounced past him. "Let's show him the Hunting Stones, Barkkit!"

Tallkit stared at his denmates. They were three moons older and twice his size, but he was determined to keep up with them. "I thought we were going to climb Tallrock again," he protested. "I *know* I'll make it this time." His eyes stung in the bright, cold air. He'd only opened them for the first time a few sunrises ago and they were still slowly adjusting to sunlight after the cozy gloom of the nursery.

He blinked up at the high slab of granite where Barkkit had told him Heatherstar stood to address the Clan. It loomed, jagged and dark, from a wide, sandy crater, which encircled it like an empty pool.

The Meeting Hollow.

Tallkit gazed into it wide-eyed. At the bottom, Heatherstar, Hawkheart, and Reedfeather huddled beside the stone, their breath billowing as they spoke.

Hawkheart looked up and caught Tallkit's eye over the rim. "Our youngest kit is exploring again," he murmured.

Tallkit shifted his paws. The dark glint in the medicine cat's gaze made him nervous. Palebird had warned him to stay away from the gray-brown tom; he had little patience for kits.

"Stay under cover, Tallkit." Hawkheart narrowed his eyes. "We don't want you attracting buzzards to the camp."

"Buzzards?" Tallkit's heart lurched.

"Kits are their favorite prey," Hawkheart warned. "And they can spot you from Highstones."

Reedfeather's whiskers twitched. "Don't scare the poor kit." There was a purr in his throat as he nodded to Shrewkit, who had popped up beside Tallkit. "What are you showing him today?"

Shrewkit flicked his tail. "The Hunting Stones."

Heatherstar shook frost from her thick gray pelt. "Be careful," she cautioned. "The stones will be icy."

"Don't come mewling to me if you sprain a paw," Hawkheart called.

"Come," the WindClan leader urged her deputy and medicine cat. "It's too cold to sit here. Let's go to my den."

As Heatherstar hopped out of the Meeting Hollow, Hawkheart and Reedfeather followed, their tails twitching as they ducked into the shelter of the leader's den beneath a gorse bush at the far end of the clearing.

"Can we play sliding in the hollow?" Barkkit mewed.

"I want to go to the Hunting Stones," Shrewkit insisted. He scraped up a pawful of snow and flung it at Barkkit. The wind snatched the flakes and tossed them back into his whiskers.

As he sneezed, Barkkit purred with amusement. "Wow! You're scary!"

"I'll show you!" Shrewkit hurled himself at his brother and sent him rolling over the grass.

Tallkit backed away as their dark brown pelts scuffed the snow. *It must be fun to have a littermate to play fight with. If only Finchkit hadn't died.*

Shrewkit leaped free of his brother's grip. "Look at Tallkit!" he teased. "He's blinking like he's just opened his eyes!"

Tallkit bristled. "I'm nearly half a moon old and Sandgorse says I opened my eyes quicker than *any* kit in the nursery." He glared at his denmates. "I'm just not used to snow." The ground sparkled, and the heather that formed the camp boundary—so dark against the sky yesterday—now glittered brightly with frost. What would the moor look like when the heavy snows came and the world turned completely white? Palebird had warned Tallkit that leaf-bare hit WindClan hardest of all the Clans, because the moor touched the sky. But this also made them more special, and safer.

"We're closer to Silverpelt than any Clan," she'd told him as she snuggled him in their mossy nest. "Which means that StarClan watches us more closely."

Tallkit heard worry in her mew. "Is that why we tunnel under the moor?" he asked. "To hide from the dead warriors in other Clans?"

"Don't be silly." Palebird had licked his ear. "We tunnel because we're stronger and cleverer than all the other Clans together." Her washing became brisker, silencing him.

"I'm going to the Hunting Stones!" Shrewkit charged across the grass.

Barkkit raced after him. "What about sliding in the hollow?"

"There's not enough snow for real sliding." Shrewkit veered away from Tallrock.

"You're just scared." Barkkit swerved after his brother, sending a shower of frozen flakes up from his paws.

"Am not!" Shrewkit called back.

Tallkit followed, not caring where they chose to play. It felt great to be outside, the grass cold on his pads as he raced across it.

"Watch out!"

Tallkit skidded to a halt as Cloudrunner yowled at him. The pale gray tom was crossing his path with Aspenfall. The warriors were heading to the prey heap, carrying fresh-kill. Wind-ruffled from the moor, they'd brought food for the Clan. Tallkit gazed at them, impressed by their long legs and wiry tails. They were moor runners, which meant they served WindClan by hunting and patroling the borders, and Tallkit could smell heather on their pelts.

In the brittle patch of bracken where the tunnelers made their nests, Woollytail looked up from washing his mud-streaked belly. Like all the cats who served the Clan by carving out new tunnels and shoring up old ones far beneath the moor, his pelt was permanently stained with sand and dust. He nodded at the rabbit swinging from Cloudrunner's jaws. "Did you catch that on the high-moor?"

"Yes." At the prey heap, Cloudrunner kicked away a stale mouse left from the previous day's hunt and dropped his catch. "You're right, as usual, Woollytail."

Tallkit blinked at Woollytail. "How did you know?"

"I can smell the sand in its fur." Woollytail flicked his tail and returned to washing.

Hickorynose, his tunnelmate, shifted on the bracken beside him. "You only find sand tunnels on the high-moor." The brown tom lifted a forepaw and rubbed dirt from his ear. "Not like the gorge tunnel. *That's* all soil and grit. But it'll open the way to fresh prey beside the river."

Cloudrunner snorted. "If you ever find a way to stop the cave-ins."

Aspenfall laid a vole beside the rabbit. "The grit makes it

unstable. It's not safe to tunnel there."

Woollytail narrowed his eyes. "It is if you know what you're doing."

Tallkit glanced from tunneler to moor runner as an awkward silence fell between them.

Heatherstar cut through it. She padded from her den and followed the rim of the Meeting Hollow. Passing the grass nests of the moor runners, she brushed by Cloudrunner and stopped beside the bracken patch. "Will the new tunnels be ready before newleaf, Woollytail?"

Woollytail sniffed. "It takes time to shore up the roofs."

Heatherstar flicked her tail. "I'm sure you'll find a way." She turned back to the prey heap and sniffed Cloudrunner's rabbit.

Does Heatherstar ever patrol underground? Tallkit watched the WindClan leader curiously. She'd trained as a moor runner, but surely as leader, she needed to understand what it was like to be a tunneler too.

"Hurry up, Tallkit!" Barkkit called.

Tallkit jerked his attention away and scurried after his denmates. Barkkit and Shrewkit were already at the Hunting Stones. The smooth, low rocks huddled like rabbits in the grass near the elders' den. Sprigs of heather poked between them and moss clumped at their base. Shrewkit leaped onto the highest stone and crowed down at Barkkit. "I am leader of the Hunting Stones!"

Barkkit scrambled onto the boulder beside him. "I'm deputy!"

Tallkit reached the rocks and waded through the thick

moss at the bottom. Reaching up with his forepaws, he kicked out with his hind legs and tried to jump up beside Barkkit. His claws slithered on the frosty stone and he slid back into the chilly moss.

"Hey, Wormkit!" Shrewkit called down. "Why don't you tunnel underneath? You're not supposed to be a moor runner like us!"

Tallkit's pelt pricked with confusion. "I'm not Wormkit. I'm *Tall*kit!"

"You're going to spend your life wriggling underground like a worm, aren't you?" Shrewkit taunted. "That's where you should be now—*under* the rocks, not on them."

Tallkit frowned. He knew that his mother and father were tunnelers, but did that really mean he couldn't play on the Hunting Stones?

Barkkit reached down with his forepaw. "Ignore him and try again, Tallkit!" he mewed.

Tallkit leaped for his denmate's paw and felt it curl beneath his own. He churned his hind legs while Barkkit heaved. Scrabbling against the stone, he flung himself onto the rock. "Thanks!" He sat up beside Barkkit, his pads stinging on the frozen rock.

He gazed across the camp. Sun shone from a crisp, blue sky, thawing the grassy hummocks, which bulged like clumped fur across the frosty clearing. The tunnelers' bracken patch glowed orange while the long grass enclosing the moor runners' nests drooped lower as the frost slowly loosened its grip.

A white face appeared at the entrance of the elders' den.

"You young'uns are up early." Whiteberry slid out and sat gingerly on the cold grass a tail-length from the Hunting Stones.

Lilywhisker limped after him and stood tasting the air. She was the youngest in the elders' den, far younger than Whiteberry, Flamepelt, and Flailfoot. She'd retired to the den after a tunnel collapse had smashed her hind leg and left it useless. "Do you want to come onto the moor?" she asked Whiteberry.

The white elder looked at her. "So long as you don't try to get me down any rabbit holes."

"Not after last time," Lilywhisker purred. "I've never seen a cat chased out of a tunnel by a rabbit."

Whiteberry shifted his paws. "I *thought* it was a fox."

"Your sense of smell must be worn out." Flicking her tail teasingly, Lilywhisker hopped toward the camp entrance. Her lifeless hind leg left a trail through the shallow snow.

Whiteberry heaved himself to his paws and followed. "Yours will wear out too after a few more moons sharing a den with Flailfoot. He's got fox-breath."

"It's not that bad," Lilywhisker called over her shoulder.

"Do you want to swap nests?" Whiteberry caught up to her. "Last night he snored right in my muzzle. I dreamed I'd fallen into a badger den."

As they disappeared into the heather tunnel, a pale ginger tom nosed his way past them, heading into camp. *Sandgorse!* Tallkit lifted his tail as his father trotted into the clearing.

The ginger warrior's pelt was speckled with earth. "I've left a stack of sticks at the tunnel entrance," he called to Woollytail.

The gray-and-white tunneler lifted his nose. "Great!" he meowed. "We can start shoring up the roof this afternoon."

"You'll have to manage without me." Sandgorse headed toward the Hunting Stones. "Tallkit! I want to show you something."

Tallkit blinked excitedly at his father. "What is it?" Was Sandgorse going to show him the moor? Tallkit slid off the rock and scrambled over the tussocky grass. He skidded to a halt at Sandgorse's paws.

Sandgorse licked a sprig of moss from Tallkit's ear and spat it onto the grass. "It's time you learned to dig."

Disappointment dropped like a stone in Tallkit's belly. He didn't want to dig. He wanted to see the moor and feel the wind in his pelt.

"Tallkit's going to go worming!" Shrewkit jeered from the Hunting Stones.

Tallkit spun around crossly. "Worms don't *dig*!"

"Ignore Shrewkit!" Barkkit stepped in front of his litter-mate. "He's just teasing."

Sandgorse snorted. "Typical moor-kit, scared of getting sand in his eyes." He headed for the tunnelers' bracken patch. Tallkit scrambled after him and ducked under Sandgorse's belly as he stopped beside Woollytail's nest. Tallkit peeped out, relishing the warmth of his father's fur on his spine.

"Do you think sticks will be strong enough to hold up the roof?" Sandgorse wondered.

Woollytail frowned. "They'll do until we can roll stones into place."

"Perhaps we should take a different route to the gorge." Above Tallkit's head, Sandgorse's belly twitched.

Woollytail shook his head. "We can't be far from clay now. It'll be harder digging, but there'll be fewer cave-ins."

Sandgorse glanced toward the elders' den. Tallkit guessed he was thinking about Lilywhisker's crushed leg. "Perhaps we should explore the rabbit warrens higher up. There may be a clay seam there we can dig into."

"But we've made so much progress over leaf-bare," Woollytail argued. "It'd be a shame to start again." The tom's muscular shoulders twitched. They were as wide and toned as Sandgorse's.

Will I have shoulders like that when I'm a tunneler? Tallkit's gaze strayed across the camp to Cloudrunner and Aspenfall. They were much sleeker: built for speed, not strength. Tallkit wondered what it felt like to run across the moor with the wind rushing through his fur. Surely that would be better than being squashed underground? He imagined his ears and nose filling up with mud, and shuddered.

"Come on, Tallkit." Sandgorse's mew broke into his thoughts. His father was heading for the moor runners' nests. Tallkit scampered after him and followed him past the swishing stalks to a patch of bare earth behind Tallrock.

"There's good digging here," Sandgorse explained, running his paw over the ground. "This is where I first learned to tunnel."

Tallkit gazed down at the churned earth and wondered how many times this patch had been dug and refilled, ready for new tunnelers to practice. "Don't you ever get bored of digging?" he mewed.

"Being a tunneler doesn't just mean digging," Sandgorse retorted. "Hollowing out new earthroutes is part of being a tunneler. But we patrol them, too, and it's a great place to hunt, especially during leaf-bare. Don't forget, that's why Shattered Ice first tunneled through the rabbit warrens."

Tallkit already knew the legend of Shattered Ice. It was one of the first nursery stories Palebird ever told him. Long ago, the moor was gripped by the worst leaf-bare the Clan had ever known. There was no prey to be found in the snow-drowned stretches of heather and gorse. So one of WindClan's bravest warriors had gone into the rabbit warrens and dug deep beyond them in search of food for their Clan.

"He cared more for his Clan than his own safety," Sandgorse meowed solemnly. "And he didn't have any of the training or experience we have now."

He had only his courage and strength. Tallkit stifled a yawn.

"He had only his courage and strength," Sandgorse went on. "WindClan has tunneled ever since, learning more with each generation." He lifted his chin. "Without its tunnelers, WindClan would have suffered many hungry, preyless moons."

Tallkit's pelt pricked guiltily. How could he dream of running across the moors like Cloudrunner and Aspenfall? One day his Clan would depend on him. He should be proud to follow in his father's paw steps. Unsheathing his claws, he began to scrape at the earth, sending it showering behind him.

"Wait." Sandgorse swept his tail over Tallkit's spine. "You're not digging a hole to make dirt."

Tallkit sat back and shook his head to dislodge some flakes of dirt. There were different ways to dig?

Sandgorse thrust a paw into the soft soil and scooped out a lump of earth. Pushing it firmly to one side, he dug another. Within moments, he was hollowing out dirt, paw over paw, while a pile grew beside him, neat and compact. Tallkit felt a quiver of pride. His father looked strong and determined, as if there was no hole he couldn't dig, no earth he couldn't shape with his paws.

"Let me try." Tallkit reached down past his father and gouged out a pawful of the crumbling earth.

Sandgorse sat back. Tallkit felt his father's gaze on his pelt, warmer than sunshine. He dug harder, dragging up pawfuls and throwing them into a loose pile beside his fast-growing hole. "I'm tunneling!" he squeaked.

"Watch out!"

As Sandgorse mewed a warning, Tallkit's flank bumped his dig-pile. Cold, crumbly soil cascaded around his ears. It sprinkled over his muzzle, making him sneeze. He sat up, shaking out his fur, and stared crossly at the earth that was still showering into his hole.

Sandgorse pressed his paw against the pile to stop the flow. "Your dig-pile is as important as your hole. You must keep it compact. Press your dug-earth down firmly or you'll have to dig every pawful twice."

Tallkit frowned. This was harder than he thought.

Concentrating, he dove back into his hole and hauled up a fresh pawful of soil. He carefully patted it into the side of his dig-pile. This time it stayed where he put it, and he reached into the hole with both paws and began scooping, paw over paw, taking time to press each lump into his pile just as Sandgorse had done.

"Very good, Tallkit." There was pride in Sandgorse's mew.

Tallkit swallowed back a purr and kept digging. The hole was so deep now that his hind legs ached each time he reached down.

"Slow down," Sandgorse warned.

"I'm okay—" As Tallkit answered, his hind paws shot out from beneath him. Muzzle first, he crashed into the hole. Pain seared through his paws as they twisted the wrong way, his claws bending back as they caught on the soil. A wave of earth smothered him, choking him and pushing him farther into the hole. *Help! I'm being buried alive!*

Teeth sank into his tail, dragging him up. "Are you okay?" Sandgorse let go and stared into Tallkit's face.

"No!" Tallkit's muzzle throbbed and his claws burned. "I can't do this! I hate digging holes, and I don't want to be a tunneler!" A wail rose in his belly as soil stung his eyes. "Palebird!" Chest heaving, he turned and raced for the nursery.

CHAPTER 2

❧

Sandgorse bounded after him. "*You were* doing really well."

"I was not!" Anger surged through Tallkit as his eyes watered from the grit. "I fell in! And hurt my claws!" He stumbled to a halt outside the nursery and held up a paw.

"You just snagged them. They'll be okay."

Tallkit blinked through tears. "You don't know that!" Hazily he spotted Palebird's black-and-white pelt at the nursery entrance.

"Tallkit!" She slid onto the grass. "What happened?"

Tallkit flung himself against her soft fur. "I fell in and soil got in my eyes." He screwed them up as Palebird began to lap at them gently.

"Is that better?" She paused and waited while he opened them gingerly. The stinging had stopped. He shook his head, spraying earth from his ears.

"I hurt my paws, too."

Palebird leaned down and sniffed them. "They're fine," she mewed. "Let's go inside."

"Tallkit!" Sandgorse stepped closer. "You can't give up yet!"

"Leave him," Palebird murmured. "He's frightened."

19

Tallkit glanced over his shoulder. Sandgorse's green eyes were round with worry. "I'll try again later," he meowed reluctantly.

"We'll see." Palebird nosed him gently into the den.

"He's got to learn—"

Tallkit didn't hear the rest of his father's mew. Palebird's fur was swishing in his ears as she guided him to their nest. He curled into the soft sheepswool lining. "Where's Brackenwing?" Barkkit's mother was gone. "And Mistmouse?" The ginger queen's nest was empty and there was no sign of Ryekit, Doekit, or Stagkit.

"Brackenwing's at the prey heap." Palebird settled into the nest beside him. "Mistmouse went hunting."

"Hunting?" Queens didn't hunt. They looked after their kits.

Palebird sighed. "She's missed being out on the moor these past moons. And her kits don't need her anymore."

The entrance to the nursery rustled as Brackenwing pushed her way in. She carried with her the scent of fresh rabbit. "Who's missed the moor?" Heather rustled as she settled into her nest.

"Mistmouse," Palebird told her.

Brackenwing ran her tongue around her lips. "I haven't felt the wind in my fur for too long," she mewed wistfully.

Tallkit nestled against Palebird. "Do you miss being underground?" She'd been a tunneler before he'd been born.

"Of course."

Tallkit wasn't convinced. Who'd *want* to spend the day in the dark?

Brackenwing flicked her tail over her paws. "You won't be tunneling for a while, Palebird." The ginger queen's mew sounded ominous.

Tallkit's gaze flicked anxiously toward his mother. "Why not?"

"My kitting was hard. I lost Finchkit." Palebird shifted beside him. "It'll take me a bit longer to recover."

Tallkit searched her gaze. He could never tell whether his mother was sad or just tired. "Why did Finchkit die? Did you kit her wrong?"

"Hush!"

Brackenwing's sharp mew surprised him. Had he said something bad? Palebird *liked* talking about Finchkit. "Did StarClan want her?" he pressed.

Palebird sighed. "I guess they did."

But not me. Why had StarClan left him with Palebird? Perhaps they wanted him to cheer her up. "What color was Finchkit's pelt?" Tallkit asked.

Palebird's gaze clouded. "Ginger, like your father's."

"I don't know why you gave Finchkit a name," Brackenwing muttered.

"She *needed* a name," Palebird answered.

"She only lived for a moment." Brackenwing frowned. "StarClan would have named her."

Tallkit felt his mother tremble. Talking about Finchkit didn't seem to be cheering her up. He pawed at her cheek softly, trying to distract her. "I've got sand in my ears."

"Have you, dear?" Palebird leaned down and began washing his ear fur.

Relieved to feel her soften beside him, Tallkit snuggled closer. He didn't even remember Finchkit. *Am I supposed to?*

A shadow darkened the nursery entrance. "Have you calmed him down yet?" Sandgorse stuck his head through the gorse. "The sooner he starts digging again, the better."

"I've just gotten him cleaned up," Palebird objected.

"We'll practice some other skills," Sandgorse promised.

Tallkit ducked out from under his mother's muzzle. "Are you sure it's okay?" he mewed, blinking up at her. He didn't want to leave Palebird if she was still sad, but Sandgorse sounded so eager for him to go.

"Whatever you want, dear." Her gaze drifted away.

Tallkit felt a jab of disappointment. Didn't she want him to stay? He stood up. *She wants me to train so I can be as strong as Sandgorse.* He clambered over the side of the nest. "See you later."

Palebird didn't answer. She was staring blankly at the den wall.

"Come on, Tallkit." Sandgorse brushed his way through the nursery entrance.

Tallkit followed. He was pleased to see his father's gaze brighten as slithered onto the snowy grass beside him.

"I knew one little fall wouldn't put you off." Sandgorse whisked Tallkit forward with his tail. "Let's practice moving stones. Tunnelers have to learn to move rocks much heavier than themselves."

"Really?" Tallkit scampered at his side as they crossed the camp.

"It's an important skill." Sandgorse nodded toward a row

of rocks clustered beside the elders' den. "Let's try these. Just small ones to begin with."

Small ones? Tallkit stared at the stones. They were as big as sparrows.

Sandgorse stopped beside the nearest, and beckoned Tallkit closer with a twitch of his tail. "Grab it with your forepaws, and use your weight to roll it toward you."

Tallkit swallowed. "Won't it squash me?"

"The first rule of tunneling is that you're always stronger than you think," Sandgorse told him.

Brown fur flashed at the corner of Tallkit's gaze.

"I touched your tail! *You're* the rabbit now!"

"Did not!"

"Did so."

Shrewkit and Barkkit were chasing each other over the Hunting Stones. Heather sprigs quivered in their wake.

Sandgorse nudged the rock toward Tallkit. "Roll this one."

Tallkit stared at it.

"Why do I always have to be the rabbit?"

"You don't!"

Flattening his ears to block out the sound of his denmates playing, Tallkit reached up and rested his forepaws on the rock. With a grunt, he tried to heave it toward him. His belly tightened with the effort, but the stone didn't move.

"Let's try a smaller one." Sandgorse pushed another stone closer.

As Tallkit reached for it, Flailfoot padded out of the elders' den. His black pelt moved like a shadow against the frosty gorse. "He's a bit young to be moving rocks."

Sandgorse sniffed. "It's never too early to start learning tunneling skills."

Flailfoot sat down. "I didn't move my first stone till I was an apprentice."

Tallkit gritted his teeth. *I'm going to move it!* Hissing under his breath, he heaved. His claws slipped. His hind legs buckled. With a gasp, he fell backward and landed on his tail.

"Nice move, Wormkit!" Shrewkit called from the Hunting Stones.

Tallkit turned on him, ears flat. "I'm *learning!*"

"Take no notice," Sandgorse advised. "Shrewkit thinks like a moor runner. He doesn't understand patience."

Tallkit's heart sank. Would he have to spend the whole day trying to shift this dumb rock while Shrewkit and Barkkit played Rabbit on the Hunting Stones?

Heatherstar's mew rang through the cold air. "Let all cats old enough to catch prey gather beneath Tallrock."

Tallkit jerked around. The WindClan leader stood on top of the dark stone in the middle of the Meeting Hollow.

"Wait here," Sandgorse ordered. He trotted across camp and bounded into the sandy hollow.

Flailfoot brushed past Tallkit. "Try starting with a smaller stone," he suggested as he headed after Sandgorse.

Tallkit sat back on his haunches and watched his Clanmates streaming toward Tallrock. Aspenfall and Cloudrunner bounded down into the snow-whitened circle, lithe and light-footed. Redclaw and Dawnstripe followed. Meadowslip and

Larksplash were already staring up expectantly at Heatherstar. They shifted to let the other moor runners settle beside them.

Sandgorse headed for the opposite end of the hollow, where the tunnelers sat, and stopped beside Woollytail and Hickorynose. Flailfoot jumped stiffly down beside them. Tail high, the old tunneler nodded to Reedfeather. The WindClan deputy, who was sitting at the foot of Tallrock, dipped his head in return.

Barkkit bounced toward Tallkit, eyes bright. "Aren't you coming?" Shrewkit was already scrambling away across the tussocks.

Tallkit blinked. "But we're not old enough to catch prey."

"How do you know?" Barkkit shrugged. "You've never tried. Besides, we won't sit with the warriors. We can watch from over there." He pointed with his nose to where Shrewkit was threading his way through the long grass that edged the moor runners' nests. "Come on."

As Tallkit scampered after Barkkit, the camp entrance shivered. Lilywhisker and Whiteberry hurried in.

"Have they started?" Lilywhisker called to Flailfoot as she limped across camp.

"Not yet." Flailfoot padded to the edge of the hollow and reached up to steady Lilywhisker as she scrambled down on her three good legs. She joined the tunnelers while Whiteberry headed for the moor runners on the far side of the hollow.

Mistmouse paced the rim, brushing past her mate,

Hareflight. The brown tom stood as stiff as the trunk of a gorse bush, as though his claws had taken root. Tallkit paused beside the moor runners' nests and watched them curiously. Mistmouse's kits, Ryekit, Stagkit, and Doekit, were standing beside the two warriors.

"In here." Barkkit nudged Tallkit into the grass beside Shrewkit.

Tallkit pushed through the long stems. "What are *they* doing at the hollow?" He jerked his nose toward Hareflight's kits.

"I don't know." Barkkit burrowed deeper into the grass and peeped out.

"Hush!" Shrewkit hissed beside them. "I'm trying to hear." His yellow eyes were fixed on the Meeting Hollow.

Heatherstar sprang down from Tallrock and weaved past her Clanmates until she reached the center. Mistmouse was fiercely smoothing the fur between Stagkit's ears. Hareflight nudged Doekit and Ryekit closer to the edge.

"Ryekit, Doekit, and Stagkit!" Heatherstar called.

Tallkit felt Barkkit stiffen beside him. "It's their apprentice ceremony!"

Tallkit leaned forward.

"Woollytail will get one of them," Shrewkit guessed.

"But Hareflight's a moor runner," Barkkit reminded him.

"So?" Shrewkit whispered. "Woollytail's been complaining for ages that WindClan needs more tunnelers. And Mistmouse will want at least one of her kits to follow in her paw steps." He glanced at Tallkit. "I feel sorry for you. Being a tunneler must be awful."

Tallkit scowled at him. "Sandgorse says it's the noblest warrior life."

"Sandgorse would," Shrewkit scoffed. "He's had so much mud in his ears it's probably filled up his head."

Tallkit unsheathed his claws, anger surging beneath his pelt. "That's not true!"

Barkkit pressed against him softly. "Just watch the ceremony," he murmured.

Stagkit was leading his sisters into the hollow. Ryekit's paws slipped and she slithered down the icy slope. Warm purrs rumbled around her as she straightened and shook out her soft gray fur.

"Rye*paw*." Heatherstar met her gaze. The new apprentice's eyes widened. "Your mentor will be Larksplash." Ryepaw purred loudly as Larksplash stepped from among the moor runners and touched her head with her muzzle.

Heatherstar flicked her tail. "Larksplash, share your speed and sharp eyes with Ryepaw so that she too may become a warrior worthy of WindClan." The WindClan leader turned to Doekit. "Doepaw," she meowed. "Your mentor will be Aspenfall."

Aspenfall pricked his ears, blinking, as though surprised.

Doepaw's pale brown pelt pricked excitedly. She puffed out her chest as Aspenfall crossed the hollow to greet her. "Aspenfall," Heatherstar meowed. "Share your courage and strength with Doepaw." Aspenfall dipped his head and touched his nose to Doepaw's ear.

Behind them, Stagkit gazed at his Clanmates.

He must be trying to guess who his mentor will be. Tallkit held his breath, as excited as if it were his own apprentice ceremony.

"It looks like poor old Stagkit gets Woollytail," Shrewkit muttered.

"Stagpaw," Heatherstar began, "your mentor will be Cloud-runner."

Shrewkit gasped. *"Cloudrunner?"*

"He's not a tunneler," Barkkit breathed.

Tallkit felt a flash of relief for his former denmate. *Stagpaw won't have to train underground!* Then guilt pricked him. He should be feeling sorry that Stagpaw would never be the noblest of warriors.

Heatherstar went on. "Cloudrunner, share your hunting skill and agility with your apprentice so he may feed his Clans for many moons to come."

Yowls of approval rose from the moor runners.

"Stagpaw!"

"Ryepaw!"

"Doepaw!"

On the rim of the hollow, Mistmouse and Hareflight twined their tails together, their eyes shining with pride.

"Cloudrunner?" Woollytail's mew rose above the cheers. Confusion clouded his yellow gaze.

Hickorynose narrowed his eyes. "Why wasn't an apprentice given to a tunneler?" he demanded.

"What's going on?" A mew sounded from the camp entrance. A gray she-cat stared at her Clanmates. Her pelt was dusted with soil.

Mistmouse turned. "Hi, Plumclaw." She shifted her paws uneasily as she faced her tunneling denmate. "I'm afraid you missed the naming ceremony."

"Did Woollytail get his apprentice?" The she-cat's gaze flashed with hope.

Woollytail shook his head. "They're training as moor runners."

"All of them?" Plumclaw's eyes widened.

Heatherstar stepped forward. "Aspenfall, Cloudrunner, and Larksplash are going to mentor Mistmouse's kits."

Plumclaw stared at Mistmouse. "Don't you want *any* of them to follow in your paw steps?"

Mistmouse dropped her gaze. Hareflight pressed close to his mate. "We've decided that we want them all to be moor runners."

"Tunneling is dangerous work," Mistmouse pointed out. "Our kits are good runners, like their father. They'll be better hunting the moors than the tunnels."

Hickorynose took a step forward, his fur bristling. "But we need more tunneler apprentices."

Behind him, Sandgorse swished his tail. "At least we'll have Tallkit in a few moons."

Tallkit's belly tightened.

"Lucky little Wormkit," Shrewkit teased.

Tallkit glared at him. "Shut up!"

Heatherstar padded toward the tunnelers. "I know you're disappointed, but Mistmouse and Hareflight want their kits to train as moor runners."

Hickorynose met her gaze. "The Clan needs tunnelers as well, Heatherstar."

"I understand your disappointment," Heatherstar

answered softly. "But Leafshine's death is still fresh in our memories."

Tallkit had heard Palebird and Brackenwing talking about the tunneler killed by the same cave-in that had crippled Lilywhisker.

"I had to respect Mistmouse and Hareflight's wishes," the WindClan leader continued.

Hickorynose dipped his head. "I guess."

Heatherstar went on. "When newleaf comes and the earth is drier, the tunnels will be safer and better for training."

Woollytail pushed past Hickorynose. "Why didn't you warn us we weren't getting an apprentice?"

Reedfeather took a pace forward. "Would you have accepted it any more easily if we had?"

Plumclaw called from the top of the hollow. "We would have known that you still respected us!"

Heatherstar lifted her chin. "Of course WindClan respects its tunnelers," she insisted. "When leaf-bare brings endless moons of snow, our tunnelers always bring us prey. We value your skills, and we want to help you keep them alive through future moons."

A growl rumbled in Woollytail's throat. "How, when you give us no apprentices to train?"

"You will have more apprentices eventually." Heatherstar flicked her tail. "For now, the ceremony is over." She turned to Cloudrunner. "Show your apprentices their territory." She dipped her head to Aspenfall and Larksplash. "Train them well."

Tallkit felt a flicker of unease as Cloudrunner hopped out

of the hollow and led Stagpaw to the camp entrance. Lark-splash, Aspenfall, Ryepaw, and Doepaw bounded after them. *How would the tunnelers get more apprentices?* Tallkit wondered. Shrewkit and Barkkit would be moor runners. Was Tallkit going to have to keep the tunnelers' skills alive all by himself?

Barkkit pressed close to him. "Sandgorse will make sure that Heatherstar chooses a tunneler mentor when it's your naming ceremony."

"Yeah." Tallkit tried to sound enthusiastic. Did he really want to spend the rest of his moons digging holes and heaving rocks?

"Redclaw, Appledawn, Hareflight!" Reedfeather called to the moor runners. "The prey heap is low. We must hunt."

Redclaw's nose twitched. "Rabbit will be easy to scent in this weather."

Appledawn sprang out of the hollow and headed for the entrance, her pale cream pelt rosy in the low sunshine.

Hareflight raced after her. "Let's hunt the high outcrops."

Tallkit watched the muscles ripple beneath Hareflight's pelt as the pale brown tom reached the camp entrance in three easy bounds. Longing pricked his belly. *I want to race on the moors. I want to be pulled by the wind, and chase rabbits beneath the big, blue sky.* Would he ever feel the same way about running through tunnels in the dark?

CHAPTER 3

Thick snow smothered the high-moor, but in the camp's sheltered dip, the heather and grass was tinged green with the promise of newleaf. Tallkit could feel the prick of fresh stems beneath his paws as he skimmed across the tussocks. Barkkit fled ahead of him, tail whipping as he plunged down into the Meeting Hollow.

Tallkit reached the edge and leaped, sailing fast and high before landing skillfully and racing on without missing a paw step. Barkkit charged ahead, kicking sand in his wake. Excitement pulsed through Tallkit's paws as he gained ground on his denmate. *He's two moons older and I'm still faster!* Tallkit pushed harder as Barkkit reached the far slope of the hollow and scrambled out.

Tallkit jumped easily up the slope, clearing it as Barkkit dived for cover beneath the thick gorse beyond. He slowed to a halt, stopping a whisker from the barrage of thorns. Pelt twitching, he paced along the edge of gorse, swishing his tail. "I know you're in there, mouse! I'm going to pull your tail!"

"Never!" Barkkit purred.

"Come out and face me, rabbit-heart!"

"Come and get me, buzzard-face!" The gorse rattled as Barkkit scrabbled deeper.

Tallkit ducked and peered under the branches. "I'm coming!"

A paw pressed on his tail. "Going tunneling, Wormkit?" Shrewkit snorted.

Tallkit spun around, bristling. "Will you drop the dumb name?" He squared his shoulders.

"But it suits you." Shrewkit's eyes gleamed. "You're going to spend your life burrowing underground."

"Ignore him, Tallkit!" Barkkit called from under the gorse. "Let's finish our game."

Tallkit held Shrewkit's gaze. "Why don't you join us?" Playing was better than arguing.

"I'm too old for kits' games."

Tallkit prickled with frustration. "Then why don't you go hunting with Redclaw?" He leaned closer. "Oh, I forgot! You're too young to leave camp."

The gorse trembled as Barkkit pushed his way out. "Stop acting like a 'paw, Shrewkit. You've got three moons left before you get your apprentice name."

Shrewkit puffed out his fur. "I don't see why I have to wait. I'm nearly as big as Doepaw."

"No kit can be apprenticed before six moons," Tallkit reminded him. "Don't you know the warrior code?"

Shrewkit flicked his tail. "Do *tunnelers* have a code?"

Tallkit flexed his claws. "We're warriors too!" he snapped. "We train to hunt and fight like moor runners. We just have *extra* skills."

"Do you mean digging?" Shrewkit sneered. "*Rabbits* can dig. It's not such a great skill."

"Yes, it is!" Tallkit felt a rush of fury. "Sandgorse is helping to build a tunnel right down to the bottom of the gorge. No rabbit could do that. No rabbit would even think of it." He fluffed out his pelt, hoping his anger would hide the fear that was pricking through his fur at the thought of squeezing down such a long, long tunnel.

"Tunnels are a waste of time," Shrewkit scoffed. "They're only good for hiding in."

"No, they're not!" How dare Shrewkit suggest that tunnelers were cowards? Being underground was far scarier than running around the moor. "The new tunnel means an extra prey run *and* a secret route in and out of our territory if we ever need it."

"Real warriors don't need secret routes. They stay in the open and *fight*."

Tallkit lashed his tail. "Tunnelers can fight underground!"

"I'm just saying I'm glad I don't have to be a tunneler's apprentice. Don't tell me you're looking forward to spending your life in the dark."

"I'm proud to follow in Sandgorse's paw steps." Tallkit shifted his paws guiltily. *I just wish I wasn't dreading it.*

Barkkit nosed his way between them. "I don't know why you're arguing," he mewed. "It's okay to want different things. If we all wanted to be moor runners we'd be just the same as ThunderClan or ShadowClan or RiverClan. But we're not; we're WindClan, and we can fight and hunt *and* tunnel."

Tallkit swallowed his frustration. Barkkit was right. Wind-Clan cats were special and it was mouse-brained to stand around arguing about it. Whipping his tail, he turned and stomped away. Sharp pain stabbed his paw. "Ow!" He lifted it, hopping. His pad stung like fury.

Barkkit bounded over. "What's wrong?"

"I stepped on something sharp." Tallkit held out his paw.

Barkkit crouched and peered at the pad. Gently he tipped it up to get a better look. "It's a gorse thorn," he mewed.

Tallkit glanced nervously toward the medicine den. "Should I ask Hawkheart to get it out?" If Hawkheart was busy, he wouldn't want to be disturbed—especially by buzzard prey.

"No need." Leaning close, Barkkit pressed his muzzle to Tallkit's pad. Tallkit felt his denmate's breath warm on his paw; then there was a sharp tug and the pain melted away. Barkkit sat up. A long thorn stuck from between his teeth. Blood glistened on the tip. He spat it out. "Lick your paw really hard," he ordered. "That'll stop it from going bad."

Tallkit lifted his paw and examined the pad. A spot of blood was welling where Barkkit had removed the thorn. He lapped it, amazed at how quickly the pain had disappeared. The blood tasted salty on his tongue. "Thanks, Barkkit." He looked at his friend. "How did you know what to do?"

Barkkit shrugged. "It was obvious."

Shrewkit rolled his eyes. "Brilliant," he snorted. "That's *really* going to help catch rabbits or fight invaders."

Barkkit tipped his head on one side. "There's more to life

than hunting and fighting."

"Is there?" Shrewkit blinked in surprise. "Don't tell me you want to be a *tunneler?*"

"That's not what I said," Barkkit mewed.

"Another digger!" Shrewkit turned his tail on his brother. He clearly wasn't listening. "That's just what WindClan needs."

Barkkit watched his brother march away.

Tallkit narrowed his eyes, confused. "Don't you want to be a moor runner, Barkkit?"

"No. I want to train as a medicine cat," Barkkit confessed.

Tallkit stared at him. "Really?"

"I'm going to ask Heatherstar if I can be apprenticed to Hawkheart."

"Hawkheart?" Tallkit echoed in astonishment. *I'd rather train as a tunneler.* "Are you sure?"

"Yes!" Barkkit's eyes shone. "I can't wait to learn about all the herbs, and how to treat different injuries."

"I can't imagine Hawkheart with an apprentice."

"Do you think he'll refuse to train me?" Worry clouded Barkkit's gaze. "Maybe that's why he's never had an apprentice before."

"No one's been brave enough to volunteer," Tallkit muttered. He purred. "He'll probably be impressed by your courage."

"Hawkheart's okay." Barkkit's anxious gaze slid toward the medicine den. "He just doesn't like being asked rabbit-brained questions, that's all."

"Then how will you learn anything?" Tallkit pointed out.

"I'll watch what he does and only ask questions when I'm sure I don't understand."

Tallkit blinked, surprised by how determined Barkkit sounded. He must have been planning this for ages. Sadness pricked his chest. "We'll never train together."

"You're training as a tunneler anyway," Barkkit reminded him.

"I'll have to learn to hunt and fight, and you would have learned basic tunnel skills." Tallkit glanced at Shrewkit, who was following Stagpaw from the prey heap. "Now I'm stuck with *him*."

"Ignore his teasing," Barkkit urged. "If you don't react, he'll get bored and back off."

"I guess." Tallkit wasn't convinced. "Let's go see if Lilywhisker needs help hunting fleas." He turned toward the elders' den.

"I'll catch up," Barkkit mewed. "I want to ask Heatherstar about becoming Hawkheart's apprentice."

As Barkkit headed for Heatherstar's den, Tallkit padded toward the thick gorse at the far end of the clearing. Flamepelt was outside the den, propped against a low hummock while Lilywhisker sat beside him, carefully grooming her lifeless leg.

Doepaw and Ryepaw were crouching in the grass beside them, eyes fixed on Flamepelt. The elder was midstory. "I took a right fork in the tunnel," he rasped. "It was darker than the inside of a rock but I could hear the rabbit a few tail-lengths ahead. It was running fast, leaving a trail of fear-scent so strong even a moor runner could follow it."

"Isn't tunnel hunting easy?" Doepaw interrupted. "There's only one way for the prey to run."

Flamepelt met her gaze. "You think it's easy to run full pelt in stone-black darkness?"

As Doepaw's eyes widened, Whiteberry padded from the gorse den. His snowy pelt glowed in the sunshine. "You've only got your ears, nose, and whiskers to guide you," he explained. "One wrong paw step and you could hit a wall."

Flamepelt leaned forward. "A dead end gives a different echo from a passage. An experienced tunneler can hear whether an underpath will open out or get narrower just by the way the air ruffles his ear-fur."

Lilywhisker lifted her muzzle. "I used to be able to hear a cavern halfway across the moor, just by the echo of my paw steps," she boasted.

Whiteberry lay beside her and stretched sleepily. "I could scent prey through a tail-length of soil."

Tallkit blinked. One day he'd learn all of these skills. He knew he should feel excited, but he could only picture darkness and mud. He shivered as though he were already belowground.

Flamepelt returned to his story. "The rabbit was well under ShadowClan territory."

"And you followed it?" Ryepaw gasped. "But it was ShadowClan prey once it'd crossed the border!"

"Tunnels belong to WindClan," Flamepelt rasped.

Tallkit padded closer. "How did you know it was

ShadowClan territory when you were underground?"

"The soil smells of pinesap," Flamepelt told him briskly, then pressed on. "The rabbit kept running. I was closing on it fast. Then I heard paw steps on the forest floor above. I was close to the surface."

Doepaw's tail twitched. "Could they tell you were there?"

Whiteberry cut in with a snort. "No overgrounder can smell through earth."

"But they might have heard my paw steps." Flamepelt lowered his voice. "If they mistook me for a rabbit, they might start digging. I couldn't risk them discovering the tunnels. So I froze." Flamepelt paused. "I could hear the rabbit racing away, and there was fresh air wafting down the tunnel. The prey was heading for an opening. I just had to hope that the ShadowClan patrol wouldn't spot it and chase it back underground."

"Did they?" Ryepaw asked breathlessly.

"The ShadowClan paw steps suddenly broke into a run," Flamepelt told her. "I heard their calls: *Rabbit! Rabbit!*" His gaze widened, flicking from Doepaw and Ryepaw to Tallkit.

The fur on Tallkit's spine lifted. "What happened?"

"Earth showered around me as they pounded overhead. I had to think fast. If they found the opening and chased the rabbit back down, they'd find me and discover the tunnel. I had to block it."

"Block it?" Ryepaw squeaked. "How?"

"I had to cause a cave-in!" Flamepelt announced. "The soil was light and soft. If I could loosen enough to block the tunnel without bringing the whole roof down, I'd be safe."

Tallkit's heart began to pound. "What if the whole roof had collapsed?" His chest tightened.

"I'd have drowned in soil," Flamepelt breathed.

"No!" Ryepaw's mew was barely a whisper.

"I could hear ShadowClan voices at the end of the tunnel, then the rabbit's paws thumping closer. Stronger steps were on its tail. The patrol was heading straight toward me." Flamepelt reached up with a forepaw. "I began scraping at the soil above my head. Claws out, I dug as hard and as fast as I could. The paw steps were thundering nearer, echoing against the walls of the tunnel. Another few moments and they'd smell me. A few moments after that, they'd crash right into me. I clawed at the roof with both paws until I heard the earth groaning. I stuck my paws in for a final pull and the roof showered down. I leaped back just in time as the whole tunnel gave way in front of me. Beyond the wall of soil, I heard the squeal of the rabbit as the ShadowClan patrol caught up with it."

"Didn't they know you were there?" Doepaw asked.

"It was too dark, and the earth-scent hid my smell." Flamepelt shrugged. "As far as they were concerned, it was just a dead-end rabbit hole. I turned around and headed for home."

Lilywhisker sighed. "I miss those days."

Flamepelt nodded. "What I wouldn't give to be running tunnels again!"

Whiteberry whisked his tail over his paws. "There were enough tunnelers back then to patrol every tunnel."

"We kept them in good condition," Flamepelt agreed.

"These days, if there's a cave-in, the Clan just thinks it's one less tunnel to patrol."

Doepaw narrowed her eyes. "Isn't it good that we don't have to send so many cats underground?" She nodded at Lily-whisker's leg. "It *is* dangerous."

"Being a moor runner's not exactly safe," Flamepelt retorted. "There are buzzards and dogs and foxes above-ground. They're just as dangerous as a cave-in. The better trained we are, the less risk there is. That's why we need to keep training our young'uns to tunnel. There'll come a time when we'll depend on the tunnels again."

Ryepaw tilted her head sideways. "But there are plenty of rabbits these days. Now our territory covers the whole moor, and even in the worst snows we can find enough to feed the Clan."

Flamepelt sat up. "What if another Clan decides to invade our territory?"

Doepaw bristled. "We'd fight them off."

Flamepelt's tail twitched. "Tunnels give us an advantage in battle."

Tallkit glanced from elder to apprentice. Had moor runners and tunnelers always disagreed like this? How had WindClan stayed together for so many moons if the two sides felt so differently?

CHAPTER 4

❧

The camp entrance swished as Sandgorse padded into camp, Plum-claw and Mistmouse at his tail. Mud streaked Sandgorse's pelt and his shoulders sagged. Tallkit hurried to greet him.

"Hi, kit!" Sandgorse meowed. "Have you had a good day?"

"Yes! Flamepelt's been telling us about the time he chased a rabbit all the way under ShadowClan territory."

"Ah, that's a good story." Sandgorse ran his tail along Tall-kit's spine. The tip felt wet and smelled of mud. "We've been working on the gorge tunnel."

"Sandgorse!" Heatherstar leaped out of the Meeting Hollow and crossed the camp. Reedfeather bounded after her. "How's the work going?" Heatherstar prompted. The leader's gaze flicked over the muddy, bedraggled pelts of Plumclaw and Mistmouse, and there was a flash of concern in her eyes.

"It's fine," Sandgorse reported. "We've shored up the stretch beyond the peat ridge. It's steep there, but we've pulled up clay from lower down and strengthened the tunnel walls."

Reedfeather narrowed his eyes. "It seems like a lot of work."

Plumclaw shook out her pelt. "It'll be worth it when it's finished."

"When will that be?" Heatherstar asked.

Mistmouse exchanged glances with Sandgorse. "It's hard to say," she meowed. "We're tunneling in territory we haven't worked before. It's difficult to predict whether we're going to meet sand, clay, or stone next."

Reedfeather moved beside Heatherstar. "It sounds dangerous."

"It's challenging." Sandgorse puffed out his chest. "But we're learning a lot. And when it's done, WindClan will have a secret route from the top of the moor right down to the river."

"What about the cliff face?" Heatherstar's ears twitched. "You can't tunnel through rock."

"We've planned for that," Plumclaw explained. "There's a seam of clay just as the river drops into the deepest part of the gorge. We plan to dig up through that and meet the tunnel coming down."

"Won't RiverClan be able to see it from the bottom of the gorge?" Reedfeather asked.

"There are brambles," Sandgorse told him. "The entrance will be hidden." He looked at Tallkit. "I can't wait to show you," he purred.

Tallkit felt a rush of pride. Sandgorse could do things even the Clan leader couldn't. "I can't wait to see it!" he mewed.

"You may be apprenticed in time to help finish digging it," Sandgorse purred.

Tallkit stiffened. Suddenly he imagined himself at the bottom of a long tunnel, far from the sky, digging in the dark through filthy clay, desperately trying to find his way through to fresh air. He swallowed as his chest tightened. "Yes," he whispered shakily.

Heatherstar fluffed up her fur. "You'd better get dry," she advised the tunnelers. "This chilly wind will give you greencough if you're not careful."

Sandgorse nodded and headed away. "Come on, Tallkit!" he called. "Help me lick the grit from behind my ears."

Tallkit scurried after him, catching up to Sandgorse as he reached the tunnelers' bracken patch. Sandgorse stopped and shook out his pelt. Tallkit screwed up his face as mud spattered him. A purr rumbled in Sandgorse's throat. "You'll have to get used to mucky fur."

Tallkit shuddered.

"You're getting him dirty!" Palebird's mew rang across the camp. Tallkit turned to see his mother hurrying toward them.

"He's helping me get cleaned up," Sandgorse objected. "He wants to get the grit from behind my ears, don't you, Tallkit?"

Tallkit gazed at his father's mud-crusted head. *Not really.*

"I guess he's got to learn how." Palebird touched her muzzle to Tallkit's head. "One day he'll be cleaning the grit from his own ears."

Sandgorse's eyes shone. "I can't wait till we can go on patrol together." He looked from Palebird to Tallkit. "Running tunnels, just the three of us."

Palebird sighed. "It may be a while before I join you."

Sandgorse looked up sharply. "What do you mean?" His gaze darkened. "Surely you'll be ready by the time Tallkit's an apprentice?"

Palebird shook her head. "I don't think I'll be strong enough."

"Of course you will." Sandgorse leaned forward and pressed his cheek against hers. "Newleaf will bring fatter prey, and you'll have your strength back in no time."

Tallkit stared anxiously at his mother. "You'll be better, won't you?"

"I hope so," Palebird murmured. Turning, she headed toward the nursery.

"Go with her, Tallkit," Sandgorse whispered. "I think she needs cheering up."

Tallkit hesitated. "What about your ears?"

"I'll wash them myself."

Tallkit trotted after his mother, scrambling over the tussocks until he caught up with her. The comforting scent of wool and milk enfolded him as they entered the nursery. Brackenwing sat up as Palebird curled into her nest. The queen's pale ginger pelt was ruffled with sleep. "Where are Barkkit and Shrewkit?" she meowed.

Does she know that Barkkit is planning to ask Heatherstar if he can become Hawkheart's apprentice? Tallkit wondered. He figured it wasn't his place to tell Brackenwing if she didn't know. "They're playing outside." He scrambled over the edge of the nest and slid in beside Palebird's belly. He was hungry.

Palebird pulled away as he nuzzled into her belly. "No, Tallkit."

Tallkit froze. *No?* He wriggled closer, closing his eyes and breathing in his mother's tempting, milky scent.

Palebird shoved him back with a paw. "I said *no*, Tallkit."

"No milk?" He stared at her in disbelief.

"It's drying up," she told him. "You're old enough to eat from the prey heap now."

"But . . ." He searched for a way to change her mind, but Palebird was staring at him blankly.

Brackenwing's nest rustled. "It's okay, Tallkit." She climbed out of the heather and leaned in to lick his ears. "Shrewkit and Barkkit have been eating from the heap for a moon. They prefer prey now."

No milk at all? Tallkit couldn't believe Palebird hadn't warned him.

His mother half closed her eyes. "You'll enjoy eating with the big kits," she murmured.

Tallkit felt Brackenwing tug his scruff with her teeth. He scrabbled at the nest, snagging wool in his claws as she lifted him out. His fur spiked. *It's not fair!*

Brackenwing lowered him gently to the floor. "Let Palebird rest." She nosed him toward the entrance. Numbly Tallkit stumbled forward. Behind him, Brackenwing was tucking wool around his mother. "You get some sleep, dear," she whispered as Palebird tucked her nose under her paw and closed her eyes.

With a pang of sadness, Tallkit slid from the den. He landed on the damp grass and fluffed his fur against the chill. Wool was tufted beneath his claws. He shook it out crossly and stared across the camp. The prey heap was stacked high. He could see a rabbit near the bottom with small, brown mouse bodies piled on top. Belly growling, he stomped toward the heap. As he reached it, he sniffed warily. Rich scents swamped his tongue. He drew back, wrinkling his nose.

"First time?" Plumclaw's mew made him jump. The dark gray she-cat nosed in beside him. "Try a mouse first. It's not too strong and it's easy to chew." She tugged one of the little, brown bodies from the heap and dropped it at his paws. "Be careful of the bones." She tapped the haunches of the mouse with her soft, gray foot. "Take a bite there."

Tallkit leaned down, trying not to breathe in the prey scent. *I want milk!* Closing his eyes, he sank his teeth into the soft flesh. Flavor flooded his tongue, pungent and warm.

"Not bad, eh?" Plumclaw purred.

Tallkit wasn't sure. He ripped a small chunk from the mouse and looked at her. The juicy meat was strange, but not horrible. He began to chew.

"There you go!" Plumclaw's eyes glowed. She hooked a bird from the pile with a claw and pointed to a patch of grass beside the heather wall of the camp. "Let's take our meal over there and stop crowding the prey heap." Grabbing the bird between her teeth, she padded across the grass.

Tallkit picked up the mouse and followed. He puffed out his chest proudly as it swung from his jaws. He felt like a moor runner bringing prey home to the Clan! He settled beside Plumclaw as she took a bite of her bird. "This is a thrush," she explained, her mouth full. "It tastes a bit woody." She swallowed. "I prefer lapwing, but we only hunt them after the breeding season."

Tallkit took another bite of mouse. He knew what to expect this time and began to relish the chewy meat.

"You'll be an apprentice soon and then you can catch your own prey," Plumclaw told him.

Catch my own prey! Tallkit wondered what tunnel-hunting was like. Chasing rabbits in the dark couldn't be as much fun as chasing rabbits on the moor. "Did you like being an apprentice?" he asked Plumclaw.

"It was great." Plumclaw tore another mouthful from her thrush.

Tallkit glanced at her from the corner of his eye. "Were you glad you were going to be a tunneler?" Could *any* cat be glad to be told they would spend their life underground?

"Of course!" Plumclaw shook a feather from her muzzle. "Both my parents were tunnelers. And I knew I'd be good at it because I'm small, and my paws are wide and strong." She held one up. Tallkit could see mud trapped beneath her claws even though the rest of her pelt was washed clean.

"Do you like being underground?" Tallkit tried to sound unconcerned. He didn't want her to guess he was having second thoughts about becoming a tunneler. What if she told Sandgorse?

"I love it," she told him. "It feels like a secret world. Above me, prey runs, warriors patrol, clouds move over the moor, and no one except my tunnelmates know where we are."

"Don't you miss the wind in your pelt?"

"No." Plumclaw looked at him, surprised. "It's snug underground. I feel safe with the earth pressing against my fur."

Tallkit swallowed. "You sound like you're half mole!"

"Maybe I am." As Plumclaw purred with amusement, Barkkit scrambled out of the Meeting Hollow. Tallkit sat up as his denmate bounced toward him.

"Heatherstar said yes!" Barkkit stopped in front of him. "I can be Hawkheart's apprentice!"

"I didn't know you wanted to be a medicine apprentice," Plumclaw purred. "Congratulations!"

"Yeah." Tallkit licked blood from his lips. "Congratulations." He couldn't help feeling a pang of envy. *You'll be doing what you want while I spend all day digging holes.*

"Tallkit?" Barkkit was frowning at him. "What's wrong?"

Tallkit lifted his chin. He wasn't being fair to his friend. "Nothing. I'm really happy for you!"

Barkkit noticed his mouse. "You're eating prey!"

Tallkit puffed out his fur proudly. "It's good."

"I like shrew best," Barkkit told him. "It tastes heathery." He glanced over his shoulder at the grassy clearing. "Do you want to play Rabbit?"

Tallkit took a quick bite of mouse and pushed the rest toward Plumclaw. "Here."

"Thanks," she meowed. "Are you sure you've had enough?"

"Plenty." Tallkit jumped to his paws. "Shall I be rabbit this time?" he asked Barkkit.

Barkkit flicked his stubby tail. "Yes."

"Okay," Tallkit mewed. "But I'm not hiding under any gorse bushes. They're way too prickly."

"Don't worry," Barkkit reassured him. "If you step on another thorn, I can always pull it out."

CHAPTER 5

♣

"Let all cats old enough to hunt gather at Tallrock." Blue sky framed Heatherstar as she called from the top. Behind her, the distant moor rolled wide and green, rippling with heather not quite in bloom.

A soft breeze tugged at Tallkit's pelt as he sat on the rim of the Meeting Hollow. His Clanmates swarmed around him, streaming down into the sandy dip. A warm newleaf had brought rich prey and now, as greenleaf set in, the Clan's warriors were plump and sleek. Tallkit glanced at the tunnelers as they clustered at one end of the hollow. Woollytail's eyes were bright and Hickorynose paced impatiently around him while Plumclaw's tail-tip flicked with excitement. Hawkheart and Reedfeather sat still as stone at the foot of Tallrock while the moor runners filled up the rest of the hollow.

"Sit down and stop fidgeting." Cloudrunner beckoned Stagpaw with a flick of his tail. Doepaw was already waiting between Aspenfall and Ryepaw.

The elders clambered stiffly into the hollow, Flamepelt leading the way. Whiteberry pressed close to Lilywhisker as she dragged her leg behind her. Flailfoot followed. "This is the ceremony I've been looking forward to," he rasped.

Tallkit's heart leaped like a rabbit in his chest.

Sandgorse stood beside him. "Are you ready?"

"Yes." Tallkit glanced at Palebird. Her round eyes, which had been dull for so long, were bright and focused.

She leaned forward and began lapping the fur on Tallkit's shoulders. "I want you looking your best," she purred.

Brown fur flashed at the entrance to the medicine den as Barkpaw hurried out. The young apprentice scrambled into the hollow and took his place beside Hawkheart. The medicine cat flashed him a reproachful look.

"Sorry, Hawkheart." Tallkit heard Barkpaw's hushed apology. "I was sorting the comfrey leaves."

Shrewpaw caught Tallkit's eye. He was sitting beside his mentor, Hareflight. Tallkit could guess what he was thinking. *You're going to be Wormpaw now.* Tallkit looked away. *I'll be an apprentice,* he told himself. *It doesn't matter whether I'm a tunneler or a moor runner.*

Heatherstar leaped down from Tallrock and crossed the hollow. She stopped in the middle and surveyed her Clan until her gaze rested on Tallkit. His pelt burned. "Tallkit!" Heatherstar called.

Palebird nudged him forward. Paws slipping on the dry sand, Tallkit scrambled down into the hollow and stopped in front of Heatherstar.

"It is rare that I give an apprentice name to only one cat." Heatherstar's blue eyes bored into him. "Let us remember your littermate, Finchkit." She glanced up at Palebird. "WindClan mourns the loss of one so young, but she is at peace, safe with StarClan."

Tallkit wondered if his littermate was watching his ceremony. Would she be jealous that she never got the chance to have her apprentice name? Perhaps StarClan would grant her one.

"Tallpaw." Heatherstar's mew jerked his thoughts back. "I have thought long and hard about who should mentor you."

Tallpaw heard murmurs of excitement from the tunnelers. "She'll choose Woollytail, surely?" Plumclaw's whisper hissed across the hollow.

Heatherstar's gaze didn't waver. "I have chosen Dawnstripe." She turned her head toward the moor runners. "Come forward, Dawnstripe."

Tallpaw gripped the earth as the ground seemed to sway beneath him. *But I'm supposed to be a tunneler.* He looked at Sandgorse, sitting above the hollow. His father's eyes glittered with outrage.

Tallpaw swallowed as Dawnstripe padded toward him. *I'm not going underground.* Relief fluttered deep in his belly.

"Heatherstar!" Woollytail's sharp mew cut across the hollow. "You promised us a tunneler!"

Paws thumped onto the earth behind Tallpaw. He spun around, heart lurching. Sandgorse had jumped into the clearing. "You've made a mistake, Heatherstar."

Heatherstar shook her head. "No, I haven't, Sandgorse."

"But I'm a tunneler. Palebird's a tunneler. We want Tallpaw to follow in our paw steps."

Heatherstar dipped her head. "I know," she meowed quietly. "But I have watched Tallpaw. He doesn't have a tunneler's nature or physique."

"That's not true!" Sandgorse snapped. "Look at this tail. It's easily long enough to pull him out of a cave-in. And he has strong paws and short fur, to keep the sand out."

Heatherstar held Sandgorse's gaze. "He can run like the wind and leap like a hare. He chases imaginary prey when he thinks no one is watching."

Palebird jumped down beside her mate. "He can chase *real* prey in the tunnels!" she hissed.

Heatherstar didn't flinch. "I've seen him when the wind's up. It gets into his fur so he can't sit still. He needs to be aboveground. He needs be true to his nature."

"*True to his nature?*" Woollytail spat. "What kit doesn't run and jump?"

Hickorynose snorted. "In leaf-bare, you said that the tunnels were too dangerous. Now you say a kit likes the wind in his fur. What excuse will you use next time you give the moor runners an apprentice?"

Sandgorse took a step closer to Heatherstar, his pelt bristling. "*Tunneling* is in his nature," he growled. "How could it not be? His kin are tunnelers stretching back for moons."

Heatherstar's tail twitched. "If Tallpaw wants to train as a tunneler later, he can. But I want him to train as a moor runner first."

Tallpaw flinched as he saw Palebird's tail droop. She clambered out of the hollow and padded, head down, back to the nursery. *Should I tell Heatherstar that I want to be a tunneling apprentice?* Tallpaw looked desperately from the WindClan leader to his father.

"He's my son," Sandgorse snarled. "I'll decide his future."

Heatherstar stiffened. "*I* decide the future of my warriors." She turned to Dawnstripe. "Share your speed and courage with Tallpaw. Make him a warrior the whole of WindClan can be proud of."

Tallpaw's heart thumped like rabbit paws on hollow earth. Dawnstripe was one of WindClan's fastest runners and had never backed down in a fight. He could learn so much from her. *I will make WindClan proud.*

He fought to stop himself from trembling as Dawnstripe touched her muzzle to his head, and he pricked his ears, listening for his Clanmates' cheers. Paws shifted on the sand around him. No cat called his apprentice name. Nervously Tallpaw glanced over his shoulder. Sandgorse had turned his tail on the ceremony. The tunnelers stared in stony silence.

"Tallpaw!" Cloudrunner was the first to call his name.

Hareflight joined in "Tallpaw!"

"Tallpaw!" Dawnstripe raised her voice above the others and led the chant, challenging the other moor runners to join in with a glare.

As more cats began to call his name, Dawnstripe nosed Tallpaw toward Stagpaw and Doepaw. "Come on," she murmured. "Greet your new denmates."

"Tallpaw! Tallpaw!" Ryepaw pummeled the ground.

Stagpaw's eyes shone as Tallpaw approached. "Congratulations."

Tallpaw's tongue felt dry. Stagpaw had never spoken to him as an equal before.

As the chanting died away, Ryepaw and Doepaw clustered around him. "The first time you see the moor is the best,"

Doepaw told him breathlessly.

"You won't believe how big it is!" Ryepaw fluffed out her gray fur.

Barkpaw raced to Tallpaw's side. "Congratulations!" he mewed. Tallpaw blinked gratefully at his friend. He still didn't know how to feel. He wanted to be a moor runner, but not if it made his mother and father so angry.

"You may think you've been given an easier path." Tallpaw turned as a gruff mew sounded in his ear. Hawkheart was standing beside him. The gray-brown medicine cat narrowed his eyes. "But it's a path that leads away from your kin. Be careful not to lose your way."

Tallpaw shook his head. "I won't; I promise!"

Barkpaw puffed out his chest. "Of course he won't!"

"Heatherstar must be crazy." Shrewpaw barged past his brother. "You should be underground, Wormkit!"

Tallpaw sniffed. "I'm not a kit. Or a worm. I'm going to be a moor runner, just like you."

Larksplash's whiskers twitched. "It'll be good to have a new apprentice in the den." She glanced at Ryepaw, her gaze warm. "A certain litter isn't too good at being ready in time for dawn patrol."

Aspenfall purred, weaving past Dawnstripe. "I bet you're an early riser, if you're anything like your father." He looked at Sandgorse. The pale ginger tunneler sat with his back to the hollow.

Tallpaw's heart twisted. He dipped his head to the moor runners crowding around him. "Thank you," he mumbled. "I must go speak with Sandgorse." He nosed his way past

Dawnstripe and Stagpaw, and jumped out of the hollow. Following the rim, he headed for his father. "Sandgorse?"

The tunneler's fur looked dull and patchy, worn thin by countless moons working underground.

Tallpaw stopped in front of his father. "Do you want me to tell Heatherstar I'd rather be a tunneler?"

Sandgorse lifted his gaze. "Is that what you want?"

Tallpaw swallowed.

Sandgorse's gaze hardened. *"Is it?"*

Tallpaw shifted his paws. "No," he mewed quietly.

"Then don't," Sandgorse snapped.

"I'm sorry," Tallpaw mewed. "But if Heatherstar had made me a tunneler, I would have trained just as hard."

"I had such plans." Sandgorse's gaze drifted toward the nursery, where Palebird was hiding.

"I know." Tallpaw tried to ignore the guilt pricking his heart. "You and me and Palebird were going to patrol together. But I promise, even though I'm training to be a moor runner, I'll be the best warrior I can be."

"You were born to be a tunneler." Sandgorse flashed an angry glance at Heatherstar as she sat, head bowed, beside Reedfeather in the hollow. "You can't change that, no matter what any other cat tells you!" Lashing his tail, he marched away.

Tallpaw watched him go, grief rising in his throat. "I'm sorry," he whispered.

Warm breath brushed his ear. *Dawnstripe.* Tallpaw recognized her scent. "There's nothing you can do," she meowed. "Leave him. He'll get used to it."

Tallpaw looked up hopefully at her. "Will he?"

Dawnstripe didn't answer. Instead she nodded toward the camp entrance. "Come on. I bet you're desperate to see what's outside." She bounded across the grass, clearing the tussocks easily.

Tallpaw raced after her, zigzagging between them. He'd jump them one day soon, when his legs were stronger from training. *As a moor runner! I'm going to be a moor runner!* He stopped at the camp entrance and watched Dawnstripe's gold-banded tail disappearing through the narrow gap in the heather that marked the entrance to the camp. For the first time in his life, Tallpaw was going to see what lay beyond the heather walls.

He pushed his way through the gap. Heather fronds swished over his pelt and he half closed his eyes as they flicked his muzzle. As soon as he cleared the branches, wind swept over his face. Opening his eyes wide, Tallpaw emerged onto a patch of windswept grass and stared at the wide heath stretching out before him.

Gray clouds massed on the horizon beyond a sea of wind-whisked heather. The moor rolled away on all sides, sloping up beyond the camp and dropping below where they stood. Gorse sprouted here and there, yellow against the green heather, clumping in thick swathes like patches of sunshine. Now that he was outside, Tallpaw could see that the Wind-Clan camp was nestled in a natural hollow, its grassy clearing hidden by the thick, leafy walls.

"What do you think?" Muzzle high, Dawnstripe stood on a grassy hillock a few tail-lengths away and looked down at him.

"It's huge!" Tallpaw whispered. He dug his claws into the grass to steady himself against the buffeting wind. He felt an urge to charge into the heather and run as far as he could, but fear rooted his paws to the spot. What if he ran all the way out of the territory? What if he couldn't find his way back to camp?

"Look!" Dawnstripe flicked her tail to the slope on the far side of the camp. Birds were swooping low to the heather, then lifting high into the sky before turning for another dive. "Lapwings," Dawnstripe explained. "They're defending their young. There must be a weasel nearby."

"A weasel?" Tallpaw blinked at her. He'd never seen one of those on the fresh-kill pile. Were weasels dangerous? He glanced around nervously.

"Stay clear of them until you've learned some fighting moves," Dawnstripe instructed. "They're fast and vicious and their bites carry infection. And they taste dreadful, so don't bother trying to catch one to eat."

Shrewpaw burst from the tunnel and stared at Tallpaw. "Looking for rabbit holes to burrow in?"

Stagpaw pushed past him. "Stop blocking the entrance, rabbit-brain."

Shrewpaw stumbled clear as Doepaw, Hareflight, Ryepaw, Aspenfall, Larksplash, and Cloudrunner streamed out behind him.

Cloudrunner stopped beside Dawnstripe. "Congratulations on getting an apprentice," he purred. "Where are you taking him first?"

Stagpaw butted in before the golden tabby could answer. "We're practicing battle moves."

Cloudrunner glanced sternly at his apprentice. "Once we've finished practicing *not interrupting.*"

"Sorry." Stagpaw dropped his gaze.

A purr rumbled in Dawnstripe's throat. "He's just excited to have a new denmate." She glanced at Tallpaw. "Are you ready?"

Tallpaw nodded. Behind Dawnstripe the moor swept down toward dense, dark green trees. Tallpaw could hear their leaves rustling from here. The trees grew so close; he imagined it being as dark as a tunnel underneath. "Is that where ThunderClan lives?" he whispered. How could they see to catch their prey?

"That's right," Dawnstripe meowed. "Don't worry, we're not going to pay them a visit!"

Larksplash paced the grass, her tortoiseshell-and-white pelt ruffled by the breeze. "I'm taking Ryepaw to the RiverClan border to refresh the scent line. Shall we travel together?"

Dawnstripe nodded. She sprang down from the grassy hillock and disappeared into a gap in the heather. Tallpaw hurried after her. As he ducked between the thick branches, he noticed that the grass underpaw was worn into a track of bare, brown earth. He smelled rabbit, though the scent was stale.

Ryepaw was trotting at his heels. "Just wait till you get to Outlook Rock," she mewed. "You can see to the end of the world from there!"

Tallpaw followed the rabbit trail as it swerved through the heather. Dawnstripe's golden tail-tip flashed in and out of sight and Tallpaw quickened his pace, worried he'd hold the others back. The trail widened until he could see Dawnstripe racing ahead. Clumps of black dirt littered the path like bunches of dark berries, and Tallpaw hopped and jumped, trying to avoid stepping on them.

"Sheep dirt," Ryepaw explained.

Alarm pricked Tallpaw's pelt. Were there sheep here? Sheep were huge. He'd seen their white backs looming beyond the camp walls. He jerked his head around. "Have you seen one up close?"

"Of course," Ryepaw purred. "They're harmless. You could walk under their bellies and they wouldn't notice. They just live to chew and make dirt." She bounded over a large clump of dirt-berries.

The ground began to slope down as heather gave way to wind-flattened grass. It felt soft and damp beneath Tallpaw's pads. Ahead of Dawnstripe, the moor rolled onward, like a gigantic, green cat sleeping under the blue sky. Tallpaw tasted the air. Sheep dirt, rabbit, and heather swamped his tongue. Was there enemy scent hidden among all that? Tallpaw closed his eyes for a moment to concentrate.

"Tallpaw, no!"

CHAPTER 6

❧

Teeth grabbed Tallpaw's scruff and tugged him with a jerk. He gasped as he felt himself swing out into open air. Twisting, his hind paws scrabbled against stones for a moment before Dawnstripe whisked him backward onto the grass and dropped him.

"Watch where you're going!" she spat, her eyes wide with horror.

Tallpaw stared at his mentor in confusion. Then his gaze slid past her to where the grass ended abruptly. There was a narrow strip of rock before the ground fell away in a sheer, jagged drop.

Ryepaw stared at him wide-eyed. "You nearly fell into the gorge!"

Larksplash stopped beside her apprentice. "We haven't lost a 'paw to the gorge in a while." Her eyes sparked.

"This is serious," Dawnstripe snapped at her Clanmate.

"I know," Larksplash meowed softly. "But I think Tallpaw's scared enough."

Tallpaw's heart pounded so loudly he could hardly hear what the other cats were saying. Trembling, he peered over the edge of the cliff. At the bottom, water roared, churning between the sheer rock walls like angry storm clouds. It looked like a huge claw had sliced a channel through the moor. Was this where Sandgorse was tunneling?

"Stay away from the edge," Dawnstripe warned. "When it rains, the grass gets slippery."

Tallpaw backed away, his heart still thumping.

Ryepaw nudged his shoulder gently with her nose. "I should have warned you," she whispered. "I forgot you've never seen the gorge before."

A distant bark sounded from somewhere downriver, beyond the end of the gorge.

Tallpaw's pelt twitched. "Is that a dog?"

Ryepaw pricked her ears. "Don't worry. It's in RiverClan territory, so it's not our problem."

"Come on." Larksplash nodded to her apprentice. "Let's go check the border. If that dog has been anywhere near, Heatherstar will want to know."

Ryepaw stretched and tasted the air. "It's with a Twoleg."

"It'll be a daft one, then." Larksplash headed away over the grass, following the line of the gorge as it sloped toward the forest. "Who'd want to hang out with a dog? Nasty, slavering things."

"Twolegs are *all* daft!" Ryepaw called, chasing after her.

Tallpaw turned to Dawnstripe as the pair disappeared down the slope. "Are there many dogs on the moor?"

Dawnstripe gazed across the heather. "They come with Twolegs, but just one or two at a time."

"Do they ever come near the hollow?" Tallpaw had only

seen sheep stray close to the camp wall.

"They don't get a chance. They make so much noise, we always have time to send a patrol to steer them away." Dawnstripe didn't sound concerned. "Their teeth are no match for a warrior's claws." She pointed her nose along the gorge. "Do you see where the land turns flat and marshy?"

Tallpaw squinted as the sun flashed from between clouds. Farther along the edge of the moor, the river emerged from the gorge and grew fat and sluggish beside low-lying meadows.

"That's RiverClan territory." Dawnstripe nodded to the forest on the opposite side of the silver river. "And Thunder-Clan sleeps and hunts among those trees."

Tallpaw wondered what it must be like to live hidden from the sky. Didn't ThunderClan long to feel the sun on their pelts or the wind in their ears? They had more in common with tunnelers than moor runners!

Dawnstripe headed away from the gorge and crossed the slope, following a ridge of earth topped with heather. It curved like an endless tail, wrapping protectively around the moor. Tallpaw's legs were aching by the time they halted at the top of a steep descent. The smooth grass swept down into a line of dense trees.

"That's the way to Fourtrees," Dawnstripe told him.

Tallpaw stared at the canopy of green leaves trembling in the breeze. "Where's the Great Rock?" He peered through the branches, trying to glimpse the huge rock he'd heard his Clanmates talking about when they returned from Gatherings.

Dawnstripe flicked her tail. "It's hidden at the moment, but you'll see it soon enough."

Tallpaw's heart leaped. He'd forgotten that he'd be allowed to attend Gatherings now that he was an apprentice. Paws pricking with excitement, he trotted after Dawnstripe as she continued around the edge of the moor. "That's ShadowClan territory," she told him as he fell in beside her.

Tallpaw followed her gaze to the swathe of pines that had taken over from the brighter green trees of ThunderClan's territory. A bare, gray strip divided the pines from the rest of the forest, cutting a path like a river across the landscape. A faint roar touched Tallpaw's ear fur and he watched tiny shapes move along the strip, flashing like drops of water in the sunshine. "Is that the Thunderpath?"

"Yes," Dawnstripe meowed over her shoulder. "You'll learn how to cross when you go to Highstones." Tallpaw's fur pricked. Dawnstripe was talking about his visit to the Moonstone, where cats shared tongues with StarClan. For a moment his head spun with excitement, and he had to stop until the ground felt steady beneath his paws again.

Ahead of them, the grass sloped more steeply and before long they were trekking through deep gorse once more. "This is the high-moor," Dawnstripe explained. "We're heading for the very edge of Clan territory."

The edge of Clan territory? Tallpaw paused and reared onto his hind legs, trying to catch a glimpse. But the ridge of earth they had been walking on had given way to a rutted sheep trail, and gorse blocked his view.

"You'll see soon enough." Dawnstripe veered onto a rabbit trail, roofed by heather fronds. Tallpaw ducked after her, his pelt pricking uneasily as the heather closed around him. The air was stuffy and still. *Imagine how much worse a tunnel would be.* Tallpaw took a deep breath and focused on Dawnstripe's golden tail as it bounced in front of him.

Suddenly he felt wind on his whiskers as the heather opened onto a grassy hilltop. Tallpaw blinked with relief as short, wind-dappled grass rolled away in front of him. He could breathe again! The grass sloped down to the Thunderpath, pale and flat and striking against the soft landscape. It was closer here, and Tallpaw flinched as a monster tore past, roaring louder than the wind. Beyond the Thunderpath, squares of grass marked out by thin rows of bushes surrounded a cluster of dark gray Twoleg nests and, farther still, tall cliffs marked the beginning of a range of jagged peaks. "Is that Highstones?" Tallpaw whispered, his gaze on the distant horizon.

"Highstones are the cliffs." Dawnstripe stood beside him, her ears stiff against the streaming wind. "You'll travel there one day, when you visit Mothermouth and touch the Moonstone."

Tallpaw shivered as the wind lifted his fur. Every WindClan apprentice shared tongues with StarClan at the Moonstone before they received their warrior name. He shifted his paws, trying to ignore his stinging pads. The long walk around WindClan's territory had left them tender and grazed. How would he ever make it to Highstones?

"Look out!" A voice echoed from the heather behind. "Mud-hole!" There was alarm in the mew.

Tallpaw whipped around and scanned the heather. "What was that?"

Dawnstripe padded toward a rabbit hole that was half-hidden between the roots of a bush. "The tunneling patrol's down there," she explained.

Another voice echoed from the darkness. "Let's shore it up with rocks."

"I shifted some back at the double fork."

"Fetch them, before there's a slide."

Tallpaw crept forward, sniffing. He smelled Plumclaw's scent, and Hickorynose. "Do you think they need help?" he asked warily. He didn't want to creep down into the earth.

"They know what they're doing," Dawnstripe told him. "They won't want us getting in the way." She headed away from the rabbit hole.

Tallpaw hurried after her. "Aren't we even going to look?" Surely the tunnels were part of WindClan territory? Their Clanmates might be in trouble.

"I'm a moor runner. I don't go underground if I can help it." Dawnstripe shook her pelt as though she were shaking out soil. "One of the tunnelers will take you down during your training and teach you the basics of hunting and patrolling down there."

Tallpaw tried to ignore the tightening in his chest. *I will be able to breathe underground; I will.* Instead he gazed toward the distant horizon, relishing the wind that lifted his fur. He lifted his chin. *If Shrewpaw, Ryepaw, Stagpaw, and Doepaw can survive basic tunnel training, so can I.* As Dawnstripe headed through a gorse patch, Tallpaw raced to catch up. He was relieved to feel the ground smooth underpaw, well trod by sheep. His paws burned with every step and he winced as he hopped over a lump of dirt-berries. "Where are we going now?"

"Camp." Dawnstripe glanced at him. "You must be tired."

"No," Tallpaw lied. "I could stay out for days."

A purr rumbled in Dawnstripe's throat. "Did you like what you saw?"

Tallpaw nodded enthusiastically. "I didn't imagine Wind-Clan territory was so huge."

"We guard the edge of the world," Dawnstripe told him. "The other Clans sit cozy in their marshes and woods, fed by the river and sheltered by our moor. They never know the true taste of the wind or the scent of first snow. There's no Clan cat faster or more nimble than a WindClan cat." She glanced at Tallpaw's long, black tail. "You'll have good balance. It won't be long before you can outpace a rabbit even on rough ground."

"I was named for my tail." Tallpaw puffed out his chest. He remembered what Sandgorse had told Heatherstar: that it was a tunneler's tail and would make it easy to drag him from a cave-in. Relief flooded Tallpaw's pelt. He'd never have to face a cave-in now that he was going to be a moor runner. Then he pictured Sandgorse's eyes, dark with disappointment. Guilt formed a lump in his throat as the gorse opened onto heather and Tallpaw glimpsed the hollow cradling the camp. He broke into a run, overtaking Dawnstripe and racing for the entrance. His paws skidded on the grass as he swung around and ducked through the gap in the heather to burst into the clearing beyond.

Barkpaw called from outside the medicine den. "You're back!" He raced across the tussocks and skidded to a halt in front of Tallpaw. "What did you see?"

Tallpaw winced at the sharp tang of herbs wafting from his friend. "Everything! Fourtrees, ThunderClan territory, and RiverClan and ShadowClan. And the Highstones." His pelt pricked suddenly. "And the gorge."

"Ryepaw said you nearly fell into it." Barkpaw rubbed green sap from his nose.

"Is Ryepaw back already?" Tallpaw scanned the camp and spotted her sharing prey with Shrewpaw and Stagpaw outside the apprentices' den. She had feathers in her whiskers.

"She and Larksplash caught a grouse," Barkpaw told him.

Tallpaw could smell its scent wafting across the grass. His belly rumbled. "Do you want to share a mouse?"

Barkpaw glanced back at the medicine den. "I'll have to check with Hawkheart."

"I'll fetch one from the prey heap." Tallpaw headed across the grass. His paws stung and he almost tripped.

"Are you okay?" Barkpaw darted in front of him. "Is it a thorn?"

"My pads are sore from walking." Tallpaw lifted a forepaw and sniffed it gingerly. There was a faint scent of blood.

Barkpaw leaned closer. "It's just a bit grazed," he told him.

"Mine were the same after Hawkheart took me out herb-gathering the first time. Your pads will toughen up."

"Are you checking for sores, Wormpaw?" Shrewpaw was marching toward them, puffing feathers from his muzzle.

"Stop calling me that!" Tallpaw glared at him. "Heather-star made me a moor runner, remember?"

"A real moor runner wouldn't look so tired," Shrewpaw snorted. "You were born to be a tunneler. Stick to digging, Wormpaw, and leave moor-running to cats with tougher pads."

CHAPTER 7

❧

"Wake up, sleepy slug."

Tallpaw felt a paw brush his ear. Blinking, he jerked up his
head. Sunshine was streaming under the gorse, flooding his
nest. It silhouetted Dawnstripe at the den entrance.

"I didn't think *anyone* could sleep longer than Shrewpaw."
Dawnstripe flicked her tail. "But he's been pacing the entrance
with Hareflight since the sun touched the heather."

"He's just showing off," Tallpaw growled under his breath.
He hauled himself to his paws. His muscles ached after yesterday's trek and his pads were still sore. Why hadn't Shrewpaw
woken him? They were supposed to be training together.

"Hurry up." Dawnstripe turned and stalked away.

Pelt pricking with irritation, Tallpaw clambered out of his
nest. It wasn't as soft as his nest in the nursery, or as warm.
The gorse bush that overhung the apprentices' den didn't stop
the breeze from swirling in straight over Tallpaw's nest. By
leaf-bare it would be freezing. Stagpaw, Doepaw, and Ryepaw
had already made nests at the back of the den, pressed against
the smooth boulder that held back the roots of the bush. Tallpaw eyed his denmates' nests jealously and decided to collect
heather and snagged wool as soon as he got the chance, to

make his own nest so deep and well protected that no wind could reach through it.

"Stop dawdling, Tallpaw!" Hareflight called.

Shrewpaw was pacing beside his mentor while Dawnstripe talked quietly with Cloudrunner, muzzles close. Stagpaw and Doepaw were at the prey heap sifting through yesterday's catch, and Ryepaw was hauling a wad of sheepswool toward the elders' den.

Everyone's been awake for ages! Tallpaw shook out his pelt and hurried toward Dawnstripe. He ached all over. "My legs hurt," he complained.

"They need exercise." Dawnstripe's gaze flicked toward him briefly before returning to Cloudrunner.

"But they feel—"

Dawnstripe cut him off. "You'll be okay once we're out on the moor."

Tallpaw twitched his tail crossly. Palebird would have fussed over him. Sandgorse would have told him that it was growing pains and that he was turning into a fine warrior.

Where is Sandgorse? Tallpaw scanned the clearing. He hadn't seen his father since his naming ceremony. He'd gone to his nest straight after training yesterday and was asleep by the time Sandgorse's patrol had returned from the tunnels.

"You managed to wake up, then, Wormpaw." Shrewpaw was staring at him.

"Yeah, bug-breath," Tallpaw hissed back.

Dawnstripe spun around. "Only kits name-call," she snapped.

"Shrewpaw started it," Tallpaw defended himself.

Dawnstripe looked at him sternly.

Shrewpaw's whiskers twitched. "Perhaps *tattle*paw should go back to the nursery."

Tallpaw dug his claws into the ground. He wanted to rake Shrewpaw's nose.

Dawnstripe stepped between them. "We're meeting up with the older apprentices later, to help with their final assessment."

Tallpaw blinked. "How?" He pictured himself being mauled in a mock battle.

"They need a lure for their tracking exercise," Dawnstripe told him.

Shrewpaw wove around Cloudrunner. "Can I help, too?"

The pale gray tom dipped his head. "Ask Hareflight." He turned to Dawnstripe. "Let's meet at Outlook Rock."

"Okay," Dawnstripe agreed. "I want Tallpaw to warm up first."

"I'm already warm," Tallpaw told her. The greenleaf sun was hot on his pelt, even though it had hardly lifted above the heather.

"I meant I want you to stretch your muscles," Dawnstripe told him. "You'll need to lose yesterday's stiffness before you work with the older apprentices."

Tallpaw's pelt burned, and not from the sunshine. He glared at Shrewpaw, ready for a stinging comment. A gray pelt slid in front of him, distracting him.

"Hi, Hickorynose," mewed Tallpaw.

The tunneler padded past Tallpaw without speaking and

pushed his way through the entrance tunnel. Sandgorse followed.

Tallpaw darted forward. "Sandgorse!"

But Sandgorse didn't seem to hear him. Tallpaw stared in surprise as his father ducked into the tunnel and disappeared.

Dawnstripe's whiskers brushed his ear. "He must be thinking about the new tunnel," she murmured. "Mistmouse was saying they've reached a tricky seam of gravel."

"I guess." Tallpaw stared sadly at the trembling heather. Were the tunnelers going to treat him like he was from a different Clan now?

Hareflight marched past Shrewpaw. "Let's get going."

Dawnstripe followed him. "Come on, Tallpaw. Let's race some of that stiffness from your legs." She ducked through the gap. Shrewpaw pushed in after her. Tallpaw followed, wondering if it was possible to race stiffness away.

A light breeze whisked his ears as he emerged onto the smooth grass. He scanned the moor for a sign of Sandgorse, but his father had already disappeared. Dawnstripe's golden tail flashed between two bushes. Tallpaw could hear paw steps thrumming, and raced after her. He zigzagged along the weaving track, narrowing his eyes against the twigs that lashed his face. Would he ever know all the trails on the moor as well as Dawnstripe seemed to? She ran ahead, sure-pawed, making each twist and turn as easily as a rabbit. Tallpaw felt awkward, jerking around the corners, tripping on roots, and trying not to fall.

The trail lightened up ahead and the heather suddenly

opened onto a clearing on the hillside. Dawnstripe skidded to a halt. "This is where you'll do most of your training." She nodded to the wide sweep of grass. Boulders clustered at the far end of the sheltered space.

Hareflight and Shrewpaw burst from the heather behind them and stopped. Hareflight flicked his tail. "Three laps," he ordered Shrewpaw.

Shrewpaw tore away, following the line of bushes around the edge of the clearing. He sped over the grass, fast as a skimming bird.

Tallpaw blinked at Dawnstripe. "Me too?"

"Just once around," she told him.

Tallpaw hared after Shrewpaw as fast as he could. He didn't want to lag behind his denmate.

"Take it easy!" Dawnstripe called after him. "You're just warming up, remember?"

So's Shrewpaw! Tallpaw raced harder.

His lungs ached. A cramp stabbed his ribs. Shrewpaw was already halfway back. At this rate, the dark brown tom would lap him by the time he reached Dawnstripe. Tallpaw forced himself to keep going. The grass flashed beneath him as he fought for each breath. Shrewpaw slithered past Hareflight and Dawnstripe. Tallpaw began to gain ground. Dragging in another breath, he hurtled the last few tail-lengths and skidded to a halt beside Dawnstripe.

He collapsed onto the grass, flanks heaving. "Fast, huh?" he gasped, pleased with his effort.

"It's not a race." His mentor leaned over him. "The best warrior is the one who's still fighting at the end of the battle.

Don't use up all your strength in the first fight."

Tallpaw looked up at her, eyes glazed as he panted.

"Come on, Shrewpaw!" Hareflight called to his apprentice. "Longer strides!"

"Watch him," Dawnstripe ordered. "See how much land he covers with each step. Watch how he stretches forward each time his paws leave the ground. Speed is vital, but you need to be in control of the speed." She nosed him to his paws. "You're fast, but you run like prey, not a hunter."

Hareflight was still watching Shrewpaw. "Nice paw-work," he called as Shrewpaw swept past. Tallpaw felt the wind from his pelt.

He watched how Shrewpaw curved his spine with each stride, stretching his forepaws and tucking his hind legs in close before thrusting himself out flat again. "Can I try again?" he asked Dawnstripe.

"Got your breath back?" Dawnstripe asked.

"Yes."

"Don't aim for speed," Dawnstripe warned. "You need your strength later."

Tallpaw dipped his head and padded away. He broke into a run, not pushing hard at first but gaining rhythm and speed as he crossed the grass. He focused on each bound, curving his spine the same way Shrewpaw did, and reaching out with his forepaws a little farther before they touched the grass. He pushed harder with every stride until he was aware of nothing but the steady thrumming of his paws and the way his breath fell in time with his pace. He was suddenly moving with ease, as though the wind were carrying him while the grass slid beneath him like air beneath a swallow's wings.

"Very good!" Dawnstripe's mew surprised him. He'd completed a circuit of the training ground already, so focused that he hadn't seen her. He pulled up, slowing to a trot before turning and padding to her side.

Hareflight dipped his head. "Nice work, Tallpaw."

"You learn quickly," Dawnstripe meowed.

Shrewpaw slewed to a halt a few tail-lengths away. "Not bad for a tunneler."

I'm not a tunneler! Tallpaw choked back the words.

Hareflight glanced up the hillside. "We should meet the others."

Tallpaw followed his gaze. "Is Outlook Rock over there?" He squinted across the heather but could see nothing but blue sky arcing over the moor.

Dawnstripe headed up the slope. "I'll show you."

Outlook Rock stuck out from the moor-top like a snipe's beak. Below it, the land dropped away, the valley so steep and long that Tallpaw couldn't tell whether the white shapes in the meadow below were sheep or dandelions. He padded gingerly over the stone, feeling the wind tug at his pelt as he peered over the edge. The whole world rolled out before him, fading against the clouds on the distant horizon. Dizzy, Tallpaw shrank back. What if a gust of wind lifted him off? The granite beneath his paws was too smooth to grip.

"Look ahead, not down," Dawnstripe warned from behind him.

Tallpaw fixed his gaze on the horizon. Highstones gleamed palely in the sunshine. Beyond them, mountains nudged at the sky. Movement flickered at the corner of his vision and he found himself twitching, his gaze flitting from a wind-ruffled tree to a distant monster flashing along a Thunderpath. A buzzard swooped in the distance, snatching his attention up to the sky.

"They're coming!" Shrewpaw's call made him turn.

Cloudrunner, Aspenfall, and Larksplash were leading their apprentices up the slope. Dawnstripe beckoned Tallpaw with a flick of her tail and he hurried to her side as Stagpaw, Ryepaw, and Doepaw leaped onto Outlook Rock. The three apprentices looked somber and focused as they lined up along the rock and sat down.

"What are they doing?" Tallpaw whispered to Dawnstripe.

"They're being tested on their observation skills," Dawnstripe hissed back. "Keep quiet so you don't disturb them."

Cloudrunner stood behind Stagpaw. "What do you see?" he asked his apprentice.

"Red monster; lapwing diving for insects; a Twoleg walking across the Thunderpath." Stagpaw leaned forward and squinted. "Dog running along a hedgerow."

"Which way?" Cloudrunner prompted.

"Toward the scent line."

"How long before it reaches it?"

"Long enough for a runner to fetch a patrol from camp."

"Good." Cloudrunner looked over his shoulder at Aspenfall. "Doepaw's turn."

"Twoleg climbing a fence; rogue crossing the Thunder-path."

Tallpaw watched her steadily scan the landscape. His attention had been caught by one movement after another, and his neck ached from jerking his head around. Doepaw seemed to be directing her gaze at each place in turn, picking objects out with fixed concentration before shifting her head.

Ryepaw was even better. "The Twolegplace loner is sunning himself on his green-patch. There's a heron fishing the stream beside Long Wall."

Dawnstripe leaned down to Tallpaw. "Ryepaw has the best eyesight in WindClan," she whispered.

Tallpaw glanced up as a buzzard swooped high overhead. Ryepaw's gaze remained trained on the land stretching below her. "How come they don't get distracted?" he asked.

"Training," Dawnstripe breathed.

Larksplash padded from the rock. "Nice work," she told Ryepaw. "Let's test your hunting skills."

Tallpaw felt Dawnstripe press against him. "This is where you help out."

Tallpaw gulped. "How?"

Cloudrunner paced around the older apprentices as they assembled on the grass, their eyes wide with anticipation. "We need to test your tracking skills." His gaze flashed toward Tallpaw. "You'll be the rabbit, Tallpaw. Stagpaw, Ryepaw, and Doepaw will hunt you."

"They'll catch Tallpaw easily," Shrewpaw snorted. "I should be the rabbit."

Hareflight narrowed his eyes. "You're good at open-running,

Shrewpaw. But in the heather, I think Tallpaw will have the advantage."

Shrewpaw bristled. "Why?"

"He's smaller," Hareflight explained. "And more nimble."

Tallpaw's heart was speeding. His denmates were going to *hunt* him? He leaned closer to Dawnstripe. "What will they do when they catch me?" he asked in a nervous whisper.

Dawnstripe purred. "Don't worry. They're being tested on how they pursue you," she whispered. "They need to work together to track you down. Aspenfall and Cloudrunner will be watching to see how they manage to stay out of sight while still giving one another tail signals."

"So I just need to keep running." Tallpaw's pelt tingled. He knew how to run!

Cloudrunner flicked his tail. "Head for that boulder," he told Tallpaw.

Tallpaw narrowed his eyes. Beyond a vast stretch of heather and gorse he could just make out a tall stone standing against the sky.

"Try to reach it without being caught." Cloudrunner crossed the grass and whispered into Tallpaw's ear. "Switch course a couple of times. Include a double-back. Make it as hard as you can for them to run you down."

Tallpaw nodded, dazed. At the last sunrise, he had been a kit, living with his mother in the nursery. This was his first ever taste of warrior training, and he was already being lined up as prey for bigger, stronger, faster cats.

It's my second day. How am I going to outwit three trained apprentices?

CHAPTER 8

Tallpaw felt Dawnstripe's tail sweep his spine. "You'll do fine," she murmured. "Just keep moving, and think like a fox."

"A fox?" Tallpaw had no idea how a fox thought. He'd never even seen one.

"Be smart." Dawnstripe nosed him away.

Tallpaw slid into the nearest bank of heather. Quiet as he could, he darted between two stems, hoping he'd find a rabbit trail that would lead closer to the rock. The gap opened for a few tail-lengths but ended in a thick gorse stump. Tallpaw's heart quickened. The apprentices would find him straight away. Shrewpaw would laugh at him for the rest of the day—for the rest of their *lives*, probably. Tallpaw turned and pushed through the thick heather branches, wincing as he forced his way past. He struggled onward until finally he burst out into a gap between the bushes.

A sharp tang touched his nose. Tiny dirt-berries! He'd found a rabbit track. The trail led among the stems. Tallpaw raced along it. Instinctively he kept low, crouching down so that his spine didn't set the heather quivering and give his position away.

Am I going the right way? Where's the rock?

He couldn't see it through the heather, but if he stretched up his head to get his bearings, the others would spot him. He tasted the air, hoping for a clue. *Peat and heather.* And the familiar scent of Stagpaw. Was the young tom close?

Tallpaw pushed on harder, twisting his ears back for sounds of pursuit. Paw steps thrummed behind him. *Switch course.* Cloudrunner's instruction echoed in his ears as the path forked ahead. Tallpaw swerved, taking the trail that sloped upward. He could feel the ground trembling. More paw steps pounded behind. The apprentices were on his tail.

The path sloped steeply, growing rocky, which forced Tallpaw to slow down so he didn't trap his paw and break his leg. He told himself that his pursuers would have to slow down too. After a frantic scramble over the stones, the trail emerged from the heather onto a grassy hillside. Tallpaw flattened his ears and ran faster. Remembering his practice earlier, he lengthened his stride. The grass blurred beneath him. Snatching a breath, he glanced over his shoulder.

Stagpaw exploded from the heather. Ryepaw and Doepaw fanned out behind. Tallpaw saw Stagpaw's tail flick one way, then the other. They were planning to surround him! He swerved sideways, his paws skidding on the grass as he switched direction. Cutting across the apprentices' path, he blocked their attempt to trap him from on both sides.

"Come on, Stagpaw! Think!" Aspenfall called from higher up the slope.

Wind streamed through Tallpaw's whiskers. Exhilaration

pulsed in his belly. He was running fast as a bird. But the apprentices were gaining on him.

Double back. He was smaller than his pursuers, and that made him nimble. He slowed, gradually at first. *They'll think they've outrun me.* Tallpaw glanced over his shoulder, pleased to see triumph flash in Ryepaw's eyes. She was in the lead now, Stagpaw racing just behind, matching her stride step for step. Beside him, Doepaw veered away.

Tallpaw saw the she-cat narrow her eyes. *She's going to try to overtake me and block my path.* Suddenly he slammed his paws hard into the grass. He spun around, leaving deep scars in the turf, and charged straight back toward the apprentices. Their eyes stretched wide in astonishment.

Surprised, huh? Ears flat, tail streaking behind, Tallpaw raced down the slope through the gap between Stagpaw and Doepaw.

"Don't let a kit outpace you!" Cloudrunner yowled from above them.

Kit? I'm an apprentice! Tallpaw sprinted down the hillside. The rock flashed at the edge of his vision. He'd have to change course to reach it. Stagpaw, Ryepaw, and Doepaw were still trying to turn, slithering clumsily on the grass behind him. Tallpaw needed to make a break for the rock before they found their footing. He darted sideways, his hind paws slipping out from under him. His belly hit the ground but he scrambled up and kept running. Stagpaw was pulling closer. He could hear the young tom's breath. Ryepaw and Doepaw pounded at his tail. He was closing in on the rock. If he could just keep running, he'd make it. Excitement thrilled through him.

Then paws grasped his flanks. A swift push sent him sideways. The world spun as Tallpaw tumbled over the grass and skidded to a halt.

"Great chase!" Stagpaw leaned over him.

"Are you okay?" Doepaw pushed past her brother and looked anxiously at Tallpaw. Ryepaw was just behind, panting too hard to speak.

"Yeah, I'm fine." Tallpaw scrambled to his paws, struggling to catch his breath.

"Good work!" Cloudrunner ran across the grass toward them, Dawnstripe at his heels.

"You nearly made it!" Tallpaw's mentor skidded to a halt in front of him, her eyes shining.

Stagpaw nudged him with a shoulder. "I thought you'd outrun us for a moment," he panted.

Aspenfall, Larksplash, and Hareflight pounded across the grass with Shrewpaw trotting behind much less eagerly.

Hareflight reached them first. "That was impressive."

Shrewpaw glared at Tallpaw. "*I* would have made it to the rock."

Doepaw swished her tail. "I don't think so, small-paws."

Tallpaw wanted to purr, but he was still trying to get enough air inside him.

Cloudrunner jerked his nose toward Fourtrees. "Let's test your hunting skills."

Ears pricked, looking as if he'd done nothing more strenuous than chase a leaf, Stagpaw led the way down the slope.

As the apprentices disappeared into the heather with their mentors, Dawnstripe tasted the air. "It smells like they'll find good hunting there."

Tallpaw stuck out his tongue. He couldn't taste anything but the wind.

Dawnstripe shook out her golden pelt. "Don't worry, Tallpaw. Before long you'll be able to scent prey halfway across the moor."

"I'm hungry." Shrewpaw glanced hopefully at the thick line of trees running along the bottom of the moor. "Can we hunt too?"

"Battle moves first," Hareflight told him.

"With *Tallpaw*?" Shrewpaw's tail drooped. "He won't know any."

Hareflight glared at his apprentice. "Then teach him some."

Shrewpaw stomped across the grass and stood a tail-length away. His brown pelt looked like a stray piece of wood against the windswept moor.

Dawnstripe swept Tallpaw forward with her tail. "He'll need to learn defensive moves first," she called to Shrewpaw. "Attack him, but don't forget that it's his first session." She nodded to Tallpaw. "The simplest defense is to raise your forepaws. Don't jab out wildly. Focus on protecting your muzzle and pushing your attacker away."

Tallpaw nodded, trying to remember everything Dawnstripe was saying. He could still feel his heart pounding from the chase. He curled his hind claws into the grass to steady himself, then fixed his gaze on Shrewpaw.

Shrewpaw's eyes glittered. "Ready?"

Tallpaw nodded. Letting out a ferocious yowl, Shrewpaw flew toward him. Tallpaw gasped and lifted his paws. He was too slow. Claws raked his nose. With a yelp, Tallpaw tripped over his own tail and rolled onto the grass.

"Shrewpaw!" Hareflight's mew was sharp. "Dawnstripe warned you that it's Tallpaw's first time."

As Tallpaw scrambled to his paws, he saw Shrewpaw roll his eyes. "Why do I get stuck training with a kit?"

Tallpaw faced him, nose stinging. "I'm not a kit," he hissed. "Try again."

Shrewpaw crouched, wiggling his hindquarters. Tallpaw watched him. As Shrewpaw leaped, he reared and lifted his forepaws, quicker this time. Shrewpaw hit him more slowly and Tallpaw found it easy to flip him away with a sharp shove. As Shrewpaw rolled dramatically onto the grass beside him, Tallpaw felt a twinge of satisfaction.

Then claws jabbed his ribs. Tallpaw gasped. Shrewpaw had thrust out a hind leg as he rolled and caught him in the side.

"Sorry!" Shrewpaw jumped up. "It was an accident."

Yeah, right. Tallpaw narrowed his eyes. *I bet we're supposed to keep our claws sheathed in practice!*

"Try it again," Dawnstripe encouraged. "This time, move as you push him away, Tallpaw. You need to land ready for the next attack."

Tallpaw nodded and faced Shrewpaw once more. Shrewpaw's tail-tip was flicking. *You still think I'm a tunneler.* Tallpaw flexed his claws, fighting the urge to unsheathe them. *I'll show you.*

Shrewpaw sprang into the air. Tallpaw froze for moment, then, seeing daylight beneath the young tom's belly, he ducked beneath it and bucked like a rabbit. He felt Shrewpaw's weight on his back, and pushed his spine into his denmate's belly. Shrewpaw yelped as Tallpaw tossed him backward. Tallpaw turned on his hind paws. Shrewpaw was writhing on the grass. Tallpaw reared over him and Shrewpaw stared up, his eyes wide with shock.

Forepaws raised, Tallpaw showed his teeth for a moment before dropping onto all fours and padding away. "How was that?" he asked Dawnstripe.

Dawnstripe blinked at him. "Not exactly what I expected."

"It was excellent," Hareflight purred. "Great work, Tallpaw."

Shrewpaw clambered to his paws, scowling. "He was supposed to be practicing defense moves, not attack."

Tallpaw prickled. Everything he did seemed to annoy Shrewpaw. He lifted his chin. "I was defending myself. It's not my fault if you can't keep your balance."

"You cheated, Wormpaw." Shrewpaw stalked past him and pushed into the heather. "Can we get something to eat now?"

Dawnstripe and Hareflight exchanged glances before Hareflight hurried to catch up with his apprentice.

"Well done, Tallpaw." Dawnstripe fell in beside him as they followed the others along a narrow trail.

"Thanks." Satisfaction warmed Tallpaw's pelt.

"Don't worry about Shrewpaw," Dawnstripe reassured him. "He's used to training with older apprentices. Hareflight will have a word with him about his attitude."

"A tabby can't change his stripes." Tallpaw sniffed. "Shrewpaw was born with a burr in his fur. I'll just have to put up with it."

"Come and share this rabbit!" Barkpaw called from beside the Hunting Stones as Tallpaw ducked into camp. The scent of fresh prey reached Tallpaw's tongue. He bounded over the tussocks and stopped in the patch of sunshine where Barkpaw was tearing flesh from a rabbit carcass. Suddenly realizing how tired he was, Tallpaw flopped down beside his friend.

"Here." Barkpaw shoved the rabbit toward Tallpaw.

"Thanks." Tallpaw leaned forward and took a bite.

"How was training?" Barkpaw asked.

Tallpaw glanced at Shrewpaw, who was sniffing disdainfully at a vole on the prey-heap. He wished he could tell Barkpaw what a pain in the tail Shrewpaw had been. But they were littermates. And a true warrior didn't complain about his Clanmates. "It was great." The memory of chasing across the grass with the apprentices at his heels thrilled Tallpaw once more. He felt a stab of delight as he remembered flipping Shrewpaw onto his back. "I learned a lot."

Barkpaw took another bite of rabbit. "I learned how to make a dressing for scratches today," he told Tallpaw with his mouth full. "It draws infection out of rotten wounds."

Tallpaw's belly tightened. "That sounds . . ." He searched

for words while he fought back queasiness. ". . . interesting."
I'm glad I'm training as a warrior.

"I made it for Whiteberry's ear." Barkpaw kept on chewing.
"He's got an infected tick bite. I added juniper sap. That'll
loosen the tick. It was so swollen I thought its skin would
burst."

Tallpaw stared at him, the scent of rabbit suddenly making him feel sick. "How's Hawkheart?" he asked, changing the
subject.

"He's a really good teacher," Barkpaw mewed. "It's hard
keeping up but I'm learning so much."

Tallpaw noticed Shrewpaw heading toward them. Ignoring his queasiness, he took a bite of rabbit. Shrewpaw reached
them as he was swallowing. The dark brown tom flung a
mouse onto the ground. "Have you cured anyone yet?" he
asked, settling down beside Barkpaw.

Barkpaw swallowed. "I won't know until tomorrow."

Tallpaw pulled another mouthful of flesh from the rabbit.
Shrewpaw munched on his mouse. Barkpaw glanced uneasily from one to the other before blurting out, "It must be fun
training together."

Tallpaw met Shrewpaw's gaze, wondering what the brown
tom would say.

Shrewpaw shrugged. "It's okay."

Tallpaw blinked, surprised at Shrewpaw's reply. "Yeah,"
he agreed. Why should they make Barkpaw worry that they
weren't getting along?

He ate till his belly was full, then heaved himself to his

paws. "I'm going to stretch my legs," he told Barkpaw. "I don't want to stiffen up. Dawnstripe's taking me out again later." He nodded at Shrewpaw and headed across camp.

Palebird was crouching outside the nursery. Meadowslip paced beside her. The gray queen had only just moved to the nursery, swollen with Hickorynose's kits. Her belly swayed as she padded back and forth, tail twitching and ears flicking as if she was too restless to sit still.

Palebird gazed blankly across the camp. Tallpaw frowned. Why wasn't his mother restless, too? Didn't she ever wish she were out on the moor? Or back in the tunnels? Wasn't she bored stuck in camp?

Tallpaw stopped beside her. "You should come and watch me train."

"What, dear?" Palebird looked up at him distractedly.

"It'd be good for you to get out of the camp."

Brackenwing leaped out of the Meeting Hollow and hurried over. "Don't bother Palebird," she warned. "She needs rest."

Tallpaw scowled. *She's been resting for six moons. She must have recovered from kitting by now.*

"She hasn't been sleeping well," Meadowslip explained.

"Tell me about it later, Tallpaw," Palebird murmured. "I'm sure you've had fun."

Tallpaw's tail whipped crossly and he slouched away from the nursery, eyeing Barkpaw and Shrewpaw. They were chattering like thrushes now that he was gone.

Behind him, Tallpaw could hear Meadowslip talking to

Palebird and Brackenwing. "Do you think the visitors will return this greenleaf?"

Tallpaw's ears pricked. *Visitors?*

"I'm sure they will," Brackenwing answered the young queen. "I can't remember a time that they didn't."

Tallpaw stopped and sat down. He needed a wash after his meal. He might as well wash here, where he could listen to the queens.

"I hope Wee Hen made it through leaf-bare." Brackenwing lowered her voice. "She was very frail last time we saw her."

"Whiteberry will be disappointed if she doesn't come," Meadowslip commented.

Tallpaw cleaned his muzzle with a freshly licked paw.

Brackenwing purred. "Wee Hen and Whiteberry could swap stories from dawn to dusk. There was talk of her settling with the Clan once."

"*Settling* with us?" Meadowslip sounded shocked. "How would we explain her to the other Clans?"

"WindClan wouldn't be the first to take in a rogue," Brackenwing pointed out.

"But we're the only Clan that lets visitors share our dens and our prey every greenleaf," Meadowslip replied. "What would the other Clans say? What if they thought we were training rogues to attack them?"

Tallpaw lapped the fur along his spine as it lifted with interest. He'd never heard of *visitors* living with the Clan. Why hadn't anyone mentioned them before?

"Who cares what the other Clans say?" Brackenwing

sniffed. "They huddle in the marshes and woods, hiding like prey from the wind and the sun. We live with our tails touching the sky. If we want to share our territory, that's our choice."

"Tallpaw!" Dawnstripe called from the camp entrance. Tallpaw jumped to his paws, his fur still wet from washing. Dawnstripe's whiskers twitched as she beckoned him with her tail. "Put your tongue away and let's practice some battle moves."

Tallpaw hurried after her as she ducked through the heather. "Who are the greenleaf visitors?" he asked as he caught up to her on the smooth grass outside camp.

Dawnstripe paused, her eyes narrowing. "Who told you about the greenleaf visitors?"

"Meadowslip and Brackenwing were talking," he told her.

"You shouldn't eavesdrop."

"I wasn't," Tallpaw protested. "They weren't exactly whispering." He frowned at Dawnstripe. "Are the visitors a secret?"

"We don't talk about them when they're not here, and especially not outside the Clan." Dawnstripe headed along the sheep trail that wound through the gorse patch.

Tallpaw trotted after her. "Why do they come?"

Dawnstripe didn't look back. "They just always have."

"Do they live in camp with us?"

"Just for greenleaf."

"Do they join patrols and hunt for the Clan?"

"Sometimes."

Tallpaw stopped. "Are they rogues?" He stared after Dawnstripe. Why was she acting like he'd discovered a secret? If they came every greenleaf, he was bound to know eventually.

Dawnstripe halted and turned around. "I guess you could call them rogues. They don't follow the Clan code."

"Do we *have* to let them stay with us?" Tallpaw unsheathed his claws. Did WindClan really let a band of rogues take over their camp and their prey every greenleaf?

Dawnstripe swished her tail. "Of course not. We choose to let them stay, and make them welcome."

"But rogues are bad, aren't they?" Tallpaw tipped his head on one side.

"Not all rogues are bad." Dawnstripe kept going along the trail. "Not *these* rogues."

Tallpaw trotted after her. "Then why's it such a secret?"

"It's best the other Clans don't know."

"Why?" *Is WindClan breaking the warrior code?*

"You sound like a kit." Dawnstripe nosed her way out onto a stretch of grass. "Stop asking questions and show me that move you used on Shrewpaw this morning."

CHAPTER 9

Tallpaw paced the camp entrance. Dew soaked his paws. The sun was just lifting over the horizon. Its rays spilled over the heather, setting the purple flowers alight until the moor glowed. Tallpaw was the first cat awake, eager to leave for the dawn patrol. He'd poked Shrewpaw as he padded out of the den, but the dark brown apprentice was still half asleep. Through the gap beneath the gorse, Tallpaw could see him blinking groggily over the edge of his nest.

The long grass rustled beside the Meeting Hollow and Dawnstripe slid out. She yawned and stretched, then padded over the tussocks. "Good morning, Tallpaw."

"Hi, Dawnstripe." Tallpaw flicked his tail. "Are we going to check *all* the borders?" This was his first dawn patrol.

Dawnstripe shook her head. "That would take too long." She jerked her muzzle toward the long grass where more cats were emerging into the open. "Stagleap, Ryestalk, and Larksplash will patrol the moor-edge and gorge with us. Hareflight, Shrewpaw, Doespring, and Appledawn will re-mark the borders near Fourtrees and ShadowClan."

Shrewpaw padded, yawning, from the apprentices' den. "Is

there time to raid the prey heap before we leave?" His belly growled.

Tallpaw glanced across the clearing. There was only a stiff vole and a squashed mouse in the pile. "Perhaps you'll catch something while you're patrolling."

Dawnstripe's ear twitched. "No hunting until the borders have been checked."

Shrewpaw's belly rumbled louder.

"Heatherstar will send out a hunting patrol soon." Dawnstripe tipped her head sympathetically. "There'll be prey on the heap by the time you get back."

"How can you be hungry?" Tallpaw was too excited to eat. He padded around Dawnstripe.

Shrewpaw sat down and began to wash his face. "I've done dawn patrol before, remember?"

"You can't be bored of it!" Tallpaw tasted the air, wondering what the moor was like this early. "What if we see an intruder?" he asked Dawnstripe. "Can we chase it?"

"Larksplash is leading the patrol," Dawnstripe meowed. "You'll have to ask her."

Larksplash was already heading toward them. Tallpaw raced to meet her. "If we spot an intruder, can we chase it?"

"It depends." Larksplash padded past him.

Tallpaw bounced after her. "On what?"

"On whether it's a sheep or a dog or a rogue." Larksplash stopped beside Dawnstripe. "If it's a threat to the Clan, then we chase it."

Tallpaw's imagination began to whirl. What if they

surprised a RiverClan patrol trying to invade the moor? What if a stray dog needed to be chased off? "When are we leaving?" he mewed to Dawnstripe.

Larksplash answered. "When Ryestalk and Stagleap stop gossiping and join us."

The young warriors stood at the top of the Meeting Hollow with Doespring. They'd been warriors for a half moon. Tallpaw had watched their ceremony, secretly proud that he'd helped with their assessment. He'd nearly outrun them then, and he was even faster now. With a little more training, he was sure he'd be the fastest cat in the Clan.

"Ryestalk!" Larksplash flicked her tail and the gray she-cat looked up.

"Coming!" Ryestalk leaped over the tussocks with Stagleap close behind. "Sorry!" She skidded to a halt on the wet grass.

Stagleap's eyes brightened. "Is Tallpaw patrolling with us?"

"Yes." Tallpaw puffed out his chest.

"Want to race?" Stagleap plucked the ground excitedly.

"Yes, please—"

Larksplash stepped between them. "We're patrolling, not racing," she meowed sternly. "I want your attention focused on the borders."

Tallpaw glanced at his paws, peeking at Stagleap from under his fur.

The dark brown tom's whiskers were twitching with amusement. "Sorry, Larksplash." He straightened his tail respectfully, but his whiskers kept twitching.

Tallpaw swallowed a purr. "No racing, I promise. No

having fun whatsoever on the dawn patrol."

Huffing, Larksplash turned away and headed through the entrance.

Ryestalk brushed past Tallpaw. "She doesn't mean to be bad-tempered," she whispered. "She's just not a dawn cat."

"I know the feeling." Shrewpaw stared blearily at the rest of his patrol as they headed toward him.

"You'll feel better once the wind's in your fur," Ryestalk promised as she followed Dawnstripe through the entrance.

Outside, the air was sweet with heather blossom. The sun was climbing into a pale blue sky. Tallpaw narrowed his eyes against the glare. He could make out pockets of mist pooling in dips and hollows across the moor. Heat would burn them away before long. It was going to be another scorching day.

Tallpaw felt the breeze in his tail. "Which way?" he asked Larksplash.

She was already heading upslope, toward the high-moor. "We'll reset the markers along the Thunderpath first."

"But there's no Clan beyond that border." Tallpaw caught up to her, weaving around a clump of heather to stay near her. "Why do we have to mark it?"

"There are rogues and loners out there," Larksplash reminded him. "It's only fair to warn them that they've reached Clan territory."

I thought we welcomed rogues. Tallpaw glanced over his shoulder at Dawnstripe. She was watching the horizon. Was she looking out for their greenleaf visitors?

Stagleap caught up. "I know you said no racing." He turned

his round, amber gaze on Larksplash. "But we're not at the border yet."

Ryestalk popped up beside her brother. "We'd get there quicker if we ran."

Larksplash rolled her eyes. "Okay, then. But don't get too excited, and be careful of the Thunderpath."

"We're not 'paws anymore," Stagleap retorted.

"Tallpaw is," Larksplash reminded him. "So *be careful*."

Stagleap caught Tallpaw's eye. "Ready?"

"Ready!" Tallpaw tensed, feeling energy surge beneath his pelt.

"Go!" Ryestalk crashed away through the heather.

Stagleap chose a wider course, skirting the bushes and charging for the stretch of grass beyond. *Grass makes for easier running.* Tallpaw raced after Stagpaw. His paws skidded in the dew as he swerved around the heather. Ryestalk exploded from the bushes beside him as he veered onto Stagleap's trail. She whisked past him with a yowl of triumph. Tallpaw dug in his claws and pushed harder.

The ground sloped steeply ahead of them. Ryestalk pounded over the grass but she couldn't match her brother's strength. Stagleap streaked higher. Stretching farther with each stride, Tallpaw found his rhythm until he was skimming the ground, hardly touching it with his paws. Wind streamed through his whiskers as he ran past Ryestalk. Stagleap was only a tail-length ahead. The top of the moor loomed above him, the blue sky stretching out endlessly beyond.

As Tallpaw drew closer, Stagleap crested the rise and

began to charge down the other side. Tallpaw glanced back. Ryestalk was lagging but she put on a spurt of energy to crest the rise and hurtled down after them. The slope gave Stagleap an extra burst of speed. His wide shoulders and stocky build might slow him uphill, but here he could use his strength to race harder than ever.

Tallpaw lengthened his stride, but Stagpaw was pulling farther ahead. As the slope flattened out beside the Thunderpath, the young warrior slowed to a halt and lifted his tail in victory.

"Nice try," Stagleap puffed as Tallpaw reached him.

"I'll get you one day," Tallpaw panted.

Ryestalk pulled up beside them. "I'm hopeless on grass!" She struggled to get her breath. "I'd rather sprint over rabbit trails."

"You're better at twists and turns," Stagleap agreed. "Next time we'll race through heather."

The Thunderpath glittered in the sunshine a few tail-lengths away. Tallpaw looked along it as he caught his breath. He'd never been this close. "Where are the monsters?" It was deserted.

"They come later," Stagleap told him.

Ryestalk glanced over her shoulder. "We've passed the scent line."

Tallpaw tasted the air. The acrid tang of the Thunderpath mingled with stale WindClan scent.

"Let's start resetting the markers." Stagleap turned back. "Before Larksplash gets hissy."

As Tallpaw followed, he spotted Dawnstripe's golden pelt flash farther up the slope. She was bounding toward him, her tail bushed. "I don't want to see you so near to the Thunderpath again!" she snapped as she reached him.

Tallpaw stared at her in surprise. "But it's deserted."

"Monsters travel as fast as birds. And they're bigger than you can imagine." Dawnstripe glared at him.

"But it's—"

Dawnstripe narrowed her eyes. "When I tell you something, you *listen*; you don't argue."

Tallpaw's throat tightened with anger but he swallowed it back. *I can't wait to be a warrior!*

Tallpaw helped the young moor runners to mark the border that ran level with the Thunderpath, following the high-moor toward the gorge.

I'm bored. Tallpaw stopped to spray another clump of heather. Wearily he watched Larksplash double back to follow yet another scent trail that had crossed the boundary. At this rate, they'd be marking borders till nightfall.

"Is that RiverClan?" Dawnstripe called after Larksplash.

The tortoiseshell warrior sniffed the heather. "Just a Twoleg."

"Did they have a dog with them?" Ryestalk hurried to taste the scent.

Larksplash shook her head.

Stagleap climbed a hummock and lifted his chin. "There's been no dog on this part of the moor in a moon."

Ryestalk looked at him. "Since *you* started patrolling, I suppose."

"Can we keep moving?" Tallpaw's legs itched. He wanted to run. Why couldn't they find a fresh rabbit scent—something he could *chase*?

Stagleap bounded from the hummock and marched along the scent line, tail high. "They're scared of my scent."

"Who are?" Tallpaw was puzzled. "Rabbits?"

Stagleap flashed him a look. *"Dogs!"*

Tallpaw snorted, ducking as Stagleap launched a play attack and swiped his ears.

"We're patrolling the border," Dawnstripe reminded them sternly.

Tallpaw frowned. Weren't they allowed to have any fun? He stopped and sprayed a gorse stem halfheartedly.

In the distance he could hear water. At least they were nearly at the gorge. After that, they could head for camp and do some proper training. He followed Larksplash as she disappeared into a patch of heather. He pushed through the whippy branches, the rest of the patrol at his heels. The path wound through hummocks, spiky twigs pressing in on all sides. The pollen-heavy blossom made Tallpaw sneeze, and he was relieved when the heather opened onto grass near the cliff top.

Larksplash, Ryestalk, and Dawnstripe fanned out and sniffed at the scent line that ran along the top of the gorge. Tallpaw crept forward and peered over the edge. Greenleaf had calmed the water and it flowed smoothly far below, winding between the cliffs. "Is it deep?" he asked Stagleap.

Stagleap shrugged. "How would I know?"

Tallpaw scanned the sheer rock face, spotting a narrow ledge at the water's edge. It ran the whole length of the gorge, opening out at the end onto grassland. "Have you ever been down there?"

Stagleap shook his head. "It's too dangerous in leaf-bare. In newleaf, there's snowmelt and the river covers it."

"But it's a good route to get to the Twoleg bridge without being seen by RiverClan." Tallpaw nodded toward the wooden pathway spanning the river, just visible beyond the gorge.

"Are you planning to invade RiverClan territory?" Stagleap teased.

As he spoke, Tallpaw felt a faint shudder in the ground beneath him. His fur lifted along his spine. "What was that?"

Before Stagleap could answer, yowls echoed behind them. Tallpaw spun around, scanning the moor. He could see nothing but birds swooping across the heather. Larksplash tasted the air. The yowls sounded again, deep and hollow, strangely muffled.

Ryestalk's gray fur stood on end. "What is that?"

Tallpaw darted to the edge of the gorge and looked over. Was someone calling from the bottom?

"It's coming from here!" Dawnstripe was sniffing at a rabbit hole a few tail-lengths away. She backed away as the yowls grew louder.

Sandgorse burst out of the hole. Fur spiked up, eyes wide,

he glanced over his shoulder as Mistmouse hurtled out on his heels. "Are you okay?" He circled his mud-streaked tunnel-mate, sniffing her anxiously.

"I'm fine," she panted. Her pelt was thick with mud.

Sandgorse stuck his head down the hole and yowled. Tall-paw pricked his ears as distant yowls sounded back.

"They're safe." Sandgorse straightened up. He seemed to notice Larksplash for the first time. "Just a cave-in. The others are safe. Hickorynose and Woollytail are experts. They'll find their way out through a lower entrance if they need to." He shook out his pelt.

Tallpaw rushed over to his father. "What happened?"

Sandgorse touched his nose to Tallpaw's head. "Too much sunshine," he explained matter-of-factly. "Makes the soil shrink. Rocks drop and we get cave-ins." He looked at the wide, blue sky. "We could sure use a few days of rain."

Tallpaw winced. What if Sandgorse had been caught in the cave-in? In the last half-moon, he'd been aware of more and more distance between himself and his father. Sandgorse spoke to him, but not often, and not with the warmth he'd had before. If he could just see how well Tallpaw was doing with his training, he would understand that he had chosen the right path, and everything would be okay again.

Sandgorse padded away, weaving between Dawnstripe and Stagleap. "Are you patrolling the borders?"

"We've nearly finished," Dawnstripe told him. "No sign of intruders."

The tunneler gazed across the heather. "We've been digging all night."

Ryestalk blinked at him. "Aren't you tired?"

Sandgorse's eyes shone. "We're so close to breaking through to the gorge." His ears twitched excitedly. "I'm not resting till it's done."

Mistmouse peered down the tunnel. "What about the cave-in?"

"We'll clear it in no time." Sandgorse nosed past her, his mew echoing as he stuck his head into the hole. "The soil's light. It'll be easy to burrow through." He ducked out and looked at Dawnstripe. "This is the perfect time to give Tallpaw some tunneling experience."

Tallpaw's pelt bristled. He forced it flat. "But we're patrolling the borders."

Sandgorse kept his gaze on Dawnstripe. "You said you'd nearly finished."

Dawnstripe glanced at Tallpaw. "Heatherstar does want every warrior to spend a day underground," she conceded.

"At *least* a day." There was an edge to Sandgorse's mew. "How will moor runners appreciate the importance of the tunnels if they don't know what it's like to be underground?"

"Of course." Dawnstripe shifted her paws.

Please, no, Tallpaw begged her silently.

"Then it's settled." Sandgorse beckoned Tallpaw with a flick of his tail.

Tallpaw looked hopefully at Dawnstripe. "Is it?"

"You might as well go with him." Dawnstripe dipped her head. "When you're finished, come and find me in camp."

"Okay." Swallowing, Tallpaw padded toward his father. The rabbit hole loomed in front of him like a black mouth sucking him in. *There can't be more than one cave-in today, surely?*

Sandgorse purred. "I'm glad you finally have a chance to see what tunneling's all about." For the first time in a half moon he gazed at Tallpaw with pride.

Tallpaw gritted his teeth. He couldn't let his father down now. "I'm looking forward to it," he lied. Perhaps once he was underground, he'd understand why his father thought being a tunneler was so special.

CHAPTER 10

❧

"You first, Mistmouse." Sandgorse stood aside to let the pale tabby she-cat scramble into the burrow. Behind her, Tallpaw paused. "Go on," Sandgorse urged. "Don't let the darkness put you off. Remember you have ears and whiskers as well as eyes."

Tallpaw crept in. The earth was loose beneath his paws and he unsheathed his claws, digging them in to stop himself from sliding as the tunnel sloped steeply down. Blackness wrapped around him as the entrance faded behind. Tallpaw strained to see the walls of the tunnel, or where he was placing his feet, but no light eased the darkness. He could hear his father behind him, Sandgorse's breath warm on his tail as the air at his muzzle turned cold. Tallpaw's pelt, hot from the sun a few moments ago, felt the chill, and he bushed out his fur.

Sandgorse purred. "If you think this is cold, wait till we're deeper." Tallpaw tried not to imagine it. "Listen." Sandgorse paused. Tallpaw stood still. He could hear Mistmouse's fur brushing the walls ahead.

"Wait, Mistmouse!" Sandgorse called. Her paw steps stilled. "Can you hear it?" Sandgorse asked.

Tallpaw pricked his ears. "Hear what?"

"Keep listening."

Tallpaw strained to hear, closing his eyes to block out the stifling darkness. Muffled paw steps sounded at the edge of his hearing.

"That's your patrol, heading along the gorge," Sandgorse mewed softly.

"How do you know?" Tallpaw whispered.

"Three sets of paw steps, heading away from us."

Tallpaw was impressed. "It could have been rabbits," he suggested.

"No." Sandgorse shifted his paws. "They thump; they don't patter."

"Can you tell if it's sheep?"

"Of course. Their steps are harder, while a dog's resonate more deeply in the earth."

Mistmouse moved ahead of them, stirring the darkness with thicker shadows. "Your father can tell ThunderClan paw steps from WindClan," she told Tallpaw with a hint of pride.

Sandgorse's tail whisked the side of the tunnel. "ThunderClan high-step like deer," he growled. "When they pass overhead on the way to the Moonstone, they prance over us like they own the moor."

"Typical ThunderClan," Mistmouse huffed.

Sandgorse snorted. "They have no idea we can track them from underground. We know exactly when they arrive and when they leave WindClan territory."

"We'd know if they dared stop to hunt," Mistmouse added.

Tallpaw felt a nudge from behind. "Let's get going,"

Sandgorse prompted. "Hickorynose and Woollytail are probably already digging through the cave-in from the other side. They'll need our help."

Tallpaw blinked, wishing his eyes would adjust to the darkness. But without a spark of light, he began to realize that he was utterly blind here. Mistmouse's paws scurried ahead and Tallpaw followed, pressing back the queasy feeling in his belly. *Sandgorse won't let anything happen to me.*

Tallpaw's whiskers dragged along the tunnel sides, sending shivers through his fur. A sudden gap in the wall on one side surprised him, along with the blast of cold air that struck his flank.

"That tunnel leads toward the high-moor," Sandgorse told him.

"Do you know where you are all the time?" Tallpaw was amazed. He felt as helpless as a mouse—as though the earth had swallowed him like prey.

"Every tunneler knows each twist and turn," Sandgorse meowed. "We can get to any part of our territory from here, and cross any border."

Tallpaw's thoughts quickened. Having the tunnels meant that WindClan could thwart any invasion and outwit any enemy. No wonder the tunnelers defended their skills so fiercely. "Has Heatherstar been in the tunnels?" he asked.

"She comes on patrol occasionally," Sandgorse replied. "But she doesn't really understand the darkness, or the power it gives to a warrior. She's a moor runner who can only imagine hunting and fighting overground."

"I can hear them." Mistmouse slowed down.

Tallpaw nearly bumped into her. Stopping clumsily, he strained his ears and heard muffled mews ahead. He felt Sandgorse press behind him.

"Make way, Tallpaw." Tallpaw squeezed against the side of the passage to let his father pass. "They're digging," Sandgorse reported. "We should start work this side and meet them in the middle."

Tallpaw heard Mistmouse begin scooping earth with her front paws. The tunnel was wider here. Tallpaw could feel space around his whiskers. There was enough room for Sandgorse and Mistmouse to work side by side.

"We always work in twos," Sandgorse told Tallpaw, pushing a heap of dirt back toward him. "If there's a cave-in, you never leave your companion. It's the most important rule of tunneling. Another cat's life is as precious as your own. Never forget it for a moment."

Mistmouse chimed in. "One tunneler dies; two tunnelers survive."

Tallpaw reached for the earth Sandgorse had kicked back to him. "What do I do with this?" Surely it was dumb just to fill up the space behind?

"Spread it out," Sandgorse told him. "As thin as you can, even if it means dragging it right back up the tunnel."

Tallpaw was still pushing loose soil around when he heard a stone scraping earth. He felt its hardness against his muzzle as Sandgorse pushed it back toward him. "How do I get rid of stones?" Tallpaw called.

"Press it into a crevice, if you can find one," Sandgorse

meowed over his shoulder. "Keep it close. We never get rid of stones; they're useful for shoring up walls."

Tallpaw grabbed the stone in his paws. It was bigger than the sparrow-sized rocks he'd practiced on as a kit, but he heaved it backward, grunting at the effort. *You're always stronger than you think.* Sandgorse's lesson came back to him. And it was true: Even in the cramped space, Tallpaw found he could tug the stone back up the tunnel until he felt a dent in the earth wall. Pushing hard, he pressed the stone into the earth, then returned to haul some more of the soil that Sandgorse and Mistmouse had dug out. Scrabbling with his forepaws, Tallpaw dragged a pile of earth backward, leaving a trail of loose dirt in his wake.

His paws were clogged with grit and he could feel soil deep in his pelt. Fighting the instinct to wash it out, he kept hauling earth, spreading it back up the tunnel. Each time he hurried back for another load, he trampled the loose earth harder into the tunnel floor. As he reached for another pile, he suddenly realized that he'd forgotten he was working in the dark. And he was warm!

"They're close!" Sandgorse called excitedly. "Can you hear them, Tallpaw?"

Tallpaw listened and heard Woollytail's growl. Hickorynose answered, his gruff mew echoing beyond the wall of dirt.

Tallpaw's pelt pricked. "Won't it collapse again if we clear away the blockage?"

"All the earth's fallen that's going to fall," Sandgorse reassured him.

"How do you know?"

"Listen." Sandgorse scraped back more pawfuls of dirt, then halted. "Do you hear loose dirt? Or falling stones?"

"No." Tallpaw felt a quiver of relief.

"And there's no creaking above," Mistmouse added. "The earth will hold." As she spoke, Tallpaw felt fresh air on his whiskers.

"Sandgorse!" Woollytail's delighted mew echoed around the walls of the tunnel.

"Is Hickorynose all right?" Mistmouse asked.

"I'm fine!" Hickorynose called from farther down the tunnel.

"Great." Tallpaw felt his father's tail swish past his nose. "Now we can get back to finding the gorge."

Tallpaw tasted the air. "I smell heather!" The sweet scent of blossom touched his tongue.

Sandgorse's tail flicked past his nose. "There's an airhole ahead," he explained. "A small crack up through the earth to the moor."

Tallpaw strained his eyes and saw shapes in the darkness: Woollytail's spine; Hickorynose's ears silhouetted against it.

Light! And air! Tallpaw felt a rush of excitement.

"Let's head for the river," Mistmouse urged.

"Are you still trying to tunnel through the clay seam to get to the river?" Tallpaw asked, remembering a discussion from moons ago.

"That's right." Sandgorse nudged him forward as the others headed away. "It's hard gauging our depth exactly, but yesterday I hit clay."

Tallpaw glanced up as he passed below the airhole, blinking into the pale light seeping from the moor. "You found the seam?"

"That's what we've been digging through all night." Sandgorse's mew was filled with warmth. "We should break through to the other side soon. I'm so pleased you're here to see it happen! The first ever tunnel from high-moor to the river!"

Tallpaw felt the air dampen and fade as the soil around him thickened to mud. He was sharply aware of the airhole fading into the distance, and with it, the light and the scent of heather. He followed the sound of paw steps, staying close to the warmth of Mistmouse's tail. As the tunnel twisted and turned, he quickly learned to recognize changes in the thickness of air that warned of a turning ahead. But his chest was tightening and he found himself snatching for each breath.

"Sandgorse?" he called nervously.

"Nearly there." Sandgorse's reply was muffled.

"Sandgor—" A hard wall of mud slapped Tallpaw's muzzle. He yelped, half in pain, half-surprised.

Sandgorse stumbled back. "Turn to your right! Concentrate!"

"Sorry." Tallpaw pricked his ears, focusing harder on the space ahead.

The air ahead seemed to tremble, and as he pushed on, the earth throbbed around him.

"What's that?" Tallpaw froze. Was the tunnel about to collapse?

"It's just the river," Woollytail called. "We're at the end of the tunnel. A few more scoops and we'll be in the gorge."

In the gorge! Fresh air! Tallpaw's chest relaxed a little. They were probably only a tail-length from the wind and the sun.

Sandgorse pushed past him. "Wait here."

Tallpaw heard paws scraping dirt.

"The clay's wetter here!" Hickorynose sounded jubilant. "We must be close."

Tallpaw hung back, listening above the hum of the river. The tunnelers' pelts brushed against one another; clay squelched beneath their paws. Tallpaw could hear their breathing as they worked. "Should I dig, too?" he offered. Anything to get them into daylight faster.

Splat. A hunk of clay landed in front of him. Mud spattered his nose.

"Start packing the dug clay into the walls," Mistmouse ordered.

Tallpaw wrinkled his nose as he scooped up a pawful of slippery earth and smeared it against the side of the tunnel. He felt the earth trembling beneath his pads. The river must be very close.

Splat. Another lump landed at his paws. *Splat. Splat.*

The tunnelers were tossing clods so fast that Tallpaw hopped back to avoid them. He snatched another pawful and slapped it against the wall. Working as fast as he could, he gathered pawful after pawful of clay, spreading it along the passage behind him until he could hardly squeeze past the fresh, slimy layer. He paused for breath, his muscles aching. He must look like a mud-drowned rat by now.

"Tallpaw?"

As he turned back for more mud, he felt his father's breath near his muzzle. "What?"

"This is what I always dreamed of," Sandgorse mewed softly. "You working beside me. Digging a new tunnel together, a tunnel that may be the one to change WindClan's destiny forever."

Tallpaw stiffened. Did Sandgorse think he'd change his mind about becoming a moor runner now that he'd been underground? Another gob of clay splatted in the passage beside Tallpaw and his father darted back to help the others.

"Are we nearly there?" Tallpaw called above the rumbling of the river. His ear fur quivered. *Has it gotten louder?*

"We'll hit air any moment!" Sandgorse sounded as excited as a kit at his naming ceremony.

"Wait!" Mistmouse snapped from somewhere in the darkness.

"What is it?" Woollytail's mew was edged with alarm.

The tunnelers paused. A long, mournful creak echoed along the passage. It sounded like stone flexing, with the deep suck of mud gradually releasing its grip on a hillside that had stood for moons.

"StarClan, help us." Hickorynose's mew was barely more than a whisper.

"What's happening?" Tallpaw asked nervously.

"Run!"

Paws scrambled in the darkness. Tallpaw felt fur press against him.

"Tallpaw!" Sandgorse's yowl pierced his ear fur. *"Run!"*

Shock pulsed though Tallpaw. Spinning around, he pelted up the tunnel. "Sandgorse!" He glanced over his shoulder into blackness.

"Behind you!" Sandgorse called. "Hickorynose? Woolly-tail? Mistmouse?"

"Here!"

"Here!

"Here!"

"Faster, Tallpaw!" Sandgorse urged, panic edging his mew.

Behind them, an earsplitting roar shook the earth as water exploded into the tunnel. Tallpaw's pads slithered on the mud. Ears flat, he flailed in the darkness, skidding against walls as the tunnels twisted.

"Let me through." Sandgorse barged past him. "Keep your nose to my tail and run!"

Tallpaw obeyed, too frightened to speak. He couldn't run properly here. There was no space to curve his spine or stretch his legs. Terror pulsing through every hair, he focused on the touch of Sandgorse's tail-tip on his nose. Water roared behind them like wind caught in a valley. It charged after them, making the ground tremble.

Just keep running!

Tallpaw's chest heaved. There was no air here! How could he breathe? Panic flared inside him, but he kept running until light flashed ahead—brighter, brighter, now dazzling—and they were out, bursting from the tunnel like rabbits chased by a fox.

Tallpaw collapsed on the grass. Through glazed eyes he saw

Hickorynose flash past him with Woollytail and Mistmouse. They had all made it. With a sigh, Tallpaw shut his eyes, his breath slowing.

Paw steps paced the grass beside him. "I can't believe we got it wrong."

Tallpaw pricked his ears. Sandgorse sounded *annoyed*. Wasn't he scared?

Hickorynose grunted. "I'd been counting the tail-lengths, and I was sure we had two more to go before we reached the river."

"We didn't take enough notice of the easy digging in leaf-bare," Woollytail huffed angrily. "We reached the water faster than we expected."

Tallpaw opened his eyes.

Mistmouse was peering down the rabbit hole. "At least the flooding will let us know where the river is."

Tallpaw sat up. "We nearly drowned! You can't go back down there!"

"But we *didn't* drown," Sandgorse pointed out. "And we've learned a lot for next time."

"Next time?" Tallpaw shook his ears in disbelief. "Are you planning to carry on with the tunnel?"

"Of course." Mistmouse looked over her shoulder at him. "Now that we have a tunnel with water in it, we'll know what level to aim for on the wall of the gorge. Obviously the new tunnel will have to come out higher next time."

"Should I fetch Plumclaw?" Hickorynose suggested. "She'll want to be part of this."

"Yes." Woollytail turned excitedly in a circle. "We'll be through to the gorge by moonhigh."

"But it's dangerous!" Tallpaw's heart seemed to beat in his throat.

"Not if you know what you're doing." Sandgorse's eyes were bright with exhilaration. Had he *enjoyed* racing the river? Tallpaw winced. His father had even more courage than he thought.

"Why don't you go back to camp?" Sandgorse meowed. "Have a rest and get cleaned up. Then you can come back and help us with the new section."

Come back? Tallpaw decided he'd rather face a patrol of ShadowClan warriors.

Sandgorse was purring. "We'll break through to the gorge together, Tallpaw. Palebird will be so proud of us."

Tallpaw backed away. "No." His throat was dry. "Never."

Shock flashed through Sandgorse's gaze. "But you saw how it was! Didn't you feel it? The excitement! The danger!" He looked across the moors. "You can't want to go back to running through heather after that."

"Yes!" Tallpaw jumped up, bristling with frustration. "Why don't you get it? Just because *you* love tunneling doesn't mean I do! I'm not you! I thought we were all going to *die* down there. I'm a moor runner, not a tunneler!"

CHAPTER 11

"When can we start using the tunnel?" Cloudrunner asked Hickorynose.

Tallpaw pricked his ears. Had the tunnelers dug all the way through to the gorge? The cats around him shifted to hear the answer. Above, the full moon turned their pelts silver as they waited to leave for the Gathering. Larksplash and Appledawn sat beside Reedfeather. Stagleap plucked at the grass while Doespring gazed dreamily at the stars. Hareflight and Shrewpaw practiced battle moves a few tail-lengths away. Tallpaw was quivering with anticipation, though he was trying to hide it. This would be his first visit to Fourtrees, his first meeting with the other three Clans.

Hickorynose paused before replying to Cloudrunner. "We need to shore up the walls and roof before it's safe for moor runners," he warned.

The pale gray tom's fur pricked along his spine. "And you really think this is going to make a difference for us all?" Cloudrunner meowed.

"It's a good route down to the gorge," Heatherstar reminded him.

Reedfeather's eyes flashed. "Quicker for getting to River-Clan territory."

"Why would we want to go there?" Cloudrunner stared at his deputy.

Reedfeather shrugged. "There might be a war between the Clans."

"The Clans haven't been at war in moons," Cloudrunner huffed.

"Maybe there are other reasons for needing to visit our neighbors," Reedfeather meowed. He turned his gaze away. "War is not the only connection between us."

Tallpaw impatiently kneaded the grass with his claws. Why was Reedfeather going on about visiting RiverClan? The only place outside the moor that they needed to reach was Four-trees!

"Don't worry; we'll be leaving soon," Dawnstripe promised.

"I'm not worried." Tallpaw padded past her, avoiding her gaze. He knew he should feel excited about his first Gathering, but instead he felt nervous. His quarrel with Sandgorse yesterday had unsettled him. Why was his father so obsessed with him being a tunneler? *How can I enjoy training to be a moor runner? Sandgorse makes me feel like a traitor.*

Barkpaw hurried from the medicine den. "Hawkheart says I can come!" He glanced over his shoulder at the medicine cat, who was crossing the tussocks behind him.

Tallpaw lifted his tail in greeting as his friend reached him. "Is Shrewpaw coming too?"

"Didn't he tell you?" Barkpaw looked surprised.

"Shrewpaw doesn't tell me anything." Tallpaw had given up trying to be friends with his denmate.

"Why should I?" Shrewpaw paused from practicing battle moves. "You're wasting your time and Dawnstripe's by training as a moor runner. You're a tunneler."

"No, I'm not!" Tallpaw snapped.

"You will be one day." Shrewpaw glanced meaningfully at the bracken patch. "Sandgorse will make sure of that."

"Sandgorse respects what I want." Tallpaw's heart twisted. *If only it were true.*

"Of *course* he does," Shrewpaw sneered.

"In the end, we all decide our own destinies," came an unexpected voice.

Tallpaw spun around in surprise as he heard Hawkheart's deep growl behind him. The medicine cat stalked past and settled beside Heatherstar.

Cloudrunner was still bickering with Hickorynose. "I don't see why we *need* a route to the gorge."

"You'll appreciate it one day." Hickorynose sounded weary from the long nights of digging.

Tallpaw had watched Heatherstar spend most of the day persuading him to attend the Gathering. "One of the tunnelers should come," she'd insisted, sitting beside the bracken patch while Hickorynose and his tunnelmates finally got a chance to clean the clay from their paws. They'd opened the tunnel by moonhigh, just as Sandgorse had promised. But they spent till dawn safeguarding against cave-ins and mudslides, and returned to camp more anxious than exhilarated.

"The whole Clan should be represented." Heatherstar had challenged one tunneler, then the next, until finally Hickorynose had looked up.

"What does it matter?" he'd grunted. "The other Clans don't know a tunneler from a moor runner."

Plumclaw sniffed. "Tunnelers don't need to share gossip with the other Clans."

Heatherstar had bristled. "The Gatherings aren't for sharing gossip," she'd snapped. "They keep harmony between the Clans."

"Harmony!" Woollytail had snorted. "The Clans are just there to spy on one another." He'd returned to washing, tugging grit from between his claws.

"Well?" Heatherstar glared at the tunnelers, her tail flicking. "Who's coming to the Gathering?"

Hickorynose sighed. "I will."

Heatherstar had nodded. "Then you'd better get some rest."

Now, in the moonlight, Tallpaw thought Hickorynose still looked tired despite his sleep. He yawned as Cloudrunner complained to Stagleap.

"The gorge tunnel will be as steep as a cliff," the pale gray moor runner fretted. "You won't get me down it."

Stagleap shrugged. "Tallpaw said it's not that steep."

"He says they dug the slope long and shallow," added Doespring.

"Yes, it's not too bad," Tallpaw meowed.

Cloudrunner turned and stared at Tallpaw. "You've been *down* it?"

"He helped dig it out," Stagleap announced.

Tallpaw shifted his paws uncomfortably as he remembered how terrified he'd been with the river roaring at his tail like an angry swarm of bees. And Sandgorse *still* wanted him to be a tunneler. *Just because it's right for him doesn't make it right for me!*

"Ready?" Dawnstripe's mew surprised him.

"Ready?" Tallpaw echoed, lost in his own thoughts.

Dawnstripe rolled her eyes. "The Gathering, remember?"

Heatherstar was already heading out of the camp.

"Of course I remember!" Tallpaw glanced at the bracken patch. Was Sandgorse watching him leave for his first Gathering? He scanned the nests for eyes flashing in the darkness, but there was no sign of any cats looking at him. Tallpaw glanced at the nursery, relieved to see Palebird sliding out of the gorse.

She nodded to him. "Good luck, Tallpaw."

"Good luck, Tallpaw," Shrewpaw mimicked.

Barkpaw growled at his brother. "Leave him alone. It's his first Gathering!"

"Poor little Wormpaw has to go without his mother."

Tallpaw unsheathed his claws.

"Come on." Dawnstripe nosed her apprentice away from his denmate.

Growling under his breath, Tallpaw followed Stagleap through the heather. Doespring met him on the grass clearing outside camp, Ryestalk at her side. "Are you excited?" Her amber eyes were bright. It was her first Gathering as a warrior.

Tallpaw shrugged. "I guess."

"You *guess?*" Ryestalk followed Cloudrunner and Hareflight across the grass. "It'll be great!" she called, disappearing into the heather.

Hawkheart shadowed Whiteberry and Flamepelt, his sharp gaze flicking over the elders. "You should be resting in your nest, Whiteberry," he muttered.

"I'm not letting a few aching joints keep me away from a Gathering," Whiteberry rasped.

"I gave him the heather blossom we gathered." Barkpaw trotted after his mentor.

Hawkheart's gaze narrowed. "How much?"

"Half a pawful, soaked in water. Like you showed me."

Hawkheart nodded. "Well done." His gaze flicked back to Whiteberry. "Has it helped?"

"I was fine before." Whiteberry limped along the trail after his Clanmates. "Don't waste your herbs on me."

"Poor Barkpaw." Shrewpaw stopped beside Doespring. "Imagine spending your life listening to elders complain."

"He's had plenty of practice, growing up in a nest with you," Doespring meowed sharply. Shrewpaw scowled at her and trotted ahead to catch up to Barkpaw.

Stagleap ripped at the grass. "Hurry up, Tallpaw!" Beyond him, the heather rippled as WindClan moved though it.

"What's Fourtrees like?" Tallpaw meowed.

"Weird." Stagleap shouldered his way through the bushes.

Tallpaw slid after him, following the trail. "How?"

"You'll see."

Doespring was pushing at Tallpaw's heels. "Should we race?"

"No thanks." Tallpaw wasn't in the mood for running.

Stagleap glanced back, his eyes flashing in the darkness. "*I'll* race you!"

Tallpaw leaned aside to let Doespring pass. "See you there!" she called as she broke into a run. The two warriors hared away, their paws thrumming the ground. Tallpaw trudged after them, following their scent through the heather.

Paw steps sounded behind him. "I thought you loved racing?" Dawnstripe had caught up to him.

"I don't feel like it," Tallpaw murmured.

Dawnstripe walked in silence for a few moments. "What's the matter?" she asked at last.

"Nothing."

"You've been in a bad mood since you went tunneling yesterday."

"So?"

"So, you hardly heard a word I said in training today," she persisted. "You didn't even *try* to outstalk Shrewpaw, and your hunting stance was the worst I've ever seen."

"Maybe I'm not meant to be a moor runner." Tallpaw let gloom swamp him.

"Don't be silly." Dawnstripe was brisk. "You're the best runner I've seen. Now, tell me what happened in the tunnels that upset you. Is it Sandgorse?"

Tallpaw sighed. "He didn't even see me off to my first Gathering."

"It's going to take Sandgorse time to accept that you want

to be a moor runner," Dawnstripe told him. "No cat can change his feelings overnight."

"Doesn't he want what's best for me?" Tallpaw asked crossly.

"Of course he does," Dawnstripe meowed. "But he still thinks being a tunneler is best for you."

"Is he right?" Tallpaw's belly tightened.

"Do you want to train as a tunneler?" Dawnstripe prompted.

"No!" The word burst from Tallpaw before he had a chance to think. "Never! I don't want to spend my life in the dark with soil in my fur and mud in my claws!"

"Okay." Dawnstripe padded steadily beside him. "So you're going to have to put up with Sandgorse's disappointment. You can't change the way he feels. The only thing you can change is how you feel."

"I feel bad."

"But not bad enough to become a tunneler just to please Sandgorse."

"I guess not." Tallpaw followed the trail as it wound out from the heather. Moonlight shone on the slope ahead.

Dawnstripe kept pace with him, her long strides carrying her easily over the flattened grass. "Then let Sandgorse sulk if he wants to, and concentrate on becoming the best moor runner you can be. Your Clan needs good warriors, and I think you can become one of the best."

Tallpaw glanced at his mentor. "Really?"

Paw steps thrummed toward them. "Come on!" Stagleap slowed to a halt in front of them. "I've already beaten Doespring to the top of the hollow."

Doespring charged up behind him. "You did not!"

"Okay," Stagleap conceded. "You were a whisker ahead." He blinked at Tallpaw. "Heatherstar and the others are waiting for you to join them before they go down. Hawkheart's getting restless."

Dawnstripe bounded forward. "Quick, Tallpaw. It's your first Gathering. Enjoy it!" She hared away over the grass with Stagleap and Doespring on her tail.

Tallpaw raced after. He caught up to his Clanmates at the top of a steep slope. Ahead, treetops swished in the moonlight. The air was thick with the taste of earth and thick, damp foliage. *Fourtrees.*

"You took your time," Hawkheart growled.

"Sorry." Tallpaw peered into the trees, waiting for his eyes to adjust to the darkness. The ground sloped steeply away beneath his paws, and through gaps between the trunks, he could make out a clearing filled with moonlight.

"Let's go." Heatherstar flicked her tail and the WindClan warriors streamed down the slope.

Tallpaw bounded after them, feeling the soft grass give way to crumbly earth. Ferns swished against his pelt and brambles twitched as he hopped over their trailing branches. As he reached the foot of the slope, he slowed to a stop. Four gigantic oaks stood in the center of the hollow, their trunks thicker than Tallrock back in the WindClan camp. Above his head, branches creaked. Tallpaw pressed his ears flat, unnerved by the noise. Even when the wind howled across the moor, the heather only whispered in reply. The bark of the trees glowed silver, and the canopy of leaves blocked out the sky until the wind tugged at them, revealing glimpses of stars.

"We're the first!" Doespring stopped beside him. "Look!" Her mew echoed around the walls of the hollow. "It's the Great Rock."

Tallpaw followed her gaze, his heart quickening as he saw the stone looming palely in the shadows, bigger than any boulder on the moor. As the branches moved overhead, moonlight dappled the rock. Tallpaw tensed as he felt the ground tremble. Was the Great Rock *alive*?

"Someone's coming!" called a voice behind him.

Doespring tasted the air. "It's ThunderClan."

As she spoke, dark shapes bounded down the far slope. Their paw steps set the earth shaking as they spilled into the hollow. Tallpaw backed away. He'd never seen such huge cats, wide-shouldered and stocky with long fur and sharp claws that glinted at the ends of their toes.

"Greetings, Heatherstar." A fox-furred tom, his muzzle crisscrossed with old scars, dipped his head to the WindClan leader.

"It's good to see you, Pinestar," Heatherstar responded politely, her eyes glinting in the moonlight.

"Hawkheart! Any news this moon?" A ragged gray tom shambled toward the WindClan medicine cat.

"That's Goosefeather," Doespring whispered to Tallpaw. "He's ThunderClan's medicine cat."

Tallpaw heard a purr in his other ear. "Goosefeather talks to himself," Stagleap whispered. "The ThunderClan apprentices told me that he walks in the woods chatting to the trees and the squirrels."

Doespring snorted with amusement.

"Hello, Goosefeather." Hawkheart welcomed his fellow medicine cat.

Barkpaw stood beside his mentor and nodded, looking overawed.

"Have you killed anyone recently, you old herb-muddler?" Hawkheart joked.

Goosefeather snorted. "Not on purpose."

Tallpaw's eyes widened as he watched ThunderClan warriors weave among the WindClan cats, exchanging greetings like old friends. "Is it okay to talk to the other Clans?"

"So long as clouds don't cross the moon," Doespring reminded him. "If they do, StarClan is warning us that the truce is over."

"Be careful what you say," Stagleap added. "If you say too much, you might give away WindClan secrets. If you say too little, the other Clans will accuse you of being hostile."

Tallpaw swallowed. "How will I know if I get it right?"

"Just listen and be polite," Doespring advised. "If you talk to the apprentices, don't say more than you need to. If they talk about training, join in, but don't share WindClan battle moves."

"Here comes ShadowClan!" Stagleap's hiss made Tallpaw stiffen.

The bushes on the slope stayed almost silent as shadows moved between them. Tallpaw's pelt pricked. These cats hardly rippled a leaf as they slunk into the hollow, silent as prey. Tallpaw wrinkled his nose. ShadowClan brought with them a stench of pinesap and dank moss. "Do they always smell like that?"

"You'll get used to it," Stagleap promised. "They probably think we smell odd."

Tallpaw lifted his chin. "No one could find the scent of the wind *odd*."

Doespring shrugged. "Maybe *they* do. Perhaps that's why they hide in the forest."

"That's Cedarstar." Stagleap pointed his muzzle at a dark gray tom. The ShadowClan leader's white belly flashed beneath him as he joined Heatherstar and Pinestar at the foot of the Great Rock.

Tallpaw watched a gray tabby approach Reedfeather. "Is that Stonetooth?" he asked, half recognizing the cat from one of Flailfoot's stories.

"Yes. He's been ShadowClan's deputy for so long, only the elders remember who came before him," Doespring meowed.

"And there's Sunfall." Stagleap nodded toward a golden tabby. ThunderClan's deputy was pacing around the clearing, dipping his head to warriors, sharing words with one group before moving on to the next.

Whiteberry limped across the clearing and touched muzzles with a small ginger she-cat. "Littlebird." His eyes flashed with mischief. "You haven't missed a Gathering in moons. Come to gossip, eh?"

"Of course." She swept her tail over her paws as she sat down.

A graying ThunderClan tom hurried to join them. "How's hunting?" he asked as he reached them.

"Not bad, Mumblefoot," Whiteberry rasped. "Though with only two apprentices, it's a long wait for fresh prey to arrive."

Littlebird snorted. "You should go out and hunt your own."

"If only!" Whiteberry sighed. "My legs are too slow."

"Your claws are still sharp," Littlebird countered.

Tallpaw's ears pricked as Shrewpaw's mew sounded from below one of the oak trees. "Of course, I'm the *fastest* apprentice." Three apprentices were gathered around the dark brown tom, their eyes round. "And there's no cat faster than a Wind-Clan cat."

A white ShadowClan apprentice lashed his tail. "Any cat could run fast on the moor. You've got the wind at your tail and no trees to get in your way."

"You think it's easy living on the moors, Blizzardpaw?" Shrewpaw flattened his ears.

A silver-furred she-cat with pale blue eyes stared at him. "WindClan cats think they're so special."

"That's because we are." Shrewpaw stuck his nose in the air.

"You're as puffed up as the sheep that live on your dumb moor." The silver apprentice lashed her tail.

"Moonpaw." A sleek gray ThunderClan tom hurried over to her. "Don't forget the truce."

"But Shrewpaw's showing off!" Moonpaw protested. "All WindClan cats are show-offs."

Tallpaw noticed Hawkheart's head turn toward the squabbling apprentices. "Stormtail!" he called to the gray ThunderClan tom beside Moonpaw. "Can't ThunderClan keep its 'paws under control?"

Moonpaw's gaze flashed toward the WindClan medicine cat. "Don't worry," she growled. "I won't break the truce." As she stalked away, Stormtail hurried after her, throwing an apologetic look at Hawkheart.

Tallpaw suddenly realized that his heart was racing. The rustling leaves and the babbling voices made his ears twitch. Words were tossed back and forth like prey between paws. How would he ever learn the names of all the cats in other Clans? Would he ever know what to say? Could he ever feel at ease here, trapped beneath trees?

"Look, Doespring!" Stagleap's mew surprised him. "There's Nettlepaw!" He jerked his nose toward a white ShadowClan she-cat with ginger patches. "Let's find out if she passed her assessment!"

Tallpaw stared as they raced away across the clearing. He glanced around, feeling suddenly exposed. Should he follow them? Or join Shrewpaw with the other apprentices? Uncertain, he dropped into a crouch and watched the Clans blend together in a haze of pelts. *Where's RiverClan?* Tallpaw dug his claws into the earth, feeling for vibrations, but the pattering of paws in the clearing blotted out distant tremors. He tasted the air. A tang that tasted of rancid water was drifting into the hollow.

"Sorry we're late!" A huge tom bounded down between brambles and crossed the clearing to Heatherstar. His fur shone in the dappled moonlight, so thick that Tallpaw could only guess at the sturdy muscle moving beneath. *That must be Hailstar.* Tallpaw watched the RiverClan leader's Clanmates stream into the hollow. They slid as easily as fish among the other Clan cats until the clearing was teeming with bodies. Tallpaw glanced up, wishing he could see wide-open sky. But he was underneath one of the Great Oaks, and branches blocked his view. *It's like being underground.* His tail twitched nervously.

A familiar scent wafted over him as a pelt brushed his flank. "You'll get used to it." Cloudrunner nudged him. "Next time won't seem so strange."

Tallpaw straightened up. "How can any cat live under trees?"

Cloudrunner shrugged. "I guess a cat can get used to anything."

Pale fur moved at the side of the Great Rock. Heatherstar was jumping to the top with Cedarstar, Pinestar, and Hailstar close behind.

"Follow me." Cloudrunner headed into the crowd.

Tallpaw kept close to the pale gray warrior, his whiskers brushing pelts as they weaved between the Clans. He flattened his ears, trying not to breathe too deeply amid the jumble of scents. He pretended he was moving through heather, relieved when Cloudrunner stopped beside Stagleap and Doespring.

Tallpaw nosed in beside Stagleap. "Can I sit here?" he whispered.

"Of course." Stagleap shifted to give him room.

Doespring leaned around her brother and blinked at Tall-paw. "Can you see from there?"

"Just about." As Cloudrunner squeezed in behind him, Tallpaw stretched to peer over the heads of Hareflight, Shrew-paw, and Appledawn, who were lined up like stones in front of him, their eyes lifted toward the Great Rock. Larksplash, Ryestalk, and Dawnstripe flanked them while Hickorynose wheezed as he settled down behind.

Cedarstar stepped forward and spoke first. "ShadowClan is well," he declared. Tallpaw watched his amber eyes glint in the moonlight as he scanned the Gathering. "Our nursery is full." The ShadowClan leader's gaze warmed. "Three new kits have been born to Silverflame."

Tallpaw noticed the ShadowClan cats around him exchange knowing, worried glances. Was there a secret behind this good news?

"Prey is plentiful in the forest and greenleaf has been kind." Cedarstar stepped back and nodded to Pinestar.

As the ThunderClan leader began to speak, his Clanmates shifted below, fluffing out their fur. *Why are they so pleased with themselves?* Tallpaw wondered. They lived in a forest, hiding like prey among the trees. No Clan lived like WindClan, on top of the whole world, close to the sky with their tails in the wind.

"Greenleaf has been kind to ThunderClan, too," Pinestar meowed. "The woods are prey-rich. StarClan blesses us this moon." His gaze darkened. "There have been dogs in the forest, but our patrols have driven them back into Twoleg territory."

Stagleap leaned close to Tallpaw. "Perhaps I should offer to scent mark their borders for them," he whispered. "That would scare the dogs away."

"Hush," Dawnstripe hissed. Stagleap sniffed and turned his gaze back to the Great Rock.

Hailstar had stepped forward. "The newleaf rains have fed the river, bringing more fish this greenleaf than RiverClan can eat."

"Don't the other Clans ever go hungry?" Tallpaw whispered.

Cloudrunner's breath touched his ear. "That's what they want you to think," he muttered. "No Clan would admit to hunger." He nodded toward two burly ThunderClan warriors. "Look at the scars on their muzzles. They've hardly had time to heal."

Tallpaw peered through the half-light. Cloudrunner was right. The warriors' noses carried the mark of fresh injuries.

"It looks like those dogs put up a fight before they were chased back to Twoleg territory," Cloudrunner commented. "Pinestar didn't mention *that*."

Heatherstar was taking her place at the front of the Great Rock. "Prey is running well on the moor. Stagleap, Doespring, and Ryestalk have become warriors. And we have a new apprentice." Tallpaw froze as her gaze locked with his. "Tallpaw!" Heatherstar called proudly.

"Tallpaw!"

"Tallpaw!"

"Tallpaw!"

Around him cats raised their voices, calling his name. Tall-paw shrank beneath his fur. No one had warned him about this! Eyes glowed warmly as they fixed on him. Tallpaw tried to sit up straight, forcing his ears not to flatten as his name rang around the hollow.

He sagged with relief when they fell silent and Heatherstar spoke again. "The nursery is empty, though with StarClan's blessing, not for long. The long, warm days have brought health and full bellies to WindClan. Soon it will bring kits to make WindClan even stronger." Tallpaw leaned forward, waiting for her to announce WindClan's greatest achieve-ment: the tunnel leading to the gorge. But the WindClan leader stepped back, nodding to the other Clan leaders.

In the hollow, the cats stood up and began to move, break-ing rank and clustering into groups.

"Is that it?" Tallpaw blinked up at the Great Rock. "Isn't Heatherstar going to mention the tunnel?"

Stagleap stared at him. "Why should she? It's just a tunnel. The other Clans wouldn't understand."

"We never tell them about our tunnels." Ryestalk flicked her tail.

Doespring stood up and shook out her pelt. "They'd think we'd turned into rabbits."

Tallpaw narrowed his eyes. Surely news about the latest tunnel would just prove WindClan's strength? Why keep it a secret, if the aim of a Gathering was to make the other Clans think WindClan was as strong as they could possibly be?

Cloudrunner brushed past him. "The tunnels give us tactical advantage," he murmured. "It's best we don't share news about them with the other Clans."

Tallpaw turned and dipped his head to Hickorynose, hoping the old tunneler understood that *he* appreciated the tunnel. But Hickorynose was shouldering his way through the crowd, gaze low, heading for an empty slope where he stopped and sat apart from all the other cats.

"Come on." Stagleap nudged Tallpaw with his muzzle. "Meet Shimmerpelt."

"Shimmerpelt?"

Doespring rolled her eyes. "She's in RiverClan. Stagleap's got a massive crush on her."

"But I thought that was forbidden." Tallpaw was confused.

"It's forbidden to take a mate from a different Clan," Stagleap meowed breezily. "But that doesn't mean you can't talk to them." He padded away, Doespring at his heels.

"I'll stay here," Tallpaw called after them. He just wanted to watch for now. He gazed around the clearing, surprised to see the Clans at ease, sharing tongues as though there were no borders anywhere in the forest. Heatherstar and Pinestar talked in low murmurs, their heads close. Dawnstripe and Appledawn purred loudly as two ThunderClan toms demonstrated comical battle moves, fighting more like hares than warriors. At the edge of the clearing, Reedfeather sat close to a RiverClan she-cat. His tail whisked against her soft, pale brown flank as he talked, and Tallpaw was surprised by the warmth in Reedfeather's gaze. When the RiverClan she-cat got to her paws and padded toward the edge of the clearing, Reedfeather followed.

"Tallpaw!" Dawnstripe's call caught his attention.

He turned. His mentor was at the far side of the clearing, beckoning him with her tail. He hurried toward her and she nodded to a dark gray tom, who smelled of sap. "This is Frogpaw of ShadowClan." She glanced past him. "And his sisters are over there." Tallpaw followed her gaze toward a mottled she-cat and her pale gray littermate.

Frogpaw sniffed. "They're called Newtpaw and Ashpaw."

"I thought you might like to meet some apprentices from another Clan," Dawnstripe told him. "They are our neighbors, after all."

Tallpaw twitched an ear. "I guess."

"How long have you been training?" Frogpaw asked.

"Just a moon." Tallpaw didn't like the way the young tom was eyeing him—like a hunter assessing prey.

"Who's this?" Newtpaw nosed past her brother.

"He's the new WindClan apprentice." Ashpaw poked her muzzle close and sniffed. "He smells like heather."

Tallpaw glared at her. *And you smell like nettles.*

"WindClan!" Heatherstar called from the slope. "The rabbits will start running early. We should return to camp and sleep while we can."

Tallpaw felt a ripple of relief. He wasn't going to have to share tongues with these stinky cats.

"Why did you introduce me to them?" he hissed to

Dawnstripe as he ran after her. Around him, his Clanmates streamed up the slope toward the moor.

"Know your enemy," Dawnstripe told him. "If you meet them in battle, you'll recognize their scent and their strength."

"Will I?" Tallpaw wasn't convinced he'd be able to tell the three apprentices apart from their smelly Clanmates.

"What did you think of Frogpaw?" Dawnstripe pressed.

"He looked at me as if he was trying to work out how strong I was."

"And Ashpaw?"

"She's not shy." Tallpaw felt a prickle of irritation. She'd sniffed him like she was checking stale scent. "Nor is her sister."

"You have a sense of them, then." Dawnstripe pushed through a patch of ferns.

Tallpaw followed in her paw steps, the fronds whisking his flanks. "I guess."

"When battle comes, it will help, I promise."

Tallpaw didn't answer. How could knowing that the three young ShadowClan cats were bad-mannered and pushy help him in fight? Suddenly he felt bone-weary. By the time he reached the top of the slope, his paws ached. He was usually fast asleep in his nest by now. He followed Dawnstripe across the grass, comforted as the scent of peat and heather flooded his nose. He glanced up at the sky, relieved to be in the open. Moonlight shone on the pelts of his Clanmates as they crossed the moor ahead of him.

By the time they reached camp, he was yawning. "I'm so tired."

"Hush," Dawnstripe cautioned him. "The Clan will be sleeping."

"Lucky Clan," he muttered.

Dawnstripe stopped suddenly, her pelt bushing.

"What is it?" Tallpaw hissed.

Dawnstripe was staring at the walls of the camp. Heatherstar stood frozen outside the entrance while her Clanmates paused around her, their ears pricking.

Voices sounded from inside.

"They're here!" Larksplash was the first to move. She raced toward the entrance, ducking past her leader and plunging into the heather. "The visitors! They've come at last!"

CHAPTER 12

❧

Tallpaw raced into the camp after Dawnstripe. The whole Clan
was awake, swirling between the moonlit tussocks so that the
clearing looked as busy as Fourtrees. Strange cats appeared
among Tallpaw's Clanmates. A black-and-white she-cat paced
beside a gray tom. Her ginger-and-white companion stood,
eyes bright, near the edge of the Meeting Hollow while a
large, creamy-brown tom tasted the air. Beside them, a tawny
tom, short-furred and thin, glanced around curiously.

Tallpaw opened his mouth and let their scent bathe his
tongue. He could taste Thunderpaths, stale food, and a smoky
smell, like the grimy clouds that sometimes drifted from Twolegplace.

"Who are they?" Barkpaw's eyes were wide.

Tallpaw stopped beside him. "They're *the visitors.*"

Shrewpaw nosed his way among his Clanmates, snatching
sniffs of the newcomers.

Redclaw blocked his path. "They're our guests, not prey.
Treat them with respect."

Shrewpaw lifted his chin. "What are they doing here?"

"They've come to share food and stories," Redclaw told
him.

Heatherstar weaved between her Clanmates and dipped her head to the black-and-white she-cat. "It's good to see you again, Bess." Her eyes flicked over Bess's companions. "Where's Wee Hen?"

Bess shook her head. "'Twas a hard cold-season," she meowed softly. "But she died warm and full-fed."

Heatherstar's tail drooped. "She'll be missed."

Whiteberry hurried over the tussocks, his eyes clouding. "Did she have any words for me?" he asked hopefully.

Bess met his gaze. "She asked that you share her stories with your young'uns."

"Of course." Whiteberry's tail quivered and he turned to the creamy-brown tom. "It's good to see you, Algernon."

The tom whisked his tail. "We decided it were well time we tasted heather once more."

Tallpaw shifted his paws, unnerved by the strangeness of having cats who weren't Clanborn right inside the camp. And they spoke so strangely. "I didn't believe they'd actually come," he murmured, half to himself.

Barkpaw jerked around. "You knew about them already?"

Tallpaw blinked at him. "Didn't Hawkheart warn you?"

"*Warn* me?" Barkpaw narrowed his eyes. "Who are these cats?"

Tallpaw shrugged. "All I know is that they're rogues and they come every year to spend greenleaf with WindClan."

Barkpaw gazed at the strangers. "Why?"

"Because they always have." Tallpaw repeated Dawnstripe's words, still not understanding why that made it okay for WindClan to share nests and prey with rogues.

"Reena!" Larksplash bounded over the tussocks toward the young ginger-and-white she-cat. "You've grown!"

"Oh my tail and whiskers!" Reena looked surprised. "So have you!"

Meadowslip and Brackenwing hurried after Larksplash and crowded around Reena.

"How was leaf-bare?" Meadowslip asked.

Brackenwing ran the tip of her tail along Reena's spine. "Did you find somewhere warm to shelter?"

"We stayed cozy," Reena reassured them. Her gaze flicked over Larksplash. "Are you a warrior yet?"

"I've been a *mentor*," Larksplash purred.

"A mentor?" Reena looked impressed. "You were hardly more than a 'paw the last time we were here." She glanced around the Clan. "Who've you been mentoring?"

Ryestalk padded forward. "Me." Her nostrils twitched.

"And who are you?" Reena cast an admiring gaze over the young warrior.

"I'm Ryestalk."

"Well, I'm Reena, and I'd be honored to touch noses with you." She leaned forward, sticking out her muzzle.

Ryestalk glanced at Larksplash. "It's okay," Larksplash reassured her. Gingerly Ryestalk touched her nose to Reena's, then hopped back.

Barkpaw growled under his breath. "I hope they haven't brought whitecough with them."

Tallpaw breathed in the scent of the visitors. "They smell clean and healthy to me."

Barkpaw was still scowling. "I'd like to look them over in

the medicine den before they start mixing with the Clan. Hawkheart says strangers bring sickness."

The tawny brown rogue had wandered over to the Hunting Stones and stood watching the Clan in silence, his eyes glittering. Beside him, the small, dark gray tom shifted his paws warily.

Aspenfall approached them, ears twitching. "Sparrow." He nodded to the tawny-colored tom.

"Aspenfall." Sparrow matched Aspenfall's respectful tone.

The dark gray rogue lifted his head. "I hope cold-season was kind to the Clan."

"Leaf-bare was long, Mole," Aspenfall told him. "But the prey kept running and our nests were warm."

"Bess!" Cloudrunner bounded across the clearing and touched noses with the black-and-white she-cat.

Tallpaw felt fur brush his flank. Palebird slid in beside him. "It's good to see old friends," she murmured.

"Have you known them long?" Tallpaw asked.

"They've been visiting since before I was born," Palebird replied. "At least, Algie and Bess have. Reena is their daughter. Sparrow and Mole joined them later."

Tallpaw glanced at the gray tom. "They have weird names." He could understand Sparrow and Mole, but Reena, Algie, and Bess felt strange to his tongue.

"Bess was named by Twolegs," Palebird explained. "Algernon, too. They were kittypets once, I think. And Bess gave Reena her sister's name."

"Is that Palebird?" At mention of her sister, Bess turned

her head. "You look thin." She padded over, her eyes round with worry. Reena followed her.

"I haven't been well." Palebird sighed.

Bess was staring at Tallpaw. "Who's this?"

"My son, Tallpaw." For once, pride warmed Palebird's voice.

"He's a fine one," Bess purred.

"I kitted another." Palebird's mew wobbled. "But she died."

"Oh, Palebird." Bess's eyes clouded. She pressed her cheek against Palebird's. "You poor duckling."

Reena stood silently behind her mother. Tallpaw shifted his paws, his tail pricking self-consciously as the two she-cats shared a long moment of grief. He couldn't help noticing how clean Bess's white paws were. And Reena's ginger pelt shone in the moonlight. He always imagined rogues would be ragged and dirty.

Barkpaw nudged him. "I think Hawkheart wants me." Hawkheart was beckoning from the rim of the Meeting Hollow, his gaze as watchful as Sparrow's. Barkpaw crossed the clearing, then followed his mentor to the medicine den.

Across the clearing, the elders clustered around Algernon while Sandgorse purred loudly. "Tell us more, Algie," he urged.

But Mistmouse circled the clearing without taking her eyes off the visitors, while Hickorynose sat close to Woollytail, muttering under his breath. Tallpaw narrowed his eyes. *Not everyone wants them here.*

"He's a thoughtful one, young Tallpaw." Bess's mew jerked Tallpaw's attention back.

"I was just watching the Clan," he mewed quickly.

Bess glanced over her shoulder. "They'll take a while to get used to us again," she meowed. "Once we've proved we can earn our keep, the icy ones'll thaw."

"Earn your keep?" Tallpaw didn't understand.

"Catch their own food," Palebird explained.

Bess threw a wink at Whiteberry across the bracken patch and added, "We may even catch a little extra for the old'uns."

"They'll be grateful for it," Tallpaw admitted. "So will I. With just the two of us, we have trouble catching enough prey for them."

"Two of you?" Reena looked confused.

"Me and Shrewpaw," Tallpaw explained. "It's our job to take care of the elders."

As Tallpaw spoke, Heatherstar lifted her muzzle. "It's late. We should rest. Who will share their dens with our friends?"

"Bess must stay in the nursery," Palebird called. On the far side of the clearing, Meadowslip nodded.

"Would Mole like to bed down with us?" Flamepelt suggested. "The elders' den is the warmest place in the camp besides the nursery." He glanced at Mole. "Not that you're as old and frail as us!" he added.

Mole dipped his head. "You're very kind," he mewed. "And I suspect there's not many moons between us."

Redclaw lifted his tail. "There are spare nests in the long grass for Algie and Sparrow."

"Thanks, Redclaw." Algie headed for the moor runners' patch.

Sparrow narrowed his eyes. "Thank you," he meowed

before padding after his companion.

Bess glanced at her daughter. "What about Reena?"

Palebird frowned. "There's not much room in the nursery now that Meadowslip's so close to kitting."

"There's room in the apprentice den." Tallpaw surprised himself, the offer tumbling out before he'd even thought about it.

"Thanks, Tall." Reena strutted past him, tail flicking. "Just tell me which nest is spare and I'll happily bed down."

"Er, it's Tallpaw, actually." Tallpaw hurried after her, wondering what Shrewpaw would say about an extra denmate. *Reena had better not try to call him "Shrew"!*

Reena had already picked out a nest at the back of the den by the time Shrewpaw reached the gorse bush. It was Ryestalk's old nest, and Reena sneezed as dust wafted up from the wool lining when she curled down into it.

Shrewpaw glared through the den opening. "What's she doing here?"

"She needed a place to sleep," Tallpaw explained. "We've got spare nests."

"They're apprentice nests," Shrewpaw snapped. "Not for rogues."

"We're only rogues till you get to know us." Reena peeped over the top of her nest, her eyes twinkling. "Until then, why don't you pretend I'm a little old egg just waiting to hatch and keep your claws sheathed? No sense in killing prey before it's worth eating."

Shrewpaw blinked. "Pretend you're an egg," he echoed.

"Yep." Reena buried her nose beneath her paw, muffling her mew. "Just a chick in a shell." She peeped out and caught Tallpaw's eyes. Her gaze sparkled with laughter.

Tallpaw swallowed back a purr as Shrewpaw climbed, frowning, into his nest. Having visitors might be fun, he decided as he settled down to sleep.

CHAPTER 13

❧

"Rabbit!" Dawnstripe dropped into a crouch, her gaze fixed on a small, brown shape bobbing up the slope. Tallpaw pressed his belly to the ground. He glanced at Reena.

She was already flat against the grass, her tail twitching behind her. "I see it," she whispered. "What now, Tall?"

"Tall*paw*," he hissed under his breath.

Reena had joined Tallpaw for his training session while Shrewpaw patrolled the boundaries with Hareflight. Their pelts were wind ruffled after a morning practicing prey-hunting skills. Now they had a chance to test them for real.

"Should I stalk from behind while you two get either side?" Reena was proving to be a natural at planning an attack, even though she didn't have the speed of a WindClan cat.

Dawnstripe narrowed her eyes. "Can you move in without alarming it, Reena?" She glanced at Tallpaw. "We'll need time to cut off its escape routes." She pointed her muzzle toward a cluster of sandy dips in the grass beside the grazing rabbit. "If it gets to that warren, we've lost it."

"I'm good at moving quietly," Reena promised. "And Tall-paw's fast enough to catch that critter at the mouth of its hole!"

Tallpaw twitched his tail with pleasure. Training with Reena was far better than training with grouchy Shrewpaw. Dawnstripe nodded him to the wind side of the rabbit. She trusted him to gauge his own scent drift. Tallpaw licked his nose and felt for the breeze. He could probably get halfway to the rabbit before it picked up his smell. Dawnstripe began stalking over the grass, keeping low.

Tallpaw nodded to Reena. "Good luck," he whispered, and crept slowly upslope, keeping to one side of the clear grass while Reena padded forward.

The rabbit bobbed farther along the hill, nibbling at green-leaf shoots. Dawnstripe moved in steadily. Tallpaw padded over the soft grass without ruffling it. He paused as he neared the rabbit. Any closer and the wind would carry his scent straight to it. He glanced across the slope at Dawnstripe. She was close to the warren. He waited until she'd slid into place and blocked the rabbit's path to safety.

Reena was moving in behind, her ginger-and-white pelt bright against the grass. But she was creeping slowly with movements so tiny, no prey would notice. The rabbit hopped a few more steps. Tallpaw sped up. He saw Dawnstripe nod and broke into a run, racing for the kill. Reena surged forward. Dawnstripe leaped. The rabbit bolted, kicking grass in its wake as it fled upslope.

Tallpaw plunged into a flat-out sprint, Reena close on his heels. Dawnstripe closed in from the side. The rabbit was only a tail-length away. Tallpaw pounced, claws unsheathed.

He hit bare grass. "Where'd it go?" Blinking, he spun around. The rabbit had disappeared.

Reena scrambled to a halt, ears flat. "It found a hole." She sniffed at an opening in the ground, covered by long grass that was crushed flat where the rabbit had plunged through.

Dawnstripe lashed her tail. "There's no way we could have seen that hole—" As she spoke, paw steps echoed from inside. Fur exploded from it as the terrified rabbit hurtled out.

Tallpaw didn't stop to think. He sprang forward, slamming his paws onto the rabbit's spine, and sank his teeth into its neck to give a killing bite.

Gray fur flashed at the edge of his vision. "I thought I smelled rabbit." Tallpaw looked up to see Woollytail emerge from the hole.

"What were you doing in there?" Reena blinked at the tunneler, her eyes clouded with confusion. "Were you waiting for it?"

"No," Woollytail meowed. "It surprised me as much as I surprised it. One moment I was propping up a crumbling roof; the next, paws are thumping toward me. I'm not going to ignore prey if it's running toward me, so I chased it." He broke into a purr. "I didn't realize I was part of a hunting team."

Dawnstripe lifted her tail. "We're lucky you were down there."

Tallpaw licked blood from his lips, the warm tang making his belly rumble. "Who's in there with you?"

"Sandgorse and Plumclaw are working on the second gorge tunnel," Woollytail explained. "I was on my way back to camp when I saw the crumbling roof. I thought I'd fix it before it caved in."

Dawnstripe was looking confused. "Second gorge tunnel?" she echoed. "Isn't one enough?"

"Not with the river being so unpredictable," Woollytail meowed. "After the first one flooded, we knew we were going to need more than one route. You never know—"

Dawnstripe cut him off. "The first one *flooded?*" Her gaze snapped to Tallpaw. "What does he mean?"

Tallpaw backed away from the rabbit. "The tunnel kind of flooded while I was working on it with Sandgorse."

"*Kind of* flooded?" Dawnstripe's eyes widened.

Woollytail shook earth from his pelt. "It was just a miscalculation," he told her. "We dug too low the first time. The new tunnel's at the right level now, but come leaf-bare and snowmelt, the river's going to fill it, so we need a second one, higher up."

Dawnstripe was staring at Tallpaw as though Woollytail hadn't spoken. "Were you okay?"

Tallpaw tried to stop his pelt from pricking at the memory. "I didn't even get my paws wet."

Woollytail snorted, amused. "He's a great tunnel runner."

Dawnstripe's tail bushed out. "You had to *run?*"

"It was either that or drown," Woollytail told her.

"You could have been killed!" Dawnstripe's fur lifted along her spine. Tallpaw couldn't tell if she was more frightened or angry.

"I was okay," he reassured her. "Sandgorse was with me."

"Tunneling near the gorge is too dangerous," Dawnstripe declared.

Reena stepped forward, her eyes round. "Why do you tunnel *at all*?"

"WindClan cats have always tunneled," Woollytail mewed.

Reena peered into the rabbit hole. "And there are cats underground right now?" She sounded amazed.

"Of course."

Reena shuddered. "Do you sleep down there?"

Tallpaw's pelt pricked with irritation. Why was she acting like it was so creepy? "Sandgorse and Palebird are tunnelers, too," he huffed. "They're all WindClan warriors, you know."

"Sandgorse and Palebird kitted you, right?" Reena's eyes rounded with curiosity as he nodded. "Why aren't *you* a tunneler, then?"

Tallpaw dropped his gaze, feeling hot beneath his pelt. "Heatherstar thought I'd make a better moor runner."

"Moor runner," Woollytail muttered under his breath. "We've too many runners. Not enough diggers."

Dawnstripe had been pacing. She stopped in front of Woollytail. "Does Heatherstar know about the flood?"

"Why should she?" Woollytail answered. "She's no tunneler."

"We need to tell her."

Tallpaw's belly twisted. He sensed trouble.

"Hey, *Wormpaw!*"

Shrewpaw. Tallpaw turned and saw his denmate charging toward him. *That's all I need.* Hareflight bounded after his apprentice.

"We're going to Outlook Rock." Shrewpaw stopped beside

them. He glanced at Reena. "Do you want to come with us?"

"They look busy," Hareflight warned. "Don't let us hold you up, Dawnstripe."

"I'm returning to camp with Woollytail," Dawnstripe growled.

Hareflight pricked his ears. "What's wrong?"

"Nothing." Dawnstripe glanced at Woollytail. "But could you take Tallpaw with you to Outlook Rock?"

Hareflight swished his tail. "Of course."

"What about me?" Reena stepped forward. "Can I come?"

Shrewpaw looked at Hareflight. "Can she?"

"She doesn't need to know *everything* about how WindClan trains its warriors." Hareflight swapped looks with Dawnstripe. "Perhaps you could take her back to camp?"

Reena's shoulders slumped. "I'll be no trouble; I promise."

"Bess'll be missing you." Dawnstripe beckoned Reena with her tail. "Let's go." She grabbed Tallpaw's rabbit in her jaws as she and Woollytail started to walk away. His tail-tip was flicking angrily.

"Come on, then, you two!" Hareflight broke into a run, heading uphill.

Shrewpaw darted after him. Tallpaw followed, giving one last glance at Dawnstripe, Woollytail, and Reena.

Clouds were gathering on the horizon as they reached Outlook Rock. Hareflight stood on the grass where the stone jutted over the slope. "Shrewpaw, you go first. Remember, observation is an important part of your final assessment."

Shrewpaw padded to the edge. Peering down at the

meadows and forest stretching below, he began to list what he could see. "Monster. Dog by the Twolegplace. Buzzard circling Highstones . . ."

Tallpaw stuck close to his denmate, trying to spot each new find as Shrewpaw listed it. "Can I try?" he asked Hareflight, before Shrewpaw could call everything in sight. At this rate there would be nothing left for him to point out.

"Swap places," Hareflight ordered.

Shrewpaw turned and pushed past Tallpaw. Tallpaw's heart lurched as his paws slithered on the smooth rock. Carefully he took Shrewpaw's place, bracing himself against the breeze. "I can smell the Thunderpath," he called to Hareflight. "It smells as though monsters have been traveling it all day." He scanned the land, struggling to find something Shrewpaw had missed. On a treetop beyond the cluster of Twolegplace, he could make out some movement, and recognized the dark feathers of a bird of prey. Half guessing, he began to describe it. "A buzzard is teaching its fledglings to fly."

"How can you see that?" Shrewpaw nosed in beside him.

Tallpaw gripped with his claws, trying to keep his place. "There!" He flicked his muzzle toward the distant tree.

"That's not a buzzard," Shrewpaw scoffed.

Tallpaw glanced back at Hareflight. The brown warrior was squinting. "It's the right color."

"How can you see fledglings?" Shrewpaw challenged.

"Why else would a buzzard be balancing on the edge of its nest in the middle of greenleaf?" Tallpaw retorted.

"Nice guesswork, Tallpaw," Hareflight praised him.

"Is that what we're practicing?" Shrewpaw sneered. "*Guessing?*" He turned his tail on Tallpaw and stomped back to Hareflight's side. "I thought we were practicing our observation skills."

Tallpaw growled under his breath. Training with Reena—even if she couldn't get his name right—had been much more fun.

The sun was sliding toward Highstones as they reached camp. Tallpaw's belly was rumbling. As he followed Hareflight, Shrewpaw, and Dawnstripe toward the entrance, he smelled Sandgorse and Plumclaw's fresh scents on the grass. The tunneling patrol must have returned recently. He pushed through the heather tunnel, his heart quickening as he saw Sandgorse, Plumclaw, Woollytail, Hickorynose, and Mistmouse gathered in the Meeting Hollow. Heatherstar and Reedfeather faced them stiffly.

Hareflight trotted into camp behind Tallpaw and stopped. "Looks like the tunnelers have got more news about the gorge tunnel."

"Great." Shrewpaw sounded unenthusiastic. He padded past his mentor. "Can I get something to eat?"

Hareflight nodded. "You too, Tallpaw," he meowed. "You must be hungry."

"Thanks." Tallpaw crossed the tussocks, his gaze lingering on the Meeting Hollow.

"Tallpaw!" Reena's mew made him spin around.

The rogue she-cat was settled in a patch of sunshine beside

the elders' den. A lapwing lay beside her, half-eaten. Its rich scent washed Tallpaw's tongue.

"Do you want some?" Reena called. "I can't eat all this."

Gratefully Tallpaw hurried toward her. "What happened to the rabbit we caught?"

"Dawnstripe gave it to the elders."

Whiteberry stuck his head out of the den. "It was very tasty." His gaze moved toward the Meeting Hollow. "Reena said that the tunnelers had helped catch it."

Tallpaw took a bite of lapwing, his belly growling. "Woolly-tail flushed it out of a hole for me," he told Whiteberry with his mouth full.

"Perhaps Heatherstar's giving the other tunnelers hunting tips." Whiteberry sniffed. "They've been talking since Sand-gorse's patrol got back."

From the bristling of the tunnelers' fur and the dark look in Heatherstar's eyes, Tallpaw guessed they weren't talking about hunting. Besides, tunnelers were already as good at hunting as moor runners, in their own way.

"Great lapwing," he told Reena, suddenly aware that she was watching him. "Did you catch it?"

Reena nudged him with a paw. "Don't be silly," she purred. "That's proper moor hunting. Give me a barn full of mice and I'm as fast as the next cat, but chasing birds through heather takes more skill than I've got."

"You wait till the end of greenleaf." Tallpaw ripped away another mouthful of bird flesh. "You'll be plucking buzzards from the sky."

Reena purred. "You think?" She didn't sound convinced.

Tallpaw stiffened as Heatherstar and Reedfeather left the Meeting Hollow. He searched the tunnelers' faces as they headed for the prey heap. What had they been discussing? Tallpaw quickly swallowed his mouthful of lapwing as his father veered toward him. He leaped to his paws. Had Sandgorse heard how he'd caught the rabbit? Was he coming to congratulate him? Then Tallpaw caught sight of Sandgorse's expression, and his heart sank.

Behind him, the gorse rattled as Whiteberry ducked back inside her den. Reena shifted her paws. She looked uneasy. She must have seen the thunderous look on Sandgorse's face, too.

"Hey, Sandgorse." An ominous feeling sat like a stone in Tallpaw's belly.

Sandgorse stopped in front of him, eyes blazing. "Why did you have to tell Heatherstar that you nearly drowned?"

"I—I didn't!" Tallpaw backed away. "It was Woollytail. He told Dawnstripe."

"You're such a coward, you can't even own up to your own mistake!"

"What mistake?" Why was Sandgorse so angry?

"It's bad enough that my son is too rabbit-hearted to go underground," Sandgorse snarled. "Now I discover that he's so scared of getting his paws wet he wants to stop *everyone* from going underground!"

"I don't!" Tallpaw's heart pounded in his throat. What had Heatherstar told the tunnelers?

"Thanks to you and your tattling, Heatherstar's ordered us to close off the gorge tunnel and stop all work there." Sandgorse leaned closer, his breath hot on Tallpaw's muzzle. "*You* get a fright, and a project that *we've* spent moons on has to be abandoned."

Tallpaw shrank as his father showed his teeth. "Just because you don't want to be a tunneler," Sandgorse hissed, "doesn't mean you have to spoil it for everyone else! From now on, stay away from me and the tunnels!"

CHAPTER 14

Tallpaw hung his head over the side of his nest and peered out from under the gorse. The clearing was empty. While the Clan slept, the waning moon silvered the tussocks and spilled shadows across the Meeting Hollow. Tallpaw blinked up at the stars. *Are you there, StarClan? Can you see me?* He wondered if Finchkit was watching him. Would *she* have been such a disappointment to Sandgorse? Maybe she would have known how to make Palebird happy.

Shrewpaw and Reena were snoring gently in the nests behind him. Loneliness hollowed out Tallpaw's chest until he couldn't bear it any longer. He crept from his nest and slid out of camp. Beyond the heather walls, a soft breeze tugged his fur. The moor stretched before him, drenched in moonlight. Tallpaw broke into a run, relishing the wind against his fur, lengthening his strides until he felt like a bird skimming the grass. He headed for the moor-top, skirting the heather, staying in the open, out of breath by the time he reached Outlook Rock.

Up here the wind pushed hard enough to make him pad warily across the stone, taking care not to slip. He stopped at the edge and stared across the sleeping valley. Far beyond the meadows, an owl screeched. Tallpaw narrowed his eyes, seeing wings flutter in the top of a distant oak. An owl lifted and circled up into the peat-black sky. *Is that what it feels like to join StarClan?* Tallpaw imagined lifting off from Outlook Rock and spiraling into the stars.

The grass rustled behind him. Paws brushed the rock.

Tallpaw spun around. "Who's there?" He could just make out the outline of a cat against the dark bulk of the moor.

"It's me—Sparrow." The tom's mew was soft. "Is that Tallpaw?"

Tallpaw dipped his head. "Yes."

"Are you supposed to be out here by yourself?"

Tallpaw turned back to the horizon. "Probably not."

"Do you mind if I join you?" Sparrow jumped onto the stone and sat down beside Tallpaw. "I couldn't sleep."

"Do you ever wonder what it would be like to fly?" Tallpaw murmured. He gazed at the owl as it swooped low over a meadow.

"I would think it's hard work." Sparrow's tail whisked over the rock. "If you stop flapping, you fall. I'd rather feel the earth beneath my paws, know where I am just by looking around me."

Tallpaw glanced at him. "Do you like being a rogue?"

Sparrow's eyes glinted. "Is that what I am?"

"That's what warriors call cats who don't live in Clans."

"Then I guess I'm a rogue."

"Why are you here?" Tallpaw asked.

"I couldn't sleep," Sparrow repeated.

"Not on the rock. I mean, why are you staying with Wind-Clan?"

"It's where my friends wanted to come," Sparrow meowed. "So I came too." He gazed into Tallpaw's eyes. "Why are *you* here?"

Tallpaw blinked. *What did he mean? Why am I with WindClan? No, that's a dumb question.* "Do you mean why am I on Outlook Rock?"

"If you like." Sparrow turned and stared across the valley.

"I couldn't sleep, like you."

"Something bothering you?"

Sandgorse. Sadness and anger welled up until Tallpaw's throat tightened. "My father hates me. He wants me to be a tunneler, but I hate tunneling." Once Tallpaw started talking, he couldn't stop. "I tried going underground but the river broke through the clay and chased us and now Heatherstar's found out and banned them from tunneling and Sandgorse thinks it's all my fault because I'm a coward." The words rushed from Tallpaw so fast it surprised him. He stopped and took a deep breath.

Sparrow hadn't moved. He sat as still as the rock, gazing out to the horizon. "*Are* you a coward?"

Tallpaw bristled. "No!"

"Then Sandgorse is wrong," Sparrow meowed simply.

"I was scared, though," Tallpaw confessed. "When the tunnel flooded."

"I'd have been scared, too." Sparrow shifted his paws. "No

cat wants to be trapped underground in a flood."

"Sandgorse wasn't scared," Tallpaw pointed out.

"Sandgorse has been facing floods for moons."

"Perhaps I should become a tunneler." Tallpaw sighed. "If I faced floods for moons, I might get used to it too."

Sparrow caught his gaze and held it. "Is that what you want?"

"It's what Sandgorse wants."

"But is it what *you* want?"

"No." Tallpaw's pelt pricked with frustration. He'd been over this before. "But what I want doesn't seem important."

"It doesn't seem important to Sandgorse." Sparrow blinked. "But I'm guessing it's important to you."

Of course it's important to me!

"You should spend more time aiming for what *you* want," Sparrow meowed. "And less time worrying about what your father wants."

That's easy to say. Tallpaw twitched his tail.

"Sandgorse chose his own destiny," Sparrow went on. "Why should he get to choose yours, too?"

In the end, we choose our own destinies. Hawkheart's words echoed in Tallpaw's mind. "You're right!" Tallpaw stared at Sparrow. "Why should Sandgorse get to choose my path as well as his own? My paws are my own; I'll decide what to do with them." Energy surged through him.

Sparrow stood up and turned toward the moor.

"Are you going?" Tallpaw called.

"I want to see what the night prey's like in the heather,"

Sparrow told him. "I'm sure the elders will like waking up to a full prey heap."

Tallpaw watched him pad across the rock. "Thank you," he meowed.

Sparrow glanced back. "What for?"

Before Tallpaw could answer, the rogue slipped into the shadow of the moor. Tallpaw turned back to the valley and gazed at the stars on the horizon, his heart feeling lighter and freer than it had in moons.

You chose your destiny, Sandgorse. I'll choose mine.

"You're still half-asleep!" Dawnstripe nudged Tallpaw's shoulder as he dragged his paws toward the entrance. His feet felt as numb as stones and his mouth was dry. He'd sat on Outlook Rock until the horizon had started to lighten. Only then did he return to his nest. He'd managed to snatch a short sleep before the sun rose, but it wasn't enough to stop his eyelids from drooping as he headed out on patrol with Aspenfall, Dawnstripe, and Stagleap.

"Bring back a mouse!" Lilywhisker called from outside the elders' den. "Flailfoot's starving."

Tallpaw frowned. Hadn't Sparrow restocked the prey heap like he'd promised?

"Reedfeather's patrol will be back soon," Dawnstripe called back. The WindClan deputy had taken Doespring and Appledawn hunting.

Mole padded from the gorse and stopped beside Lilywhisker, his nose twitching. "I smell rabbit." As he spoke, the entrance tunnel shivered and Sparrow padded into camp. A plump rabbit hung from his jaws.

Lilywhisker's eyes lit up.

Dawnstripe purred. "You're just in time." She flicked her tail toward the elders' den. Sparrow nodded and carried his catch across camp.

Belly rumbling at the scent of fresh prey, Tallpaw stumbled dozily after the rest of his patrol.

"Excuse me." Hickorynose shouldered past with Mistmouse, Plumclaw, Woollytail, and Sandgorse behind him.

"Why can't tunnelers wait their turn like other warriors?" Aspenfall grumbled under his breath as he halted to let the tunneling patrol through the entrance first.

Tallpaw snapped his head up and tried to catch Sandgorse's eye. Before he pushed his way through the heather, his father shot him a look that stabbed Tallpaw's heart.

Dawnstripe brushed softly against Tallpaw. "Why don't you run to the first marker?" she suggested. "It might wake you up a bit." Tallpaw heard sympathy in her mew. *She saw how Sandgorse looked at me.*

"Okay." Running wouldn't make Sandgorse's angry stare hurt any less, but Tallpaw was grateful that his mentor cared. As he raced onto the grass, he saw the ginger tip of Sandgorse's tail snake into the bushes. *Why can't I have normal kin who care about my training and who are proud of me?*

Scowling, Tallpaw rounded the edge of the camp and raced for the first marker. As he neared the border with Fourtrees, he began to pick up scents from the forest. Somehow the wind carried scents more easily from this side of the moor—including, when the breeze blew in the right direction, the harsh smell of Twolegplace. Tallpaw paused and tasted the air. Something was different; there was a faint, ominous tang below the scent of the bright-yellow gorse flowers and the tiny, purple blooms on the heather. His hackles rose.

Not dog. Not Twoleg. He sniffed again. *Sparrow?* Perhaps the rogue had left scent when he was hunting. It didn't smell like Sparrow, but it *was* familiar. *I smelled it at the Gathering!* Concentrating, Tallpaw sifted through his memory of the scents he'd learned at full moon. *Pinesap? Stale river water? Neither! It's ThunderClan!*

Tallpaw scanned the heather. The scent was fresh. A ThunderClan cat had passed this way since dawn. He had to tell Dawnstripe. He whirled around and raced back toward camp. Plunging through a swathe of bristly gorse, he exploded out on the other side. Dawnstripe, Aspenfall, and Stagleap were padding across the grassy clearing, following his trail to the border.

"Invasion!" Tallpaw skidded to a halt, panting.

Aspenfall's pelt bushed up. "Where?"

Tallpaw tasted the air. ThunderClan scent was wafting from the slope behind him to the moor-top. He scanned the hillside. Thick-furred tails bobbed through a swathe of dark-green bracken. "Everywhere! ThunderClan has invaded!" Hurtling forward, he streaked past his patrol.

"Tallpaw!" Dawnstripe yowled after him.

He glanced backward. She was staring at him wide-eyed.

Why wasn't she following? Tallpaw pounded upslope and crashed into the bracken. ThunderClan scent flooded his nose as he pursued them though the feathery fronds. He burst onto open grass, astounded to see the ThunderClan patrol already nearing the moor-top. Two broad-shouldered warriors, one tortoiseshell, one gray, were leading two younger cats at a calm, purposeful walk.

How dare they trespass so deep into WindClan territory? They weren't even trying to hide! Tallpaw raced toward them. "Weasel hearts!" he screeched.

The ThunderClan patrol turned and stared at him. The tortoiseshell arched her back, eyes wide.

"Tallpaw!" Dawnstripe's yowl sounded behind him.

"I'll hold them off!" Tallpaw unsheathed his claws, ready to sink them into the first warrior he reached. Paw steps thrummed behind him. His patrol was catching up. He wouldn't have to fight alone.

The ThunderClan cats backed away, their ears flat.

Tallpaw leaped at the gray warrior. "Trespassers! Wind-Clan, attack!"

CHAPTER 15

✿

"Tallpaw!" Claws grabbed his flanks and dragged him backward. "Stop!"

Tallpaw slammed to the ground as Dawnstripe knocked his legs from under him. His chin hit the grass with a thump. He struggled to his paws and glared at her. "What are you doing?"

She glared back. "They're *allowed* to be here."

Tallpaw blinked.

"It's their route to Mothermouth."

Tallpaw's pelt burned. *What a rabbit-brain!* Swallowing, he turned and faced the ThunderClan warriors. "Sorry," he mumbled.

Dawnstripe nodded toward the younger cats. "Fuzzypaw and Robinpaw are probably going to share tongues with StarClan at the Moonstone. That's right, isn't it, Dappletail?"

The tortoiseshell let her fur lie flat again. "Yes. Thank you, Dawnstripe."

The gray warrior's whiskers twitched. "I thought we were going to get shredded for a moment."

Tallpaw fluffed out his chest. "I could shred—"

Dawnstripe padded in front of him before he could finish. "You know how eager apprentices can be." She dipped her head to the gray tom. "Windflight, I'm sorry if he alarmed you."

Fuzzypaw peered around Dawnstripe at Tallpaw. "We thought he was a rabbit," he mewed.

Tallpaw shook out his black-and-white fur. "You must have some weird-looking rabbits in the forest."

Robinpaw sniffed. "Not as weird-looking as you."

"I'm sure you'll want to be on your way," Dawnstripe meowed firmly. As she shooed them away with a flick of her tail, Aspenfall and Stagleap caught up.

Aspenfall's gaze flashed toward Tallpaw. "You managed to stop the war, then?"

"Only just," Dawnstripe muttered.

"Your apprentice is very fast," Windflight meowed generously.

"That's true," Dawnstripe agreed. "He'll be a good warrior when he's learned a little common sense."

"I forgot about the routes to Mothermouth over the moor." Tallpaw felt the fur bristle along his spine. *"Okay?"*

Stagleap nudged his shoulder. "Come on. Let's check the border anyway." He headed down the slope, weaving through the bracken stems.

Relieved to escape the stares of the ThunderClan apprentices, Tallpaw padded after him, breaking into a run when he reached a flat stretch of grass. He hared after Stagleap, the wind streaming through his pelt. Pushing harder with every stride, Tallpaw realized how easily he was gaining on the stocky, young warrior. He curved his spine deeper, stretched out farther, and within moments he was neck and neck with Stagleap. He relaxed, matching his pace to Stagleap's.

Stagleap glanced sideways at him as the moor sloped more steeply toward the Fourtrees border, and both cats slowed. "Have you grown?"

"You've shrunk," Tallpaw teased. He could taste the air growing rich with the scent of tree sap as the sweet smell of heather faded behind them.

Stagleap pulled up first as they reached the scent line, and Tallpaw scrambled to a halt a moment later, skidding across the border half a tail-length before leaping back onto Wind-Clan territory. Through the trees, he could just make out the tops of the Great Oaks at Fourtrees.

"This way." Stagleap led him along the trees toward a thicket of brambles that spilled out of the trees nearer to ShadowClan territory. Tallpaw swerved to avoid the tangle of prickly branches, glad that the brambles on the moor were few and far between. He'd hate to be trapped among thorns, unable to run without snagging his pelt at every turn. He sniffed gingerly at a bramble tendril, scared a prickle might lose its grip and let a branch whip across his muzzle.

The fresh scent of pinesap bathed his tongue. *ShadowClan?* There was bound to be ShadowClan scent here, Tallpaw reminded himself. They were tail-lengths from the border. And yet the scent smelled fresh, as though many pelts had brushed past not long ago. Tallpaw glanced at Stagleap.

Should he say something?

His ear twitched. He wasn't ready to make another rabbit-brained mistake. Not so soon. There was probably a good reason that there was ShadowClan scent here. Perhaps a ShadowClan patrol was on its way to the Moonstone, too. Perhaps the jumble of smells had drifted over the border and clung to the brambles. Surely if something were wrong, Stagleap would have noticed it?

Stagleap was veering away from Fourtrees and heading for the ShadowClan border line as it sloped toward the Thunderpath. Tallpaw knew that the ShadowClan camp was on the far side of the Thunderpath, but they had spread their scent marks on this side too, along the edge of the trees as far as the hollow with the Great Oaks. WindClan didn't object; they didn't want the trees for themselves.

Tallpaw caught up to his Clanmate. "Did you smell anything?" he asked casually. "Back there, I mean."

"Only the wind." Stagleap paused as Aspenfall and Dawnstripe appeared at the crest of the hill. He called to them. "Has ThunderClan declared war?"

Aspenfall's tail quivered. "They know it was an honest mistake."

Dawnstripe pulled up beside Tallpaw. "How's the border?" She sniffed the air. "Have you started marking it?"

"Not yet." Tallpaw realized that he'd been so busy worrying about ShadowClan scent, he'd forgotten to leave his own. He quickly sprayed a clump of grass and followed Stagleap down the slope. After a few strides, he paused and scanned the hillside. Far away, along the Thunderpath, he could see the ThunderClan patrol, specks now. Tallpaw winced as he imagined the story the apprentices would tell on their return, of a rabbit-brained WindClan apprentice who thought they were attacking WindClan at a steady walk.

He suddenly noticed that Stagleap had slowed. The dark brown warrior sniffed the grass, padded forward a tail-length, then sniffed again. His hackles rose.

"Is something wrong?" Aspenfall asked.

"I keep getting whiffs of ShadowClan on this side of the border."

Aspenfall trotted over and ran his muzzle across the grass. He wrinkled his nose.

Dawnstripe opened her mouth. "I can smell it from here," she growled. "A ShadowClan patrol has crossed the border."

"They didn't go far." Stagleap was checking the grass deeper into WindClan territory. "There's no scent here."

"Why would they cross at all?" Aspenfall asked.

Tallpaw glanced up the slope toward the brambles. "I smelled ShadowClan up there, too."

Aspenfall jerked his head up and stared at him. "Why didn't you say?"

"I thought they might be on their way to the Moonstone like the ThunderClan cats."

"ShadowClan doesn't need to cross our territory to reach the Moonstone," Aspenfall snapped. "Their camp is on the other side of the Thunderpath, just like Highstones."

Tallpaw gulped. "There were *a lot* of scents up there."

Aspenfall broke into a run and bounded up the slope. Dawnstripe raced after him with Stagleap at her heels. Tallpaw followed, his heart pounding. What had he done? He caught up with his Clanmates as they investigated the bramble thicket.

Aspenfall dodged back and forth, sniffing leaves. "There are too many scents to count."

"Why didn't you mention this before, Tallpaw?" Dawnstripe's pelt was spiked along her spine.

"I didn't want to be wrong again." Tallpaw felt cold. "What does it mean?"

"A huge ShadowClan patrol has crossed the border." Stagleap had his muzzle pressed to the ground, following a line of trampled grass across the moor. "They headed this way."

"Toward the camp!" Aspenfall charged past Stagleap and plunged into the heather.

Dawnstripe launched herself across the grass. "Come on, Tallpaw!"

Tallpaw bolted after her, Stagleap racing at his side. Tallpaw ran faster than he'd ever run before. Stagleap fell behind as Tallpaw pushed harder, hearing nothing but the blood roaring in his ears. Aspenfall and Dawnstripe were just a few paces ahead of him, swerving along a rabbit trail through a dense swathe of gorse and then bursting into the clearing outside camp.

Yowls rang out beyond the heather wall. An agonized screech. A terrified wail.

Dawnstripe skidded to a halt. Tallpaw slammed into her

flank as Aspenfall pulled up beside her. "Why are we stopping?" Tallpaw gasped.

Stagleap caught up with them, panting.

"Fetch the patrol that's hunting near the RiverClan border!" Dawnstripe ordered Tallpaw. "We'll need every spare warrior."

"I want to fight!" Tallpaw protested. If it hadn't been for him missing the first signs of invasion, they might have stopped the ShadowClan patrol from reaching the camp.

"I'll go." Aspenfall hurtled away.

"Okay, then." Dawnstripe stared at Tallpaw. "Are you ready?"

Tallpaw nodded. "Ready."

"Come on!" With a battle yowl, Dawnstripe raced through the entrance. Tallpaw shot after her, Stagleap crowding his heels. Tallpaw burst out of the heather, claws unsheathed, and stared in horror.

The camp seethed with snarling cats. Tails lashed. Paws flailed. The stench of pinesap mingled with the tang of blood. At the center Stonetooth, the ShadowClan deputy, reared up on his hind paws, teeth bared.

"Spare no one!" he snarled, slamming his paws down on Hareflight's spine. Hareflight rolled clear and leaped to his paws, hissing.

Tallpaw looked around, frozen.

"Circle the clearing and pick off the outsiders!" Dawnstripe ordered before she leaped into the middle of the fighting. As she disappeared beneath a huge tabby, Tallpaw scanned the edges of the camp.

Algernon and Bess were outside the nursery: one ducking,

the other slicing at ShadowClan attackers. Meadowslip and Palebird were nowhere to be seen, so Tallpaw figured they must be inside the nursery. Reena crouched in the entrance, slashing at any ShadowClan muzzle that came near.

Shrewpaw and Hareflight wrestled a ShadowClan tom at the entrance to the medicine den. Hareflight grasped him in his claws and dragged him backward. Unbalanced, the ShadowClan warrior kicked out. Quick as a bird, Shrewpaw swooped and sank his teeth into the tom's hind legs.

"Nice move, Shrewpaw!" Brackenwing called to her kit across the clearing. Without pausing for breath, she ducked and spun around, knocking a ShadowClan she-cat to the ground with a well-aimed blow.

Sparrow crouched at the entrance to the elders' den, pelt bushed up. Redclaw was braced at his side as two ShadowClan toms stalked toward them.

"You need rogues to defend you?" one of the ShadowClan warriors sneered, showing his teeth.

Sparrow lashed out and knocked him flying. Redclaw lunged and sent the other tom reeling with a blow to his muzzle.

Heart pounding in his ears, Tallpaw crept forward. *Circle the clearing and pick off the outsiders.* He recognized Frogpaw's dark gray pelt from the Gathering. Belly flat to the grass, the Shadow-Clan apprentice was creeping up on Ryestalk as she grappled with Newtpaw. Newtpaw dived beneath Ryestalk and flipped her onto her back, then started battering Ryestalk's muzzle. Ryestalk thrashed like wounded prey, trying to find her paws, her soft belly exposed. Frogpaw crouched even lower.

He's going to attack! Tallpaw raced toward him, yowling in fury. The ShadowClan apprentice leaped up, eyes wide. Tall-paw slammed into him. Frogpaw staggered backward, eyes flashing with rage. Hissing, he reared up and sliced Tallpaw's muzzle. Pain scorched through Tallpaw, but rage kept him on his feet. He narrowed his eyes and lashed out, keeping his hind paws firmly planted on the grass.

Ryestalk rolled past him, her claws dug deep into Newt-paw's flanks. "Are you okay?" she yowled to Tallpaw.

Tallpaw dodged a blow from Frogpaw and hooked the apprentice's legs from beneath him with a well-aimed kick. "I'm great!"

As Frogpaw hit the ground, Tallpaw sank his claws into the ShadowClan cat's shoulders. "Who smells of nettles now?" he growled, pressing Frogpaw's muzzle into the grass.

Suddenly claws pierced his flanks. Tallpaw yelped as he was dragged backward. He tried to struggle free but his pelt was caught fast.

"You smell worse than nettles!" Ashpaw hissed in his ear. "You smell of sheep dirt!" She flung him to the ground and plunged her paws into his belly.

Gasping, he tried to roll aside, but Frogpaw had leaped up and was pummeling Tallpaw's muzzle with a flurry of blows. Tallpaw's thoughts spiraled into panic. He flailed desper-ately, trying to break free, but Ashpaw and Frogpaw had him pinned to the ground.

Gray fur flashed at the corner of his eye. "When you hear the next yowl, get to your paws and start swinging," came a gruff voice. *Mole!*

The rogue grabbed Frogpaw and dragged him backward. Frogpaw screeched with fury. Tallpaw kicked free of Ashpaw and jumped to his paws. While Mole flung Frogpaw onto his back, Tallpaw flew at Ashpaw, claws stretched. Ashpaw's eyes widened with shock as his claws raked her muzzle.

Tallpaw kept swinging. "The only thing you'll be smelling for a while is *blood!*" he screeched. He kicked off with his hind legs and hurled himself at the ShadowClan apprentice. She rolled underneath him and crouched against the grass while he sank his teeth into her shoulder. Screeching with pain, she tore free and raced for the entrance. Newtpaw was ahead of her, her tail bushing as she fled the WindClan camp.

Aspenfall was chasing a tabby tom across the clearing. Redclaw hissed at a white warrior as he fled while Hareflight and Dawnstripe herded a gang of yowling ShadowClan warriors toward the entrance. *We've driven them out!* Tallpaw realized. As he felt a rush of triumph, a screech sounded from the Meeting Hollow. Tallpaw rushed to the edge and looked down.

In the shadow of Tallrock, Heatherstar reared over Stone-tooth. She slammed her paws down, sinking her claws deep into his pelt. Blood dripped from above her eye and she blinked it away. "Why did you attack us? Why?" She shook the ShadowClan deputy savagely.

"Why shouldn't we?" Stonetooth hung limp in her claws, his eyes shining with hate. "We could hunt on these moors just as well as you."

Heatherstar's eyes flashed. "The moors are ours and always

will be." She hauled Stonetooth to his paws and flung him toward the edge of the hollow. "Run after your weasel-hearted Clanmates before I rip you to shreds."

Stonetooth climbed out of the dip, leaving blood in his wake. "We've seen your weaknesses, you rabbits!" he snarled. "Next time, we'll drive you from your dens for good." Hissing at the watching WindClan warriors, he limped out of the camp.

Heatherstar turned to her medicine cat. "Check the injured, Hawkheart." She shook her head, sending scarlet droplets onto the churned-up sand. As Hawkheart moved toward her, she stepped back. "I'm fine," she meowed. "Start with the others."

Hawkheart turned and scanned the clearing. "Barkpaw!"

Tallpaw jerked around. Where was Barkpaw? He felt a surge of relief as he saw his friend hurrying out of the elders' den. "No injuries there!" he called to his mentor.

As he spoke, Reedfeather crashed through the entrance. "We've gotten rid of Stonetooth." The WindClan deputy lashed his tail. "Appledawn and Doespring are chasing him back to his own territory."

"Hawkheart!" A panicked cry rose from the tunnelers' nests. Redclaw was leaning over Brackenwing. His mate was sprawled in the long grass, unmoving. "She's bleeding!"

"Barkpaw," Hawkheart ordered, "fetch spiderweb and thyme leaves." He raced across the camp, clearing the Meeting Hollow in a leap. Crouching beside Brackenwing, he sniffed along her flank. "It's a gut injury." Gently he rolled the pale ginger she-cat onto her side.

Tallpaw crept closer, wincing as he saw blood flooding from Brackenwing's belly. Brackenwing groaned, her eyes rolling back until only the whites showed.

Redclaw leaned close to her cheek. "It's okay. Hawkheart will fix you."

Hareflight and Cloudrunner crowded at the edge of the bracken. Palebird nosed past Algie and Bess. "Brackenwing?"

"What's wrong?" Meadowslip was just behind her, her kit-swollen belly swaying.

Lilywhisker and Flailfoot watched, trembling, from the entrance to elders' den. "It looks bad," Flailfoot whispered.

Tallpaw stumbled aside as his mother pushed past. "Brackenwing!" Palebird's voice cracked as she crouched beside her friend.

Barkpaw raced out of his den with a wad of cobweb and leaves clamped between his jaws. He dropped them at Hawkheart's side and stared at his mother. "Brackenwing?"

The she-cat's eyes were closing. Redclaw looked at Hawkheart, his eyes as round as an owl's. "Can you save her?"

Hawkheart touched the small wad of web with his paw. "It's too late," he growled softly. "She's lost too much blood."

"Brackenwing!" Shrewpaw pushed past Aspenfall. "Get up, Brackenwing! We won the battle!" He stared at his mother, then at Barkpaw. "What's wrong with her?"

Barkpaw met his gaze with clouded eyes but didn't answer. Beside him, Brackenwing twitched, then fell still.

"Brackenwing." With a groan, Redclaw pressed his tawny

cheek against his mate's muzzle.

"Brackenwing?" Panic edged Shrewpaw's mew.

Hareflight stepped closer to his apprentice. "She's dead, Shrewpaw," he murmured.

Tallpaw backed away, shock trembling though every hair. *She can't be dead!* His paws trembled beneath him. A thought hit him like a stone. *Why didn't I tell Stagleap about the scents?* He backed away from his grieving Clanmates, horror twisting his belly.

"This is my fault!" he wailed. "It's all my fault!"

CHAPTER 16

❧

"No." Dawnstripe *turned to face* Tallpaw. "This was ShadowClan's fault. No one else's."

Tallpaw hardly heard her. Blood pounded in his ears. *What have I done?* All around him, his Clanmates stared at him as if he'd gone mad.

Heatherstar narrowed her eyes. "What are you talking about, Tallpaw?"

Tallpaw struggled to speak. "I smelled ShadowClan scent on the bramble thicket by Fourtrees. I should have said something but I didn't."

"Why not?" Heatherstar demanded.

"I thought it was just a ShadowClan patrol on the way to the Moonstone." Tallpaw blinked at her, aware of his round-eyed Clanmates watching behind.

"You killed her!" Dark brown fur flashed at the edge of his vision. Screeching, Shrewpaw flew at him. Tallpaw gasped as his denmate crashed into his shoulder. Pain seared his nose. Claws battered his muzzle. Tallpaw lifted his forepaws and tried to push Shrewpaw away as vicious blows battered his ears.

"Control yourself!" Hareflight snatched Shrewpaw by the scruff and hauled him away. Tallpaw stumbled to regain his balance as Shrewpaw clawed the air, hissing.

"I'll never forgive you! You killed my mother." Struggling free of Hareflight, the young tom glared at Tallpaw.

Barkpaw padded from the bracken and touched his nose to his brother's shoulder. Tallpaw desperately tried to catch his friend's eye. "I'm sorry, Barkpaw."

Barkpaw didn't look at him. Instead he crouched beside Shrewpaw like a wounded rabbit. Tallpaw's heart twisted. *Oh, StarClan! Forgive me!*

"Tallpaw?" Reena's mew sounded behind Heatherstar. She crossed the grass and touched his cheek with her nose. "It wasn't your fault," she whispered.

"Reena!" Bess called across the clearing. "Come away, dear. This is Clan business."

"Oh, Tallpaw." Reena backed away, eyes soft with sympathy.

Heatherstar dipped her head. "You made a mistake, Tallpaw," she meowed. "But this is not your fault. ShadowClan killed Brackenwing. Not you."

"But—" Tallpaw tried to argue, but Heatherstar turned away.

"Let's move Brackenwing to the clearing," the WindClan leader told her Clanmates. "So that we can mourn her properly."

Tallpaw pressed himself against the wall of the camp, sheltering in the heather fronds while Aspenfall, Cloudrunner, and Hareflight lifted Brackenwing's body and carried it to a grassy hollow between the tussocks. As they laid her down, Hawkheart brought herbs from the medicine den and laid them along Brackenwing's flank. Tallpaw could smell their pungent, green odor as it masked the scent of death. Redclaw and Palebird settled beside her but Shrewpaw kept circling, his eyes dark.

"My dear friend." Palebird pressed her muzzle into Brackenwing's fur. "You're the only one who saw Finchkit before she died. No one else understood my grief."

Tallpaw wished there was some way he could comfort his mother. But he had never been able to. His chest tightened. *She won't want me. It's my fault her friend's dead.*

As the sun rose into the sky, Hawkheart moved from cat to cat, checking wounds while Barkpaw dashed back and forth to the medicine den fetching herbs to treat them. Aspenfall and Ryestalk collected the shredded gorse around the nursery and began to thread it back into the walls.

Meadowslip peeked out. "Make them thick," she mewed shakily. "I want my kits to be safe if there's another attack."

"ShadowClan won't get through this," Aspenfall promised her, weaving another thorny stem through the branches.

Stagleap helped Whiteberry, Flamepelt, and Flailfoot hook back the torn stems that dangled across the entrance to the elders' den. Lilywhisker sat back and gave directions. "Weave in some heather to soften it," she croaked. "The gorse thorns scrape my spine every time I go in."

"Tallpaw?" Hawkheart's mew surprised him.

Tallpaw glanced up at the sky. How long had he sat alone? Sunhigh had passed and the sun was sliding toward the moortop. "What?" he meowed, feeling hollow inside.

"I need to treat your wounds." The medicine cat was brisk. "Stand up so I can take a look."

"Don't bother." Tallpaw stared at the ground. The scratches Frogpaw and Ashpaw had given him were throbbing. But they felt like gnat bites compared with the stinging wounds Shrewpaw had left on his muzzle. "My wounds don't matter."

"Don't be rabbit-brained." Hawkheart crouched beside him.

"But I killed her," Tallpaw croaked.

"You're a half-trained apprentice. The safety of the Clan doesn't rest in your paws," Hawkheart told him sharply. "You weren't the only cat on that patrol. Are any of the others blaming themselves?"

Tallpaw glanced across the camp to where Stagleap was sifting through the prey heap. He hadn't detected ShadowClan's scents. *But I did. I should have told him.*

Hawkheart sniffed at the scratches around Tallpaw's ears. Tallpaw flinched as his nose touched a tender wound. "Barkpaw!" Hawkheart called across the clearing. "Bring some dock and marigold."

Barkpaw's gaze flashed toward them. Tallpaw tried to catch his eye, but his friend just nodded and headed for the medicine den. Tallpaw wondered if Barkpaw would ever speak to him again.

* * *

Once Hawkheart had left and the herbs had begun to soothe the sting of his wounds, Tallpaw tucked his paws tighter under him. Palebird and Redclaw still lay beside Brackenwing's body. Shrewpaw continued to pace in circles, while the rest of the Clan waited at the edge of the clearing for the night vigil to begin. Tallpaw watched the sun dip below the wall of the camp and huddled deeper into the heather, relieved as the shadows swallowed him.

He stiffened as the branches around him trembled. Some-one was coming through the entrance. He jerked around as Hickorynose marched into the camp. Sandgorse, Mistmouse, Woollytail, and Plumclaw followed, their eyes stretching wide as they saw the torn gorse and shredded grass littering the clearing, some of it stained ominously red.

Plumclaw's pelt fluffed. "Is that *Brackenwing*?" She charged across the clearing and gazed down at the dead warrior's body. "What happened?"

Aspenfall emerged from the nursery, his fur covered in bits of leaf. "ShadowClan attacked."

"Can't you smell their stench?" Reedfeather leaped out of the Meeting Hollow. "It seemed as if the entire Clan was here."

Heatherstar padded from her den, following the rim of the hollow and stopping beside her deputy. "It's a shame you didn't get back earlier," she mewed quietly to the tunnelers.

Sandgorse twitched an ear. "Palebird?"

Palebird lifted her head from beside Brackenwing. "I'm okay." Her mew cracked as she spoke.

Shrewpaw lashed his tail. "Brackenwing's dead and it was Tallpaw's fault!"

Sandgorse blinked. "Tallpaw? How?" Nose twitching, he peered into the shadows, stopping when he spotted Tallpaw. His eyes darkened. Heart twisting, Tallpaw looked away. *He hates me even more now.*

"Shrewpaw." Reedfeather stepped forward. "You have to stop blaming Tallpaw for something ShadowClan did. You are Clanmates. Your loyalty is to each other."

"But—"

Heatherstar didn't let Shrewpaw speak. "This wasn't Tallpaw's fault, Sandgorse. Shrewpaw speaks from grief, that's all."

Tallpaw swallowed. Was that true? No one had been near him all day except Hawkheart. Was the whole Clan grieving as much as Shrewpaw?

"Meadowslip!" Hickorynose bounded to the nursery.

Meadowslip squeezed out, dropping onto the grass and pressing her cheek to her mate's.

Hickorynose fussed over her. "Are you hurt?"

"I'm fine," Meadowslip promised. "Bess and Algie defended the den with Reena." She blinked gratefully across the camp at the rogues as they cleared scraps of heather and gorse from the bloodstained tussocks.

"I wish I'd been here to protect you," Hickorynose fretted.

Hareflight padded toward Brackenwing's body. "So do we." Hickorynose stared in surprise at the brown warrior. "The tunnelers are never here when we need them," Hareflight hissed.

Reedfeather stepped forward. "We can't keep blaming each other for this."

Woollytail's hackles rose. "This wasn't our fault."

Cloudrunner lifted his muzzle. "Where were you when we were fighting to defend the Clan?"

"We were digging tunnels so you could eat come leaf-bare!" Plumclaw snapped.

Aspenfall's tail twitched. "What good will your precious tunnels be if ShadowClan drives us from our home?"

Sandgorse narrowed his eyes. "If you'd let us dig the tunnels we need, we could defend our home more effectively!"

"You mean the *gorge* tunnel?" Aspenfall curled his lip. "How would that have helped today?"

"It would have given us an escape route!" Sandgorse snarled.

"To where?" Aspenfall challenged. "RiverClan territory?"

Sandgorse narrowed his eyes. "We could have sheltered in the tunnel. It's big enough for the whole Clan."

"You want us to leave our camp and *hide*?" Cloudrunner squared up to Sandgorse, pelt bristling. "Are you a warrior, or a rabbit?"

Tallpaw braced himself. The Clan was tearing itself apart!

CHAPTER 17

Paw steps sounded in the shadows behind Tallpaw. He scented Sparrow and looked up. The rogue had slid among the heather fronds and stood at Tallpaw's shoulder. "These are tough times, Tallpaw," he murmured. Tallpaw moved closer to the brown tom, relieved to have someone beside him.

Heatherstar pushed between Cloudrunner and Sandgorse. "We can't let this tragedy divide us," she meowed. "We are WindClan and we are strong." She dipped her head to Bess and Algernon. "And thanks to our visitors' battle skills today, we are safe. If they hadn't been here, we may have lost our home."

"What are you saying?" Hickorynose curled his lip. "That without them, ShadowClan would have won?"

Heatherstar met his gaze steadily. "Half our warriors were away tunneling. It made us vulnerable."

Tallpaw gulped. This felt like a direct challenge to the tunnelers! Beside him, Sparrow pricked his ears.

"We were lucky our visitors were with us today," Heatherstar went on. "But they won't be with us forever. What will happen if ShadowClan attacks once they've left?"

Plumclaw's eyes stretched into twin moons. "Are you saying we have to stop tunneling?"

Tallpaw's pads pricked as he watched his father's tail sweep the grass behind him.

"No," Heatherstar meowed. "But we should send out smaller tunneling patrols, and give you more training in aboveground battle skills."

Sandgorse lifted his chin. "So our skills aren't *enough* to protect the Clan?"

"I'm saying that the more skills we share, the better." Heatherstar gazed down at Brackenwing. "But first we shall join as one Clan to sit vigil for our fallen Clanmate." She crouched down and touched her nose to Brackenwing's ginger pelt.

Reedfeather joined her. As the Clan gathered around the dead warrior, Tallpaw ducked out from the heather and crossed the camp. Squeezing in beside Palebird, he pressed his muzzle to Brackenwing's pelt. Beneath her blood-soaked pelt, she felt like stone. Tallpaw leaned against his mother, breathing in the warm scent of her fur.

"Palebird?" he whispered. *Please tell me it's going to be okay.*

Palebird nuzzled closer to Brackenwing. Heart aching, Tallpaw screwed his eyes shut.

"What's this about a gorge tunnel?" he heard Sparrow whisper from the shadows behind.

Sandgorse answered him. "We spent half of leaf-bare and all newleaf digging it," he growled under his breath. "But we've had to abandon it."

"Why?" Sparrow sounded curious.

"A dumb flood scared one of the apprentices."

Tallpaw flinched. *One of the apprentices? Is that all I am to you now?*

"Why did you build a tunnel there?" Sparrow pressed.

"To give us a secret route to the river."

"Hush!" Larksplash snapped. "We're sitting vigil!"

The grass behind Tallpaw swished as Sandgorse joined his Clanmates. Tallpaw let his head drop against his mother's shoulder. Even if she didn't seem to know he was there, he could take warmth from her pelt. Tiredness crept over him as he leaned deeper into her fur. Letting go of his misery, he drifted into sleep.

The movement of Brackenwing's body woke him. Tallpaw jerked up his head and blinked. The sky was pale, the beginnings of dawn showing over the heather wall. The elders were dragging their Clanmate away.

Palebird shifted beside him. "Can I help with the burial?" She clambered to her paws.

"Yes, you can," puffed Flamepelt, who was crouched down as Whiteberry and Lilywhisker hauled Brackenwing onto his back.

Tallpaw felt cold air where Palebird had been. He stood up, his wounds stinging, his legs stiff from the damp grass. Redclaw and Cloudrunner shooed him backward to make way for the elders as they carried Brackenwing out of the camp.

Heatherstar dipped her head as they passed. "May StarClan cherish her as we did," she murmured.

The rogues kept back by the wall to the camp, looking mournful and somber. Only Sparrow's gaze glittered with something like curiosity as he watched the elders leave.

"Go and rest in your den." Tallpaw heard Dawnstripe's whisper and turned around. His mentor was gazing at him gently. "You must be tired," she murmured.

"Actually, I slept all night." Tallpaw shifted his paws guiltily. Was he supposed to stay awake?

"Then let's train." Dawnstripe whisked her tail. "The vigil is over. We might as well carry on as normal." She headed for the entrance and Tallpaw followed, relieved that Dawnstripe hadn't tried to ask how he was feeling. Her briskness was as refreshing as the wind.

They passed Sparrow and Sandgorse. The toms were talking with their heads close together, and Sandgorse's eyes flashed with excitement. Tallpaw pricked his ears.

"You say Heatherstar's forbidden you from going down there?" Sparrow asked.

"Yes," Sandgorse whispered.

Tallpaw halted and sat down, pretending to search for a flea in his tail. Why was Sparrow so interested in the gorge tunnel?

"What a waste," murmured the rogue.

Sandgorse nodded. "All that paw-work for nothing."

"You sound proud of the tunnel."

"I know it better than I know my own pelt," Sandgorse declared.

"Then surely *you* can go down there?" Sparrow reasoned.

"You know which parts are safe and which might be dangerous."

"Of course I do!" Sandgorse snorted. "I built every step of it with my own paws."

Tallpaw straightened up. What was Sandgorse thinking? Were his tunnels the only thing he cared about? Sandgorse thought he was special just because he could dig! *Rabbits dig! They're not special.* Pelt pricking, Tallpaw ducked out of camp and raced after Dawnstripe. His thoughts whirled. Perhaps Heatherstar was right. The Clans needed warriors who could fight, not tunnels.

As they reached the training ground, the sun lifted over the forest and spilled light across the grass. Tallpaw was relieved to feel warmth washing his fur. "Dawnstripe?" he asked as she halted at the head of the grass clearing.

"What?" She looked around.

"Do we really need tunnelers?"

Dawnstripe hesitated. "It's part of our tradition," she told him at last. "There's a lot of skill and courage involved. Skills that only WindClan possesses."

"So it makes us special?" Tallpaw pressed.

"Yes."

"But what use is it?" Tallpaw meowed bluntly. "What's the point of digging underground when battles are fought up here?" He gestured to the endless moor with his tail.

Dawnstripe's ear twitched. "Let Heatherstar worry about whether WindClan needs tunnelers or not. We're here to train." Tallpaw felt a prick of frustration. She hadn't answered his question. "Just one lap!" Dawnstripe flicked her tail and Tallpaw hared away across the grass. "You'll be stiff after the battle, so take it easy," she called after him.

She was right. Tallpaw tensed as pain flashed through him. But he wasn't going to take it easy. When he was running he couldn't think about anything else, and that felt good. He charged along the grass, brushing close to the heather, making as wide a circuit as he could. As he rounded the far end, he saw a creamy brown pelt slide out from the heather to stand beside Dawnstripe. *Algernon.* Tallpaw sped up, wondering why Algernon had come to the training area.

"Is everything okay in the camp?" He skidded to a halt a tail-length from Dawnstripe and Algernon.

"Of course. I just came to see what you were doing," Algernon rumbled. "I hope you don't mind."

Tallpaw shrugged. "Of course not." He peered past the rogue. Was Reena coming, too? "Where are the others?"

"Reena and Bess joined the hunting patrol," Algernon told him. "Mole wanted to hunt alone."

"What about Sparrow?"

"He went off with Sandgorse," Algernon meowed. "They were talking about some tunnel that leads down to the river."

Poor Sparrow. Tallpaw felt a flash of sympathy. Once Sandgorse got him down a tunnel, he'd talk his ears off about tunnel skills and all the rules about not leaving your tunnelmate and how to hear rabbits on the far side of the moor. He looked at Dawnstripe. "Can we practice battle moves today? In case ShadowClan attacks again."

"Yes," Dawnstripe meowed grimly. "I just hope you won't need them."

By the end of the session, Tallpaw felt much better. He was going to be the best moor runner WindClan had ever seen! While Sandgorse was grubbing around in muddy holes, *he* would be defending his Clan. *I'll avenge Brackenwing's death.* He curled his claws and imagined throwing the body of a ShadowClan warrior in front of his Clan. They'd have to forgive him then.

"Can we hunt?" he growled. He wanted to feel flesh beneath his claws. "The prey heap is empty."

Dawnstripe was deep in conversation with Algernon. He'd watched the practice session and now he leaned back on the grass, basking in the sun. "You've *lived* with Twolegs?" Dawnstripe leaned closer to the rogue. "What was it like?"

"Twolegs are funny creatures," Algernon told her.

"Dawnstripe!" Tallpaw interrupted. "Can we hunt?"

"You go." Dawnstripe flicked her tail. "We'll catch up." Tallpaw shrugged and headed downslope. "No one's hunted the burrows by the gorge in a while!" Dawnstripe called after him. "There should be plenty of prey there."

"Okay!" Tallpaw called over his shoulder as he pushed through the heather. "I'll see you there." He followed a stale rabbit track and emerged from the heather at the top of a rise. The land sloped away past a swath of gorse before flattening out to meet the edge of the gorge. Tallpaw could just make out the dimples where rabbit burrows had been dug close to the surface. Tallpaw pounded toward them. The ground thrummed beneath his paws, solid, then hollow, then solid again.

Tunnels. Tallpaw snorted. *Stupid tunnels.*

He pulled up as he neared the gorge, stepping lightly so he didn't frighten any rabbits that might be grazing near the burrows. He must be on top of the gorge tunnel by now. Was Sandgorse down there, boring the ears off poor Sparrow? He paused, feeling the ground tremble beneath his paws. Were they digging? He crouched and pressed his belly to the grass, feeling for the tremors.

The fur rose on his spine. He could feel rumbling deep in the earth. It stirred memories of the flood. Was a tunnel collapsing?

Fear flaring, Tallpaw raced for the burrows. He might be able to hear what was happening through one of the openings. Surely Sandgorse wouldn't take Sparrow anywhere dangerous? He was too experienced to lead an untrained cat into an unstable tunnel. Tallpaw slowed to a halt, jerking around, glancing from burrow to burrow. Poking his head into one, he heard the earth roar. He stiffened as the ground shook beneath his paws. Terror uncoiled in his belly.

Then claws scrabbled behind him. Tallpaw whirled around as a mud-drenched cat burst out from a rabbit hole. "Sparrow!" He recognized the rogue's eyes through his filthy pelt. Tallpaw glanced past him, expecting Sandgorse to race out behind. But he only heard the growl of earth folding in on itself, crushing air and light and everything else inside. . . .

"Where's Sandgorse?" Tallpaw stared at Sparrow. "Wasn't he with you?"

Sparrow glanced back down the hole, flanks heaving. "I lost him."

"You lost him?" Tallpaw blinked. *You left him behind?*

"Too much water," Sparrow panted. "And mud."

"You can't leave a cat underground!"

There was a flash of movement on the horizon. Dawn-stripe and Algernon were heading toward them.

"Sparrow!" Algernon's pelt spiked. "You're soaked! Are you okay?"

"I have to find my father!" Tallpaw barged past Sparrow and plunged down the hole. Darkness engulfed him. The sour smell of river water and soil flooded his nose. He raced forward, flattening his ears against the roaring earth. Hurtling along the tunnel, he crashed against one wall, then another, running blindly, panic sending his thoughts whirling.

"Sandgorse!" His yowl echoed in the darkness. The soil around him was growing looser all the time. The tunnel narrowed and Tallpaw tripped over a pile of earth. Scrabbling over it, he found himself squeezing through an ever-tightening gap. "Sandgorse!" Earth turned to mud around him. Now he was slithering though the tunnel like a snake. "Where are you?" The rumbling was growing louder. The earth was still moving. "I'm coming, Sandgorse!" Tallpaw hauled himself forward, scrabbling with his hind legs, pushing desperately on. A thunderous rumble swept toward him and the floor of the tunnel heaved beneath his paws. Mud and water filled his muzzle and terror burst his heart as the world turned black.

CHAPTER 18

Pain jolted Tallpaw awake. He was bumping over stones, being dragged from behind. Rocks jabbed his belly and scraped his legs and chin. Someone was hauling him out of the tunnel. He struggled, trying to find his paws, but claws clasped his flanks and heaved him harder. Suddenly fresh air rushed around him and he was on soft grass. He gulped in air, fresh and sweet.

"What happened?" Tallpaw coughed, spitting out mud. "Is this StarClan?" He tried to remember what he had been doing before the darkness came, but his thoughts were spinning too fast. It was like trying to catch butterflies in the wind.

A gentle paw touched his shoulder. "It's all right; you're safe now." Dawnstripe was crouching beside him. "Woollytail pulled you out."

"Out of where?" Tallpaw struggled to sit up.

Dawnstripe sniffed him anxiously. "Does anything feel broken?"

Tallpaw felt his pelt stinging where it had torn on stones, but he could move each of his legs. "I'm okay."

Woollytail paced in front of him, his gray-and-white pelt turned completely brown with smeared mud. "We'll see about that." He glanced at Tallpaw. "You should get your cuts and scratches seen to. Underground mud can be bad for you. Wounds infect easily."

"Hush." Dawnstripe waved Woollytail away with her tail. "He's already scared enough."

Scared? Tallpaw's legs buckled beneath him and he collapsed onto his belly. *Why would I be scared?* Hazily he saw Algernon sitting a little way off. Sparrow was lying on the grass beside him, his short fur spiked and filthy. *Were we both underground?* Tallpaw wondered.

Mistmouse squeezed out of a rabbit hole, her pelt slicked with mud. Algernon caught her eye. "Any luck?" Mistmouse shook her head.

Tallpaw's thoughts cleared with a jolt. "Sandgorse!" That's why he'd gone down the tunnel. "Where is he?"

Woollytail stopped pacing. His eyes were ominously dark. He turned as Plumclaw scrambled out of a second burrow. "Did you get through?" Woollytail asked.

Plumclaw shook her head. "We hit rock. Hickorynose is still trying but there's no way to dig past it."

Tallpaw's heart began to pound. "If he's still down there, you have to get him out."

Plumclaw crossed the grass toward him. "We've tried, Tallpaw, but the whole tunnel network collapsed. Floodwater's in every branch and the roofs are still caving in." She thrust her nose close to him, blinking away wet soil. "Another mouselength and you'd have drowned, too."

Tallpaw stiffened. *"Sandgorse drowned?"*

Plumclaw leaned back. "We haven't found his body, but there's no way he could still be alive down there."

"No!" Tallpaw tried to struggle to his paws, but he was shaking too much.

Woollytail glanced at Mistmouse. "There's nothing more we can do."

"We've tried everything to get to him," she meowed, ears flat. "He's down there for good."

"Maybe Sparrow can help!" Tallpaw stared at the rogue. Sparrow lifted his mud-streaked head. "Where did you last see Sandgorse?" Tallpaw demanded. "Can you lead the tunnelers there?"

"The tunnels are blocked," Woollytail reminded him.

"But if you know where to look, you might be able to dig through," Tallpaw persisted. "I'll dig through myself."

Dawnstripe pressed him back with a paw. "Tallpaw," she murmured softly. "If Woollytail can't reach him, no one can. Sandgorse is with StarClan now."

Tallpaw's hackles rose and anger surged in his chest. He glared at Sparrow. "Why did you leave him? You should have stayed with him! Don't you know that's what you do underground? You stay with your tunnelmate."

Sparrow pushed himself to his paws. "I'm no tunneler. I don't have partners. Not aboveground. Not belowground." His gaze hardened. "I was lucky I made it out. There was no way I could have helped Sandgorse. He's the one with all the skills. He shouldn't have taken me down there. He should have known it was too dangerous."

Tallpaw stared, breath catching in his throat. Sparrow was blaming Sandgorse for what happened? He stared at the other tunnelers, willing one of them to come to Sandgorse's defense. How dare this rogue blame his father for the accident?

"Woollytail?" Tallpaw croaked to the old tunneler.

Woollytail stared at his paws. "Sandgorse answered for his recklessness," he muttered.

"Are you saying this was his fault?" Tallpaw gasped.

Woollytail avoided his eye. "Come on," he grunted. "Let's get you to Hawkheart. Those wounds'll need seeing to."

Dawnstripe shoved her nose under Tallpaw's flank and heaved him to his paws. Algernon darted over and pressed against his shoulder. With Dawnstripe pushing on the other side, Tallpaw managed to stagger forward. As they climbed the slope, he felt strength beginning to seep back into his paws, though his breath was hard to catch. He stopped and coughed up more muddy water, then moved on, thankful for Algernon and Dawnstripe's help. He could hear paw steps behind and looked back to see Woollytail helping Sparrow back to camp. Tallpaw growled under his breath. How could Woollytail help the cat that had killed his tunnelmate?

He staggered wearily through the entrance. Aspenfall paused on a tussock and stared at the mud-streaked cats. "Any news?"

Palebird hurried out of the nursery. "Did you find him?"

Tallpaw stared blankly at his mother.

"No," Dawnstripe answered for him.

"Sandgorse!" As Palebird collapsed, Meadowslip hurried to her side.

Tallpaw closed his eyes. "He's dead," he whispered. His legs crumpled beneath him and choking mud seemed to swamp him once more. He could feel the suffocating weight of earth and water, and he imagined his father thrashing against the flood as it grew heavier and heavier until at last he was pinned without light or air, lungs screaming, heart bursting.

"Tallpaw?" Hawkheart leaned over him. "Swallow these leaves."

A pungent scent wafted beneath his nose. Numbly he lapped up the green specks beside his mouth.

"Bring more thyme, Barkpaw," Hawkheart called. "And some of the poultice we made for the wounded warriors."

"Are you all right, Sparrow?" Bess's anxious mew sounded nearby. Tallpaw opened his eyes and saw the black-and-white cat pacing around the brown warrior. Reena was sniffing at his filthy pelt.

"I'll live." Sparrow shook out his fur, showering his companions with muddy water.

Hawkheart turned his head. "All Sparrow needs is a good wash," he growled. "Help him get cleaned up." He nosed Tallpaw onto his side and began sniffing his scratches. "Great StarClan, what a mess."

"I had to drag him out," Woollytail meowed.

"He's pretty shredded," Hawkheart muttered. "But no deep wounds."

Paw steps pattered closer and a wad of herbs landed beside Hawkheart. "Is he okay?" Tallpaw recognized Barkpaw's mew.

"He'll be fine." Hawkheart began to lap herbs into a wound on Tallpaw's pad. Tallpaw winced at the pain but held still.

"Go and soak moss in the spring," Hawkheart told Barkpaw. "Plenty of it. I want you to wash as much of this mud out of Tallpaw's fur as you can."

The medicine cat's mew faded into buzzing, and darkness swallowed Tallpaw. Hawkheart poked him sharply. "Stay awake. You've had a shock. You can sleep later." He began pressing the herbs more firmly into Tallpaw's wounds. The pain jerked Tallpaw into wakefulness.

"These will heal in no time," Hawkheart promised. "We just have to get you clean." He nosed some more pungent thyme toward Tallpaw. "Keep chewing this. It'll help."

Tallpaw lapped up another tongueful of shredded leaves and began chewing. His thoughts started to clear. By the time Barkpaw returned and began sluicing his pelt with soaked moss, he was able to turn and watch.

"I'm sorry about Sandgorse." Barkpaw didn't lift his eyes from what he was doing.

"I'm sorry about Brackenwing," Tallpaw meowed.

Barkpaw didn't reply, just kept washing Tallpaw's pelt. The long, cool strokes lulled Tallpaw and eased his pain.

"Do you want some food?" When Barkpaw had gone to rinse out the mud-filled moss, Reena clambered over a tussock and sat down beside Tallpaw. "You haven't eaten all day." She twitched her tail toward the prey heap, stacked high with fresh-kill.

Tallpaw shook his head. "I'm not hungry, thanks."

"Then I could just sit with you," Reena offered.

Tallpaw shook his head. He didn't want company. His pain

was all on the inside now, too deep for anyone to touch. He could see Palebird outside the nursery staring into space, her eyes glazed. For a moment Tallpaw understood why she always seemed so distant. If she didn't let herself feel anything, she might protect herself from her grief for Finchkit. Now he wanted to do the same. "I'd rather be alone," he mumbled.

"Are you sure?" Reena leaned close, the scent of rabbit on her breath.

"I'm sure." Tallpaw watched her pad away to the Hunting Stones, where Bess, Algernon, and Mole were tucking grass around Sparrow.

Bess pulled up a pawful of moss from beneath one of the rocks and packed it beneath Sparrow's shoulder. "Is that more comfortable?"

Sparrow wriggled. "Much better," he purred.

Tallpaw growled under his breath. Anger felt better than grief. He watched the sun sink below the heather. It glowed on Dawnstripe's pelt as she padded toward him. A mouse dangled from her jaws. She stopped beside him and dropped it at his paws. "You should eat something," she meowed.

How did Dawnstripe think he could eat? Didn't she know he'd just lost his father? "I told Reena: I'm not hungry," Tall-paw muttered.

"It won't always feel this bad," Dawnstripe promised.

He glared at her. "Yes, it will!" he snapped. "I'll never feel happy again. StarClan doesn't want me to be happy. They should have taken me, not Finchkit." He glared across the camp at Palebird. "Maybe Sandgorse wouldn't be dead if my sister were alive."

Dawnstripe stiffened. "Don't say things like that!"

"I've done everything wrong," Tallpaw snarled. "If I'd insisted on being a tunneling apprentice, Sandgorse would have been exploring the gorge tunnel with me, not Sparrow. *I* wouldn't have left him behind."

"You're upset." Dawnstripe got to her paws. "You're not thinking straight. I'll come and check on you later, when you've had some rest." She padded away and settled down beside Redclaw and Appledawn, but her gaze flashed anxiously toward Tallpaw as she shared tongues with her Clanmates.

Appledawn's voice carried on the breeze. "Sandgorse should never have taken Sparrow down those tunnels."

Tallpaw sat up.

"Heatherstar said they were dangerous," Redclaw agreed.

Tallpaw bared his teeth at the tawny warrior. "Sparrow made him go down there!" he hissed across the clearing. "The nosy rogue wouldn't stop pestering Sandgorse until he showed him the tunnels! And then he left Sandgorse down there to die!" Rage pulsed like lightning in his paws.

On the other side of the clearing, Sparrow stood up. "I'm sorry your father is dead, Tallpaw. But he told me it was safe when it wasn't. How was I supposed to know what would happen? I'm no tunneler. I believed him. When the river burst through, I didn't have time to save him. I barely saved myself."

"If there was time to save yourself, there was time to save Sandgorse," Tallpaw snapped. "You *left* him to die."

"Enough!" Heatherstar leaped to her paws and marched across the clearing. "The Clan has seen too much grief this moon. Go to your nest, Tallpaw. Words won't change anything now."

Tallpaw met her gaze. He was trembling with fury.

"Go," Heatherstar repeated.

Tallpaw glanced around at his Clanmates. They stared at him, frozen in shock. Prey hung from Cloudrunner's mouth. Lilywhisker's eyes were round. Flamepelt sat stiffly beside her. Stagleap, Ryestalk, and Doespring blinked at him like birds lined along a branch. Shrewpaw narrowed his eyes while Barkpaw sat like stone at the entrance to the medicine den.

Whipping his tail, Tallpaw turned and stalked to his nest. He climbed in and thrust his nose under his paw. When sleep came, it was filled with dreams. Mud pressed around him, sucking at his fur; water dragged him through endless tunnels, and in brief flashes of light from somewhere above his head, Tallpaw saw Sandgorse, mouth open, shrieking for help, only to be hauled away by another surge of mud.

"Tallpaw." Breath touched his ear. Tallpaw jerked up his head. Barkpaw ducked away. "How are you?"

Beyond him, Tallpaw could see the camp through the gorse opening of his den. A bright moon lit the tussocks. "Is it nearly dawn?"

"Not yet." Barkpaw reached into Tallpaw's nest. Tallpaw smelled the tang of ointment. "I just want to put some herbs on your wounds," Barkpaw told him. "Hawkheart's worried about infection."

Tallpaw leaned back and let Barkpaw spread the thick paste of herbs onto his grazes. "I had nightmares," he meowed.

"They'll pass." Barkpaw avoided Tallpaw's gaze.

"I don't want to sleep again." The thought of returning to his dreams made Tallpaw's belly harden.

"You need to rest." Barkpaw sounded very far away. Even in this half light, Tallpaw could see tiredness shadowing his friend's eyes. Barkpaw was still wrapped in grief for Brackenwing.

Tallpaw understood. Loneliness jabbed his belly. If only they could share their grief. But Barkpaw seemed too far away. Did he still blame Tallpaw for Brackenwing's death?

Tallpaw blinked open his eyes in the pale light of dawn, surprised to find that he'd slept again after Barkpaw had left. He peered out from the gorse bush and saw Reedfeather calling patrols for the day.

"Aspenfall, Cloudrunner, and Doespring," the deputy ordered, "take Mole hunting with you. Hareflight, Stagleap, and Shrewpaw, check the ShadowClan and Fourtrees border. Dawnstripe and Redclaw, patrol the rest."

Tallpaw watched his Clanmates charge out of camp while Reena and Bess headed for the elders' den. "We've come to clean out your bedding," Bess called through the entrance.

Lilywhisker padded out, yawning. "You'll have to wake the others. Flamepelt's snoring like a badger."

Tallpaw hauled himself to his paws, wincing as his scratches stung.

"Stay in your nest." Hawkheart's stern growl surprised him. The medicine cat slid into the den. Tallpaw sat down as Hawkheart sniffed his wounds. "There's infection in your forepaw. I can smell it," he told Tallpaw. "I'll dress the wound again. Then stay off it. You're confined to your nest until it's healed."

"I can't stay here," Tallpaw argued. "I hate it. I just sleep and have nightmares."

"You don't have a choice." Hawkheart dabbed fresh herbs onto Tallpaw's wounds. "You have to get well. There's been too much loss. First Brackenwing, then your father."

"But—" Tallpaw began to argue but Hawkheart silenced him with a look.

Tallpaw lay back in his nest as the medicine cat left. The low gorse roof seemed to press down on him. His breath quickened in the stale air. Tallpaw longed to be on the moor. He needed to feel the wind lifting his fur, filling his chest. Fear churned in his belly. He couldn't stay here for days. As his mind spiraled into panic, Sparrow bounded past the den, crossing the tussocks with ease.

Tallpaw sat up. *He hardly has a scratch on him. He must have fled the cave-in at the first drop of soil! Weasel-hearted coward!*

"Sparrow!" Hickorynose called to the rogue from the prey heap. "Do you want some fresh-kill?"

"Yes," Sparrow called. "I'm starving."

Hickorynose tossed a mouse to the rogue's paws and Sparrow crouched to eat it.

Tallpaw's belly rumbled. *Isn't anyone going to offer me any prey?*

I'm still their Clanmate, after all. He sank his claws into his bedding. *They don't care if I eat. As far as they're concerned, I killed Brackenwing. Poor Sparrow's only crime was to follow a foolish warrior down an unsafe tunnel.* He hissed, curling his lip as he watched Sparrow lick his lips. *No one blames him. They're too dumb to see what's under their whiskers.*

"But I blame you," he growled through gritted teeth. "You killed my father!"

CHAPTER 19

Tallpaw was roused by the sound of paws scurrying across the star-lit clearing. He peeked through the gorse opening and saw Hawkheart heading for the nursery. *Is Meadowslip having her kits?* It had been a quarter moon since Sandgorse had died. Her kits were well overdue.

Palebird's face appeared at the nursery entrance, eyes round with worry. "They're coming," she whispered to Hawkheart. The medicine cat shooed her back and slid into the den.

Tallpaw rested his muzzle on the soft wool lining of his nest. Being stuck in camp since the accident had made him feel tired, not rested. He didn't think about running anymore, or the feeling of wind in his fur. Every time he imagined prac-ticing battle moves with Dawnstripe again, or running across the moor, guilt tightened his throat. Sandgorse would be watching from StarClan, his eyes dark with disappointment. *You were born to be a tunneler.* His father's words rang in Tallpaw's head. *You can't change that, whatever any other cat tells you.*

He must have dozed because it was light when the chat-ter of his Clanmates woke him. They were clustering outside the nursery. Lilywhisker and Whiteberry had pushed their way to the front. Larksplash and Appledawn circled Palebird beside the Meeting Hollow. They were showering her with questions.

"Is Meadowslip okay?"

"How many kits are there?"

"What did Hickorynose say when he saw them?"

For once, Palebird's eyes were bright. Tallpaw climbed out of his nest, pricking his ears as she answered the warriors' questions. "Three kits," she announced. "Hickorynose is delighted. He's named the tom Hopkit. One of his paws is a little crooked, but he'll be fine. There's another tom—Pigeonkit. He's dark gray and white, and there's a she-kit, Sorrelkit. She's gray and brown." Palebird sat back, ears twitching with delight. "They are beautiful! Hungry the moment they arrived."

Heatherstar purred. "WindClan will have more warriors."

Plumclaw eyed her sharply. "Let's hope Hickorynose *insists* they become tunnelers."

"Let's hope they grow up healthy and strong," Heatherstar meowed.

Bess nosed in among the Clan cats. Reena's ginger fur flashed beside her. They seemed as excited as the warriors. Sparrow watched from a tussock, staring at the nursery with an unreadable expression while Hareflight and Redclaw paced excitedly beside him.

"This is the first good thing to happen to WindClan in moons," Hareflight enthused.

"The rogues have brought luck to the Clan," Redclaw gushed.

Luck? Tallpaw bristled. He imagined the pleasure he'd get from sinking his claws deep into Sparrow's short, brown fur.

"Tallpaw!" Reena slid from the crowd and hurried over to him. "Isn't it great? Kits in the camp! I can't wait to see them!"

"What do you care?" Tallpaw sniffed. "They're Clan kits, not rogues."

Reena stopped in front of him, eyes flashing. "Of course I care!" she exclaimed. "They're WindClan cats."

"Stop acting like you're one of us," Tallpaw growled. "If you hadn't come, Sandgorse would still be alive."

Reena gasped. "We helped you fight off ShadowClan!"

Tallpaw curled his lip. "Sparrow took my father into a tunnel and left him to die."

Sparrow's head turned. Tallpaw watched the rogue's expression from the corner of his eye. He looked more curious than angry. Tallpaw dug his claws into the ground. Was Sparrow too much of a coward to fight for his honor? "Weasel-heart," he hissed.

Reena's eyes blazed. "Don't you dare blame Sparrow for Sandgorse's death!" she spat. "Your father knew those tunnels were unsafe, but he took Sparrow down there anyway. Sparrow could have been killed too!"

"But he wasn't," Tallpaw mewed coldly. He looked at Sparrow, but the rogue had turned back to Hareflight and Aspenfall. "Now he's got more friends in WindClan than I have."

"You've turned mean, Tallpaw," Reena spat. "*That's* why you've got no friends anymore. Whenever a cat comes near you, you bite their head off."

"So?" Tallpaw hissed. "At least I don't *kill* them."

"See what I mean?" Reena's gaze hardened. "Why don't you talk to me once you've finished feeling sorry for yourself?" She turned and stalked away, her tail twitching angrily.

Paws thrummed the grass as Shrewpaw whisked past. "Hey, Reena!" Together they disappeared among the cats gathered outside the nursery.

Tallpaw headed for the camp entrance. *Let them all chatter like starlings. I don't care.*

"Wait for me." Flailfoot's mew rasped behind him.

"I'm just going for a walk," Tallpaw muttered. "Don't try and stop me."

"I wasn't going to." Flailfoot fell in beside him. "Is this your first time out since the accident?"

"You mean since Sandgorse was killed." Tallpaw pushed through the heather.

Flailfoot followed. "If you want to put it that way."

"Then, yes. It's my first time." Outside camp, the wind snatched at Tallpaw's fur and he shivered, forgetting how cold it could feel. He took the rabbit trail that led to the grassy slopes below the moor-top. The blossom was beginning to fade, but as it dropped from the bushes it gave a far sweeter scent than before. Tallpaw breathed it in, opening his mouth to let it bathe his tongue.

Flailfoot padded alongside him. "You must have missed the moor."

"I guess."

They weaved on in silence, the bushes brushing Tallpaw's pelt, sprinkling his fur with purple blossoms. As they broke from the heather onto the grassy slope, Tallpaw felt the wind tug his ears. He'd also forgotten how it could spark excitement in his paws. Suddenly he wanted to run until his chest hurt. He glanced at Flailfoot.

The old tom's whiskers twitched. "Go on," he urged. "Run. I can tell you're longing to."

Tallpaw plunged forward, his legs stiff at first, but loosening as he hared across the grass. Ears flat, tail streaking behind, he raced as hard as he could. He screwed up his eyes as the wind battered his face, and felt the rush of air as he crested the moor-top and saw meadows and valleys stretch before him. Flailfoot was a speck far behind, his black pelt a smudge on the grass. Tallpaw whirled around in a broad circle and raced down to meet him.

"Feeling better?" Flailfoot asked as Tallpaw slowed to a halt in front of him.

"Yes." The restlessness that had suffocated Tallpaw while he was stuck in the camp had disappeared.

Flailfoot headed upslope. Tallpaw paced beside him, catching his breath. "The sun feels hotter out on the moor."

Flailfoot purred. "There's no better feeling than the sun on your pelt."

Tallpaw stared at the old tunneler. "You *like* it?"

Flailfoot kept walking. "Of course. The sky, the wind, the wide-open moor—they're all in the blood of every WindClan cat. Even tunnelers."

"I thought tunnelers preferred being underground."

"We get used to working in the dark," Flailfoot told him. "And the challenge of building tunnels safely makes it interesting. But it always feels good to come up to the surface." He winked at Tallpaw. "We're not worms, you know."

Tallpaw looked up. Gray clouds were drifting in from the mountains, swallowing the blue sky. "I love being in the open more than anything else," he confessed. "Sandgorse never understood that."

"I think he did," Flailfoot murmured. "In his own way."

"No." Tallpaw stiffened. "I disappointed him so much," he mewed. "By not wanting to be a tunneler."

"Every tunneler dreams of passing on their skills to their kits. Of working side by side with their own kin."

"Mistmouse didn't," Tallpaw reminded him. "She's glad that Doespring, Stagleap, and Ryestalk are moor runners."

Flailfoot stopped and looked directly at Tallpaw. "Sandgorse wanted you to be happy, you know."

"He had a strange way of showing it." Tallpaw remembered the furious glare his father had given him after Heatherstar had announced that the gorge tunnel was to be shut down.

"He didn't know he was going to die," Flailfoot rasped. "If there'd been more time, he would have come to accept that your dream was not his. There would have been time to forgive and forget."

Tallpaw's throat tightened. He pictured Sandgorse puffing out his chest as Heatherstar gave Tallpaw his warrior name. He stopped walking, his paws suddenly as heavy as stones.

"Sandgorse loved you, Tallpaw." Flailfoot began to head downhill, back toward the camp. "Whatever your differences. Never forget that."

Tallpaw stayed where he was. Up here, there was nothing between him and StarClan but the sky. *Is Flailfoot right, Sandgorse?* He stared up at the clouds but there was no reply. Tallpaw shook himself and sprinted down the slope, quickly catching up with Flailfoot. "What was my father like?" he asked breathlessly. "When he was in the tunnels?"

"Sandgorse was a great planner," Flailfoot told him. "He could pick out a route overground, then dig it exactly the same underground, paw step for paw step. He knew the tunnels under this moor better than any other tunneler." Flailfoot's eyes glowed. "But he hated worms."

"Worms?"

"Yes." The old tunneler purred. "Every time we hit worm soil, he'd send his tunnelmate in first. He always said he'd rather be plastered whisker to tail in clay than get a worm under his claw."

Tallpaw purred, amused that his father could be so squeamish, but sad that he was only just hearing about it. *Why didn't I know this before?*

They were nearing the hollow and Tallpaw could see the walls of camp silhouetted in the early-morning light. He glanced at Flailfoot. The old tunneler's eyes were half-closed. He was enjoying the last moments of sun on his pelt before they headed into the shadows. Did tunnelers *really* love the open moor as much as their Clanmates? Tallpaw had never imagined that they enjoyed being aboveground. He'd thought that they tunneled because they loved the dark and the closeness of earth around them.

"Tallpaw!" Dawnstripe called to him as he nosed his way into camp. "Good news!" She raced across the tussocks to meet him. "Hawkheart says you're fit enough to start training again!"

Tallpaw halted. "Really?"

Flailfoot flicked his tail along Tallpaw's flank. "Congratulations!"

Plumclaw and Woollytail looked up from the bracken patch. "There you are, Flailfoot!" Plumclaw called. "We wondered where you'd gone."

"Tallpaw?" Dawnstripe leaned closer. "Did you hear what I said?" Tallpaw nodded. "Aren't you happy?" Dawnstripe's eyes flashed with worry.

Tallpaw lifted his muzzle. "I want to train as a tunneler."

Woollytail jumped to his paws. "What did you just say?" He bounded across the clearing toward Tallpaw.

Plumclaw trotted after her denmate. "That's wonderful news!"

Dawnstripe blinked. "But you're going to be a moor runner."

"I've changed my mind." Tallpaw spoke slowly, more certain that he was making the right decision with every word. "I want to continue what my father was doing. I want to learn his skills and pass them on to my kits when the time comes."

"But you're a great moor runner," Dawnstripe argued. "And

you've learned so much already."

"I know," Tallpaw mewed. "But everything has changed; don't you see?"

Dawnstripe shifted her paws. "I suppose I'd better speak with Heatherstar."

"Thank you." Tallpaw touched his muzzle to her cheek. "I'll miss training with you; I really will, but this is something that I have to do." His grief was floating away like mist. "I must honor Sandgorse's memory and protect the skills he valued."

Dawnstripe backed away. "If you're sure."

"I'm sure."

She turned and headed for Heatherstar's den.

Woollytail stopped beside him. "Do you really mean this?"

Tallpaw nodded. "Completely."

"Don't do this for your father's sake." Woollytail lowered his voice. "Sandgorse would never want that. He was tough on you, I know. But tunnelers *have* to be tough. It doesn't mean he didn't understand. He was proud to see you fight for what you truly wanted, even if that wasn't what he'd hoped for. He'd have been proud to see you as a moor runner, you know."

"Don't talk him out of it!" Plumclaw shouldered her denmate aside. "Sandgorse would have been so happy! We need more paws."

Tallpaw met her eager gaze. "Tunneling is in my blood, Plumclaw. I just never realized it before."

CHAPTER 20

❧

"Is it true?" Barkpaw lifted his head from the spring that bubbled just outside the camp wall. "You're becoming a tunneler?"

Tallpaw padded down the slope and stopped beside him. "Dawnstripe's asking Heatherstar right now." He crouched at the water's edge. Finding Barkpaw here had surprised him. Tallpaw had grown used to the medicine apprentice avoiding him whenever he could. They'd hardly spoken in the quarter moon since Sandgorse's death. Tallpaw wasn't sure if it was because they were both lost in grief, or because Barkpaw blamed him for Brackenwing's death. He didn't dare ask.

Barkpaw hauled a dripping wad of moss from the spring. "You don't have to do this, you know."

"I want to." Tallpaw dipped his head and began lapping at the cool, fresh water.

Barkpaw sat down, letting the moss drain beside him. "Why?"

Tallpaw flicked his tail. "I don't expect you to understand."

"You were doing so well with your training." Barkpaw tipped his head on one side. "And you loved being a moor runner."

"I'll love tunneling, too." Tallpaw sat up, water dripping from his chin.

"Even Shrewpaw was impressed by your hunting skill." Barkpaw didn't seem to be listening to anything Tallpaw said. "Though he'd never admit it."

"This is something I have to do." Tallpaw licked his lips. "For my father's sake."

"But you're not Sandgorse!" Barkpaw leaned forward. "You don't have to live his life for him just because he's dead."

"That's not what I'm doing," Tallpaw growled under his breath.

Barkpaw's gaze burned into Tallpaw's. "You think you'll feel better if you follow his wishes, don't you?"

Tallpaw looked away first. "The Clan needs tunnelers more than ever. It's my duty to follow in Sandgorse's paw steps."

"It's your duty to be the best warrior you can, for your Clan," Barkpaw argued. "And you could have been the best moor runner ever."

"I can be the best tunneler ever." Tallpaw turned and bounded up the bank.

"This won't bring Sandgorse back, you know!" Barkpaw called after him.

"I know that! This is about *me*, not him!" Tallpaw marched back to camp, pelt twitching. *Why can't Barkpaw try to understand?*

"Hey, Wormpaw!" Shrewpaw was waiting inside the camp entrance. "I hear you're going to train where you belong, at last."

Tallpaw shrugged. "Relieved that you don't have competition anymore, *weasel*paw?"

Reena trotted across the clearing. "Arguing again, Tallpaw?"

"He started it!" Tallpaw bristled.

Shrewpaw glanced at Reena. "Tallpaw would argue with his reflection in the spring," he sniffed. "I can't wait to train without him snarling at me."

Tallpaw unsheathed his claws.

"Let all cats old enough to catch prey gather beneath Tall-rock." Heatherstar's call made Tallpaw spin around. Was she going to announce his new mentor? Excitement rippled through his pelt. Would she choose Woollytail? Sandgorse would be pleased to see his old friend training Tallpaw. Tall-paw raced for the Meeting Hollow, leaping down onto the sandy earth as his Clanmates streamed across the clearing to join him. Tallpaw watched Dawnstripe sheathe and unsheathe her claws as she sat opposite him, her eyes round with worry.

Don't be upset. Tallpaw felt a prick of guilt. *Please understand that I have to do this.*

Heatherstar stepped to the edge of the rock. "Meadow-slip's kits have brought new life to WindClan. Let us pray that Hopkit, Sorrelkit, and Pigeonkit grow into strong, healthy warriors."

Murmurs of approval rippled though the Clan. Tallpaw lifted his chin. *Me next.* The WindClan leader caught his eye, her shoulders stiffening. Tallpaw paused. *Is she angry about my change of heart?*

"WindClan," Heatherstar began, "you have known for some time that I have had doubts about our tunneling."

"What is she talking about?" Plumclaw hissed.

"Hush." Hickorynose stared up at their leader.

"Tallpaw has asked to train as a tunneler," Heatherstar went on. "I can only admire his loyalty to the memory of his father. Sandgorse's death shook us all. We will grieve him for many moons to come." She glanced sympathetically at Palebird. "Tallpaw's wish to learn the skills that led to his father's death shows true courage."

Tallpaw padded forward expectantly.

"However." The sharpening of Heatherstar's mew made him stop. "I have thought long and hard," the WindClan leader went on. "And I've decided that there will be no more tunneling for WindClan."

Tallpaw blinked. *What?*

"This is not a decision I take lightly, but I hope that many of you will support me."

Reedfeather, at the base of the rock, nodded solemnly. Aspenfall and Cloudrunner exchanged approving looks.

"We do not need the tunnels," Heatherstar explained. "Prey has run aboveground for many leaf-bares. We have improved our hunting skills, learned to work in teams. Even in the harshest weather, we have been able to catch prey aboveground."

Plumclaw's tail whipped over the sandy earth.

Heatherstar pressed on. "WindClan's tunneling skills have served us well for countless moons, but a new dawn is coming. Our moor-running skills are more important. We have enemies to fight aboveground. And we *must* fight them. We can't hide in our tunnels and hope they will go away. We must train hard and become warriors to equal any Clan." She lifted her muzzle. "It will take time and effort, but we will become stronger than WindClan has ever been. In moons to come, the other Clans will fear us."

"They fear us already!" Plumclaw yowled.

"You saw Stonetooth when ShadowClan attacked." Heatherstar's gaze fixed on the dark gray tunneler. "He spoke as though we were vermin to be cleared from the moor."

"They think of us as rabbits!" Redclaw growled.

Aspenfall clawed the earth. "We must prove that we are warriors!"

"What about our tunneling skills?" Woollytail growled.

"They won't be forgotten," Heatherstar promised. "Our tunnelers won't have to retrain as moor runners. Their duty now will be to block all the tunnels, making them safe for future generations of WindClan cats."

"*Block* them?" Plumclaw stared at her in amazement. "What about all our hard work digging them?"

"I don't want to lose another cat in those tunnels," Heatherstar insisted. "And no more cats will train as tunnelers. Ever."

Rage surged through Tallpaw. How could she deny him his entire future? "Then Sandgorse died for nothing?" he hissed.

Hickorynose padded forward and smoothed Tallpaw's bristling pelt with his tail. "Not for nothing, Tallpaw," he meowed gently. "His death will be the last death in the tunnels."

Tallpaw stared at him. "You sound like you *want* to stop tunneling!"

Hickorynose glanced at the nursery. "I don't want my kits to die like Sandgorse." He dropped his gaze. "Or Leafshine," he added, remembering the tunneler who'd died in the same accident that had crippled Lilywhisker. "But I'll tell them of my days in the tunnels and make sure that WindClan will always remember what we achieved."

Mistmouse nodded. "Stagleap, Doespring, and Ryestalk are happy as moor runners. Our young deserve to run with the wind in their tails."

"Our days of hiding are over," Cloudrunner declared.

"Hiding?" Disbelief flooded Woollytail's gaze.

"Cloudrunner only meant that it's time we faced the world with our heads held high." Larksplash paced around him. "Once every cat in WindClan has battle skills, we'll be the strongest Clan of all." She glanced up at the sky. The thick bank of cloud had reached the sun. Rays spilled over the edge for a moment before the cloud swallowed them. "We live closest to StarClan. We will make our ancestors proud!"

"WindClan!" Shrewpaw began to cheer.

"WindClan!" Aspenfall joined in.

"WindClan!"

"WindClan!"

Tallpaw stared in shock as his Clanmates cheered for the end of the tunnels. Woollytail backed away from them. From the rim of the hollow, the rogues watched, their pelts pricking in surprise. Sparrow's eyes were thin, yellow slits. Tallpaw showed his teeth. *You started this when you killed Sandgorse. You've spoiled everything.*

"Tallpaw." Palebird's mew startled him. He jerked around and met her gaze, a muzzle-length from his. "I'm glad you can't become a tunneler."

"But it's what Sandgorse would have wanted!"

"He wouldn't have wanted you to die as he did." Palebird reached forward and touched her nose to his cheek. "And I couldn't bear to lose another cat I love."

Tallpaw stared at his mother in confusion. He couldn't remember the last time Palebird had told him that she loved him. He should have been ecstatic. But Heatherstar had snatched away his dream. And all around him his Clan were cheering. Had *everyone* gone mad? He scrambled out of the Meeting Hollow and raced out of the camp, crashing through the heather. *No one can stop me from being what I was born to be!* He pelted upslope to the warren where Woollytail had helped them catch a rabbit. Sheep were grazing the moor beyond. *They haven't blocked the tunnels yet!* The rising wind ripped at Tallpaw's fur. Rain began to spray his muzzle. It hardened as he climbed, lashing his pelt by the time he reached the warren. *I'll teach myself to tunnel, like Shattered Ice!*

Tallpaw stopped at the first rabbit hole he reached and stared into the darkness. A worm of fear stirred in his belly, and his breath quickened as he remembered the suffocating closeness of the walls and the roar of the river chasing him. Every hair on his pelt bristled. *Don't go down there!* He pushed back the thought. *I will be a tunneler! I'll make Sandgorse proud of me!* He dove into the tunnel, scrabbling to push himself through the narrow gap.

"Oh no, you don't!"

Teeth clamped around his tail and hauled him backward. Dawnstripe dragged him from the rabbit hole, her eyes blazing. "Those tunnels are out of bounds!" she spat. "Didn't you hear Heatherstar?"

"I don't care!" Rain battered his ears.

"You're going to be a moor runner!" Dawnstripe yowled over the rising wind. "And I'm going to be your mentor until you get your warrior name."

Tallpaw glimpsed two pelts streaking toward them. "Is he okay?" Hareflight called through the rain. Shrewpaw raced past his mentor and skidded to a stop on the grass in front of Tallpaw.

"Poor Tallpaw," he snorted. "Won't Heatherstar let you become a wormpaw?" He nodded toward the entrance. "Why not go down there anyway? You know you were born to live underground."

"Shrewpaw!" Dawnstripe glared at the apprentice. "Show some respect to your Clanmate."

Hareflight joined them. "Stop teasing him, Shrewpaw!"

"This has gone beyond teasing!" Dawnstripe snapped. "If Shrewpaw were my apprentice, I'd claw his ears."

Shrewpaw flung a scorching look at Dawnstripe. "Why are you siding with a tunneler?"

Hareflight paced around Tallpaw. "You shouldn't have run out in the middle of a Clan meeting," he fretted. "You worried everyone."

Tallpaw flattened his ears. "No one's worried about me. I killed Brackenwing." He thrust his nose toward Shrewpaw. "Remember?"

A growl rumbled in Shrewpaw's throat.

"The visitors will think we can't control our apprentices," Hareflight went on.

Tallpaw turned on him. "Who cares what that bunch of rogues thinks?" he hissed. "If they had any sense of honor, they'd have left after they killed Sandgorse."

Dawnstripe lashed her tail. "No one killed Sandgorse!"

"You're hare-brained!" Shrewpaw snarled. "You're an embarrassment to WindClan with your dumb accusations! Nobody likes you. You *should* be underground! We won't miss you."

Blood roared in Tallpaw's ears. He lunged for Shrewpaw. Sinking his claws deep into his shoulders, he rolled the apprentice onto the soaking grass. Shrewpaw yowled, scrabbling at Tallpaw's belly with his hind claws. Tallpaw raked his denmate's muzzle, sending blood spraying across the grass before jaws closed around his neck fur and hauled him off. As Dawnstripe dropped him, Tallpaw shook out his pelt. Hareflight was holding Shrewpaw back by the scruff.

"Tallpaw!" Dawnstripe's eyes were round with shock. "You can't attack your Clanmate! No matter how he provokes you!" She pointed her muzzle toward the sheep. "Go and use up the rest of your anger collecting wool for the elders."

Tallpaw stomped away, his pelt spiking as rain lashed it. His belly churned. Shrewpaw's words rang in his ears.

Nobody likes you. We won't miss you.

CHAPTER 21

Tallpaw shivered. The wind, which was whipping the moor, carried
the chill of coming leaf-fall. While the Clan moved restlessly
around him, he stared across the valley toward Highstones.
Below him, the trees in the fields had turned as mottled as a
tortoiseshell's pelt, with flashes of orange and gold among the
fading green leaves.

"Are you coming to say good-bye?" Dawnstripe called to
him above the noise of the wind.

Tallpaw looked past her to the rogues lined along the ridge.
They were leaving at last. In the two moons since Sandgorse's
death, Tallpaw had hardly been able to bear looking at them.
Watching his Clanmates treat them as though nothing had
happened—as though Sandgorse were still alive—soured
every mouthful of prey. How could his Clan be so unfeeling?

"Come on," Dawnstripe urged. "Heatherstar expects
WindClan apprentices to show courtesy to our guests."

Tallpaw's tail twitched. "All right, I'm coming." He followed Dawnstripe across the grass, passing Appledawn and
Hickorynose. They had already said their farewells. Meadowslip had stayed in camp with her kits.

The elders were touching noses with the rogues. Lilywhisker leaned forward and pressed her muzzle to Bess's. "Take care," she rasped. "I hope leaf-bare treats you well."

"Good-bye, Sparrow." Flamepelt dipped his head. "Good hunting."

Mole lifted his tail. "Thanks for sharing your den."

Lilywhisker's eyes misted. "We'll miss your stories."

Shrewpaw slid past Tallpaw and stopped in front of Reena. "You were a great denmate."

Reena's eyes glowed. "So you didn't mind sharing with a rogue after all?"

Shrewpaw dropped his gaze. "Sorry if I was a bit unfriendly at the start."

Reena winked. "You're forgiven."

Fur ruffling self-consciously, Shrewpaw hurried back to Hareflight's side.

Heatherstar padded forward with Reedfeather beside her. "WindClan wishes you well." She looked expectantly at Tallpaw. He was the only cat who hadn't exchanged words with the rogues.

"I hope you find somewhere to stay," Tallpaw meowed stiffly. *And that you never come back.*

Heatherstar seemed satisfied. She turned to Sparrow. "The WindClan that you've known for countless moons is on the edge of great change." She glanced at Hickorynose and Woollytail standing side by side with Mistmouse and Plumclaw. "If you come again, you'll find a Clan no longer divided into moor runners and tunnelers, but united as warriors, as strong as any Clan."

Tallpaw pricked his ears. *If you come again?* Heatherstar had said *if.* Perhaps there wasn't room for visiting rogues anymore. Tallpaw waited for Sparrow's answer. Was he going to mention Sandgorse? Surely the rogue would acknowledge the cat who'd died so that he could look at WindClan's tunnels?

Sparrow dipped his head. "I wish you all well."

Was that it? Tallpaw stared at him in disbelief. It was as though Sandgorse had never existed at all.

Algernon stepped forward, purring. "Thanks for your kindness."

Bess whisked her tail. "Let's hope cold-season is kind to us all." She turned and began to head downslope. Sparrow followed, Mole and Algernon at his heels. Reena bounded after her mother and fell in beside her.

Lilywhisker sighed. "Sparrow was a great hunter." She eyed Tallpaw and Shrewpaw pointedly. "He *always* made sure the elders and queens had something to eat."

"We won't let you go hungry," Tallpaw growled. He watched the rogues move over the grass below. Who knew where they were heading? They were already fading to specks as they neared the Thunderpath.

The wind pulled at Tallpaw as though it wanted to whisk him after them. He dug his claws into the grass. *This is my home.* He focused on the rogues again. Sparrow's fur was a dark smudge against the grass. Rage surged in Tallpaw's belly. *How can you just leave?* Sparrow would carry on with his life, unremorseful and unpunished while Tallpaw was left alone.

Tallpaw fought to stop his pelt from bristling. *Because of you, Heatherstar closed the tunnels. I can never follow in my father's paw steps or live the life he wanted me to live. You killed him; then you destroyed his dream and mine.*

"Tallpaw?" Doespring's gentle mew jerked him back.

"What?" He shook out his pelt, suddenly realizing the grass at his feet was shredded. He sheathed his claws quickly.

"We're leaving." Doespring tipped her head toward their Clanmates. They were moving steadily across the moor like birds crossing the sky. Heatherstar headed the flock, Reedfeather at her side. Woollytail kept close to Palebird, their pelts brushing from time to time as they padded over the grass. Tallpaw narrowed his eyes. His father's old tunnel-mate never seemed to leave Palebird alone now. He'd have to make sure that his mother didn't mind.

"Come on!" Doespring bounded away.

Tallpaw plunged after her, his paws thrumming the earth. He slowed as he neared his Clanmates, not quite catching up while Doespring weaved among them and fell in beside Stagleap and Ryestalk.

He'd be a warrior soon, then a senior warrior like Hareflight. One day he'd be an elder, limping like Whiteberry and sharing stories from moons ago with his denmates. Above the vast sky stretched toward distant horizon. The Clan looked small and fragile beneath it. Was this it? His life laid out before him like an old story, told again and again through countless moons?

Tallpaw's chest tightened. Suddenly he felt trapped, as

though he were in the tunnels once again.

"Tallpaw!" Dawnstripe called from ahead. "Let's hunt!" She veered away from her Clanmates, doubling back upslope. "I'll race you to Outlook Rock!"

Tallpaw hared after her, running faster than the wind, desperate to escape the anxiety that beat inside him on frantic wings.

Tallpaw plunged through the gap in the heather and skidded to a halt in the clearing. Flanks heaving, he glanced over his shoulder as Shrewpaw burst through after him. Tallpaw flicked his tail. *I beat you.*

"I stumbled on a rabbit hole," Shrewpaw panted.

"Shame." Tallpaw headed for the prey heap. He'd been training all day and his belly was growling.

Lilywhisker and Flailfoot lay outside the elders' den, basking in the dying sun. With leaf-fall coming, its warmth was fading. Lilywhisker sighed wistfully. "I wonder where Bess and Algernon are now?"

"The den's too quiet without Mole's snoring," Flailfoot commented.

"I hope they've found a warm place to shelter," Lilywhisker fretted.

The rogues had been gone for days, but the Clan kept chattering like birds, worrying where they were and how they'd find enough prey now that the weather was turning.

"I miss Reena," Shrewpaw declared, stopping beside Lilywhisker.

Lilywhisker looked up at the apprentice. "She'd make a good warrior with the right training."

Shrewpaw gazed at the moor that loomed up beyond the heather walls. "But she'd never give up traveling."

Frowning, Tallpaw hopped over the tussocks. Reena would never give up eating other cats' prey, or sleeping in nests that other paws had woven. *That* would be too much like hard work. He dragged a rabbit from the prey heap and carried it to a soft tussock beside the bracken patch. He liked to eat here. Sandgorse's nest still carried his scent—stale now, but familiar.

As he took a mouthful, he saw Dawnstripe and Hareflight pad into camp. They nodded to each other as they parted at the entrance.

"Tallpaw." Dawnstripe headed toward him. "Your battle moves were lazy today. What's up?"

Tallpaw stared at her, his mouth full. "Nothing."

"Really?" Dawnstripe narrowed her eyes. "You seemed to be thinking about something else. You have been for days. With your assessment coming up, you really should be concentrating on your warrior skills."

Tallpaw swallowed. "I'll try harder," he promised. What did it matter? His Clan would go on with or without him, just as it had done with Sandgorse.

A thought flashed in his mind. *We're just visitors, like the rogues. We arrive, we eat, we sleep, and then we move on to StarClan.* The only difference was that Clan cats stayed in one place their whole life. *I'll only ever see heather and grass and sky.* Tallpaw felt Wind-Clan's borders pressing closer.

"Well?"

Tallpaw suddenly realized that Dawnstripe was staring expectantly at him. He'd been so lost in thought that he'd missed something. "What?"

"The Moonstone," she meowed, exasperated. "Aren't you excited?"

Tallpaw pricked his ears. "Are we going?"

"I just told you!" Dawnstripe's tail twitched. "We're going tonight. Finish your meal quickly and go to Hawkheart to get traveling herbs."

Tallpaw nodded, feeling hope spark deep inside him. He was going to see something new after all!

In the medicine den, his belly full, he peered around the scooped-out cave. The screen of gorse on the open side made it very dark, and the jumbled scent of herbs made Tallpaw's nose wrinkle. How could Barkpaw smell *anything* after living in here?

"They're beside the grinding stone."

Hawkheart's mew made him jump. He hadn't spotted the medicine cat standing in the shadows. Hawkheart padded across the sandy floor, tipping his nose toward leaves heaped beside a smooth, wide stone at the side of the gorse cave. There were two piles.

"Do I eat them both?" Tallpaw asked.

"You can if you want," Hawkheart grunted. "But I wouldn't if I were you. They taste foul and Shrewpaw might be annoyed that you'd eaten his."

Tallpaw's heart sank as Shrewpaw slid into the den, his

dark brown pelt hardly visible in the gloom. He spotted Tall-paw and rolled his eyes. "Oh no, you're not coming to the Moonstone, are you?"

Tallpaw stepped closer, fluffing out his fur. "So what if I am?" he growled.

Hawkheart pushed between them. "One day you're going to need to start behaving like Clanmates," he snorted.

Tallpaw scowled. It wasn't his fault that Shrewpaw was so mean.

Hawkheart pawed a pile of herbs toward him, and pushed the other heap under Shrewpaw's nose. "Eat," he muttered, and padded from the den.

Shrewpaw screwed up his eyes as he sniffed the leaves. "They smell foul."

Tallpaw dabbed his tongue into the herbs. The bitter fla-vor made him wince, but he wasn't going to let Shrewpaw see him make a fuss. He lapped them up and swallowed them quickly, trying not to let his disgust show. "Easy," he mewed, and headed out of the den.

Barkpaw met him outside. "Did you swallow them?" His eyes were round.

Tallpaw wrinkled his nose and nodded.

"Once the taste has gone you'll be thankful for them," Barkpaw promised. "It's a long journey and they'll give you energy."

Dawnstripe and Hareflight were pacing by the entrance.

"I'd better go," Tallpaw mewed.

"Try to remember everything," Barkpaw warned. "It will

feel like a dream, but I promise, it's all real."

"I'll try." Tallpaw bounded over the tussocks and stopped beside Dawnstripe. "How long will it take to travel there?"

Dawnstripe glanced at the sun dipping toward the horizon. "We have to reach Mothermouth by moonhigh." She glanced toward the medicine den, nodding as she saw Shrewpaw heading out. "Ready?"

Tallpaw nodded. As the bitterness of the herbs faded, he felt excitement spark in his belly. He was leaving Clan territory. He was going to share tongues with StarClan!

Outside the camp, Dawnstripe stopped. "The most dangerous part of the journey will be the Thunderpath," she warned. "Do as you're told." She caught Shrewpaw's eye as he emerged from the entrance tunnel. "And no bickering. I expect you to behave like warriors tonight." Without waiting for an answer, she pushed through the heather and led the way upslope.

On the high-moor, a cold wind sliced through Tallpaw's pelt. He shivered as he watched the sun slide down the sky far enough to touch Highstones, setting their peaks ablaze.

"Come on." Hareflight pointed with his tail to the moon, already showing in the pale evening sky. With full moon only a few sunrises away, it was almost round and dazzlingly clear. Once the sun had set it would be brilliant in the night-dark sky. "We have to hurry." The brown warrior charged over the crest of the moor and bounded down the steep slope toward the Thunderpath.

Tallpaw chased after him, his paws skimming the grass. As

he broke through the scent line at the bottom of the slope, a thrill surged beneath his pelt. He was outside Clan territory! He scrambled to a halt before he crashed into the others. Dawnstripe had stopped while Hareflight and Shrewpaw padded warily toward the trail of black stone cutting across their path.

A monster hurtled past, then another, both bellowing loud enough to rattle Tallpaw's ear fur. Two more crossed behind them, traveling the other way. Suddenly the eyes of one lit up, throwing beams along its path.

"They'd be no use at night hunting," Tallpaw growled as another monster sent yellow rays shooting from its eyes. "Prey would see them coming a whole territory away." Creeping after Hareflight, he narrowed his eyes against the blinding lights. The acrid scent of the Thunderpath burned his throat and his ears ached from the monsters' roars.

Dawnstripe caught up to him. "We have to wait for a gap." She nodded toward a narrow, grass-filled ditch running alongside the Thunderpath. Hareflight and Shrewpaw were already scrambling into it. Dawnstripe followed. Tallpaw jumped down beside her, flinching as a monster sent grit showering over his pelt. He pressed his belly to the ground and shuddered as filthy water soaked his fur and monster stench rolled over him.

Eyes stinging, he stared at Dawnstripe. "Now what?"

"I'll tell you when to run," she promised.

Shrewpaw stretched up the far side of the ditch and peered over the edge. "Can I go yet?" He glanced back at Hareflight.

"Not till I say." Hareflight reared up beside him to look out.

"But there's a gap before the next monster!" Shrewpaw insisted. "I can make it."

"Look both ways—"

Before Hareflight could finish his warning, Shrewpaw leaped up onto the Thunderpath and began to race across.

"Not yet!" With a yowl of horror, Hareflight pelted after him.

Tallpaw's pelt bristled. On the far side of the path, a monster was hurtling toward the young tom. Shrewpaw stopped and stared as its eye beams lit him up like a blaze of fire. Eyes stretching in terror, he gaped at the monster. Brown fur blurred as Hareflight hurled himself at Shrewpaw. They tumbled away together as the monster raced past, wailing.

"Did they make it?" Tallpaw whispered.

Dawnstripe was peering over the edge of the path. Her whole body was stiff, her pelt spiked up along her spine.

"Did they make it?" Tallpaw demanded. He scrambled up to look for himself.

Ears showed in the grass on the far side of the Thunderpath. Two pairs of eyes flashed. Hareflight and Shrewpaw were staring back at them across the stone.

"They made it," Dawnstripe breathed, slumping down with relief.

Tallpaw's heart pounded. "It's our turn." He swallowed hard.

"Don't go till I say," warned Dawnstripe.

Tallpaw didn't intend to. Standing on Outlook Rock, he'd seen birds peeling fresh-kill from the Thunderpath. He wasn't going to be crow-food before he'd seen the world beyond Clan territory.

Dawnstripe's head twitched as she watched the monsters flash past. Then she grew still, her gaze fixed farther down the path. She checked the other way. "Ready?" she hissed.

Tallpaw tensed. "Ready."

A monster sped past one way, then the other.

"Now!" Dawnstripe leaped from the ditch. Tallpaw scrambled after her. "Just run!" Dawnstripe yowled, pelting across the hard, black path.

Tallpaw's pads stung as he pushed against the stone. It was sharp with grit and grazed his paws, but he kept running, his gaze fixed on the verge ahead. He dived onto the grass, blood roaring in his ears, and skidded to a halt. "Dawnstripe?"

He glanced back, relieved to see her panting, a muzzle-length behind. Hareflight padded up to meet her. "I'll never get used to it," he growled.

"It'll be quieter on the way back," Dawnstripe panted. "The monsters sleep at night."

Tallpaw tasted the air. The strange scents reminded him of Bess and Reena and how they'd smelled when they first arrived—like stale food and smoke. But he could also smell prey. He ducked beneath a long row of bushes and pricked his ears, listening for the scurrying of tiny claws.

"Tallpaw!" Dawnstripe poked her head in beside him. "Not this way."

Disappointed, he trotted after her as she led the way along the line of bushes, turning as the path led them upslope. They trekked through meadows of long, wet grass that soaked Tallpaw's belly fur and chilled his paws until they were numb. The land sloped up, then down, until Tallpaw's legs ached with walking.

The stars were shining in a peat-black sky by the time the lush fields gave way to stubby grass. The land steepened and the grass turned to stones beneath their paws. Hareflight shook out his fur. Dawnstripe paused and gazed across the rocky soil. Tatty heather dotted the slope, clinging to the stony ground with spindly roots.

Tallpaw looked up. Highstones rose above them, so tall they blocked the mountains behind. Moonlight washed the rocks like water. He could hear Shrewpaw panting and glanced over his shoulder. The young tom's eyes were clouded with exhaustion, his shoulders drooping. For a moment, Tallpaw felt a flash of sympathy for his denmate. "We're nearly there," he mewed.

Dawnstripe lifted her golden muzzle and stared up the slope. Higher up the slope, a hole yawned, square and black. "Mothermouth," Dawnstripe whispered.

Tallpaw scrambled toward the hole, forgetting his tiredness as excitement pulsed in his paws. Stones cracked behind him as Hareflight, Dawnstripe, and Shrewpaw followed. Tallpaw looked over his shoulder at the valley that stretched back toward the moor. They'd come so far! WindClan territory seemed suddenly small, dwarfed by the wide, star-specked sky.

Are you there, Sandgorse? Tallpaw tipped back his head and stared into the sky, searching Silverpelt for a star that outshone the rest. *Can you see me?*

"Come on, Tallpaw." Dawnstripe's hushed mew sounded above him. She'd climbed past him onto a smooth ledge, her moonlit fur bright against the gaping hole behind. She was sitting on the threshold of Mothermouth. Hareflight and Shrewpaw sprang up beside her. Nose twitching, Tallpaw scrambled up the last tail-length.

The ledge was smooth and icy cold beneath his paws. Wet stone scent rolled from the freezing darkness. *So this is Mothermouth!* Tallpaw padded from moonlight into shadow, his heart pounding as the greatest tunnel of all swallowed him whole.

CHAPTER 22

❧

"Let me lead." Dawnstripe's mew was barely a whisper as she padded past him through the darkness.

Tallpaw was happy to fall in behind her, staying close enough to feel her tail-tip brush his cheek. He could feel Shrewpaw's breath warm on his rump, and Hareflight's solid paw steps sounded reassuringly from the rear. Tallpaw's heart fluttered like a caught sparrow. This tunnel was far bigger than the tunnel he'd walked with Sandgorse, but it was still a tunnel, still a long way from light and space and air. Tallpaw felt the immense darkness pressing around him. His throat tightened until the air seemed too thick to breathe.

You're following in the paw steps of countless cats. StarClan will keep you safe.

Dawnstripe's tail slid ahead; Tallpaw sped up, frightened of losing the feel of its soft tip on his nose. Cold air swirled around him, piercing his pelt. He sensed the huge weight of rock hanging above his head. Ahead, the distant echo of dripping water hinted at deepness he was frightened to imagine. How long till they reached the Moonstone? Steadying his breath, he focused on his paws, trying to relish the solidity of the stone beneath them, constantly stretching his muzzle to keep contact with Dawnstripe's tail.

"I smell fear-scent. Aren't you feeling at home, Wormpaw?" Shrewpaw snarked.

"Be quiet, Shrewpaw!" Hareflight's angry hiss sounded from behind.

Tallpaw's mind swirled. He fought back panic. Every paw step was taking him farther from the light. Could he find his way out if the others weren't here? A stream of cold air suddenly buffeted his flank. Another billowed from the other side. There must be more tunnels branching off this one, snaking deep into the earth.

Please let me out! As a terrified groan welled in his throat, the air around him changed. It became still, the vicious chill easing. Tallpaw halted as Dawnstripe's paw steps fell silent.

"We're here," she announced softly. "In the cavern of the Moonstone."

Shrewpaw pushed past Tallpaw, rocking him on his paws. "Where is it? Where's the stone?"

"There must be a cloud covering the moon." Hareflight's deep mew sounded close to Tallpaw's ear. "Just wait."

Tallpaw strained to see through the darkness. His nose twitched as he smelled the familiar scent of heather. Fresh air must be flowing into the cavern from somewhere above them. Suddenly a beam of silver light sliced down through the dark. Tallpaw blinked as it cast a glow over a huge stone in the middle of the cavern. *The Moonstone!*

The surface of the rock glittered like sunshine on water,

sending light rippling across the dark walls. Tallpaw backed away, bristling.

"Don't be afraid." Dawnstripe stepped forward and crouched beside the stone, the silver light drenching her pale golden fur. "Come and touch your nose to it. You too, Shrewpaw."

Shrewpaw was circling the stone, his tail spiking. "Do we have to touch it?"

Hareflight stooped beside Dawnstripe. "You won't share with StarClan until you do."

Shrewpaw padded warily toward the Moonstone and, hunkering down, stretched his muzzle forward. Tallpaw watched his denmate's eyes close. Shrewpaw's ruffled fur smoothed out, and his whole body softened as if he had drifted into the best sleep ever.

"Come on, Tallpaw." Dawnstripe coaxed him forward. "StarClan will welcome you."

Tallpaw padded closer. His heart seemed to swell in his chest. *Will I see Sandgorse? Or Brackenwing?* Hunching beside the rock, he narrowed his eyes against its glare. He took a deep breath and touched his nose to the sharp stone.

At once he was plunged into darkness, sucked down by currents too strong to resist. But somehow there was nothing to be frightened of, and Tallpaw let himself fall until his vision cleared. He felt his paws sink into muddy earth; rain lashed his pelt and battered his ears. Tallpaw peered through the storm. Was this StarClan? A churned field stretched away on one side, while a hedge pressed at his other, rattling as a cold wind shook it.

Tallpaw saw several solid-looking shapes ahead, ears and tails silhouetted in the rain. *The rogues!* He recognized their dripping pelts as they trudged beside the hedge, trying to find some shelter from the storm. One by one, they clambered over the snaking roots of a lightning-blasted tree. Tallpaw crept after them, ducking under the low branches as though he was stalking prey. He halted beside the charred tree and watched them disappear along the trail.

This isn't StarClan! This is just a dumb dream! Frustration flared inside him. *Where's Sandgorse?* Curling his claws into the wet earth, he screwed his eyes shut and tried to sleep once more.

Darkness engulfed him and he was swirling through emptiness again. More shapes flashed on the edge of his vision: a Twolegplace, a dense forest, a chattering river sparkling in sunlight. Tallpaw blinked open his eyes, desperate to find himself in StarClan's territory.

The Moonstone gleamed at the end of his nose. He was back in the cavern. Where was StarClan? Fear wormed in Tallpaw's belly. They hadn't shared anything with him! He backed away from the Moonstone, noticing that Shrewpaw was still resting peacefully by the stone.

Were the ancestors ignoring him because of Brackenwing? Or was StarClan angry because he hadn't been able to follow in his father's paw steps? Tallpaw's heart twisted. *I tried!*

Dawnstripe blinked open her eyes and stretched. She met Tallpaw's gaze. "Did you dream?"

Before he could answer, Shrewpaw jumped up. "Wow! I

saw the star and some old cat called Dais—"

"Hush." Hareflight stirred beside him, his mew thick with sleep. "You don't share your StarClan dreams with any cat."

Dawnstripe nodded. "You keep the secrets they share with you in your heart."

"Unless you're a medicine cat and StarClan speaks to your Clan through you." Hareflight stretched, arching his spine and quivering.

Dawnstripe padded toward the cavern entrance. "Let's get back to the Clan." Shrewpaw bounded past her. "I'll lead!" Dawnstripe called. "I don't want you getting lost."

Hareflight and Shrewpaw fell in behind her and Tallpaw followed last, glancing over his shoulder at the Moonstone as he headed out of the cavern. The huge rock glittered frostily in the moonlight. A pang tugged at Tallpaw's belly. *StarClan, why didn't you share with me?* Cold air washed his pelt as he stepped into the darkness, trailing a little behind his Clanmates. Numbness set into his paws, and Tallpaw had to force himself to keep plodding upward, following the scent and sound of his Clanmates as they led him out of the hill.

Hareflight and Shrewpaw were already scrambling down the rocky slope when Tallpaw emerged into moonlight.

"I thought we'd lost you," Dawnstripe murmured. She waited for Tallpaw to jump down from the ledge, and fell in beside him. Tallpaw walked in silence. As they reached the meadows, he hardly felt the wet grass drag along his flanks. All he felt was tiredness, growing heavier with each paw step.

The sky was turning pale beyond the moor-top as they

neared the WindClan border. The Thunderpath was quiet and they crossed it easily, just as Dawnstripe had promised.

Dawnstripe peered closely at Tallpaw as the ground began to slope up toward the moor. "Are you okay?" she prompted.

"I'm fine." Tallpaw padded past her without meeting her gaze. "Just tired." He glanced up the slope to the top of the moor, then back toward Highstones. They seemed to catch fire as the rising sun turned them red, then yellow, paler and paler against the lightening sky. The jagged peaks loomed over the valley, piercing the clouds. To Tallpaw, the moor hardly seemed big enough to contain WindClan, hemmed by forest, crushed by the sky, cut off short by the river in the gorge.

But this is home! Breaking into a run, he bounded past his Clanmates and raced down the hillside toward camp. The Clan was already stirring. Lilywhisker and Whiteberry yawned at the entrance to their den. The Meeting Hollow looked as crowded as a burrow full of rabbits as the Clan gathered around Reedfeather, waiting for his orders for the day's patrols.

"Tallpaw!" Hopkit scrambled across the tussocks, stumbling each time his twisted paw buckled underneath him. "Did you see the Moonstone?"

"Yes." Tallpaw nuzzled his head. The kit's wide, friendly gaze seemed to banish the darkness of Mothermouth.

Sorrelkit raced after her brother, her gray-and-brown fur spiked with excitement. She stopped beside Tallpaw and began sniffing his pelt, her mouth open as she tasted the strange scents he'd brought back. She glanced over her shoulder at Pigeonkit. "He smells funny."

Pigeonkit pushed past her and inspected Tallpaw closely. "Your fur's all wet."

"We've been trekking through long grass," Tallpaw explained.

"What did you see?" Sorrelkit flicked her short tail.

"The Moonstone."

Sorrelkit widened her eyes. "Was it big?"

"Bigger than Tallrock, and it shone like the stars."

"Did you touch it?" Hopkit leaned back, his fluffy ears pricked.

"You'll have to wait till it's your turn to visit it." Tallpaw was too tired to talk. "Isn't it time you had your first taste of mouse?"

Pigeonkit puffed out his chest. "I've already tasted it!"

"So have I!" Sorrelkit announced.

Tallpaw spotted a bird on the prey heap. "What about lapwing?" he asked.

"Meadowslip's worried we'll swallow the feathers," Hopkit mewed.

"What if I pluck it for you?" Tallpaw offered.

Sorrelkit raced around him. "Will you?" she squeaked.

"Come on." He headed toward the prey heap.

Pigeonkit and Sorrelkit streaked ahead. "Wait for me!" Hopkit was struggling to keep up, his crooked paw twisting beneath him.

Tallpaw turned back and tucked his nose under the black tom's belly. "Hang on!" he warned, flipping the kit onto his shoulders. Tallpaw purred as the young kit dug his tiny claws into his pelt, and carried him over to his littermates.

Bright sunshine turned the distant trees golden. Tallpaw took a step forward, bringing him right to the edge of Outlook Rock. Under the sweep of empty, blue sky, he could see sheep and Twolegs, dogs and monsters. He could even see a hare sitting in the middle of a distant meadow. The air around him was completely still, as though the world were holding its breath.

"A black-and-white dog is chasing sheep in the hill-meadow," Tallpaw reported.

Dawnstripe shifted behind him. "And?"

"There are grouse beside the copse." Tallpaw imagined padding beneath the distant trees, new scents bathing his tongue, the grouse within stalking distance. His mouth watered. "There's a fire in a Twolegplace." The scent of smoke touched his nose and he glimpsed a plume rising from the top of a Twoleg nest. Feathers flashed in the sunshine and Tallpaw's gaze flicked toward a hawk as it dived out of the sky. He scanned the meadow where it swooped, trying to pick out its prey. His paws itched to be there. He could snatch the prey out of the bird's path. "Hawk hunting rabbit."

"I'm impressed." Dawnstripe got to her paws. "You haven't missed anything." Her pads scuffed the rock. "Let's move on to your battle-skills assessment."

Tallpaw turned from the edge of the rock, dragging his gaze from the distant fields. He followed Dawnstripe to the training ground, the trail so familiar now that he didn't even have to think about where to put his paws. His thoughts were still on the hawk. He'd traveled across the meadow it had hunted in. Now he was back inside WindClan's borders while it was crouching in a treetop, feasting on its catch. Yearning pricked beneath his pelt. What was it like to hunt only for yourself, to have the freedom to go wherever you wanted, without boundaries or codes pinning you down?

"Tallpaw?" Dawnstripe's mew jerked him back. "Are you ready?"

Shrewpaw was waiting in the middle of the clearing with Hareflight. "How did Tallpaw do at Outlook Rock?" the brown warrior asked.

"He passed the assessment easily," Dawnstripe replied.

"Good." Hareflight flicked his tail. "Shrewpaw hunted well."

"I'm pleased to hear it." Dawnstripe gestured with her tail to send Tallpaw over to his denmate. "Time to test their battle skills," she meowed to Hareflight. "If they perform well enough here, they'll have passed everything."

Tallpaw trotted across the grass. Shrewpaw eyed him belligerently. Tallpaw sighed, wishing his denmate weren't so competitive. They could pass this assessment easily if they each gave the other a chance to show off his skills. He crouched in the grass, relaxing the muscles along his spine. *A warrior moves with ease, not stiffness.* Dawnstripe's advice rang in his ears. *No claws, no teeth unless there's a real battle. Fight with your wits as well as your paws.* Tallpaw made sure his claws were well sheathed and kept his gaze fixed on Shrewpaw, bracing himself for his denmate's first move. "Ready when you are," he mewed.

Shrewpaw narrowed his eyes. "Why don't *you* attack first?"

"If you like." Tallpaw wasn't going to let Shrewpaw unsettle him. He focused on Shrewpaw's left shoulder, then leaped for the right. His feint worked. Wrong-footed, Shrewpaw staggered sideways.

Shrewpaw's eyes blazed. "Cheater."

"It was a fair move."

Shrewpaw lunged at Tallpaw. Grasping Tallpaw's shoulders, he kicked a hind paw out from under him. *Good move.* Tallpaw was impressed and let Shrewpaw roll him onto his side. As soon as their backs were to their mentors, Shrewpaw sank his claws into Tallpaw's pelt. "You won't fool me twice, *Wormpaw.*"

Tallpaw flinched. "No claws, remember?"

"We're training to be warriors, not kits!" Shrewpaw hissed in his ear.

Tallpaw dug his hind claws into the grass and thrust Shrewpaw backward. Pain ripped through him as Shrewpaw tugged a lump of fur from his flank. *Don't let him put you off!* Tallpaw leaped to his paws. Shrewpaw faced him, eyes gleaming. Tallpaw backed away. *Let him think he scared me.* He felt a twinge of satisfaction as he saw triumph flash in Shrewpaw's gaze. *Come on, Weaselpaw.*

Shrewpaw sprang. Tallpaw glanced at his denmate's paws. His claws were sheathed. *For now.* He knew that Shrewpaw would be digging them in the moment they were out of sight of Hareflight and Dawnstripe. He leaped sideways.

Shrewpaw twisted to counter his move and Tallpaw shoved his muzzle beneath Shrewpaw's belly. Ducking under him, he felt Shrewpaw writhe on his shoulders before tumbling to the ground. Tallpaw dropped and rolled in the other direction, scrambling to his paws in time to face Shrewpaw as the young tom jumped up.

"That was a coward's move," Shrewpaw growled, just loud enough for Tallpaw to hear.

"Really?" Tallpaw spat. "It must be one you taught me."

Shrewpaw curled his lip. "I'm going to take a piece of your ear back to camp for that."

"I'd like to see you try!" Tallpaw lunged at Shrewpaw, turning on his forepaws and swinging his hind legs around. He kicked out and sent Shrewpaw staggering backward. But Shrewpaw recovered quickly and lunged at him. Tallpaw swallowed back a yelp as claws stabbed his flank. Teeth gripped his hind leg and jerked it from under him. As Tallpaw hit the ground with a thump, Shrewpaw leaped on him.

Pain flared white-hot along Tallpaw's spine as Shrewpaw pushed his muzzle and churned his hind claws against his back. Couldn't Dawnstripe see what was going on? Tallpaw pushed the thought away. He didn't want Dawnstripe rushing to his rescue as if he were a kit. He twisted his head and clamped his jaws around Shrewpaw's foreleg, just hard enough to get a grip, careful not to draw blood.

"Don't you know any *warrior* moves?" Shrewpaw snarled. "I fought better when I was a kit. No wonder you couldn't save your father!"

Fury roared through Tallpaw, stripping sense from his thoughts like wind tearing up heather. Without thinking, he unsheathed his claws and bit down on Shrewpaw's foreleg so hard he tasted the young tom's blood. Shrewpaw screeched and dragged himself free. Tallpaw plunged after him, grabbing him with outstretched claws, and hauled him back. Flinging him to the ground, he slammed his hind legs into Shrewpaw's belly and began battering him with blows that sent fur flying across the grass. The heather swam at the edge of Tallpaw's vision and the dark shape of Shrewpaw seemed to fade beneath him. In its place, Tallpaw saw the short, brown pelt of Sparrow.

"*You!*" He dragged the rogue onto his side, dripping blood from his scratched muzzle into the rogue's dark, expressionless face. "You deserve to die."

"Tallpaw!" Dawnstripe's yowl seemed to come from far away. The tug of her teeth in Tallpaw's scruff startled him. He felt himself being yanked back, clear off his paws.

Hareflight lunged in front of him, shielding Shrewpaw. "What in StarClan's name are you doing?" The brown warrior stared at him, horror widening his eyes.

Tallpaw blinked. Shrewpaw was trembling, bloody and tattered, on the ground beside his mentor.

What have I done?

CHAPTER 23

Dawnstripe glared at Tallpaw, her pelt spiked with rage. "No claws, remember?"

Tallpaw stared back, shock pulsing through him. "I'm sorry!"

Beside him, Hareflight checked Shrewpaw's wounds. Shrewpaw squirmed away from his mentor. "I'm okay," he insisted.

He doesn't want to admit that I nearly shredded him. Tallpaw winced as he recalled the fury that had driven him on. *How far would I have gone if Dawnstripe hadn't stopped me?*

Dawnstripe smoothed her chest fur with a couple of licks. "It's been a stressful day," she meowed. "You just got carried away."

Hareflight eyed Tallpaw warily. "I guess."

"Sure." Shrewpaw nodded as he shook out his pelt, hiding his scratches.

"It won't happen again," Tallpaw promised, but inside he felt a stab of panic. Would he fail his assessment because of this? He could have *killed* Shrewpaw because he'd lost control of his rage. *I don't deserve to pass the assessment.* His pelt pricked with shame. *True warriors don't hurt their Clanmates.*

Dawnstripe headed into the heather. "Let's get back to camp."

Tallpaw trailed behind his Clanmates, dreading what Dawnstripe would have to tell Heatherstar. Doespring and Stagleap were just leaving the camp as they reached the clearing outside.

Stagleap lifted his tail excitedly. "How did the assessment go?"

Doespring's eyes widened as she saw Shrewpaw's bloody nose. "What happened to *you?*"

Hareflight padded forward. "Tallpaw forgot he was fighting a Clanmate."

Stagleap stared at the clumps of fur hanging from Shrewpaw's pelt. "Did you think you were fighting a ShadowClan patrol?"

Tallpaw looked at the ground, his pelt hot.

Shrewpaw shrugged. "He just got lucky with a few swipes."

"Go to Hawkheart," Hareflight told him. "Get those scratches seen to while Dawnstripe and I speak with Heatherstar."

Stagleap shot Tallpaw a questioning look, but Tallpaw wasn't about to tell him anything. "I'm going to get a drink," he muttered, and followed the trail that skirted the camp wall to the spring. As he rounded the corner, he slowed. He could hear mews up ahead. Two cats were already beside the water.

"Are you sure?" Tallpaw recognized Woollytail's rasping mew.

Palebird answered him. "Yes. In two moons' time."

Tallpaw pricked his ears.

"What about Tallpaw?" Palebird meowed. "We should tell him first."

"Of course," Woollytail answered. "He'll be pleased. It's been a hard greenleaf for all of us. This will cheer him up."

Tallpaw's pelt pricked uneasily. *What will cheer me up?*

Palebird lowered her voice. "I think I should tell him by myself."

Tallpaw brushed past the heather and faced his mother. "Tell me what?"

"Tallpaw!" Palebird's eyes brightened. "I have good news." *Why is Woollytail looking so worried, then?* Palebird gazed fondly at Woollytail. "I'm expecting kits."

Tallpaw glared at him. "Yours?"

The tunneler lifted his muzzle. "Yes."

"You're going to be a brother at last," Palebird gushed.

"But what about Sandgorse?" Tallpaw blinked at Woollytail. "You were his friend. How can you—"

"Sandgorse would be pleased." Woollytail cut him off. "He wouldn't want to see Palebird grieving for the rest of her life. You should be pleased for your mother." Palebird's eyes shone. "She hasn't been this happy for a long time," he went on.

Tallpaw's heart twisted. *Sandgorse and I couldn't make you happy. But Woollytail can.*

"You'll still be her first kit," Woollytail told him gently. "Did you really think you'd be her last?"

Tallpaw looked at the two cats. Woollytail's eyes begged

him to understand, while Palebird seemed oblivious that she'd caused him any pain. "Whatever makes her happy," he growled, turning away. Mouth still dry and tasting of Shrewpaw's blood, he marched into camp.

The Meeting Hollow was buzzing. Tallpaw's Clanmates were streaming into it, their pelts ruffled with excitement. Cloudrunner looked over the rim. "Hurry up, Tallpaw, or you'll miss your own naming ceremony!"

Aspenfall and Larksplash settled near the edge of the hollow. Mistmouse and Appledawn were discussing something animatedly while Plumclaw, Hickorynose, and Meadowslip sat close together. Tallpaw realized that for the first time, tunnelers and moor runners were sitting together.

Hopkit, Sorrelkit, and Pigeonkit leaned over the edge. "Why can't we sit next to you?" Hopkit called to his mother.

Meadowslip shooed them away with a jerk of her muzzle. "Go and sit beside the nursery. You can see well enough from there. Heatherstar doesn't need kits under her paws. This is an important ceremony."

Tallpaw spotted the Clan leader standing in the middle of the hollow. Reedfeather stood a few paces behind while Hareflight and Dawnstripe flanked him. Shrewpaw was with his father. Redclaw puffed his chest out proudly and glanced up at the pale sky. Was he wondering if Brackenwing was watching?

Dawnstripe caught Tallpaw's eyes, beckoning him with a flick of her tail. Did this mean he'd passed his assessment? Her eyes shone and she gave him a tiny nod. He'd passed!

Tallpaw stared numbly back at her. Palebird had found a new family to replace her old one. What did it matter if he had a warrior name? She would have a litter of kits to look after soon. They'd make her happier than he ever had.

"Come on, Tallpaw." Woollytail padded up behind him and nudged him forward.

Beside him, Palebird purred. "Your naming ceremony! So much good news in one day!"

Tallpaw narrowed his eyes. *For you, maybe.* He padded across the tussocks and slid down into the hollow.

Heatherstar dipped her head. "Leaf-bare is coming, but we will face it with two new warriors." She looked at Shrewpaw. "Your warrior name will be Shrewclaw, in honor of your skill at hunting and fighting. You have trained well and are worthy of your warrior name."

Shrewclaw fluffed out his tail and purred.

"Tallpaw." Heatherstar's eyes glowed as she gazed at him. Tallpaw shifted his paws. "Your father always meant to name you for your long tail, and so I give you your warrior name in honor of him. Talltail, one day you will be a greater warrior than even you can imagine. Sandgorse would be proud of you."

Talltail stared at his leader. He should have felt happy, but the numbness wouldn't shift. Instead it wrapped itself tighter around his heart. Heatherstar held his gaze, her eyes searching his as if she was trying to tell him something. *Is she just being kind because she knows I don't fit in?* Around him, the air filled with the calls of his Clanmates.

"Talltail!"

"Shrewclaw!"

They lifted their voices to the afternoon sky, celebrating WindClan's newest warriors.

Talltail glanced over his shoulder at Palebird. She was pressed against Woollytail, her eyes bright. Talltail swallowed back the sadness welling in his throat. *Is she proud of me, or just happy about the kits?* Surrounded by his Clanmates cheering his name, he had never felt more alone.

The stars shimmered in a peat-black sky. Perched on the edge of Outlook Rock, Talltail gazed beyond the mountain peaks that edged the horizon like jagged teeth. What lay beyond? Had any cat traveled that far? His breath billowed in front of him, the stone slab cold beneath his paws. The chilly leaf-fall night carried the distant scent of a leaf-bare frost.

He was sitting vigil with Shrewclaw, their first night as warriors. As a fox barked far below, an owl flapped up from a distant tree. Talltail pricked his ears to see if he could hear the beat of its wings on the crystal air. A light twinkled in Two-legplace, catching Talltail's eye. Did a kittypet live trapped inside those walls? Snug and warm, blissfully unaware of the warriors on the moor? How many lives were being lived out there, beyond his view?

Talltail's thoughts drifted to Sparrow and the other visitors. Had they passed that Twoleg nest? Perhaps that's where they holed up for the winter. Maybe they were kittypets in leaf-bare, just playing at being rogues when the warm weather came. He shifted his paws, trying to ease the stiffness in his legs.

"Too cold for you up here?" Shrewclaw whispered. "You could go hide in a tunnel. I won't tell."

"Sure you wouldn't." Talltail twitched the tip of his tail with irritation. Was Shrewclaw going to keep on taunting him now they were warriors? He slid a look at his denmate. "Don't you get bored of throwing the same old insults?"

"Not at you."

"We're not supposed to be talking." Talltail watched a wisp of cloud drift over the moon. "StarClan won't approve."

"They probably don't approve anyway," Shrewpaw hissed. "You don't deserve your warrior name after fighting like that in the assessment."

"You were the first to unsheathe your claws."

"That was just to give it a bit of edge," Shrewclaw snapped. "I wasn't trying to rip your pelt off." A growl rumbled in his throat. "You caught me by surprise. Next time, I'll shred *you*."

"There won't be a next time."

Heatherstar's mew made Talltail jump. He turned and saw her purple gaze blinking from the shadowy grass. She padded onto the rock. "You do know that you shouldn't be speaking at all, let alone threatening each other?" Her gaze flicked from Talltail to Shrewclaw.

Talltail squirmed, feeling like a scolded kit. "Sorry, Heatherstar."

"Talltail started it," Shrewclaw muttered.

Heatherstar silenced him with a look. "I just wanted to check on my newest warriors." Her glaze slid past Talltail to the starlit view beyond. "How's the valley tonight?"

"Chilly," Shrewclaw told her.

Talltail looked out beyond Highstones. "Endless," he whispered, letting a note of longing creep into his voice.

Heatherstar's eyes glittered for a moment; then she turned away. "Stay silent," she reminded them as she padded onto the grass. "StarClan is watching."

Talltail stifled a yawn. The sky beyond ThunderClan territory was beginning to lighten at last. Shrewclaw's head was drooping beside him. Talltail flicked him with his tail.

Shrewclaw jerked up his head. "What?"

"It's nearly dawn," Talltail hissed.

"I knew that," Shrewclaw grunted.

Talltail stared out from the rock, watching the valley wake. Monsters began to roar along the Thunderpath. In the Twoleg den far below, a dog barked insistently until a Twoleg barked back, and the dog fell silent. The meadows and copses stirred into life as dawn turned the moon-drenched leaves from silver to green, and finally the sun lifted its head over the forest and set Highstones alight.

Talltail heard paw steps brushing the grass behind. He tasted the air before he turned. *Reedfeather.*

"You're still awake." Reedfeather sounded pleased.

Talltail stretched, arching his spine until his tail quivered. He straightened and shook the damp morning chill from his fur. Beside him, Shrewclaw yawned. "I'm glad I got my warrior name before leaf-bare," he meowed. "I'd have frozen to death sitting out here all night."

"Would a little hunting warm you up?" Reedfeather offered.

Shrewclaw blinked. "Now?"

"Sounds like a good idea to me." Talltail padded off the rock. He needed to stretch his legs and he was as hungry as a fox.

The heather rustled as Doespring and Aspenfall appeared.

"They're awake!" Aspenfall called.

"Of course!" Shrewclaw bounded off the stone slab beside Talltail.

"You must be frozen," meowed Doespring. She sniffed Shrewclaw's dew-specked pelt. "And tired."

"Not too tired to hunt," Reedfeather meowed. "They're joining our patrol. They can rest afterward."

Talltail tasted the air. "Where are we hunting?"

Reedfeather nodded toward a patch of heather that caught the first rays of sunlight on the hillside below. "Prey will be waking early there." He trotted down toward it, Aspenfall at his side. Shrewclaw ran to catch up while Doespring fell in beside Talltail.

"Isn't it great about Palebird's kits!" she purred.

"Any excuse to stay in the nursery," Talltail grunted.

Doespring stared at him. "Aren't you pleased?" she meowed. "They'll be your kin."

"Yeah." Talltail kept his eyes on the patrol ahead.

"When did you turn so selfish, Talltail?" Doespring protested. "Palebird's lost so much. You should be pleased for her."

"*Should* I?" Talltail stopped dead and curled his claws into the grass. "I'm a warrior now; I can have my own opinion. Palebird should have stayed faithful to Sandgorse. It's only been a few moons since the accident. Anyone would think she's glad he's gone so she can have Woollytail as her mate!"

Doespring's tail twitched. "You think too much about yourself, and not enough about your Clan, Talltail." She narrowed her eyes. "You say you're old enough to have your own opinion. But you're also old enough to understand that loyalty to your Clan is more important than anything. Palebird is happy. So's Woollytail. It's great news that there'll be more kits in WindClan. You're the only one who's not pleased."

Before he could argue, she broke into a run. "I'll race you to the warren," she called to the cats ahead as she hared past them. They charged after her.

Shrewclaw veered toward the heather, nose twitching. "Rabbit scent!"

Doespring swung around and gave chase with Aspenfall and Reedfeather on her tail. Talltail watched them plunge into the bushes. He didn't want to follow. He'd rather hunt alone, with no one telling him how he should feel. He tasted the air as he headed for the moor-top. A rabbit had definitely passed this way not long ago.

Talltail padded forward, stepping lightly over the grass. Low, grassy lumps covered the ridge ahead of him. *Burrows.* He dropped into a crouch and began to stalk, belly to the ground. Something twitched at the edge of his vision. He turned slowly and saw a pair of long, brown ears sticking above the grass. *Rabbit.*

Talltail held his breath. The rabbit bent its head to graze. Talltail crept closer, low as a snake through the grass. He could hear the rabbit munching. In the distance the heather rustled as his Clanmates crashed through it. *Can't they hunt quietly?* Eyes fixed on his quarry, Talltail leaped.

The rabbit raced away, its fear-scent filling the air. Talltail hurtled after it. Now the creature was less than a tail-length away. Timing his strides to match the rabbit's, Talltail pounced. "Got you!"

His heart sank as his paws hit bare grass. "Where are you?" He whirled around, spotting a burrow that reeked of fear-scent. *You can't hide in there!* Talltail plunged into the darkness. Tiny paws scrabbled a fox-length ahead of him. Reaching forward, he grabbed the rabbit's fluffy haunches before it could disappear into the maze of tunnels. It squealed as Talltail hauled it out and nipped it quickly with a killing bite. As he sat up, the scent of blood and fresh earth filled his nose, blotting out all the other scents of the moor.

"What in the name of StarClan are you doing?" came a disbelieving voice. Aspenfall was standing at the edge of the heather.

Talltail nudged the rabbit with a paw. "Hunting." He spat out a tuft of fur.

"We don't hunt underground anymore, remember?" Aspenfall looked round-eyed with concern. "Heatherstar said it wasn't safe."

"I was chasing it from the ridge over there," Talltail explained, pointing with his tail. He felt hot underneath his pelt. Why was Aspenfall questioning his catch? Had he forgotten that Talltail was a warrior now, just like him?

"Well, the tunnels are forbidden now," Aspenfall meowed.

Shrewclaw slid out of the heather behind the gray-and-white warrior. "Has Wormcat been digging tunnels?"

Anger surged through Talltail. He kicked the rabbit toward his Clanmate. "No, I've been catching prey."

Aspenfall took a step forward. "Calm down, Talltail. It's going to be hard for all of us to remember that we don't have the tunnels to hunt in. Come on, let's get that rabbit back to camp."

Talltail picked up the fresh-kill and clamped it hard between his jaws to stop himself from responding to any more of Shrewclaw's barbed comments. *I'm a warrior now,* he told himself. *Things have changed from when we were apprentices.* The rabbit bounced heavily against his front legs, making him stumble. So many things had changed, in fact, from Palebird expecting Woollytail's kits to the tunnels being shut down forever, that Talltail hardly recognized WindClan at all.

CHAPTER 24

❧

Talltail sat stiffly in his nest. Through its thick, wool lining, he could feel the moor ring with ice; every paw step, every clattering sheep hoof shivered through the frozen earth. His breath billowed up into the clear, black sky as he peered over the frost-wilted grass that edged the moor runners' nests. Even without the tunnels in use, the warriors still slept in two groups, preferring to keep their own nests for now. But when the next litter of kits passed their final assessment, would they share a single sleeping area?

Talltail pricked his ears, straining to hear the noises from the nursery. Stagleap was fast asleep in the nest beside him. Cloudrunner and Appledawn snored muzzle to muzzle. But Redclaw, Larksplash, and Dawnstripe were sitting up like Talltail, listening as another moan rose from beyond the thick gorse walls of the nursery.

Woollytail paced anxiously outside with Hickorynose next to him. Mistmouse and Plumclaw huddled at the rim of the Meeting Hollow.

"She'll be fine," Plumclaw reassured Woollytail as he passed.

Woollytail grunted, the fur rippling along his spine.

"Hawkheart's with her," Mistmouse soothed. "He's done this countless times."

Hopkit, his black fur sticking up in tufts, scrambled from the elders' den, where he'd been sent with Pigeonkit, Sorrelkit, and Meadowslip to wait out Palebird's kitting. "Are they here yet?"

Sorrelkit pushed past her brother. "Hawkheart's still in there, rabbit-brain. Of course they're not here yet."

Talltail jumped out of his nest. He knew he wouldn't get back to sleep again. Palebird sounded like she was struggling, her groans growing more desperate. Talltail padded toward the elders' den and stopped beside Hopkit. "These things take time," he muttered, trying to reassure himself as much as the kit.

Pigeonkit stuck his nose from the den entrance. The white patches on his pelt glowed against his dark gray fur in the moonlight. "Did Meadowslip make all that noise when she kitted us?" he mewed.

Talltail's ear twitched as a low, agonized wail echoed across the clearing. "I can't remember," he lied. Meadowslip's kitting had been much quieter than this. Was something wrong? His paws pricked with worry.

Meadowslip nudged Pigeonkit out of the way and padded out of the elders' den. "She's tougher than you think," she murmured to Talltail, gazing toward the nursery.

Talltail tipped back his head and looked up at Silverpelt. The ancestors wouldn't let Palebird lose kits twice, would they?

Lilywhisker slid out behind Meadowslip. Her amber eyes shone in the moonlight. "The first one is always the hardest. Second kits come easier."

Talltail stood and watched the nursery as Pigeonkit, Sorrelkit, and Hopkit weaved around him.

"We won't be the youngest anymore!" Hopkit mewed.

"I can't wait to show the new kits around camp," Sorrelkit declared.

"It'll be a few days before they're allowed out of the nursery," Meadowslip warned her.

Pigeonkit flicked his tail in the air. "We can teach them how to play Rabbit Run."

"And show them the Hunting Stones." Hopkit limped toward the smooth rocks and scrambled onto the highest one.

Talltail remembered one of his earliest days outside the nursery, when Sandgorse had tried to teach him to dig. The memory sent a shiver along his spine. If only he hadn't fallen into that hole, he might have chosen to be a tunneler from the start. Everything might have been different.

Sparrow would still have come. Talltail stiffened. *He would still have persuaded Sandgorse to risk his life in the tunnels.* The dark anger that lurked in the pit of his belly wormed up to his throat.

Pigeonkit stared at him. "Why are you growling?"

Talltail blinked. "I was just thinking about something else," he meowed quickly, shaking out his pelt.

Barkpaw squeezed out of the nursery and followed the rim of the Meeting Hollow toward the medicine den.

Talltail bounded toward him. "How is she?" he demanded,

slithering to a stop on the frosty grass in front of the young tom.

"She's tired." Barkpaw's eyes were dark.

Talltail's belly fluttered. "She will be okay, won't she?"

"I can't make any promises." Barkpaw met his gaze. "But Hawkheart knows what he's doing. She's in good paws." As he hurried away toward the medicine den, Talltail glanced anxiously at the nursery.

Ryestalk climbed out of her nest in the long grass and crunched across the clearing. "You were born on a night just like this, Talltail." She fluffed out her pelt.

"How do you know?" He didn't look at her. "You were hardly more than a kit yourself."

"I was young, but my eyes were open, and my ears worked perfectly." Ryestalk flicked her tail. "You were a squealer! Stagleap picked you up and put you outside the den one night, just so he could get some sleep." Her eyes flashed as if she expected him to purr with amusement. When he didn't, she went on. "Sandgorse heard you and took you straight back in. Poor Stagleap got an ear chewing for being so rabbit-brained."

The entrance to the medicine den rattled. Barkpaw scurried out with a wad of leaves in his mouth. Talltail wrinkled his nose at the sharp herb tang as the apprentice trotted past.

"Palebird's lucky to have two medicine cats to look after her," Ryestalk meowed. "She'll get through this, Talltail."

As Barkpaw pushed his way back into the nursery, a shrill, puny mew sounded through the gorse wall. Ryestalk's eyes lit up. "That's the first one!"

Hawkheart stuck his head out. "Come in, Woollytail. Meet your first kit."

Woollytail stared at the medicine cat like he'd just been dropped on the Thunderpath and a monster was headed for him. Hickorynose nudged him toward the gorse den. "Go on," he urged.

"I won't know what to do!" Woollytail whispered.

"Just welcome your new kits to WindClan. You'll be fine." Hickorynose walked his friend closer to the entrance and watched the tunneler squeeze through the thorny entrance.

Palebird shrieked. Talltail's heart lurched. A tiny mewling drifted from the nursery. Then there was silence. Talltail held his breath. He heard fur swishing inside. Hawkheart was murmuring to Barkpaw. Woollytail's strained mew was quickly hushed. The tunneler slid out of the nursery, his eyes wide and glittering. Talltail rushed toward him, shouldering past Appledawn, Ryestalk, and Hickorynose as they clustered around for news.

"Is Palebird all right?" Talltail begged.

"She's great." Woollytail met Talltail's gaze. "Come and meet your brothers and sisters."

Weak with relief, Talltail followed Woollytail into the nursery. Barkpaw scooted to the edge to make room as they squeezed in.

Hawkheart lifted his head from Palebird's nest. "She's very tired," he warned them.

Just enough moonlight filtered through the gorse for Talltail to make out his mother sprawled in her nest, her pelt wet and ruffled, and her eyes glazed. Four tiny shapes squirmed at her belly. Talltail crept closer, his nose wrinkling at the pungent scent of herbs and newborn kits. Woollytail crouched at Palebird's head and started licking her ears.

Hawkheart stood up with a grunt and headed for the entrance. "She'll be back on her feet in a day or two," he pronounced. "Don't keep her awake too long."

Palebird stared at him in dismay. "You can't leave! How am I going to feed all these kits? There are so many!"

"There are only four, and they'll do the work," Hawkheart told her briskly. "You just have to lie still."

"What if I don't have enough milk?"

"Of course you will." Hawkheart slid from the den. "Come on, Barkpaw," he meowed over his shoulder. "Palebird can manage without us now."

Palebird gazed up at Woollytail with anxious eyes. "Will I really be able to look after them?"

"Of course." Woollytail lapped her cheek fondly. "You'll be a fine mother with these little ones, just like you were with Talltail."

Talltail's heart felt as if something was squeezing. He gazed down at the kits, trying to make one out from another as they huddled together. "Have you named them?"

"Not yet," Woollytail told him. "Palebird's too tired."

The kits had better get used to that, Talltail thought bitterly.

The smallest kit—a black tom, his pelt still slick from his kitting—began to climb the side of the nest, hauling himself up with his tiny claws. Talltail reached in and grasped him gently by the scruff. *Stay warm, little one.* He swung him toward Palebird's belly.

"Careful!" she snapped. "You'll hurt him!"

Stinging as though Palebird had raked his muzzle, Talltail laid the kit beside his littermates. He backed away. "I was just helping." Grief hollowed his belly as he slid from the den.

Barkpaw was waiting outside. "They're perfectly healthy," he meowed, as if he thought Talltail was still concerned.

"Good." Talltail headed for the entrance, his heart aching.

"Where are we going?"

We? Talltail glanced at his friend. It felt like a long time since Talltail had heard Barkpaw say *we*. "I'm going to feel the wind in my fur." He fixed his eyes on the gap in the heather. "Do you want to come with me?" He braced himself for Barkpaw to make excuses and return to his den. "You must be tired," Talltail prompted. The moon was sinking, which meant dawn was close, but there was time for Barkpaw to rest before his morning duties. "Hawkheart probably has a busy day planned for you."

"I don't feel like sleeping yet," Barkpaw told him. "That was my first kitting." He ducked through the entrance first.

Talltail followed, and they began to climb the slope, following the trail around the heather. "Is Palebird really okay?" Talltail meowed in a rush.

"Really." Barkpaw's pelt brushed his as they climbed.

"She looked tired."

"It was a hard kitting."

"None of them died, though." Talltail thought of Finchkit.

"They're survivors, like you," Barkpaw purred.

They walked in silence for a while. Talltail gently steered his friend toward Outlook Rock. "I love this view," he mewed as he led Barkpaw out across the stone.

Barkpaw peered into the night-shadowed valley. "Why? Everything is so dark and far away."

Talltail sat down, beckoning Barkpaw to sit beside him with a flick of his tail. "Just wait."

"For what?"

The sky was growing pale as the sun pushed up toward the horizon behind them. Glancing over his shoulder, Talltail saw weak rays seeping through the bare branches of Thunder-Clan's forest. "You'll see in a moment," he told Barkpaw. As he spoke, the sun lifted above the trees. Sunlight swept the moor and lit up the tips of Highstones.

Barkpaw gasped. "I've never seen that!"

"Can you see the mountains behind?"

Barkpaw narrowed his eyes. "There are mountains?"

"And more land beyond them, probably," Talltail meowed, paws pricking. "Places no Clan cat has ever seen."

"Or will ever see," Barkpaw commented.

Talltail turned. "Why not?"

"Why would any cat trek that far from home?"

"To see what was there!"

Barkpaw shrugged. "I've been to the Moonstone, and that's far enough. There's plenty to see on the moor. I still haven't learned every herb that grows here."

"Don't you want to find *new* herbs, growing in places other cats haven't been?"

Barkpaw stared across the valley. "I couldn't possibly go wandering off. My Clan needs me."

Talltail shifted his paws. "I wish WindClan needed *me*."

"Of course they do!"

Talltail shrugged. "I thought I could replace Sandgorse by becoming a tunneler," he murmured. "I thought they'd need me then. But Heatherstar said we didn't need tunnelers anymore. Now Palebird has had Woollytail's kits. So she doesn't need me either."

"She does!" Barkpaw exclaimed. "And the kits will need you, too."

Talltail shook his head. "It's more than not being needed," he sighed. "That's just part of it."

Barkpaw frowned. "What do you mean?"

"I . . . I can't help feeling that I have to find Sparrow."

"Why?" Barkpaw's eyes went round with confusion.

"He killed Sandgorse." Talltail searched his friend's gaze for some trace of understanding or sympathy. Didn't any of his Clanmates realize what Sparrow had done?

"But Sandgorse's death was an accident," Barkpaw meowed. "It wasn't Sparrow's fault."

Not Sparrow's fault? Talltail's anger swelled until he felt it block his throat, choking his words. Why didn't anyone see that a rogue had caused the death of a Clan cat and walked away unpunished? He glowered at the valley. *You're out there somewhere, I know.* He pictured Sparrow stretching happily in a pool of dawn sunshine. *You think you can go unpunished forever, but I won't let that happen.* Talltail's claws scraped the rock. *One day, you'll be sorry.*

Barkpaw followed his gaze. "Each cat has his own destiny to follow," he murmured. "And only StarClan knows where that leads."

"What if it leads beyond the Clan?" Talltail growled.

Barkpaw's tail twitched. "Beyond the Clan?"

"What if my destiny is out there?" Talltail nodded toward the valley. *What if my destiny is to avenge Sandgorse's death?*

"On your own?"

"Yes." Talltail glared at the distant fields, scanning for brown pelts moving across the grass.

"Do you want to be a rogue?" Barkpaw demanded. Shock edged his mew.

"Of course not." How could Barkpaw be so narrow-minded? "Can I only be a warrior inside warrior territory?" Talltail turned his gaze on Barkpaw. "The warrior code must reach beyond borders, surely? Courage, honor, and loyalty don't end at a scent line."

"You're just feeling unsettled because of the kits." Barkpaw climbed to his paws and stretched. "Once you've gotten to know them, you'll feel differently. There's room for all of you in the Clan, you know."

"Maybe." Talltail watched Barkpaw pad toward the grass. *But I doubt it.*

"I'd better get back," Barkpaw called over his shoulder. "Hawkheart will be looking for me."

Talltail turned his gaze back toward the valley. *Where does my path lead?* He glanced at the sky. *Are you going to tell me, StarClan?* His heart sank when there was nothing but silence, no change in the shape of the clouds overhead or in the sound of the wind. But his warrior ancestors hadn't shared with him at the Moonstone; why would they guide him now? Perhaps even StarClan didn't know what lay ahead for him.

A bird called from the valley. Another answered it. Tall-tail tipped his head on one side to listen. Those birds weren't troubled by the idea of dead birds watching them, making decisions on their behalf. Why should he wait for his ancestors to make up their minds?

I choose my own destiny. Nothing can stop me—not even StarClan.

CHAPTER 25

❧

Talltail hopped from his nest, ready for the dawn hunting patrol. Stagleap and Shrewclaw were still snoring, not even stirring as he picked his way between their nests. They must have returned late from last night's Gathering. Talltail had slept through their return. Why wait up and hear news they'd be sharing all day anyway?

He padded out of the long grass. Freezing fog filled the camp. Dawn light seeped through the mist as Talltail sniffed at a frosty mouse. It was all that was left of the prey-heap pile. He picked it up and carried it to the nursery, thrusting it through the entrance to give it a chance to thaw. It should be soft by the time that Palebird, Meadowslip, and their kits woke.

It had been a quarter moon since Palebird had kitted Wrenkit, Bristlekit, Rabbitkit, and Flykit. Talltail was proud of them. They had already explored the whole camp, asking questions, begging for badger rides, and getting under everyone's paws.

As he leaned into the nursery now, Palebird lifted her head sleepily and peered through the half light. "Is that you, Talltail?"

"Yes. Do you need something?" Talltail pricked his ears.

"Go away," Palebird grunted. "You're disturbing everyone. The kits kept us awake half the night because you made them so excited about the Gathering."

As Talltail ducked out of the den, a gorse thorn stabbed his ear. It stung less than Palebird's words. Appledawn was stretching his spine at the edge of the long grass where the warriors slept. Hareflight stood yawning at the rim of the Meeting Hollow while Cloudrunner sniffed the empty patch where the prey heap should have been.

Cloudrunner lifted his head. "It looks like we've got some hunting to do," he commented.

"I'm ready." Talltail flexed his claws.

Appledawn headed for the entrance, Hareflight at her side. Cloudrunner raced past them and led them out of camp. Talltail felt their paw steps ringing through the ice-bound earth. He gave chase, catching up on the grass clearing outside. He stopped and scanned the moor. "Which way?"

"There'll be prey near Fourtrees," Cloudrunner guessed. "Anywhere close to the woods, when it's this cold." The pale gray tom crashed away through the frost-whitened heather. Talltail veered around the bushes, running hard so that he was ahead of the patrol when they broke from the other side. He heard their paws thrumming behind him and pushed harder.

"Why don't you hunt down by the RiverClan border?" Cloudrunner panted when he caught up to Talltail at the edge of the trees. "Hareflight and I will search the brambles." He glanced at Hareflight as the brown tom slithered to a halt, narrowly missing getting poked in the eye by a branch.

Appledawn pulled up behind him, her flanks heaving. "It's a bit early for a race!" she panted.

Cloudrunner nodded to her. "You can hunt the RiverClan border with Talltail." He nodded toward the scrubby hillside that linked the woods above Fourtrees to the river. Suddenly the warrior's eyes narrowed. Talltail jerked around, following his gaze.

Two dark pelts were weaving between the bushes just below the border with RiverClan.

"The river must be frozen if they're hunting on land," Hareflight meowed. "They won't like eating mice instead of fish."

"They didn't mention it at the Gathering," Cloudrunner growled.

Talltail snorted. "Of course not. Clans don't admit when they're starving, remember?" He quoted the warrior's words back at him.

Cloudrunner's pelt rippled. "Just keep your eyes open. Hungry Clans cross borders."

Of course they do! Otherwise they'd starve. Talltail headed downhill, Appledawn hurrying to keep up. "I hope we get a rabbit," she meowed. "I'm starving."

"If we could use the tunnels, we'd find plenty," Talltail muttered. Bushes dotted the slope as it flattened toward the RiverClan scent line. The soil felt crumbly beneath Talltail's paws, sandy enough to resist freezing even after several dawns of frost. This area was popular with rabbits because it was easy to dig at the height of leaf-bare, though the burrows became unstable in warmer weather.

"We might as well re-mark the border while we're here." Appledawn padded toward a bramble spilling over the grass and brushed past it.

Talltail headed for a clump of ferns farther along. As he marked the icy fronds, he felt the earth tremble. Paw steps were heading this way. Talltail pricked his ears and let the fur lift along his spine. Something was running at full pelt, not even slowing as it approached the scent line. The ferns swished and a rabbit hared out past his nose. A she-cat exploded after it, with a tom at her heels.

RiverClan scent bathed Talltail's tongue. He recognized the ginger-and-white pelt of Nightsky as she streaked after the rabbit. Piketooth raced after her, ears flat, eyes wide. Talltail watched, rooted to the spot with surprise. The rabbit veered across the slope and Piketooth peeled away, picking up speed as he hit the open grass of WindClan territory. He outflanked the rabbit and drove it back toward Nightsky. Eyes gleaming, she pounced, killing it with a sharp nip to the spine.

"Why are you standing here like a lump?" Appledawn's hiss sounded in Talltail's ear. "They're on our territory!" She darted forward.

Talltail followed and quickly overtook her, slowing as he neared the RiverClan cats. They spun around, bristling. Nightsky stood in front of her catch. Piketooth showed his teeth. Talltail scrambled to a halt, blocking them from Appledawn's line of sight. The RiverClan cats looked lean and hungry, their pelts dull.

"Quick," Talltail hissed to Nightsky. "Take the rabbit and get back to your own territory."

The RiverClan she-cat stared at him.

"Hurry!" Talltail hissed. He could hear Appledawn racing up behind him.

Nightsky grabbed the rabbit and fled back to the border. Piketooth tore after her, flashing a shocked look at Talltail as he passed.

"What in the name of StarClan are you doing?" Appledawn gasped, skidding to a stop beside Talltail.

"I tried to stop them!" Talltail meowed. "But they were too quick for me. They must be starving!"

"*We'll* be starving if you give away all our prey!" Appledawn spat.

Fur flashed at the edge of Talltail's vision. Hareflight and Cloudrunner were running down the slope. On the other side of the border, Talltail was relieved to see Nightsky and Piketooth disappear into the ferns.

Cloudrunner pulled up beside Appledawn. "What happened?"

"Talltail just let a RiverClan hunting patrol steal our prey!" Appledawn snarled.

Talltail bristled. "It was their prey. It came from their territory."

Appledawn lashed her tail. "Once it crosses the border, it's our prey."

Cloudrunner faced Talltail. "Is this true?"

"They took their prey back over the border, yes." Talltail lifted his chin.

"You let them kill it on our land, though," Appledawn put in.

"They killed the rabbit before I reached them. And they're clearly starving." Talltail couldn't understand why his Clanmates were so unforgiving. "Are we supposed to *want* other Clans to starve?" *Is that what warriors do?*

Hareflight stepped forward. "We take care of our own Clan first." He glanced up the slope toward camp. "We have hungry cats, too."

"Then let's hunt," Talltail meowed lightly. "We haven't lost a rabbit; we've just seen one cross the border and go back again. Come on, let's check out that gorse over there."

"Your Clanmates aren't happy with you." Heatherstar sat at the back of her den, half-hidden in shadow.

Talltail stood in front of her, feeling slightly baffled. Why was everyone making such a fuss about the RiverClan rabbit? "It was prey from their territory." He was tired of explaining.

"So you keep saying." Heatherstar sighed. "But we have to feed our own Clan first."

"*They* flushed it out," Talltail reasoned. "It never would have run into our territory if RiverClan hadn't chased it there."

Heatherstar leaned forward. "What's wrong, Talltail?" Her eyes were round with curiosity.

Talltail's fur pricked along his spine. "Why does there have to be anything wrong?"

"I know you've had a hard time." Heatherstar's mew was sympathetic. "Palebird never got over Finchkit—"

"She got over her enough to start a new family with

Woollytail," Talltail muttered.

Heatherstar blinked. "Losing Sandgorse was a shock for you, I know. And I'm sorry you weren't able to follow in his paw steps, but I had to think of the whole Clan." Heatherstar took a breath. "If there's ever anything you want to talk about, I want you to know you can come and talk to me. Or Dawnstripe." She frowned. "I worry that you hold back from your Clanmates. You keep too much to yourself. Being part of a Clan means sharing in all things."

Talltail flicked his tail, feeling more and more uncomfortable. "May I go now, please?"

Heatherstar nodded. "Of course. But remember, you can always talk to me."

"Thanks." Talltail turned and headed out of the den.

Barkface, who had been given his medicine cat name just a few days before, was waiting for him in the clearing. "I have to talk to you," he hissed urgently.

"What about?"

"Just wait!" Barkface led him to the spring outside the camp wall and stopped in the clearing. The water bubbled beside their paws, lapping over the rim of ice around the edge of the little pool. "Do you remember what you said at Outlook Rock?" He faced Talltail with his ears pricked. "After Palebird kitted? You asked what would happen if your destiny led you beyond the Clan," Barkface prompted.

Talltail nodded. "So?"

"You said that it was possible to be a warrior even beyond Clan borders."

"I still believe that."

Barkface went on. "You wanted to find out what was out there."

Talltail's paws pricked with impatience. "Why are we going over this again?"

"I was out on the moor at sunrise," Barkface mewed in a rush. "I was picking sheep sorrel to ease Flailfoot's fever, and I found a tuft of black-and-white fur."

Talltail stared at him. "How's that important?"

"*You're* black and white!"

"Are you saying you found my fur?" Talltail looked along his flank. "I don't think I've lost any."

"No!" Barkface leaped up the ridge of earth above the spring and paced along the top. "Don't you see? It was a sign."

"A sign?" Talltail was confused.

"As I held it up and looked at it, the wind whisked it from my paw and carried it over the moor like a puff of smoke. It just vanished."

Talltail frowned. "What are you trying to say? That I'm about to vanish?" Anxiety began to worm in his belly.

Barkface was quivering. "I just know it means something. It *felt* important, like StarClan had sent it. And after what you said about your destiny leading you outside the Clan, well, maybe you were right. Maybe this was StarClan's way of saying they agree."

"You think StarClan *wants* me to leave?" Talltail felt cold. Was that why they hadn't shared dreams with him at the Moonstone? "Do *you* think I should?" His throat tightened.

"No!" Barkface scrambled down the bank and stopped a whisker from Talltail's muzzle. "Of course you don't have to. But if you truly believe that your destiny lies beyond our borders, I think StarClan wants you to follow it."

Talltail saw his friend's eyes glow with conviction. *He just wants me to be happy.* Slowly he nodded. "Thanks for telling me, Barkface." He climbed up the bank and padded over the grass. "I'll have to think about it."

"Do what you feel is right, Talltail," Barkface called after him.

Talltail lifted his muzzle and gazed toward the moor-top. He could picture the valley beyond as easily as if it were the WindClan camp. He'd memorized the fields, the roll of the hills, the tracks left by rivers and Thunderpaths on the countless patrols he'd spent on Outlook Rock. He could picture it just as Sandgorse could picture the tunnels running below the moor.

His paws itched with sudden excitement. He belonged out there, and StarClan agreed. His destiny was to leave his territory and track down the cat who'd killed his father. He saw it clearly now. His Clanmates didn't think Sparrow had done anything wrong, but StarClan understood. They were telling him to avenge Sandgorse's death.

Energy surged beneath his pelt.

I have to leave the moor! My destiny lies beyond the Clans!

CHAPTER 26

❧

Talltail hurried back to the camp. He had to tell Heatherstar. He should leave as soon as he could. That's why the weather had been so cold and dry. *StarClan must be preserving Sparrow's scent trail for me to follow!*

"Talltail! Talltail!"

As he crossed the tussocks, Rabbitkit, Flykit, Wrenkit, and Bristlekit came tearing toward him. He hopped clear as they swarmed around his legs. "I can't play now," he told them briskly. "I have to speak with Heatherstar."

Bristlekit stared at him with round eyes. "But you just spoke with her!"

Wrenkit glanced over her shoulder. "She's busy." The WindClan leader was with Reedfeather in the Meeting Hollow. The two cats sat, heads close, deep in conversation.

"She won't be too busy for this." Talltail tried to move forward, but Rabbitkit clung to his leg. "Give us a badger ride!" she squeaked. "Cloudrunner says we're too big now."

Talltail felt a pang as he met the young cat's gaze. He would miss his half sister growing up. He'd never even know her warrior name. "Okay," he conceded, and crouched down.

Before he had time to protest, all four kits had scrambled onto his back. They clung to his fur with thorn-sharp claws.

Lilywhisker purred outside the elders' den. "Come and see this, Flailfoot. Talltail's bringing us some prey."

"No, he's not!" Flykit wriggled on Talltail's back.

Talltail's whiskers twitched. "Yes, I am. I'm going to feed you to Lilywhisker and Flailfoot. Elders love the taste of fresh kit."

"No! No!" Flykit squealed in horror. "I want to get down."

Stomping his paws like a badger, Talltail carried the kits toward the elders.

Lilywhisker licked her lips. "You're just in time, Talltail. I'm getting hungry."

"No!" Flykit squealed.

"Don't be silly," Wrenkit chided. "*Of course* they won't eat us."

"But what if they did?"

Talltail felt Flykit scrabble along his spine. "It's okay, Flykit." He stopped beside Lilywhisker. "We're just pulling your tail."

Lilywhisker reached forward and swung Flykit off Talltail's back by his snowy scruff. Talltail hunkered down and let the others scramble off. He watched as the kits swarmed over Flailfoot, his heart aching at the sight of the kits and elders. There was so much he would miss. And yet his destiny lay elsewhere—with revenge for his father's death. *And then what?*

Talltail pictured the mountains beyond Highstones. There was so much to discover out there, enough to fill countless lifetimes.

"Lilywhisker." He dipped his head solemnly to the elder.

"Thank you for your kindness these past moons."

The old cat blinked in surprise. "Er, okay." She looked as if she was about to question him, so Talltail backed away.

"I have to speak with Heatherstar," he meowed. He turned and trotted over to the Meeting Hollow. "Heatherstar? Can we talk?"

She looked up, her eyes darkening, and nodded to Reed-feather. "We can continue this later," she murmured to her deputy, and leaped out of the hollow. "Follow me, Talltail."

He followed her to her den, sliding into its shadow for the second time that day. "I have to leave WindClan." He blurted out the words before Heatherstar had even sat down.

"Leave WindClan?" She repeated his words almost absently, her gaze wandering as though she was remembering something from a long time ago. "Okay," she murmured at last.

Wasn't she going to ask him why? "Sparrow was never punished for killing Sandgorse," he told her bluntly. "I have to find him and make him pay for what he did."

"And that's why you're leaving." Heatherstar curled her tail over her paws. "Couldn't you wait for him to return next greenleaf and punish him then?"

Talltail shifted his paws. Why was she being so calm? He was going to leave WindClan! "There's more to it than that," he admitted. "I . . . I want to see what lies beyond the Clans. Don't you?"

Heatherstar shook her head. "The Clan has always been as much as I need."

"But my Clanmates don't understand me. Some of them don't even like me."

"You could change that," she meowed softly. "They respect you. But they can sense your anger and unhappiness. It makes their pelts prick."

"That's why I need to go," Talltail confessed. "I feel trapped here." Thoughts of tunnels—roaring water and pressing earth—swamped him. He struggled to catch his breath. "I need fresh wind in my pelt."

"You feel trapped by your home?" Heatherstar tipped her head questioningly. "Are we trapped by the sky, or the earth?" she asked. "Are we trapped because we need prey to live? Or water to drink? Or air to breathe? We depend on all these things, but they don't make us feel trapped." Her eyes burned in the darkness. "Can you imagine what your life will be like without the protection of your Clan? You will have to hunt for yourself, heal yourself if you get hurt. There will be no one to share your victories. Or your defeats."

Talltail's ears twitched. "But I will be free."

"You will be free to discover where your heart truly lies." Heatherstar's mew was barely a whisper. She seemed to be talking to herself.

Talltail leaned closer. "Barkface had a sign from StarClan."

"Barkface is a talented young medicine cat." Heatherstar's eyes sparked. "But it is Hawkheart who reads signs from StarClan."

"The sign said I should leave."

"A cat decides his own path."

"Don't we have to do what StarClan tells us?"

Heatherstar purred. "Our ancestors were all cats like us once. They know we shape our own destinies."

Talltail's fur tingled. "I'm leaving," he meowed. "Now."

"I understand." Heatherstar sighed and stood up. "I know there is nothing I can say to change your mind. But say farewell to your Clan first."

"Do I have to?" Talltail swallowed. He didn't need to explain himself. He only needed to tell them what he planned to do. He followed Heatherstar out of the den, around the rim of the hollow, and stopped beside her at the head of the grassy clearing.

"WindClan!" Heatherstar beckoned her Clanmates forward with a flick of her tail. "Talltail has something to say."

Aspenfall padded from the prey-heap pile. Cloudrunner got to his paws and crossed the tussocks. Hareflight and Shrewclaw fell in beside him. Mistmouse and Hickorynose climbed from their nests in the bracken patch. Woollytail nearly tripped over Hopkit, Sorrelkit, and Pigeonkit as they dashed ahead of Meadowslip and barged past their Clanmates.

Redclaw halted as the kits bounced past him. "Watch out!"

Wrenkit scrambled over the bumpy clearing with Bristlekit and Flykit at her heels. They crowded around Palebird as she padded out of the nursery.

"What does Talltail want?" Flykit asked his mother anxiously.

Palebird stooped to smooth the white fur between his ears with her tongue. "I don't know."

Lilywhisker, Flailfoot, and Flamepelt padded from the elders' den, eyes sparking with curiosity, while Hawkheart ducked out of the medicine den.

"Do you know what this is about?" he asked Barkface, who was just behind him. Barkface looked at his paws.

Dawnstripe nosed past her Clanmates. "Talltail? What's happening?"

Talltail forced himself to take a deep breath, trying not to be alarmed by the faces staring expectantly at him. Did his Clanmates care about him after all? "I'm leaving WindClan," he announced.

"Leaving?" Dawnstripe's eyes stretched wide. "You can't!"

"I have to." Talltail dipped his head. "I'm sorry, Dawnstripe. I know you hoped I'd be a great warrior one day, but my destiny lies somewhere beyond the Clan."

"Don't be such a rabbit-brain." Woollytail stared at him, ears twitching. "This is your home."

Talltail didn't want to get caught up in an argument. He pressed on. "Look after my mother, Woollytail." He glanced at Palebird. She'd turned her attention to Wrenkit and was washing her with brisk laps of her tongue. Meadowslip nudged her and she looked up.

"What?"

"Talltail's leaving WindClan," Meadowslip told her.

Palebird's gaze sharpened with surprise. "*Leaving?* But why?"

Talltail glanced at Heatherstar. "Lots of reasons," he mewed.

Heatherstar took a step forward. "None of us is a prisoner here. I would rather Talltail stayed, just as you all would, but I will not force him against his will. Our hearts and thoughts will travel with him."

The cats stared at their leader in astonishment. Talltail realized they couldn't believe Heatherstar wasn't trying to stop him, reminding him of his loyalty to the Clan and the warrior code, the moons of training he had gone through to become a warrior, the importance of strong, young cats to catch prey and patrol borders on behalf of their Clanmates. Talltail narrowed his eyes. Did Heatherstar *want* him to leave?

Hareflight leaned forward and rested his muzzle against the top of Talltail's head. "In that case, go well, and may StarClan light your path." He sounded baffled, as if he expected Talltail to blurt out that it was all a joke.

"May StarClan light your path," murmured Cloudrunner and Ryestalk.

"Don't go!" Wrenkit dashed forward and ducked under Talltail's belly. Weaving in and out of his legs, she mewed, "You can't go. Who will play with us?"

He nosed her toward Palebird. "You've plenty of denmates to play with."

"But they can't give us badger rides!" Wrenkit wailed.

"Don't worry, dear." Palebird began washing her again. "He won't be gone long."

Talltail scanned the stunned faces of his Clanmates. "I'm going for good," he told them. "I've made up my mind. I've spent long enough looking at distant lands from Outlook Rock. I want to see them up close. I want to explore places that no Clan cat has ever been."

"Heatherstar?" Dawnstripe stared at the WindClan leader. "Are you really going to let him do this?"

"It's his choice," Heatherstar answered.

Before anyone else could argue, Talltail padded forward, pushing past his Clanmates.

"Talltail!" Doespring gasped as he passed. "I'll miss you."

"Me too," Stagleap called.

"I don't understand." Shrewclaw blinked as Talltail reached him. "How can you leave? We trained together. I thought I'd always have you to hunt alongside."

Talltail shrugged. "Hunt with someone else." He met Shrewclaw's gaze, surprised to find it darkening with sadness. "I thought you'd be glad to see the *wormcat* leave."

"I'm sorry." Shrewclaw's ear twitched. "I was only ever teasing."

"It's more fun teasing than *being* teased," Talltail commented. He pushed away his bitterness and lifted his chin. "But that's not why I'm leaving. There's something I have to do, and I can't do it here."

"Good luck." Lilywhisker's rasping mew sounded in his ear. She touched his muzzle to his cheek, and he paused for a moment to breathe in her warm, familiar scent.

"Thank you, Lilywhisker." Flicking his tail, he marched for the camp entrance, refusing to look back. He pushed through the heather, his mind whirling. *I'm actually leaving.* After dreaming about what lay beyond the Clan borders for so long, he was going to find out. Fear and excitement surged beneath his pelt.

"Talltail!" Barkface was following him across the grass clearing. "Can I walk with you to the edge of the moor?"

Talltail slowed. "Yes, of course."

Barkface fell in beside him as they skirted the heather and began to climb the slope to the moor-top.

"You weren't unhappy all the time, were you?" Barkface mewed as they neared the ridge.

"No." Talltail's heart swelled as he remembered his first day's training when he nearly outran Stagpaw. And all the times he'd skimmed the grass, fast as a bird, the wind streaming through his pelt. His first catch, his first Gathering, his first sight of the Moonstone. "But I'll only find peace when I've made Sparrow pay for killing Sandgorse."

Barkface's pelt brushed his flank. "Do you really think that will change anything?"

"Of course it will!" The dark fury that slumbered in Talltail's belly began to stir. He wanted Sparrow to suffer as Sandgorse must have suffered.

"You can always come back afterward," Barkface murmured.

Come back? Talltail didn't answer. He was never coming back.

They reached the peak of the moor. Talltail looked out across the valley, the wind lifting his pelt. "Good-bye, Barkface." He faced his friend. "You're going to be a great medicine cat." Then he bounded down the slope, all the way across the border toward the Thunderpath. He fought the urge to turn and see Barkface silhouetted against the sky. His future lay ahead of him, not behind.

CHAPTER 27

Talltail scrambled into the ditch beside the Thunderpath as a monster roared past. Flattening his ears, he waited for a gap. Sparrow was somewhere on the other side and he was going to track him down. That heartless rogue was going to pay for destroying his life.

As soon as the roar of monsters quieted down, Talltail hurtled across the flat, black stone. He scrambled through the hedge on the far side, its brown leaves rattling as he scraped between the gnarled branches and burst into the open field. *Which way would the rogues have gone?* Through stinging eyes, Talltail scanned the landscape. A muddy field stretched ahead of him, bordered on each side by brown hedges. Overhead a buzzard wheeled, its wings outstretched to catch the wind. Talltail crept along the side of the field, keeping close to the hedge as the ground sloped upward. A wide, muddy track formed the far edge of the field, uneven and specked with stones. Ditches ran on either side and Talltail hesitated, wondering whether to keep to the hedge and trek through the long, damp grass, or leap the ditch and follow the stony track.

Instinct kept him near the hedge, but the grass dragged at

his fur, soaking him until he was chilled to the bone. Nettles grew thickly among the roots of the hedge, shriveled and browned by leaf-bare but still vicious enough to sting his nose. When he got sick of trying to avoid them, Talltail backtracked, leaped the ditch, and padded warily along the open track, his heart pounding.

Every scent was new, every noise strange: a far-off whine; a distant crack; the banging of wood against wood. Talltail's sodden pelt began to spike. Had Sparrow walked this way? Talltail lifted his chin. *Sparrow* would never have let fear slow his paws. He would have walked the path as though he owned it. The arrogant tom acted like every territory was his own. Talltail flexed his claws. It was time someone taught him a lesson.

He glanced at the sky. The sun was sliding toward Highstones. Was this the way he'd come when he visited Mothermouth? He tasted the air, trying to recognize scents. A sharp Thunderpath scent bathed his tongue. His ears pricked as a low rumbling sounded nearby. Talltail froze. Something huge was growling, moving closer fast.

A huge monster lurched around the corner and bounded along the track toward him. Its round, black paws were huge, each as big as a regular monster. A Twoleg sat scowling on top, swaying and jerking as the monster bounced beneath him.

Talltail's pelt bushed up. He leaped for the edge of the path and plunged into the ditch. He tumbled to the bottom, gasping with cold as he dropped into stagnant water. The monster growled past and bumped away along the track. Trembling,

Talltail dragged himself out of the ditch. His pelt was rank with green slime, and dripping wet. He shook it, queasy at the thought of washing the putrid stench out. Angry with himself for being caught off-guard by the monster, he slunk along the hedgeside, ears pricked and mouth open, tasting for danger with every breath. The grass clung wetly to his fur and he was shivering violently by the time the hedge dwindled, leaving long strands of spiked, silver vines in its place to mark the edge of the field.

Talltail sniffed the vines. There was no scent of earth or wood to them. They ran long and barbed between wooden stalks. Beyond the row of stalks, a path of smooth, white stone stretched to a wooden wall that loomed up, taller than a tree. Eager to get clear of the soggy grass, Talltail ducked beneath the lowest vine and padded onto the white stone. The clearing was wide and square, walled by stone on either side.

Had he seen this place from Outlook Rock? He opened his mouth and let scent wash his tongue. The jumble of unfamiliar smells confused him. Pelt pricking, he pictured the view from the moor. This must be the small cluster of Twoleg dens that sat between the Thunderpath and Highstones, sheltering among the curving fields like chicks in a nest. He realized that the tall, wooden wall was part of a huge den. He remembered its roof, wide and square, towering beside a cluster of small stone dens. Lights had shone from the smaller dens and smoke had plumed from their roofs. But no light or smoke had ever flashed from the great wooden nest. Talltail sniffed it and smelled the warm scent of prey. Did Twolegs store fresh-kill there?

Keeping low, Talltail crept toward it, belly growling at the thought of an easy meal. He scanned the wall, searching for gaps in the wood. A dog barked. Talltail stiffened. The barking grew louder and sharpened into an excited yelp. He spun around to see two black-and-white dogs clear a low stone wall that surrounded one of the smaller dens and hurtle toward him. Their eyes blazed with excitement.

Talltail ran. His paws skidded on the smooth stone and he stretched out his claws, fighting to get a grip. Jaws snapped at his tail and he shot forward, heart bursting with terror. The wooden wall loomed ahead. He veered around, heading for the corner. A stone wall blocked his way. He leaped it, landing smoothly on the other side. Grass crowded the wooden wall here. Talltail plunged through it, searching desperately for a gap in the wood to squeeze through. Behind him, paws scrambled clumsily over the wall.

Talltail glanced back, relieved to see the dogs land awkwardly, crashing into each other as they fought to take the lead. Paws tangling, it took a moment for them to regain their footing. But they were fast and long-legged. He couldn't outrun them for long. Their yelping grew louder. Their breath billowed over his haunches.

Run!

Talltail's mind whirled in terror, but he forced himself to focus, his heart leaping as he spotted a split in the wood. He shot through it, splinters jabbing his pelt, his shoulders almost getting stuck as he forced his way in. Relief swamped him as he heard the dogs howling outside. There was no way they'd squeeze through behind him. He looked around, blinking as his eyes adjusted to the shadows inside the den. Pale light spilled through narrow gaps high up the walls. Bundles of dry grass loomed up on every side, bound into blocks and stacked neatly all the way to the roof. The air smelled dry and dusty, like grass in greenleaf.

Behind him the dogs scrabbled, whimpering, at the wood. Talltail spun around, his tail bushed up. A snout poked through the gap, sharp, yellow teeth showing as the dog drew back its lips and growled. With another shove, the rotten wood splintered. A paw reached in, then a shaggy, brown shoulder and a drooling, snarling muzzle.

Talltail fled as the wood split and the dogs exploded into the den, howling with triumph. He hurled himself at one of the grass piles, relieved to find the bundles tightly packed enough to support his weight as he scrambled up the side. He dug in his claws, scooting up like a squirrel. Behind him the dogs yelped and jumped, their breath hot and stinking on his tail. But this was too steep for them to climb with their ungainly paws. They slid back every time they tried to get a grip on the dried grass, landing with a snapping, yowling thud.

Talltail reached the top and peered down. Whining, the dogs paced at the bottom, their eyes blazing with fury. Outside, a Twoleg squeal made them freeze. The dogs looked at each other, glanced balefully at Talltail, then turned and ran, squeezing out through the gap they'd forced open.

Talltail sank onto the bundled grass, dizzy with relief. The ground swam beneath him, so far away he felt like he'd climbed a tree. The top of the grass stack was prickly; stalks jabbed his flank. But it was dry and warm. Mouse scent hung in the air. His belly growled, but hunting would mean climbing down from his safe nest, and the dogs might come back. Shadows swallowed the space beyond the grass stacks, growing deeper as the sun set outside. He might as well rest here for the night. Spiraling around, Talltail smoothed out a place to sleep. He curled into a tight ball and tucked his nose beneath his paws. His breathing slowed.

I made it. He'd left the Clan. He pictured his Clanmates settling down for their twilight feeding time, and waited for a prick of regret. But nothing stirred except the peace of being alone. Purring, his body softened as he drifted into sleep.

Talltail woke with a start, heart racing. *Where am I?* He blinked, recognizing the bundled grass, pale in the early light. *The wooden den.* He stretched, scenting mouse, and peered over the edge. No fresh scents of dogs. They hadn't come back. Scrambling down, he landed lightly on the smooth earthen floor.

No dawn patrol. No hunting duty. Someone else would have to clear the old sheepswool from Flailfoot's nest. Excitement surged beneath his pelt. He was free to follow his destiny!

Tiny paws scuttled at the edge of his hearing. Talltail braced himself, opening his mouth to taste the air. Mouse scents seeped from every shadowy corner. Stifling a purr of satisfaction, he crept forward. His tail whisked the stray grass stalks that littered the floor. He lifted the tip up, careful to keep quiet. Something moved in the shadows. He fixed his gaze on a flicker of brown fur and moved toward it, drawing himself silently forward, paw by paw. This wasn't how he was used to hunting, but Talltail knew there was no room to give chase in here. He had to creep up on his prey instead.

He could see the mouse more clearly now that his eyes had adjusted to the gloom. It had picked up a grass stalk and was nibbling the seeds at the tip. Talltail crept closer, holding his breath. The mouse glanced around, then went back to nibbling. Talltail showed his teeth. Then he leaped. He slammed his paws down onto the soft back of the mouse. It was already dead by the time he reached forward to nip its spine.

Sitting up, he let his purr rumble out loud, then tucked into his meal, savoring the richness of its flesh. Prey tasted different here. There was no flavor of heather and peat. It was fatty and moist and sang on his tongue. *And very easy to catch!*

A dog barked in the distance. Talltail stiffened. It was time he moved on, easy prey or not. The dogs wouldn't stay away forever. He swallowed his last mouthful and padded around the base of the grass pile, scanning the wooden wall for the hole the dogs had chased him through. It was much bigger now, jagged-edged and filled with bright light. Tasting the air warily, Talltail stuck out his head. The air was damp, and dripping grass soaked his muzzle. The hard frost had broken, giving way to low, gray clouds. A steady drizzle sprayed Talltail's face. He fluffed out his fur and padded from the wooden nest, crossing the grass toward another stone wall. The dog barked again, its companion joining in, raising their voices to a howl. They'd come looking for him soon.

Talltail broke into a run and leaped onto the wall in an easy bound. The land on the other side was wooded and sloped steeply up. To one side he could see past the line of trees to the distant Highstones. Would the rogues have gone there? Talltail narrowed his eyes. Why should they? They preferred to eat other cats' prey. Why would they head for stony, bushless slopes, where the only prey would have to be stalked with more skill than they possessed? Besides, the stones would hurt their paws. They may be used to traveling, but he guessed they only followed the softest paths that they could find.

He looked the other way, spotting a smooth, grass path at the edge of the tree line. That was the sort of route they'd choose. He jumped down and trekked along it, glancing into the shadowy woods. Would they have gone in? The trees would give shelter. He should check it out. The thought made his pelt prick. Even though the tall branches were bare, they still crowded out the sky. Taking a deep breath, he headed into the trees.

He pricked his ears, his heart quickening at the sighing of the wind above. It set the branches rattling, and as he passed a slender ash, he heard it creak ominously. Talltail darted forward, fear flaring. Did trees fall down? Was he going to get crushed? The dark gray sky glowered above, not giving enough light to throw shadows. Instead the trunks of all the trees were swallowed up in gloom, filled with brambles to trip unwary paws and holes to make him stumble.

Talltail's nose twitched. Rabbit scents hung on the damp

air. Birds, too, and other forest prey he'd smelled on trips to
Fourtrees. *Mole. Shrew. Vole.* ThunderClan prey. His prey, too,
now. His belly grumbled, but it was too dark to hunt properly.
He'd have to wait for some kind of clearing in the trees.

The ground started to slope upward, but Talltail leaped
easily up the rise and scrambled onto rocky overhangs until he
reached the crest. He was still in the forest, but it was lighter
here, the trees spaced farther apart. He breathed the damp
air, wondering which way to head. Along the ridge or down
the far side? Cat scent touched his tongue. *Tom, not from a Clan.*
His heart lurched. *Could it be Sparrow?*

Had he found him already? Perhaps this wood was where
the rogues holed up for leaf-bare, sheltering like prey beneath
the branches. Talltail leaned down and sniffed the ground.
Paws had passed this way. He walked slowly forward, muzzle close to the ground. The scent trail headed down the far
slope and disappeared beneath brambles. Screwing up his eyes
against the thorns, Talltail followed it. He ignored the prickles
scraping his spine as he wriggled underneath, and eventually
emerged onto boggy ground where his paws sank into cold
mud. The scent trail was fresher here. He was gaining ground.

Talltail's thoughts whirled. Sparrow was at the end of this
track. He *knew* it. He imagined sighting the rogue's short,
brown fur between the trees and creeping silently up behind
him. He swallowed back a growl as he pictured plunging his
claws deep into Sparrow's flesh. His pelt spiked with excitement and he hurried forward, darting over the mud as easily
as crossing grass. Bracken blocked his path but he pushed

through, ears flattening as the stench of tom led him forward. As he weaved through the tawny stems, he spotted movement ahead.

Sparrow! Fur flashed behind a bush. *I've got you!* Triumph surged through his paws. He broke into a run. With a hiss, he skidded around the bush and sprang. He landed a whisker from the tom, snarling. "You thought you'd gotten away—"

He stopped, his eyes bulging with surprise.

A shocked gray tom stared back at him, blinking. "What in the stars are you doing?"

Talltail backed away. "I—I thought you were someone else," he stammered. He smelled fear-scent on the tom and sheathed his claws. "I wasn't going to—"

"I hope not!" The tom straightened up and Talltail realized how scrawny he was. His pelt was clumped in sticky knots as though he hardly washed. Was this a kittypet? Talltail knew they were lazy, but too lazy to wash?

The tom glared at him. "Who did you think I was?"

"Just another cat," Talltail mumbled.

"Not a friend, I guess."

"Not exactly. Someone I used to know."

The tom opened his mouth, tasting Talltail's scent. "You smell of Clan," he grunted. "Were you looking for one of your own?" Talltail shook his head. "Good." The tom sat down and whisked his tail over his paws. "One Clan cat is bad enough." He narrowed his eyes. "What are you doing out here?" He snorted. "Don't answer. I don't want to know."

"I'm looking for some rogues. I really need to find them."

The tom rolled his eyes. "I said *don't* answer." He sighed heavily. "What rogues?"

"They used to visit us every greenleaf," Talltail told him.

"You're a moor cat, right?" The tom's nose was twitching. "I can smell the heather on you." He glanced between the trees. "I once knew some cats who spent time on the moor."

"Was one of them brown?" Talltail leaned forward.

"I don't remember," the tom answered.

"Did they travel in a group? A black-and-white one, and a ginger one, and a gray tom with a ruffled pelt?" Talltail's paws pricked.

"Slow down, Clan cat," the tom muttered. "I'm not used to answering questions."

Talltail took a breath. This old cat wasn't going to be rushed. He might not share anything if Talltail annoyed him. "I just wondered if you'd seen them recently," he meowed.

"Might have."

Talltail curled his claws into the earth. "This moon? Last moon?"

The tom looked thoughtful. "Last moon," he grunted eventually. "Near a Nofur's den."

"Which den?" Talltail had seen countless Twoleg dens from Outlook Rock.

"Sun-up way. Dark gray," the tom told him. "Bigger than some. It has a spike sticking up at one end like a tail."

Talltail frowned, trying to remember if he'd seen a den like that.

"Don't go inside," the tom warned. "It's colder than death

and when the Twoleg shuts the door, there's no way out." The thought seemed to alarm him. He got to his paws, his tail quivering. "I was trapped there once for three sun-ups. Glad they had a water-pool."

Talltail's mind was whirling. *Gray den with a spike.* He began to head away.

"Where are you going?" the tom called after him. "Do you want to share prey? I hear Clan cats are good hunters."

Talltail called over his shoulder. "I can't stop. I have to find this cat." His heart raced and he broke into a run, swerving clumsily between the trees.

I'm on your trail, Sparrow. You'd better start sleeping with one eye open!

CHAPTER 28
❧

Sun-up way. Talltail plunged down the hillside. *That's past ShadowClan territory.* He scrambled past a hawthorn, skidding as the slope steepened. Bracken slowed him down, dragging at his paws. He pushed through it, relieved that the slope was flattening out, and paused at the bottom to taste the air. Ahead of him the trees were thinning and light showed beyond them. Talltail hurried on, relaxing as he reached the edge of the woods and padded out onto grass. The drizzle had turned to rain and he narrowed his eyes. He'd patrolled the moor many times in worse rain than this. Keeping low, he crossed the grass, ignoring the water dripping from his whiskers. A familiar scent touched his nose. He had reached the Thunderpath.

He slowed, pelt pricking. He knew he had to cross the Thunderpath, but that would put him directly into ShadowClan territory, which might be more dangerous than anything that lay beyond. He shook the rain from his pelt and approached the Thunderpath. It was empty. Sniffing the stone, he smelled the stale scent of monsters. Nothing had passed for a while. He glanced both ways to make sure there were no monsters lying in wait, then raced across.

The stench of the ShadowClan border hit him before he was halfway across. Brambles, nettles, and ferns spilled from the thick wall of pine trees in front of him. The shadow beyond them was so dark that he couldn't see in. Heart quickening, Talltail scanned the gloom for flashing eyes. Was a Shadow-Clan patrol watching? He ducked down and crept into the grass at the edge of the Thunderpath. There was no way he could go straight across the territory. ShadowClan warriors wouldn't let him escape with his fur intact. He'd have to follow the scent line, being careful not to cross it and praying that he didn't bump into any patrols that objected to him straying so close.

He turned and started to push his way through the grass under the trees. Several monsters roared past in a herd, spraying him with muddy water. Talltail hissed and pressed closer to the tree trunks, swerving away again when the reek of Shad-owClan scent marks stung his nose. He trekked on, soaked right through his fur by the dripping grass stems. Eventually the pines began to thin beside him, replaced by rough scrub, shriveled bushes that rattled their bare branches in the wind. A smaller Thunderpath appeared ahead of him, leading away from the moor and curving around the top of ShadowClan territory. Talltail followed the new Thunderpath, hoping the grass was enough to hide him as the scrubby bushes gave way to an open stretch of marsh.

He walked faster, feeling vulnerable and cold. The scent of ShadowClan was overlaid with something stronger here: a sour, unfamiliar smell that made Talltail's belly churn. He shook rain from his whiskers and opened his mouth. He shut it quickly as a putrid stench swamped his tongue. It smelled like death and rot and stagnant water. Peering through the rain, he saw a wall of woven silver vines surrounding several huge, stinking lumps, like the backs of hunched beasts lying down. Queasy at the stink rolling from the heap, Talltail padded closer. Could this be the Carrionplace? He'd heard ShadowClan apprentices boasting about catching rats where Twolegs dumped their waste. His nose wrinkled. Who would want to eat fresh-kill from such a foul-smelling place?

The grass vanished as he drew level with the silver vines, and Talltail ran across the stretch of hard, gray stone until he reached the safety of a ditch. He scrambled down into the thick-stemmed plants, ignoring the greasy, black water that clung to his belly fur and pushing his way through until the stench of Carrionplace faded behind him. Talltail climbed out, shaking filthy droplets from his pelt. The rain hardened into hail. It stung his ears and his nose, bouncing off the Thunderpath and bombarding him until he could hardly see. Through narrowed eyes, he looked for shelter. Pine trees clustered ahead, right on the edge of the Thunderpath. Talltail broke into a run, nostrils twitching. He was still close to the ShadowClan border.

He ducked in among the pines, eyes lighting up when he spotted a hole in a gnarled trunk. He dug his claws into the cracked bark and hauled himself up until he was high enough to stick his head into the hole. Inside, leaf litter lined a crooked scoop in the wood. Talltail scrambled inside, scenting the stale smell of prey. What creature had sheltered here?

He didn't care. He was just glad to be out of the hail. He shook out his pelt and sat down. Hailstones cracked outside. The wind roared above. Talltail looked up and saw a small circle of sky where the trunk opened at the top. A hailstone bounced down and landed on his nose. He flinched and curled into the dry leaves. Flattening his ears against the spattering hail, he tucked his nose under his paw.

He must have slept, because voices woke him. Heart lurching, Talltail jerked forward and peered out from the tree. The hail had stopped and dark gray-and-brown pelts were weaving around the bottom of the trunk. The scent of ShadowClan filled the air. Talltail dodged back, fur bristling. *A patrol!* Had he crossed the border? He jumped to his paws and desperately scanned his cramped shelter. He was trapped!

"The scents are fresh." He heard a ShadowClan warrior snarl. "He must still be here somewhere."

Claws scrabbled outside the trunk. "There's a hole up there."

"Let's look."

Talltail froze. They'd think he was a spy. They'd haul him in front of Cedarstar. At the very best, he'd be sent back to WindClan. At the worst . . . He pushed away the thought and glanced up at the tiny circle of light at the top of the tree. There was a way out—if he could reach it. Digging his claws into the soft wood, he began to haul himself up. He braced his hind legs against the other side of the trunk and wedged himself high above the nest. There was a scraping noise outside and he glanced down.

A mottled tabby head poked in and sniffed the leaves. "They're still warm," he growled.

Talltail held his breath. *Please, don't look up!*

The head ducked back out. Fast as a squirrel, Talltail scrabbled his way farther up the tree trunk. Above his head, the circle of light grew until he could feel fresh air washing over him. His claws screamed with pain as he dragged himself up the last tail-length. Leaves rustled below as a ShadowClan warrior jumped into the hollow and began sniffing at the nest. "Are you sure you can't see him?" he called out to his Clanmates.

Talltail grabbed for the top of the trunk and hauled himself over the rim. Shards of bark showered down the shaft beneath him. He scrambled onto a crooked, lightning-blasted branch. Rotten with age, it creaked beneath his weight. He clung to it, flattening himself against the wood, praying it was wide enough to shield him from the gaze of the cats below.

"I heard something."

"It must be a squirrel."

"Smells like a tom."

"A cat couldn't climb that high."

"Do you recognize the scent?"

"Stagnant water and earth. Too rank for a Clan cat."

Talltail prickled with indignation.

"It could be one of those rogues we chased off last moon."

"Those cats that smelled like WindClan? Why would they come back? I clawed that she-cat's ears until she shrieked!"

He pricked his ears. *The rogues came this way!* He was still on Sparrow's trail. A surge of hope sliced through his terror.

"Let's check the Thunderpath." The ShadowClan warrior's mew echoed up the hollow trunk. "He's obviously not in here anymore."

Talltail clung to the branch, his heart pounding so hard that he feared it was ringing through the wood. Gingerly he peered down. Four warriors searched far below, picking their way among the tangled roots of the pine, sniffing every scent, their pelts bristling. Talltail's legs began to ache, his claws throbbing with the effort of clinging on. *Go away!* He willed the patrol to move on, but they circled the trees again and again, tails flicking with anger.

At last one of the warriors wandered toward the open grass. "The trail comes from this way."

"Let's track it." The mottled warrior padded after him.

Talltail watched as one by one the warriors headed away from the trees. They trekked across the grass, following his trail back along the Thunderpath. As soon as they were out of sight, he scrambled down the tree, feeling a rush of relief as his paws touched solid earth. Despite the cramp tightening his muscles, he ran fast as a rabbit, breaking through the scent line he hadn't noticed in his rush to shelter among the trees, and diving across the narrow Thunderpath into a wall of thick bushes.

He slowed, catching his breath. Not much farther on, the bushes gave way to dense woodland. Oak and ash pushed up through patches of bramble. The cloudy sky showed through their bare branches. Talltail tasted the air. There were no Clan scents here. Bracken crowded between the trunks and hawthorn snagged his pelt, but he felt safe for the first time in a long while. As he pushed on, shadows darkened around him. The sun must be sinking. How could he tell where it was when he was trapped in all these trees? Tail drooping, Talltail padded to a halt. It was pointless trying to guess which way to go. He should wait till dawn and head for sun-up.

He pushed past a clump of shriveled ferns and found himself in a small clearing ringed by trees. There wasn't enough sky to navigate by, but at least he wasn't being smothered by branches. He curled among the jutting roots of the nearest oak. His belly growled, but he was too tired to hunt. Instead he laid his chin on his paws and closed his eyes.

"Talltail!" Sandgorse's mew echoed through the dark. "Listen!"

"What is it?" Talltail looked wildly around, but all he could see was the blackness of shadow, washed with scents of trees.

"Talltail!"

"Sandgorse!" Talltail strained to hear a reply but the wind grew stronger and lashed the branches above him, drowning out every other sound. "Sandgorse?" Talltail woke with a start. Sunlight was flashing between the tree trunks and the air was still. He had been dreaming—but why hadn't Sandgorse been able to speak to him? His belly twisted with hunger and he jumped to his paws. He would have to hope that Sandgorse visited him in his dreams again. Now it was time to get moving, to put some distance between him and ShadowClan.

Above his head the small patch of visible sky was pale blue, glowing at one edge with gold-pink beams of light. *Sun-up!* Talltail whirled around until he was facing the rays from the rising sun. At last he knew which way to go. Ignoring his rumbling belly, he pushed through bracken and ducked under a bramble. A trailing branch caught his paw and he tripped, cursing as pain shot through his leg. Limping, he hurried on, but after a few paces he stubbed another paw on a jutting root, and winced as thorns stabbed his pelt. How did forest cats get anywhere?

Birds twittered in the branches, making his belly growl more loudly. He had to find food. He needed to be strong when he caught up with Sparrow. He paused and tasted the air. *Mouse.* Talltail crouched down and scanned the undergrowth. A dead leaf trembled at the bottom of a bramble. Talltail saw a flash of brown fur and pounced. The mouse shot away. Talltail darted after it, squeezing beneath the thorny branches. He exploded from the other side of the bush to see the mouse scuttle over the roots of a tree and race for the safety of a hawthorn bush.

Talltail peered through the spiky branches. He could see the mouse trembling beside the stem, and reached in with a paw. He patted the ground, his claws stretched as he tried to reach the tiny creature. It hurtled away and skittered out the other side of the bush. Talltail dodged around, his paws skidding on leaves. He glimpsed the mouse as it scuttled into a swathe of bracken, and plunged in after it. Crashing through the stems, he zigzagged after it, trying to slam his paws down on the blur of brown fur, first one way, then another, always just a moment too late.

Dumb mouse! He cursed under his breath as it disappeared through a hole in a high, wooden barrier. The scent of it filled his nose. Hungrily Talltail leaped onto the top of the wood. Ahead, red Twoleg dens blocked his view. Crowded together, with sharp edges, they seemed to glower at him through big, square eyes. Talltail blinked at them, feeling the fur rise along his spine.

A square patch of grass lay between him and the closest den. More wooden walls divided the stretch of land behind the dens into a row of tiny meadows. Talltail scanned the grass for the mouse. No sign. He padded along the top of the narrow wall, leaping the thick stalk that blocked the way to the next and peering into the little meadow. The mouse wasn't there either. Talltail curled his lip. He'd have caught that mouse on the moor. No dumb bushes or wooden walls to get in his way.

Something moved in a clump of wilting leaves below. His nose twitched. He could smell the mouse and see its brown back cowering under a leaf. Fixing his gaze on its pelt, he jumped down, his paws sinking into wet earth. He darted forward and grabbed the mouse in his teeth, killing it with a bite. Ravenous, he began to eat. *Thank you, StarClan!* The moist, fatty flesh tasted great. He chewed loudly, relishing the flavor. As he swallowed the last mouthful, a growl rumbled behind him.

Dog!

CHAPTER 29

☙

Talltail whirled around. A massive dog loomed over him, teeth glistening, eyes sparking with rage.

It lunged, and at the same instant Talltail ducked. Jaws snapped at his shoulder, tugging out fur. Screeching with pain, Talltail raced for the fence and leaped onto it, dropping down the other side. A narrow passage ran beside the red-stone den. Talltail charged along it, claws spraying grit behind him. Another tall, wooden fence blocked the end, but he scaled it and jumped down from the top.

A Thunderpath lay in front of him with a monster roaring along it. Talltail froze, pelt bushing. Behind him, the dog barked furiously. Could it get over the fence? *I'm not waiting to find out!* As soon as the monster had passed, Talltail fled across the Thunderpath. Dodging into a tiny gap between two stone dens, he raced through the bushes at the back, then hurtled past another den. Swerving onto a stone path that led between blank walls, he kept running, his breath coming in gasps. Shapes blurred around him as he ran. Monsters howled, endless fences blocked his path, but he kept dodging and jumping, refusing to give the dog a chance to catch him.

Eventually, chest heaving, Talltail scrambled to a halt. He

glanced over his shoulder. No sign of any dog. Red stone walls loomed over him on three sides. Blood welled on his shoulder where he'd lost fur. He limped toward a heap of stinking bundles that had been piled in the corner of the passage. It smelled like Carrionplace, but right now it looked like a place to shelter. Crouching behind it, he tried to catch his breath.

Sunshine sliced between the walls, striping the middle of the passage. Talltail trembled, dazed and sore. Panic began to swirl in his belly. *How will I ever find my way through Twolegplace, let alone find Sparrow?* He lapped at the patch of raw flesh on his shoulder. If only Barkface were there with soothing herbs. *You will have to hunt for yourself, heal yourself if you get hurt. There will be no one to share your victories. Or your defeats.* Heatherstar's words rang in his mind. *I can do it,* he told himself.

A clang made him freeze. He jerked up his head, pelt bristling. The noise came from around the corner. Another crash rang through the air. Talltail began to back away. A dog yelped excitedly. Talltail felt the fur rise along his spine. Had it tracked him here?

A cat screeched in alarm. It was in trouble.

Leave it. Talltail stared in the direction of the noise, his mind whirling. *I can't!* He hadn't trained to be a warrior to leave other cats in danger! He raced forward and swung around the corner at the end. A ginger tom was cowering in the corner of a walled dead end, his green eyes wide with alarm. A brown-and-white dog the size of a badger barked in his face while the tom swung out in a frenzy with his claws.

A different dog! Twolegplace was swarming with them. But this time Talltail wasn't going to run. A cat was in trouble.

Talltail focused his mind. There was rage in the tom's eyes, as if all he needed was a bit of luck for the battle to go his way. Talltail sprang onto the wall and ran along it until he was level with the dog. He stopped beside the dog, eyeing its back, then unsheathed his claws and jumped. He landed squarely on the dog's shoulders, ripping into its flesh. As the dog bucked and yelped beneath Talltail, the ginger tom reared up and swiped its muzzle. Talltail leaped down, landing beside the tom. Watching his paw movements from the corner of his eye, Talltail matched them swipe for swipe. The dog began to back away, its eyes clouding with confusion, then with fear. It snapped at the ginger cat once more, then yelped with frustration, turned, and fled.

Talltail dropped onto all fours. The tom collapsed beside him, flanks heaving.

"Are you okay?" Talltail sniffed the other cat's pelt. No blood scent.

The tom lifted his head. "I'm just catching my breath."

"Did it bite you?"

"Didn't get close enough." The tom heaved himself to his paws, staggering a little as his forepaw buckled beneath him. Talltail glanced at it. "Just a sprain," the tom told him. "I turned it on a stone while I was running." He stared at Talltail. "Thanks, by the way. I thought I was a goner."

Talltail stared at him. "Goner?"

"Dog food," the tom explained. *"Dead."*

"You shouldn't have let yourself get chased into a corner," Talltail told him bluntly.

"You think?"

Talltail tucked his hindquarters under him, ready to spring back up onto the wall and leave. It was starting to rain and he needed to find somewhere to shelter for the night.

"What's your name?" the ginger tom called. "I'm Jake."

"I'm Talltail." He hopped up onto the wall. "You should get out of here. The dog might come back."

"You're a Clan cat, aren't you?" Jake blinked up at him. "From over the fences? I've always wondered about the wild cats who live in the woods."

"That's ThunderClan." Talltail fluffed out his fur against the rain.

"So you're a ThunderClan cat."

"*Thunder*Clan?" Talltail felt a flicker of annoyance. "No way! There's more than one Clan."

"Really?" Jake's eyes bulged.

"I have to go." *I'm not here to make friends.* "Get away from here before the dog—"

"—comes back. I know. Well, thanks for helping me out."

"Be more careful in the future." Talltail sprang down the other side of the wall into another tiny meadow that backed onto a red-stone den. This meadow had shrubs growing around the edge. A hedge ran along one side and Talltail hurried across the grass and squeezed through, popping out into another little green square. He padded over it, glancing warily at the Twoleg den at the end, then tasting the air for dogs. The rain was falling heavily now, drenching his pelt. He scrambled over the far fence into an identical space. Talltail wondered why Twolegs made so many barriers. Didn't they have scent marks?

Kittypet scent touched his nose as he landed on another patch of wet grass. A ginger-and-black she-cat was sheltering under a bush near the Twoleg den. Perhaps she could give him a clue if he was headed in the right direction. He padded toward her, blinking calmly at her to reassure her.

She huddled deeper under the bush, her pelt bristling, her eyes wide with alarm.

"I only want to ask you a question," Talltail called.

She stared at him. "My Twolegs will be back in a moment. They'll chase you off." She lifted her muzzle bravely.

Talltail stopped a tail-length from the bush. "Before they do, can you tell me if you've seen any rogues around here recently?"

"Only you." The she-cat backed away.

Talltail gazed at her wearily. "I'm a Clan cat."

"A Clan cat?" Her pelt spiked. "That's worse!" Eyes sparking with terror, she scrabbled from the bush and hared toward the fence, leaping over it and disappearing.

Talltail shook out his pelt. He was tired and hungry and had no idea if he was getting any closer to the rogues. He didn't know if he would ever find his way out of this forest of Twoleg dens. And his belly was growling again. He had to find food. He hurried through the rain and leaped the next wall. A small wooden den sat at one end of the bushy clearing. It looked deserted, too small for Twolegs to live in, too ramshackle for pampered kittypets. *A good place for prey to hide.* He stalked toward it, searching the sides for a gap. There was a small hole at one corner. The edge was ragged. Small teeth had chewed it.

Rat? He'd never eaten rat. But it was food. He crept into the shadowy den, his nose wrinkling as pungent smells wreathed around him. He swallowed his rising queasiness. They were just scents. They couldn't hurt him. He slunk around the pieces of wood that littered the den floor, sniffing for prey and wondering if he'd even smell it through the stink. He blinked in the gloom. Something was lying on the ground in the corner. Talltail padded toward it, nose twitching. The soft, dead body of a rat showed in the half light. Someone had left prey behind.

Dumb kittypets. What was the point of catching prey if you didn't eat it? He crouched beside the rat and took a bite. It was so fresh, it was still warm. There was a sharp taste to its flesh, barely detectible over the thick scents swirling around the shed. *Twolegplace rats must taste different.* Hungrily Talltail took another bite. His belly heaved. *I have to eat. I have to stay strong.*

He forced himself to keep chewing despite the taste, swallowing until every morsel was gone. Relieved, he licked his lips, thinking longingly of fresh moor rabbit. The weight in his belly made him sleepy. He curled down onto the hard floor and closed his eyes, flattening his ears against the thundering of the rain. It might stink in here, but at least it was dry. Tucking his nose under his paw, he tried to ignore the tiny jabs in his belly. *I ate too fast.* He curled up tighter and let sleep enfold him.

CHAPTER 30

Talltail's belly was gripped in vicious jaws with teeth that bit through fur, skin, muscle. *What's happening?* He screeched in agony and fought to get free. He woke with a gasp, staring into the shadows that filled the wooden den. The pain in his belly didn't disappear. It hardened, making him writhe. Jerking, he vomited. He hauled himself to his paws and dragged himself from the den. *So thirsty!*

Thoughts clouded with pain, he staggered across the wet grass, lapping at the raindrops until he reached a puddle. He drank desperately, but as soon as the water hit his belly, another painful spasm seized him. He vomited again, unable to stop himself. But the tormenting thirst was still there, as if all the water in the world would not quench the fire inside him. Terrified, Talltail crouched on the wet grass and sank his claws into the earth. *StarClan, help me!* He let out a long desperate moan.

"Talltail?" A voice sounded from somewhere above him.

Had Sandgorse come to take him to StarClan? Talltail looked up weakly, then opened his mouth to release a thin stream of bile. Paws landed on the grass beside him. A muzzle reached toward his. He was dimly aware of warm breath bathing his nose.

"You ate that rat, didn't you?" The shocked mew rang in his ear. "Didn't you realize it was poisoned? I didn't think Clan cats would be so dumb!"

Jake. Talltail recognized the voice and saw ginger fur, pale in the moonlight. "Help me," he rasped.

"Wait here." Jake backed away and vanished.

Talltail was too weak to move. His body twitched, helpless with pain; he had no power to resist the spasms. Vomit dribbled from his mouth, jerked up by another convulsion. *If I die, I'll see Sandgorse.* Through his haze of pain, a pale light gleamed. *I'm sorry I didn't avenge your death.* Grief flooded him. He'd failed his father again.

He heard murmuring. It had the rumbling thickness of Twoleg mewling. *Am I dreaming?* A huge, blurry shape loomed out of the darkness. *What's happening?* Terror gripped him through the fog of pain. He tried to struggle. *I have to escape.* Vast, naked paws lifted him up. Talltail felt the ground fall away as he was swooped into the air. Something warm and yielding enfolded him, similar to the sheepswool he had used to line his nest so long ago. Then he was bouncing along, wrapped in stifling softness. Shapes whirled around him and a loud slam pierced his ear fur. He coughed up phlegm, his belly empty.

A deep, throbbing noise shook the air around him. *Monster!* Somewhere deep in Talltail's mind, fear tried to stir, but he didn't even have enough strength to be scared. Pain twisted his belly tighter and tighter until he was blind to everything but agony.

Talltail was woken by a sharp scent that reminded him of pine trees. Was he still inside the hollow trunk, trapped by a ShadowClan patrol? No, this smell was different somehow, and he was lying on a bed of sheepswool that definitely hadn't been inside that tree trunk. He forced open his eyes. They were sticky with sleep and he had to blink to clear the fuzziness from his vision. Wherever he was, it was filled with dark gray shadows. Talltail pushed himself to his paws. His belly felt crushed, but the jerking agony had gone and he didn't feel sick or thirsty anymore. He peered through the darkness and realized that there were smooth, sheer walls a muzzle-length away on every side of him. *I'm trapped!* Panic made his heart beat faster at the same time as his eyes adjusted to the light and he began to see more clearly. He was in a short tunnel with a square of silver mesh blocking the way to a pale gleam that was seeping through one end. Talltail yowled, terror making his belly twist again and awakening the pain.

"It's okay!" A familiar mew sounded through the mesh. "You're safe, I promise."

Jake! "Where am I?"

"You're in my home. I fetched my housefolk after I found you," Jake explained. "I had to fake a bellyache to get him to follow me. I knew he'd help you when he saw how sick you were."

Talltail pressed his muzzle against the mesh. "Let me out."

"I can't." Jake's ginger face stared back at him, eyes round with sympathy. "But it's okay. You're in the vet-basket."

Talltail swallowed. "Vet-basket?"

"It's a cage the housefolk use to carry me to the vet," Jake explained. "I know you hate it. I hate it too, but my housefolk will let you out soon."

"What's a vet?" Talltail could feel his legs buckling from the strangeness of everything.

"The no-fur that cured you of the poison."

"No-fur? You mean a Twoleg cured me?" Talltail's mouth hung open. "Like a medicine cat?"

Jake stared blankly at him. "I guess. It saved your life."

Talltail bristled. Why would a Twoleg save a cat's life? He tried to see through the mesh, but Jake was blocking his view. He could glimpse a roof above, white walls with clear, empty squares where he could see treetops and sky outside and, some way below his . . . his *vet-basket*, a floor of shiny, white stone. The vet-basket seemed to be balanced on a ledge halfway up one wall.

"So this is your den?" Talltail croaked.

"You could call it that," Jake meowed. "It's where I live with my housefolk. This part is my eating room."

Huge paw steps clumped behind Jake and he hopped out of the way. A moment later, a Twoleg face peered through the mesh at Talltail. Talltail's heart lurched. The wide, pink face crinkled as the Twoleg rumbled through the mesh. Then the mesh swung open and the Twoleg thrust in a huge, pink paw. Talltail hissed and pressed himself back against the end of the basket. He unsheathed his claws, ready to rake the Twoleg if it came too close. The paw was holding a shallow stone, scooped out and filled with water. The Twoleg placed it on the soft floor of the basket, then withdrew his paw and shut the mesh. Talltail waited for the Twoleg to clump away, then crept forward and sniffed the water. It smelled sour, not like spring water.

"It's okay." Jake had jumped in front of the mesh again. "You can drink it."

"It smells funny."

"It's from the tap," Jake told him. "It's not as nice as rainwater but it won't harm you."

Talltail lapped up a mouthful, wrinkling his nose. He tensed as it hit his stomach, frightened it would hurt again, but his belly only gurgled. "How long before your Twoleg lets me go?"

"My housefolk, you mean? I guess he wants to make sure you're better," Jake told him.

Talltail remembered how Hawkheart had made him stay in his nest when he was injured. Twolegs must do the same.

"I'm going out," Jake told him suddenly.

"Where?"

"Just out."

Don't leave me on my own! Talltail blinked as Jake jumped from the ledge onto the shiny, white floor, then pushed a flap in the wall and wriggled through. Fear began to spiral in Talltail's tender belly. Would he ever get out of here? The rogues would be traveling farther and farther away while he was trapped.

He edged into the shadow at the end of the basket and sat down stiffly, ashamed for wishing that Jake would come back. *Be brave! You left your Clan. You don't need anyone!*

After what felt like a whole moon, Jake dived through the flap. The Twoleg stomped into the eating room at the same moment and stroked him. Jake arched his back and lifted his tail, purring as the Twoleg showered tiny brown pebbles into a hollow stone on the floor. Jake stuck his nose in and ate. Talltail's nose wrinkled as he picked up the scent of Jake's food. He'd heard the elders talk about kittypet slop, but he never imagined he would see it close up. Then again, he'd never imagined he'd find himself inside a Twoleg den, with only a kittypet for company.

The Twoleg face loomed at the mesh again. Talltail hissed in surprise. The Twoleg purred and dropped a few brown pebbles through the mesh. Talltail hissed once more and the Twoleg clumped away. Talltail crept forward and sniffed the pebbles. They smelled a little bit like prey, but different, like the water. Why did Twolegs add weird scents to everything? Didn't they like ordinary tastes and smells?

"You can eat it, you know." Jake had hopped onto the ledge and was peering through the mesh.

Talltail took another sniff.

"It's not poisoned. It's the same stuff they give me," Jake promised. He sat back on his haunches and began to wash his belly.

Gingerly Talltail picked up a pebble between his teeth and bit down on it. The flavor was sharper than prey, but not dreadful. He ate another pellet and waited to see what his belly felt like. It twinged a little but he didn't feel sick. He lapped up the rest and listened to his belly growl appreciatively.

Talltail lifted his head as the Twoleg came back into the eating room. He arched his back as the mesh opened again, and stared at the gap, waiting for a Twoleg paw to appear. Nothing happened.

"You can come out," Jake mewed.

Warily Talltail crept to the front of the basket and peered out. The Twoleg was standing a few tail-lengths away. Jake jumped off the ledge and began winding around its legs, purring. The Twoleg bent down and ran its hairless paw over Jake's fur. Talltail shuddered. Then he spotted the flap Jake had leaped through earlier. This was his chance to escape! Darting forward, he jumped down from the ledge, his paws splaying as he hit the slippery floor. He struggled to his paws, his legs trembling, and scrambled unsteadily toward the flap.

Pain shot through his muzzle as he hit the unmoving flap head-on. He bounced off it like a kit running into a stone. Confused and hot with shame, he backed away. "It didn't open!" he hissed at Jake.

"My housefolk locked it before he let you out of the basket."

The Twoleg was bending toward Talltail. "Get away!" Talltail spat, swiping at its dangling paw with his claws.

In a flash, Jake was in front of him, shielding his Twoleg. "Leave him alone!" he snarled. "He saved your life!"

Talltail took a step back, bewildered. Twolegs saving cats?

The elders never told any stories about that. "Just don't let him touch me!" he growled.

The Twoleg's shoulders slumped. It turned and pushed through a large sideways flap in the other wall and closed it behind. Talltail's belly clenched. He looked helplessly at Jake's locked flap. "I want to make dirt."

Jake nodded toward a bright red, shallow nest filled with gray grit. "Use that."

"Make dirt *inside* a den?" Didn't kittypets have any shame?

"We all do it sometimes," Jake reassured him.

Talltail padded to the hard-edged nest, climbed over the edge, and stood on the grit. Kicking a hole, he made dirt and covered it, uncomfortably conscious that Jake was sitting only a few tail-lengths away. He climbed out again and paced the edges of the room. "Now what?"

"You have to rest," Jake told him.

Talltail's legs still felt shaky, but he didn't want to rest. How could he relax when he was a prisoner in a Twoleg den? He kept pacing, the ache in his belly nagging but not enough to stop him from moving. He gazed at the sky through the clear parts of the wall. It was growing dark. He'd wasted a whole day.

Every so often, the Twoleg returned to pour food and water or just to look at Talltail. Talltail returned its stare with a hiss and kept pacing. When the sky outside was finally black, the Twoleg brought in a big, soft shape and laid it on the floor. "My nest!" Jake mewed delightedly.

Talltail narrowed his eyes. Nests were small and woven out

of sticks and lined with moss. They weren't bright red and the size of a half a den.

Jake purred as he climbed into it and began pummeling the bottom. "You can sleep here too, if you like. There's plenty of room, and it's really soft."

Talltail looked up at the vet-basket on the ledge. He didn't want to sleep in the tiny tunnel, but he didn't want to sleep beside a kittypet either. He'd never get the flowery stench out of his pelt. "I'm not tired," he lied.

"You must be," Jake told him. "I'm always tired after I've been to the vet." He curled down into his nest. Talltail tried to catch a glimpse of Silverpelt in the night sky. Could StarClan see him here? But the clear square gaps just reflected the bright walls of the room. Anger surged through Talltail. He couldn't even *see* outside now. "I have to get out of here!"

"You will," Jake promised. "When you're better."

I didn't leave the Clan just to get trapped somewhere else! Talltail scowled at Jake. "Your Twoleg is cruel."

"No, he's not." Jake stared at him, and the tip of his tail flicked. "He's been nothing but kind to you."

"How can you stand being a kittypet?" Talltail wasn't listening. "Eating weird food. Purring at a Twoleg like you're kin." He snorted with disgust.

"He *is* like kin," Jake snapped back. "I've known him my whole life. He makes sure I'm warm and fed. And I sit with him and keep him company when he's alone. We talk to each other."

"Talk?" Jake was clearly a rabbit-brain.

Jake shrugged. "I don't understand exactly what he's saying, but I know what he means. I just say yes to everything. He seems to like that. And I've taught him the word for food. He tries to repeat it sometimes, but his accent is terrible."

Talltail could hardly believe what he was hearing. "You sound like you enjoy being a kittypet!"

"Of course." Jake went back to kneading his bed.

"Then why do you spend so much time staring into the woods thinking about Clan cats?" Talltail shifted his paws. They were growing numb with cold on the shiny floor.

Jake paused. "I guess I'm interested in how you live without housefolk, that's all." He tipped his head. "You said there was more than one Clan. How many?"

"Three more."

"What's yours called?"

Talltail hardly heard him. His gaze had slid toward Jake's nest. It looked soft. Far softer than the freezing stone. Warm, too. Shivering, he padded toward it. Jake shifted to give him room. "What's your Clan called?" he repeated.

Talltail stepped into the nest. "WindClan." It felt fluffier beneath his paws than sheepswool. He sat down, secretly relishing the comfort.

"Where do you live?"

"On the moor." Talltail crouched down and tucked his paws under him. "Below the moor is RiverClan. They live by a river and catch fish."

"How?"

Talltail glanced at him. Jake was really dumb. "They swim."

"What's the fourth Clan?" Jake started licking a paw and washing his face.

"ShadowClan. They live in the pine trees beside Thunder-Clan. No one likes ShadowClan except ShadowClan."

Jake ran a paw over his ear. "So the rest of you like one another."

"No!" Talltail's tail twitched. "If any other Clan crosses our border, we shred them." Jake's eyes widened. Talltail thought of Nightsky and Piketooth. "Okay, we don't *always* shred them," he relented. "But we're supposed to stay on our own territory all the time." He decided not to mention the Gatherings in case Jake got even more confused.

"Why are you here, then?" Jake dropped his paw and stared at Talltail. His green eyes glowed in the moonlight streaming through the clear patches of wall.

Talltail looked down at the nest. "There's something I have to do." He didn't say that he'd felt trapped living on the moor with his Clan, that he'd been burning with curiosity to find out what lay beyond the borders. From Jake's point of view, his curiosity had led him to nothing but trouble.

"Is it a warrior mission?" Jake dropped his mew to a whisper.

Talltail pricked his ears. *A mission.* He liked that idea. "Yes." It was a warrior mission, wasn't it? Or was it just *his* mission, and nothing to do with being a warrior at all? The thought unsettled him and he pushed it away quickly. He tucked his paws in tighter and closed his eyes.

"I can't believe I'm sleeping next to a warrior." Jake's soft mew was filled with awe.

"I can't believe I'm sleeping next to a kittypet," Talltail grunted. What kind of warrior settled down to sleep in a kittypet nest? In a Twoleg den! *A tired warrior.* His head began to droop.

"Talltail." He seemed to hear Sandgorse's mew far away. "You *are* a warrior. You always will be."

Am I? Talltail drifted into dreams.

CHAPTER 31
❧

Pale dawn light filtered through the clear squares high up in the wall.
Talltail lifted his head, blinking at the shiny, white room. He
stretched, carefully testing his belly. It felt much better today,
less crushed and tender. Talltail climbed quietly out of the
nest, leaving Jake snoring in a huddle. There were fresh food
pebbles in Jake's stone. Talltail's belly growled, but he wanted
to see outside before he ate. He jumped onto the ledge, then
hopped onto an even higher ledge beside a clear piece of wall.
Talltail touched his nose to it. It was cold. *It must be ice.* Talltail
wondered why it didn't melt when he breathed on it. He pushed
at it with his forepaws, hoping it would crack, but it was too
hard. Outside he could see frosty grass and whitened shrubs.
They ran down to a smooth, wooden fence; trees crowded on
the far side, sunlight flashing between their branches.

Talltail's heart ached. He should be out there, not trapped
in this Twoleg den. He dropped back onto all fours and leaned
his forehead on the transparent square.

"The window doesn't open," Jake mewed from below. He
was sitting up in the nest, his pelt still ruffled from sleep.

Window. Talltail looked back at the sheet of ice. Kittypets had funny names for things.

Jake leaped up beside him. He nodded toward the fence at the end. "That's where I keep watch for Clan cats."

Talltail pressed his muzzle against the glass. The forest seemed so close. "Is that ThunderClan territory?" he mewed.

"Yes." Jake blinked at him. "Didn't you know?"

Talltail shook out his pelt. "How would I?" he muttered. "I can't smell any scents while I'm stuck in here."

"My housefolk will let you out soon."

Talltail growled. "How soon?"

"Who knows?" Jake shrugged. "When he thinks you're well enough, I suppose."

As he spoke the big flap in the wall opened and the Twoleg came in. It started rumbling at them, its eyes shining. It was holding something flat and floppy, like a blue pelt. Its gaze was fixed on Talltail.

"What does it want now?" Talltail whispered to Jake. The Twoleg was heading toward him. Alarmed, he hopped off the window ledge and backed into a corner. He ducked as the Twoleg flapped the blue pelt toward him. He tried to escape but strong paws gripped him through the pelt and wrapped him up like a spider wrapping a fly.

"Help!" Talltail thrashed, fear flaring though him. Still smothered in the blue pelt, he was bundled into the vet-basket. The mesh slammed shut behind him and the Twoleg peered through, rumbling.

"I hate you!" Talltail hissed through the mesh.

The Twoleg leaned down toward Jake's flap. He flicked a

little stick at one side and turned to Jake, making mewling noises. Jake seemed to understand, and jumped down from the window ledge and hopped through the flap. Talltail flung himself against the mesh, yowling. Rage surged beneath his pelt as he scrabbled at the hard, silver vines, trying to bend them far enough to slide his paw out. The Twoleg turned and mewled at him.

Talltail hissed back. "I'll shred you!"

The Twoleg purred gently, then disappeared through its own flap. Breath coming in gasps, Talltail worked at the mesh. Surely it would give way eventually? His paws began to ache and his pelt grew hot. The silver vines didn't even bend. At last, when his claws were bleeding and his pads felt as if they were on fire, Talltail flopped down onto the blue pelt and shoved his nose against the mesh. He stared at the flap in the wall until Jake returned.

"Talltail?" Jake sprang up onto the ledge, smelling of wind and earth.

Talltail didn't move.

"Are you okay?" Jake's gaze clouded with worry. "Are you feeling ill again?" He pressed anxiously against the mesh. "Should I fetch my housefolk?"

"No!" Talltail sat up and glared at him. "Just tell me how to get out of here!"

"Why do you want to leave so much?" Jake looked around the room. "It's not bad here. There's plenty of food, and it's warm."

"I'm not a kittypet," Talltail growled.

"I didn't say you were. But you might as well get better properly. You nearly died."

Talltail flexed his claws. "I don't have time to stay here any longer."

"What's the rush?"

"I'm on a mission, remember?"

Jake's eyes widened. "Of course! What's the mission?"

"I'm looking for someone."

"Who?"

Talltail looked into Jake's eager green eyes. How could he explain everything that had led him here?

"Is it really that important?" Jake prompted.

Talltail dug his claws into the blue pelt. "More important than you could imagine. I have to find a rogue," he meowed. "He killed my father."

Jake bristled. *"Killed* him?"

"My father, Sandgorse, was the best tunneler in Wind-Clan. But Sparrow made Sandgorse take him into a tunnel that wasn't safe and when it collapsed, he ran away." Talltail's breath quickened as the familiar dark fury rose in his belly. "He just left my father to die."

"So you want revenge."

Talltail blinked. Jake *understood!* "I have to catch up with Sparrow before he travels too far for me to find. I'm already at least two moons behind him."

"Which means you really need to get out of here."

"Yes!" Talltail pushed helplessly at the silver mesh.

Jake thought for a moment. "I can tell you how to escape, but on one condition."

Talltail narrowed his eyes. "What?"

"You let me come with you."

"I thought you liked being a kittypet!" Talltail glanced down at the soft, red nest. "There's none of those out *there*." He flicked his tail toward the window.

"I know that," Jake told him. "I don't want to join your Clan. But if you're on a mission, I want to help."

Talltail tipped his head on one side. "Why?"

"You need me."

"No, I don't!" Talltail bristled.

Jake leaned forward. "Who ate a poisoned rat and nearly died?" His eyes flashed. "It seems to me like you could do with some help."

"But it'll be dangerous," Talltail meowed. "Why would you risk your life to help me?"

Jake puffed out his chest. "Just because I'm a kittypet doesn't mean I don't have dreams of something else." His eyes gleamed. "I don't want to spend my whole life in the wild, but I'd like to explore beyond the fences, see how other cats live. I know every paw step of the housefolk-place and I'd like to go farther."

"Really?" Talltail's ear twitched. Perhaps this kittypet could be useful. "Do you know how to get to the other side of the Twoleg dens?"

Jake eyed him suspiciously. "Can I go with you?"

"As far as the end of Twolegplace."

"Okay." Jake sat back. "It's a deal."

Talltail looked at him. "Now, how do I get out of here?"

"It's obvious, isn't it?" Jake stood up, arching his back.

"It is?" Talltail growled.

Jake rolled his eyes. "Just be nice to my housefolk," he mewed. "Act like you're completely better, and well enough to be let out. Most of all, be friendly. You can get anything out of most housefolk by being friendly."

"Friendly?" Talltail narrowed his eyes. "How? You mean all that purring and winding around its legs?"

"Exactly."

Talltail shuddered. "What if it tries to stroke me?" He imagined the Twoleg's pink paw sliding along his pelt and shuddered.

"Just purr. You might even enjoy it."

Talltail stiffened. If this was the only chance of getting out of here, he'd have to try. He watched the Twoleg flap, ears twitching uneasily. When it finally opened, his heart lurched. The Twoleg clattered in and shut the flap, then headed for the vet-basket. Talltail forced himself not to cower at the back when the Twoleg swung back the mesh. Instead he stepped out, purring.

The Twoleg's eyes lit up with surprise. It rumbled something, moving back as Talltail jumped to the floor. It stared down in amazement as Talltail weaved around its legs.

Talltail tried to pretend that the Twoleg was a tree. *I'm just leaving my scent.* "That's right," Jake urged. "Don't forget to keep purring."

Talltail realized he'd been concentrating so hard on winding around the Twoleg, he'd forgotten to purr. Did kittypets actually enjoy this or was it the only way to get what they wanted? He forced himself to purr loudly, his throat catching with the effort. The Twoleg rumbled and stepped carefully over Talltail before pouring food into Jake's hollow stone.

"Eat it," Jake ordered. "He'll know you're feeling better if you eat."

Talltail hurried to the stone and started gulping down food. He ate till his belly was bursting, then forced himself to look up at the Twoleg. He used kit eyes, pretending he was Wrenkit begging for a badger ride. "Please can I go outside?" he mewed in his most plaintive voice.

The Twoleg's face softened and it reached down with a paw. Talltail froze, forcing his claws to stay sheathed as the Twoleg ran its paw along his back. *First kittypet smell, now Twoleg stench.* Talltail gave his loudest purr, then padded toward Jake's flap and gazed longingly up at the Twoleg. "Please?"

The Twoleg mewed back.

Jake snorted. "I told you it tries to speak our language."

"Actually, I think it just called me a furball." A real purr rumbled in Talltail's throat.

The Twoleg bent down and touched the flap.

"Yes, please!" Talltail felt excitement welling as the Twoleg pulled at the side of the flap.

Jake padded closer. "Get ready."

Talltail saw the flap spring free, and in a flash he burst through and hared across the grass. He heard the Twoleg hooting behind, and the flap rattle. He glanced over his shoulder. Jake was racing after him. Talltail leaped onto the fence at the end of the grass.

Jake clattered onto the top beside him. "Follow me!" He plunged down into the long grass beyond.

Talltail dropped down after him, his pelt bushing up as ThunderClan scent filled his nose. "We can't go this way!"

Jake turned. "Why not?"

"If a ThunderClan patrol finds us, they'll shred us." Talltail nudged Jake's soft pelt. "They don't like kittypets, and they definitely don't like WindClan. Let's go back over the fence. We'll be safer in kittypet territory."

Jake looked disappointed. "But I thought we could escape into the woods."

Talltail shook his head. "You said you'd show me to the other side of Twolegplace, remember? This just takes me back to the Clans." He trotted along the edge of the trees for a few tail-lengths until he was sure he was clear of Jake's nest, then sprang up onto the fence. Jake followed.

"Hello." A soft mew made Talltail stiffen. A young, gray she-cat was staring up from the grassy square below.

"We're not here to cause trouble," he told her quickly.

Jake jumped up beside him. "Hello, Quince." There was a purr in his mew.

"Hello, Jake." Quince returned the purr. "Who's this?" She turned her round, amber eyes on Talltail.

Jake hesitated. "This is Talltail," he meowed.

"Talltail?" Quince leaped onto the fence beside them and sniffed Talltail's pelt. "That sounds like a wildcat name." She wrinkled her nose. "Ew! He smells of the cutter."

"He accidently ate a pois—"

Talltail interrupted. He didn't want every kittypet knowing he was a rabbit-brain. "I'm a WindClan warrior, actually." He puffed out his chest.

"Really?" Quince eyed him suspiciously. "Why are you hanging around Jake's home and visiting the cutter? I thought warriors were—"

"He's on a mission." It was Jake's turn to butt in. "I'm helping him. We're going to find the cat who killed his father."

Quince's eyes stretched wide. "Wow."

Talltail weaved past her and headed along the fence. "Hadn't we better be going?" He didn't want Jake inviting another kittypet along. Besides, he could hear Jake's Twoleg hooting over the fences.

Jake nodded. "Okay." He nodded to Quince. "See you around."

She watched Jake slide past. "You are coming back, aren't you?"

"Of course he is." Talltail hopped over the wooden stalk at the end and headed along the next fence.

"There's an alleyway at the end of this row," Jake called from behind.

"Great." Talltail had no idea what an alleyway was but Jake seemed to think it was good. He glanced into the forest, wondering if a ThunderClan patrol was watching. Would they be gossiping to WindClan about him at the next Gathering? It would be full moon soon. Would Heatherstar tell the other Clans that he'd left?

"There it is!" Jake squeezed past him as they reached the

last enclosed section of grass and jumped down from the fence into a passageway lined with red stone.

Talltail landed beside him. "Do you know where we are?"

"Yes." Jake quickened his pace, following a thin stream of water that ran along the crack in the middle of the path. He hopped back and forth over it, avoiding piles of clear, sharp stones. "Don't tread on the broken glass," he warned, stopping to point his nose toward shards of shiny, green ice. "If it sticks in your paw, you'll cut your tongue trying to lick it out, and the wound can turn bad easily."

Talltail nodded. He'd never seen glass before, but he'd take care to avoid it.

"This way." Jake veered toward a low wall as the sides of the alley ended. He jumped onto it and down the other side. Talltail followed, his paws stinging from the hard ground. The tall dens opened out onto a wide stretch of stone. Talltail's heart quickened as a monster rumbled past. A Thunderpath!

"Stay close to me," Jake called over his shoulder. He followed a wide, flat trail that cut between the Thunderpath and a row of Twoleg dens fronted with large windows. Monsters growled slowly beside them, their eyes beginning to light up as the sun slid behind the dens. Thin, silver trunks lining the Thunderpath flickered and blazed at their tips, throwing pools of light onto the stone below.

Talltail blinked up at them. "What are they?"

"Thunderpath lights." Jake didn't slow down, and Talltail quickened his pace. The noise and light and unfamiliar scents alarmed him, making his fur stand up and his ears swivel toward every new sound. Jake seemed unworried, his pelt smooth, his mouth open as though following a scent trail. Talltail could only smell monster fumes and carrion heaps.

"Wait." Jake stopped suddenly and pressed Talltail back with a nudge. He'd stopped beside a gap between two dens. Black sticks crisscrossed it. "Don't move. You're safe." A moment later barking exploded from the gap and a snarling muzzle poked between the black sticks. *Dog!* Talltail unsheathed his claws. Teeth glinted in the dazzling Thunderpath lights. A Twoleg growl sounded from farther down the gap, and the dog turned and ran into the shadows.

"We can pass now." Jake strolled past the gap.

Talltail hurried after him, his pelt spiking. "How did you know that dog would be there?" he gasped.

"It does that every time I come this way." Jake trotted past more windowed dens before veering away from the Thunderpath. Dusk was falling as they reached yet another row of dens, backed by tiny fenced-in meadows.

"Do you know where you're going?" Talltail wondered if Jake was just wandering aimlessly.

Jake jumped up onto a fence. "Of course."

Talltail scrambled after him. "How?" He tasted the air. Now that the Thunderpath was behind them, there was a chance of scenting whether the rogues had passed this way. He dropped down the other side of the fence and began sniffing at the bushes crowding the edge of the grass.

Jake stared down at him. "What are you doing?"

"Searching for the rogues." Kittypets were so dumb. Didn't

they know that a nose was the best tracker a cat had?

Jake landed beside him. "Don't waste your time sniffing," he mewed. "I'm taking you to a cat who knows everything that goes on around here. If the rogues have passed by here, she'll know."

Talltail blinked at him. "Who is she?"

"Just a stray." Jake flicked his tail and raced across the grass to the next fence.

Stars specked a black sky by the time they'd reached the far end of the row of dens. Jake jumped down from the last fence and turned along a wide alleyway. There were low dens here like the ones where Jake had been cornered by the dog.

"What are these dens for?" Talltail asked. "Are they for Twoleg kits?"

"Housefolk keep monsters in them," Jake explained, using a wall to jump up onto one of the roofs. Talltail sprang up after him. Ahead of them, rough stone stretched like a raised Thunderpath. He fell in beside Jake as they padded along it.

"This is the perfect place to walk." Jake sniffed the air. "No dogs or housefolk or monsters, and a clear view in every direction."

Talltail gazed around, amazed to see red stone and the lights of Twolegplace stretching as far as he could see. "Where does Twolegplace end?" he breathed.

"We're getting close," Jake answered. "But first we have to find that cat."

"The one who knows everything?"

"She lives near the end of these dens." Jake spoke with

respect, and Talltail wondered if kittypets had leaders, too.

As they reached the end of the roof, Talltail peered over the edge. "Down there?" An open space—half-lit by Thunderpath lights, half-lit by the moon—stretched ahead of them. It was crisscrossed by high, mesh fences. To one side, yellow flames burned. Talltail bristled. "Fire!"

"It's just some Twolegs keeping themselves warm," Jake explained. "There'll be cats too, hoping for food, but we'll steer clear." He fluffed out his fur. "They're not that friendly."

"Who? The Twolegs or the cats?"

"Neither," Jake told him grimly.

Talltail shivered. This felt like walking into ShadowClan territory all over again. He followed Jake from the roof, jumping down onto a hard, square ledge, then to the ground. The soil underpaw was stony. Grass poked in clumps here and there. Smashed glass was strewn everywhere and Talltail watched where he put his paws, relieved that the glinting shards were easy to spot in the half-light. He halted while Jake scrabbled through a tight gap beneath one of the high, mesh fences, then squeezed under, grit scraping his belly. Tall, gray dens loomed ahead, jagged and unlit, their windows broken, their walls cracked.

Talltail unsheathed his claws as Jake led him into the shadows and began to follow a narrow alleyway that cut between two dens. Light glowed at the end and Talltail quickened his pace, eager to be out of the pressing gloom. It felt too much like a tunnel. As he broke into a trot, Jake hissed behind him. "Slow down!"

Talltail spotted movement at the end of the alley. Shapes slid from the shadow and stood silhouetted against the light beyond. *Cats.* A tom and a she-cat, from the scent that drifted down to him. Talltail could make out the ragged ends of their ears and their clumped fur. These were fighters. He stopped. "What now?" he whispered.

Before Jake could answer, the tom growled. "We have trespassers."

"That's not good," sneered his companion.

"You're wrong, Pixie." There was malice in the tom's snarl. Talltail's belly tightened. "That's *very* good. We might have some fun with them. Let's take them to Jay and see what she suggests."

Talltail glanced at Jake, his pelt lifting along his spine. *You stupid kittypet! You've led us into a trap!*

CHAPTER 32

♣

"*Why are you bothering me with* trespassers?" A mangy, old black-and-white she-cat looked up from a dead pigeon.

This must be Jay. Talltail shifted his paws nervously. The cats had ushered him and Jake into a clearing surrounded by unlit dens and dotted with piles that stank of crow-food.

Feathers stuck to Jay's graying muzzle. She shook them away. "I'm trying to eat." As she curled her lip, Talltail saw she had no teeth. If she were in a Clan, she'd be an elder by now.

Pixie nudged him forward. "We found these two nosing around the alley," he explained.

Talltail flashed her a look. Unease was creeping beneath his pelt, but he wasn't going to show these ragged strays that he was scared. He flexed his claws. "You don't have to push."

"Are you planning on pushing back?" Pixie challenged with a hiss.

"Not yet." In the moonlit clearing he could see her scarred muzzle and thin, yellowing tail. He guessed she'd been white once.

Jake padded past Talltail. "We haven't come to start a fight," he mewed to Jay.

Talltail saw movement at the edge of his vision. He jerked

his head around, scanning the shadows. Cats were creeping forward, their eyes glinting in the moonlight. Some wore collars, but they couldn't be kittypets; their pelts were ragged and flea-bitten, their ears nicked, their noses scratched. Talltail eyed them warily, wondering if Jake understood how much danger they were in.

A russet-furred she-cat padded to Jay's side. "What are they doing here?" she asked, her narrow gaze fixing on Talltail.

Talltail stiffened. Were they going to have to fight their way out of here?

Jay shrugged. "Don't ask me, Red. It was Marmalade and Pixie who brought them." She bent down stiffly and tried to wrestle a piece of flesh from the pigeon with her gums.

The ginger tom who'd helped Pixie escort them here pushed past Talltail. "We caught them."

"Well done, Marmalade." Red met his gaze with a withering look. "Did you think they were mice?" Marmalade's pelt rose along his spine but he said nothing. Red padded closer to Talltail and sniffed him. "You smell strange. And you're small for a kittypet."

"He's not a kittypet; he's a Clan cat," meowed Jake.

Red narrowed her eyes. "Then what's he doing *here*?"

"He's with me." Jake shook out his fur. "We're on a mission. We came to ask Jay a question."

Talltail hissed in his ear. "Don't tell them everything!"

Jake blinked at him. "They're not interested."

Talltail nodded toward the cats milling in the shadows. "And we don't *want* them to be interested. They might try to stop us."

Jake frowned. "But they might be able to help us."

Talltail lashed his tail. These cats looked as helpful as a ShadowClan patrol. "Let me do the talking," he insisted.

Jay lifted her head. "That's just what I need. A *talker.*"

Talltail straightened. *Just imagine she's Whiteberry.* He was used to coaxing grumpy elders into a better mood when damp weather made their bones ache. "I'm sorry to bother you," he began softly. "But Jake said you're the only cat who knows everything that happens around here."

"That's true enough," Jay conceded, narrowing her eyes.

"We're tracking some rogues who may have passed this way two moons ago," Talltail explained as briefly as he could. "We were hoping you'd seen them."

"Why?" Jay rasped. "Are they worth seeing?"

Talltail shrugged, trying not to seem too eager. "They're just rogues."

Marmalade pricked his ears. "What does a Clan cat want with rogues?"

Red padded around Talltail. "Perhaps he wants to join them." Her gaze flicked over his pelt. "Perhaps he's bored of the Clans."

Talltail ignored her. "One of them's called Sparrow."

Jay rubbed a feather from her nose with her paw. "Why is a Clan cat traveling with a kittypet?" Her gaze rested on Jake.

Jake glanced at Talltail, as though asking permission to speak. Talltail kept his attention on Jay. "He likes Clan cats, that's all," he mewed.

"Clan cats." Jay's eyes clouded, as though she was remembering something from long ago. "I knew a cat once who liked

Clan cats." She bent down and tugged unsuccessfully at the pigeon's flesh.

Jake trotted forward. "Let me help."

Talltail's heart lurched as Jake hooked the pigeon away from Jay. He flexed his claws, ready to fight, as Red and Marmalade showed their teeth. Growls rumbled from the shadows. At the edge of the clearing, the flea-bitten cats padded closer.

"I can rip off a chunk so you can get to the soft flesh," Jake mewed cheerfully. He went on as Jay stared at him, wide-eyed. "It's okay. I won't eat any. I'll just find you a juicy bit." He nuzzled through the feathers and, holding the pigeon still with a paw, peeled off a strip. He dropped it at Jay's paws and tore off another. Then he pushed the pigeon back toward her. "It'll be easy to get into now."

Talltail blinked. Was Jake really as rabbit-brained as he seemed? He'd nearly had a swarm of spitting cats on their tails.

Jay leaned down and sniffed the hunks of flesh, dabbing a piece with her tongue. She sat up and glanced at her companions. "Why couldn't one of *you* think of that?"

Pixie bristled. Marmalade glared at Jake.

"I'm sure they did," Jake told her. "But they were too polite to offer."

Jay snorted. "Any more politeness and I'd starve to death."

As she bent and took a bite, Jake leaned closer. "Can Talltail ask you those questions now?"

"About the rogues?" Chewing, Jay tipped her head. "Go on."

Talltail pricked his ears. Perhaps Jake had just found a way to get them the answers he wanted. *Not so rabbit-brained after all, kittypet!* "I heard they might have come this way. Have you seen them?"

Jay swallowed. "Do they have names?"

"Sparrow," Talltail told her again slowly. "He's brown. He was traveling with Bess, Algernon, Mole, and Reena."

Jay poked distractedly at the pigeon with her paw. "Are they *all* rogues?"

"Yes." Talltail dug his claws into the cracked earth.

Jake nodded to Jay. "Why don't you have another mouthful of pigeon?" he suggested. "It'll help you think."

"Perhaps it will." The old she-cat pulled at the flesh with her gums, tearing a fresh morsel away, and began chewing. "Rogues, you say," she murmured, her mouth full. "Rogues with house-cat names, mind you."

"They travel together." Talltail tried to hide the impatience pricking in his fur. "They would have passed this way about two moons ago."

Jay nodded slowly, then swallowed. "Oh yes. I remember them. Red found them hunting our alleys." She looked toward the tawny she-cat. "Was that them?"

Red frowned. "Was there a black-and-white she-cat with them?"

Talltail's ears twitched excitedly. "And a small gray tom and a ginger-and-white—"

"That was them." Red nodded. "We let them take one piece of prey each, then moved them on."

"When?" Talltail's whiskers were quivering.

"Was the moon full, Marmalade?" Red asked.

Marmalade glanced at the sky. "Not as full as this."

"How long were the days?" Talltail wanted to know if they'd passed one moon ago or two.

"Not much longer than this," Red told him.

"So *last* moon?" Talltail prompted.

Jay's tail began to flick. "Whenever it was, they've gone now." She ducked down for another mouthful of pigeon. "You should go too before you wear out my ears with your questions."

Red and Marmalade padded closer to Talltail, tails flicking.

"Okay, we're going." Talltail turned away from the mangy old she-cat, beckoning Jake with a nod.

"Thanks for your help," Jake called to Jay.

Jay blinked at the kittypet. "Thanks for *yours*."

Jake purred. "I'm sure Red or Marmalade will help with your fresh-kill next time."

"Sure we will," Red hissed through gritted teeth.

Talltail nudged Jake away. "Come on." *Before you try to organize this bunch of loners into a Clan.* He steered him toward the far side of the clearing, his pelt rippling uneasily as they passed the watching strays. There was a gap between the cracked dens that would lead them clear.

"I told you she'd help," Jake purred as they reached it.

"You didn't tell me you were leading us into an enemy camp," Talltail muttered. He ducked into the alley and quickened his pace. The sooner he was away from here, the better.

Jake trotted after him. "You found out what you wanted to know, didn't you?"

"Yes. Now let's get out of here." Talltail paused and looked back. "And thanks for your help, Jake. You did well to get that old she-cat to tell us about the rogues."

Jake shrugged. "It's like dealing with housefolk. You get more out of them by being friendly."

The far side of the alley opened onto a row of neat, grassy squares. A long stretch of mesh divided them from the dilapidated dens. Talltail squeezed under the mesh, relieved to see the tiny meadows ahead. No more dodging broken glass. The grass felt soft beneath his paws. "How far is it to the end of Twolegplace?"

Jake nodded toward the large red-stone den at the end of the little meadow. "There are open fields beyond there."

Talltail followed his gaze. Beyond the den, there was nothing but wide, star-speckled sky and rolling, dark emptiness below. "The rogues would have kept going," he guessed. "Past Twolegplace."

"Or they might have turned back," Jake pointed out. "There's warmth and shelter here."

"Only if you've got a Twoleg looking after you," Talltail meowed. He started trotting toward the red-stone den. Jake stayed where he was. Talltail stopped. Was Jake going to go home now? An unexpected pang tugged his heart. He glanced over his shoulder.

Jake was sniffing the air, his eyes flashing with excitement. "I smell food." He turned and disappeared around the corner of the den. *Now where's he going?* Talltail peered around the edge of the red stone. Jake's hind legs were disappearing through a small flap, like the one where he lived. Talltail stared. *What in the name of StarClan is he doing?* His heart began to race as he stared at the flap, expecting Jake to explode out with a vicious kittypet or angry dog on his tail. But nothing happened.

As Talltail's belly began to growl, Jake's head poked from the flap. "Come and get some!" he called. "There's plenty." He licked his lips, and the scent of little, brown pellets drifted to Talltail on the breeze.

"You want me to steal kittypet food?"

Jake nodded. "Why not? There's always more."

"What about the kittypet who lives there?" Talltail asked. "Won't he mind?"

"It smells like a she, and she must be asleep upstairs, or out. There's no sign of her by the food."

"I'd rather hunt, thanks," Talltail muttered. Now that he was almost out of Twolegplace, he didn't need to eat those dry pellets anymore.

"Okay." Jake ducked back inside.

Talltail growled under his breath. He might as well catch some fresh-kill while he was waiting for Jake to stuff his belly. He began to sniff along the bushes at the grass, sticking his head under the leaves of a laurel and tasting the air. He smelled shrew. Mouth watering, he crept under the branches. The soil crunched frostily beneath his paws. Following his nose, he squeezed past the thick stem and tracked the scent to a spiky bush, then into tall grass. The stems swished as he pushed through, showering dusty seed over his pelt. The shrew smell grew stronger. Grass rustled ahead. Straining to see in the shadows, Talltail spotted a small shape moving beneath a holly bush. He pressed his belly to the ground. He'd learned from chasing the mouse into Twolegplace that hunting in thick undergrowth took more patience than speed.

The shape scuttled, then stopped. It was definitely a shrew. Talltail could make out its small, pointed nose as it snuffled among the leaf litter. Stealthily he crept forward, keeping low so that his spine didn't disturb the branches hanging above. A tail-length from the shrew, he flung his paws forward and pounced.

The shrew's paws scrabbled on the leaf litter, but Talltail was quick and pinned its tail. Hooking it close, he killed it with a bite. He gulped it down and padded onto the moonlit grass feeling pleased with himself.

Jake was lying beside the Twoleg den, belly-up, happily washing his paws. As Talltail padded toward him, he hauled himself up and belched. "Catch something?"

"A shrew."

"Was it tasty?"

"You should catch one and find out."

Jake sat back on his haunches. "Would you teach me?"

Talltail shrugged. "We're at the end of Twolegplace." He nodded to the alleyway. It would lead past the red-stone den to open fields. "You'll be going home, won't you?"

Jake looked up at the moon. "In the morning. Let's find somewhere to sleep." He gazed across the grass at a small, wooden den. "What about that shed?"

Talltail glanced over his shoulder. It looked like the den he'd been poisoned in. "No thanks. I'd rather sleep under a bush."

"Okay." Jake looked around. "Which one?" He padded toward the laurel. "This looks like it'll give us some shelter."

"What if the kittypet whose *food* you just stole comes out in the night?" Talltail didn't fancy waking up to a fight.

"Let's head toward the fields, then," Jake suggested. "There'll be a hedge or something, won't there?"

Talltail narrowed his eyes. "I thought you weren't leaving Twolegplace?"

"I want to see what it's like sleeping in the wild." Jake headed toward the alley and disappeared into the shadows.

Talltail padded after him. If this kittypet wanted to play warrior, why argue? He'd be gone tomorrow. Another pang bit his belly. He ignored it and followed Jake to the front of the den, where another tiny meadow stretched to a low, stone wall. He leaped it after Jake and trotted over a short stretch of grass that led to a rutted Thunderpath, deserted in the moon-light. They crossed it side by side, their shadows stretching across the dried mud, then jumped into the long grass beyond.

Talltail slipped into the lead. They were in wild territory now. The quiet darkness felt soothing after the glaring noise of Twolegplace. Talltail weaved through the grass and jumped over a ditch. A thick hedge edged the other side and he crept under it. The earth was dry. "Let's sleep here." He began to scoop out a hollow with his paws.

Jake watched him. "You dig your nests?"

"There's nothing to sleep on." Talltail kept on scraping. "A hollow will keep us warm."

Jake watched and then copied him, pawing at the earth until he'd dug a shallow dip. "Won't the roots make it prickly?" Jake stared in dismay at the gnarled hedge roots that he'd uncovered.

"They won't hurt you." Talltail curled into his own scoop.

"I'm not used to lumps in my nest."

"You wanted to know what it's like sleeping wild." Talltail could feel roots jabbing between his ribs too, but he wasn't going to say anything. "Besides, it's just for tonight. We'll make better nests tomorrow," he promised, closing his eyes.

Jake didn't reply, but Talltail heard his pelt swish as he settled into his uncomfortable scoop. *We'll make better nests tomorrow.* Why had he said that? Jake would be going home at dawn. *And I'll be tracking the rogues.* Excitement pricked in Talltail's paws as he pictured Sparrow, imagined sinking his claws into the rogue's fur, hearing him plead for mercy. Talltail was on his trail. He knew he would find Sparrow. And soon, very soon, he would have his revenge.

CHAPTER 33

Sunlight woke Talltail. He opened his eyes, squinting as rays sliced through the hedge. He slunk, stretching, from his makeshift den and shook out his fur. A sharp frost had hardened the earth and whitened the meadows. Ahead, the land sloped to a rugged hilltop where the sun squatted on the horizon, spilling light over the silver grass. The hedge rattled behind him.

"It looks like a good day for walking." Jake's mew was thick with sleep as he stumbled from beneath the branches. He yawned, then blinked at the hilltop. "Is that the way you're heading?"

"I guess so." The hilltop would be a good place to start. From there, he could decide which route the rogues might have taken. It looked rocky and exposed, the slope steeper and more rugged than WindClan territory. Anxiety pricked at his belly. Had any Clan cat traveled this far before?

"You don't sound sure." Talltail felt Jake's pelt brush against his as the kittypet stood beside him.

"The rogues could have gone anywhere," Talltail pointed out. He gazed across the open stretch of grassland that curved past Twolegplace. What if they'd decided to take the low path, keeping out of the cold wind?

"You've got to start somewhere," Jake meowed.

"But where?" Talltail frowned. This might have been strange country to him, but the rogues had probably walked this route for moons and knew all its secrets, all the best places to shelter and find food.

"Why don't we climb the hill, like you said?" Jake mewed. "From up there, it might be obvious which way they'd choose."

"*We?*" Talltail blinked. "I thought you were going home."

"Eventually." Jake held his gaze. "But there's no harm in seeing what's on the other side of the hill."

Talltail paused, wondering why he didn't feel irritated. This was *his* mission. He didn't need help. Especially not from a kittypet. Yet suddenly the looming hill seemed less daunting. He shrugged. "Okay."

The wind whipped his whiskers as he padded up the slope. Jake followed a few paces behind, his head switching back and forth as he scanned the landscape. When sharp, gray rocks began to jut from the grass and the slope steepened, Talltail paused and waited for him to catch up. "You're shivering."

Jake's silky fur was rippling along his spine. "I'm okay," he muttered tightly. "There'll be shelter on the other side."

"I hope so." Talltail wasn't convinced. Though he could hardly feel the wind through his short, thick fur, he knew it'd be fiercer once they'd reached the top; it was sweeping over the hilltop toward them. *What if it makes Jake turn back?* Talltail glanced anxiously over his shoulder. Twolegplace sprawled just beyond the hedge. It wouldn't take long for Jake to reach the shelter of its stone walls and tiny, fenced-in meadows.

Jake leaped past him up the rocky slope, his paws slithering on the frosty rock.

"This way's easier," Talltail called. He veered around the outcrop, following a grassy trail, but Jake scrabbled stubbornly on.

"If I can climb up Twoleg walls, I can manage this," he growled.

Talltail reached the hilltop first, and a cold blast of air snatched his breath away. He narrowed his eyes against the icy wind and tried to ignore the pang of disappointment digging in his belly. Jake would turn back now, surely?

Focusing, he surveyed the land sloping ahead. It was like being on Outlook Rock again. The view was different but he still had a hawk's eye and took only a few moments to scan the valley. The land rose and fell gently on one side; the other was steep and barren, topped by craggy peaks. A river sparkled between, meandering along the valley bottom, and in the hollow between two low hills, a dense wood nestled like moss in a nest.

"That's where they'd head." Jake's breathless mew took him by surprise. Talltail followed the kittypet's gaze toward the wooded hollow.

"If they're anything like me, they'll be looking for shelter." Jake flattened his ears against the wind.

Talltail sniffed. "If they were anything like *you*, they'd be snuggled up in a Twoleg den eating kittypet food." He paused, pelt pricking as he realized how mean he sounded. "Sorry." He caught Jake's green gaze. "I just meant they're not kittypets. They might have their own ideas about shelter."

Jake shifted his paws. "I know I'm a kittypet. I'm happy with that." He began to head down the slope that led into the valley. "It doesn't mean I can't walk a different path for a while."

Talltail bounded after him. As he caught up, a screeching cry echoed across the valley. Jake froze. "Fox!" His eyes widened with fear. "Out here? I thought they only lived in Twolegplace."

"Foxes are like rats. They live everywhere." Talltail studied the hillside. The bark had sounded close. A red pelt scurried across the grass below them.

"Where can we hide?" Jake's pelt bristled, his gaze darting across the wide stretch of grass in front of them. He nodded toward a smooth, gray boulder. "It won't see us if we crouch behind that."

"Just stand still," Talltail ordered.

"But it'll see us." Jake's mew was edged with panic. "There's nowhere to hide out here."

Talltail guessed that Jake was missing his shadowy alleys and dens. "There are plenty of places to hide." He nodded toward the long grass sprouting beyond the boulder. It stretched all the way to the bottom of the valley. They could cross the entire hillside hidden among the rippling stems. Trees and bushes lined the river where it ended. "Just imagine that the grass and bushes are walls and fences. Besides, the wind will protect us."

"The wind?" Jake blinked at him. "How?"

"It's blowing this way," Talltail explained. "We can smell the fox, but it can't smell us." He opened his mouth and let the musky scent wash his tongue as the fox slunk toward a swathe of bracken and disappeared. "See?" He flicked his tail as the fox's pelt melted among the russet fronds. "It never even noticed us."

Jake was already heading for the long grass. Talltail bounded after him, pushing through the stems a tail-length behind. He could smell Jake's fear-scent, stronger than his normal aroma, and knew he had to calm Jake down before the fox detected it. "We could beat a fox easily," Talltail called. "If we fought together."

Jake slowed. "I guess we drove off that dog."

Talltail fell in beside him. "I can teach you some battle moves if you'd like." The ground sloped more steeply as they neared the river.

"*Battle* moves?" Jake let out a tiny yelp as his paws slithered beneath him.

Talltail dug in his claws to get a better grip. "We're called warriors for a reason."

"Who do you fight?" Jake bounded down a sharp drop, scrambling to a halt as the land began to flatten out.

"ShadowClan and RiverClan mostly," Talltail replied, negotiating the drop more smoothly. "We share borders with them."

"Like fighting over fences."

Talltail's pelt ruffled. "It's more important than that," he huffed. "We're not just being selfish over a patch of ground. We're fighting for our Clan's survival! A true warrior would *die* to save his Clan."

Jake narrowed his eyes. "Is that why you're out here, risking your life?" he asked. "To save your Clan?"

Talltail hurried ahead, grass brushing his pelt. "I'm avenging my father."

"How will that help your Clan?"

Talltail turned on Jake, hissing. "My Clan has nothing to do with this!"

"It has to! You're a warrior." Confusion clouded Jake's gaze.

Talltail's thoughts whirled and tangled. *A warrior avenges the death of a Clanmate, doesn't he? I'm doing this for Sandgorse!* He stiffened. *My father wants me to avenge his death.* Sandgorse's amber gaze glowed in his mind. Then he pictured it disappearing under a deluge of mud. Blood roared in his ears.

"Talltail?" Jake was circling him. "Are you okay?"

Talltail padded past him, forcing his pelt to flatten. "I'm fine." He slid from the long grass at a point where scrubby, cow-trodden pasture sloped gently toward the river.

Jake popped out beside him. As he gazed across the valley to the wooded hollow, his belly rumbled.

"There'll be prey in those bushes." Talltail nodded toward the hawthorn that crowded the riverbank. Beyond the bare, prickly branches, sun sparkled on the rippling water. Overhead cold, blue sky stretched between the hilltops. Talltail tasted the air. The scent of fox was growing stale. The stone tang of frost was tinged with the smell of sheep, refreshing after the jumble of acrid Twoleg scents. Talltail bounded across the grass. Jake raced beside him, taking the lead and skidding to a halt by the bushes. Talltail stopped beside him, surprised to find himself breathless.

"Are you okay?" Jake leaned closer.

"Fine," Talltail panted.

"You look ruffled."

"I guess I'm still weak from the poison."

"Do you want to rest while I hunt?" Jake offered.

A purr caught in Talltail's throat. "Do you *know* how to hunt?"

"I caught a bird once." Jake puffed out his chest. Talltail tipped his head, impressed. "It was a bit injured when I found it," Jake admitted. "But it flapped a lot before I killed it."

Talltail rolled his eyes. "Let's hunt together," he suggested. He nosed his way between the hawthorn bushes. Beyond them, water lapped against the dark brown earth, deeply pitted by the hooves of animals. Talltail padded along the edge of the river, keeping a wary eye on the surface. Mouse scent touched his nose. "Wait." He dropped to a crouch, beckoning for Jake to do the same with a flick of his tail. Something was scuttling beneath the branches up ahead. He crept forward, his paws as light as falling snow, and rounded the bush. Stopping, he peered through and caught sight of the mouse. It was sitting under a branch, grasping a berry in its paws. Talltail held still. He could see Jake creeping closer on the far side of the bush. *Wait!* He willed Jake not to scare away their prey.

The mouse scurried forward. Its scent washed Talltail's

nose. Another few paw steps and he'd reach it easily. He hesitated. *Why not let Jake catch it? Every cat should learn how to hunt, even a kittypet.*

The mouse moved again. Peering under the bush, Talltail saw it skitter sideways. He was going to have to drive it straight toward Jake or the kittypet would never catch it. He lunged beneath the branches, screwing up his eyes against the prickly twigs. Paws stretched, he skidded on his belly and burst out the other side.

Jake gasped as the mouse darted toward him, then fast as a weasel, he slammed his paws down on the tiny creature.

"Bite its spine!" Talltail called.

Jake clamped his jaws around the mouse's neck and killed it with a sharp nip. Talltail wriggled out from beneath the bush, wincing as thorns jabbed his pelt. "Well done!"

Jake sat up, blinking, the mouse dangling from his mouth. He looked as surprised as the mouse. He dropped it onto the ground and purred. "I caught it!"

Talltail swallowed the urge to point out that the mouse had practically run into his teeth. "You reacted quickly."

"Thanks." Jake stared at the mouse uncertainly. "Now what?"

"You can eat it."

"What about you?"

"It's your catch."

"You helped." Jake nudged it toward Talltail with a paw. "Let's share."

"Is that okay?"

Jake cocked his head. "You share in the Clan, don't you?"

"Only if it's offered," Talltail told him.

"I'm offering." Jake nodded at the mouse. "You can have first bite."

Talltail felt Jake's gaze on him as he leaned down and bit into the warm flesh of the mouse. It tasted sweet. "Have some." He pushed it back toward Jake.

Jake took a bite, sitting up to chew. Talltail watched his eyes soften. "Do you like it?"

"Yes," Jake purred, and he took another bite, crunching through bone like a Clanborn cat. He nudged the carcass toward Talltail. "You finish it," he ordered. "You still need to get your strength back." Talltail didn't argue. His legs felt shaky from the hunt. "Do you want to rest?" Jake asked as he finished the last scrap.

Talltail looked across the stretch of meadows toward the woods. "Let's keep going." He wanted to reach the trees before dark. Woodland was gloomy enough at sunhigh. It would be as suffocating as a tunnel when dusk approached. He stood up and shook out his fur. Jake licked his lips. Together they headed across the grass, which rippled around them like water in the cold breeze.

By the time they reached the trees, Talltail's paws were trembling with tiredness. He fluffed out his fur, suddenly chilled to the bone.

Jake brushed against him. "You look exhausted."

Talltail shrugged. "I'm okay."

"Why don't we find a place to rest?" Jake glanced up at the

sun. It was beginning to slide toward the hilltop behind them. "We've traveled far enough."

Talltail's pelt twitched. "We need to catch the rogues."

"They won't be traveling fast," Jake meowed confidently. "They're rogues. They can travel where they like, when they like. What's the hurry?" Talltail was too weary to argue. He let Jake lead him into the shelter of the trees. The kittypet stared up in wonder at the crisscrossing canopy of branches. "It's like a huge den!"

Talltail didn't look. It was bad enough listening to the branches rattle in the wind. Trunks crowded around him, bushes and shadow pressing between them, trapping his paws, shutting out the breeze. Jake bounded forward and padded around a tree, staring up. A scent had caught his attention. He darted over to sniff a bramble that tumbled out from between two trunks. "It's busier than Twolegplace!" he meowed excitedly. "There are prey smells everywhere."

Talltail sat down. "Great," he muttered.

Jake glanced over his shoulder. "Look for a hollow to rest in," he mewed. He nodded toward a dip between the roots of an oak. "That might make a good nest." He ducked away past a hawthorn.

Talltail felt a twinge of anxiety as Jake's tail disappeared. "Where are you going?"

"I'll be back," Jake's mew echoed from the trees. "You rest."

Talltail padded heavily toward the oak roots. The hollow was deep, and moss grew on the damp earth inside. Talltail clambered over the edge and curled into it. The moss was wet but he was too tired to care. Closing his eyes, he must have dozed. The next thing he knew, paws were pattering across the forest floor toward him. He tensed and peeked over the rim of the nest.

Jake bounded from the trees with a wad of leaves and feathers clasped between his jaws. He stopped at the edge of the hollow and dropped them in. "You can line your nest with these." Talltail ducked as leaves, twigs, and feathers showered his pelt. He stood up and shook out his fur. "Thanks." Leaning down, he picked up a short stick between his teeth and tossed it out of the nest. "You might want to check for sharp bits next time."

"Sorry." Jake hopped down beside him and began picking twigs from the litter. He tossed them out, then paddled the soft moss with his paws. "That feels better!"

"In WindClan, we line our nests with sheepswool," Talltail remarked.

"I'll get some." Jake jumped out.

"It's okay; you don't have to." Bones aching with tiredness, Talltail sat down.

Jake was already heading toward the edge of the trees. "I won't be long!"

Talltail curled back into the moss, ignoring the dampness. He rested his nose on his paws and closed his eyes. Just a few more moments' sleep and he'd feel better. Darkness swirled through his thoughts and pulled him into tumbling dreams.

Talltail! His father's voice echoed from the shadows. Talltail, dreaming, stared around. Shadows crowded against his pelt, turning the air thick until he struggled for breath. Then something started falling on him—cold, wet earth, heavy as stones, more and more until his mouth and nose were clogged. He was inside the gorge tunnel! Suddenly eyes blinked in the blackness. *Sparrow!* Talltail recognized the cold, amber gaze of the rogue flashing in the dark.

"Where's Sandgorse? Have you left him behind?" Panic surged beneath Talltail's pelt. "Sandgorse? Sandgorse?" He pushed past Sparrow, calling into the darkness. Water rumbled in the distance, its roar growing louder, and sticky mud dragged at Talltail's legs. "You abandoned him!" Talltail turned on Sparrow, lashing his soaked tail.

But the flashing eyes had gone, and he was alone underground. More earth slid weightily onto Talltail's flank. He struggled, trying to kick free of the mud as it flooded around his paws. It lapped against his belly and dragged at his fur. "Sandgorse!" he shrieked in panic.

"Talltail!" His father's voice returned his call. "Talltail! Talltail!"

A paw shook his shoulder. Talltail jerked up his head. Jake was in the nest beside him, poking him. His eyes were wide with excitement. "You have to come and see this!"

Sheepswool surrounded Talltail, soft against his pelt. "Did you collect all that?" Talltail stared at it, still dazed from his dream.

"Yes!" Jake hopped out of the nest. "But I found something else. Come on!"

Talltail struggled to his paws, fighting the heaviness of

sleep. "I'm coming." He hauled himself out of the nest and followed Jake.

Jake padded briskly between the trees, weaving past brambles and bracken, and hopped a rotting log. Talltail scrambled over it, still drowsy. "What is it?" Irritation itched beneath his fur. Couldn't Jake have let him sleep?

"Look!" Jake stopped beside a beech trunk and nodded toward the ground. "Smell that." Talltail's nose was already twitching. "Cat scent," Jake announced proudly. "When I'd fetched the wool, I decided to have a sniff around. And I found this."

A jumble of scents clung to the leaf-strewn soil between the tree roots. Talltail leaned closer, opening his mouth.

"Is it the rogues?" Jake demanded.

There was a familiar hint to the smell. "I think it might be!" Talltail straightened up and stared at Jake, feeling a worm of excitement stir in his belly. The scents were too frozen to tell for sure. But they were definitely cat scent and *definitely* familiar. "They're stale." He unsheathed his claws and sank them into the cold, damp earth. "But we're on the right trail!"

CHAPTER 34

✤

Talltail woke in the wool-lined hollow between the oak roots. He could feel Jake breathing beside him, his pelt warm where their fur touched. He lifted his head, tasting the air. The icy chill had gone, replaced by dampness. The musty aroma of dying leaves flooded the nest.

"Jake." Talltail nudged the kittypet. Unfrozen, the cat scents they'd found last night would be much stronger. He hopped out of the nest, his paws sliding on the soggy leaves that had crunched underpaw yesterday.

Jake blinked open his eyes. "What is it?" He yawned.

"The weather's changed," Talltail told him. "There might be a trail we can follow."

Jake scrambled out of the nest, his nose twitching. He glanced at the remains of the squirrel Talltail had caught last night and licked his lips. "Should we hunt first?"

Talltail blinked. "We can hunt later." *We have to check those scents!* Heart quickening, Talltail headed for the trail Jake had led him along yesterday, mouth open, tasting for scents. He smelled moldy bark and damp leaves. Prey-scent hung heavy on the air, and the stale tang of fox.

Jake trotted after him. "Can you remember where they were?"

How could I forget? Talltail's fur rippled along his spine. It was his first real evidence that he was on the trail of the rogues. *If it is the rogues.* He broke into a run. He recognized Sparrow's scent before he'd even reached the beech where the rogues had sheltered. Loosened by the mild frost, the smell flooded the damp air, stale but clear. Talltail skidded to a halt beside the flattened leaves where the rogues had clearly spent more than one night. In the pale dawn light he noticed the bones of prey scattered nearby and spotted a thin film of fur clinging to the craggy bark at the base of the tree.

Jake stopped beside him, panting. "I thought I'd lost you for a moment," he puffed.

"I had to know if it was them." Talltail stood with his legs braced, his old rage surging back as Sparrow's scent filled his nose. He could taste Reena's scent too, and Bess's. A pang tugged his heart as he remembered how welcoming he'd been when the rogues had first arrived. How could he have been so foolish and trusting? He should have known they were trouble the moment they set paw on WindClan territory. Why didn't his Clanmates understand the threat of letting strangers into the camp? *Rabbit-brains!* They believed the rogues were their friends, even after Sparrow had caused Sandgorse's death! Talltail curled his claws into the soft earth, a growl rumbling in his throat. *I'll make you sorry!*

"Talltail?" Jake was staring at him. "Are you okay?"

Talltail flicked the tip of his tail. "I'm fine," he muttered. "I just want to find those cats."

Jake dipped his head. "We'll find them," he promised.

Talltail paced the edge of the abandoned nest until he found a scent trail leading away between the trees. It was old, but still strong enough to track. Pelt pricking, he began to follow it.

"Where are we going?" Jake called.

"Can't you smell their trail?"

Jake caught up. "I can only smell trees and leaves." He stuck out his tongue. "There are so many new scents out here. It's hard to tell them apart."

"You'll get used to it." Talltail glanced at Jake, suddenly realizing that the tom was supposed to be going home. "Aren't you heading back to Twolegplace?" he asked.

Jake blinked at him. "What? Now that we've found the trail? I can't leave you to face Sparrow alone."

"But this is my mission. I should . . ." Talltail's mew trailed away. He didn't want Jake to go. He searched the kittypet's green gaze. "You don't have to come."

"I *want* to!" Jake shifted his paws, adding quietly, "If you don't mind, that is."

Talltail glanced at the ground, feeling hot. "I don't mind," he murmured. "It's good to have company."

"That's settled, then." Jake marched away, tail high. "I know it's your mission, and I won't put my whiskers where they don't belong." He plunged past a clump of shriveled ferns. "But I can help you track Sparrow down. After that, it's up to you."

Talltail purred. "Thanks, Jake." He tasted the air. "Er, you do know that you're heading the wrong way, don't you?" The scent trail headed along a ridge in the forest floor. Jake was tramping uphill, veering away through the trees.

Jake stopped and tasted the air. "I am?" His ears flattened. "Maybe you should lead the way," he mewed.

Amused, Talltail headed along the ridge, his paws slipping on the layer of decaying leaves. He was used to grass and peat, firm turf that sprang beneath his feet. Jake trotted beside him, more at ease with the slippery trail, until brambles started to crowd the path.

"Ow!" Jake tripped over a prickly tendril, hopping on three legs and shaking his injured paw.

"Are you okay?" Talltail stopped and sniffed Jake's leg. *No blood scent.*

"I'd be better if that hadn't tripped me up." Jake glared at the bramble.

Talltail scanned the woods. The scent trail headed through bracken where fallen branches and rotting logs crisscrossed the forest floor, echoing the tangled canopy above. The rogues seemed to tackle every obstacle head-on, moving forward regardless of the territory.

"Come on." Talltail padded around the bramble, watching for spiky tendrils. He hopped over a fallen branch and pushed his way into the bracken. Broken stems showed the rogues' trail, tainted with their scent. A decaying tree lay across the path and he scrambled over it, his paws slipping on the slimy moss. On the other side, the ground turned boggy. Talltail slowed as the sucking mud dragged at his paws.

"I thought you said that rogues chose the easiest path," Jake grunted, shaking mud from his forepaw.

"It was probably frozen when they passed," Talltail guessed.

"Can you tell how old the scents are?" Jake scrambled onto harder ground and shook crumbs of leaf litter from his whiskers.

"No. The smell's quite fresh," Talltail told him. "But the frost might have preserved it." He glanced at the sky, gray above the treetops. "Come on." He pulled his paws free of the cloying mud. "If it starts raining, the scents might be washed away."

The trees here were younger and thicker, their leaf-bare branches jutting low to the ground. Talltail had to keep low, ducking one branch and leaping another like a squirrel. He heard wood crack and split as Jake blundered after him. Talltail stopped and turned, breathless, as they reached a clearing.

"This is tough going—" Jake's gaze flashed with alarm. "Look out!" He barged past Talltail, his orange pelt bushing out.

Where are you going? Talltail whipped around. A dark russet shape was blazing toward them. *Fox!*

Jake hurled himself in its path as the fox lunged at Talltail. The kittypet reared up and slashed at the fox's muzzle. The fox ducked away, showing its sharp, yellow teeth, then sprang at Jake again. Quick as a bird, Talltail shot forward, slicing the fox's muzzle. The fox yelped, eyes sparking with rage. Talltail felt fur brush his flank. Jake was beside him. Talltail reared up on his hind legs as the fox attacked again. Jake reared up too. Talltail launched a flurry of blows at the fox and Jake joined in.

The fox snapped at them—one side, then the other. Tall-tail's claws hooked flesh, and he felt blood spurt against his cheek. The fox yelped, then growled, its eyes narrowing. Tall-tail's heart lurched. *We're just making it angry!* He glanced sideways at Jake. Eyes narrow, ears flat, Jake was hissing as viciously as any warrior. He slammed a front paw against the fox's muzzle. Talltail matched his blow. They fell into a steady rhythm, lash-ing out at the fox with relentless fury. Then Talltail stumbled over a fallen twig. He lost his balance and dropped onto all fours. Jake dropped beside him. Talltail let the momentum take him down to the ground and rolled all the way over. Jake rolled with him, and they leaped to their paws beside the fox's flank and began swiping again. The fox shrieked.

"He can't fight us both!" Talltail yowled with a rush of tri-umph.

"Can you hold him while I go for his tail?" Jake called back.

"Not for long." Talltail gritted his teeth and lashed out even more fiercely as Jake darted toward the fox's haunches and clamped his teeth around the base of its tail. Talltail heard a crunch as Jake bit down hard. The fox writhed, yelping, and as Jake let go, it tore past Talltail and fled away through the trees. Talltail dropped onto all fours, panting. His forepaw stung where the fox's teeth had grazed it.

"Did it hurt you?" Jake was at his side in a moment, sniffing for wounds.

"Just a scratch." Talltail showed him the scrape along his paw. "Not deep. Barkface would treat it with dock."

"I'll find some." Jake trotted away past the ferns. He was back a few moments later with a wad of dock in his jaws. He dropped it at Talltail's paws. Lumps of fur were sticking out around Jake's neck, and his orange pelt was darkened with spots of blood.

Talltail sat down. "Are you okay?"

"I've had worse wounds from next door's tom." He dipped his head to show Talltail a long-healed nick in his ear.

Talltail sniffed it, a rush of gratitude sweeping through him as Jake's warm scent touched his nose. "Thank you, Jake," he murmured.

"What for?" Jake straightened up.

"You saved my life." Talltail paused. *"Again."*

Jake purred. "No problem." He sniffed the dock. "Do you wrap this around your paw or what?"

"You chew it and lick it into the wound," Talltail told him. Jake wrinkled his nose. Talltail's whiskers twitched with amusement. "It's okay. I can do it myself." He grabbed a leaf in his jaws and began chewing.

Jake watched as he pulped it and worked it into the scratch with his tongue. "Will that really make it better?"

"It'll stop the wound from going bad," Talltail meowed.

Jake waited until Talltail had used up all of the leaf. "Can you walk?" he asked.

Talltail's wound stung and his hind leg ached where he'd strained it, rearing up. But he wanted to keep following the rogues' scent. A heavy shower might wash it away. "I'm fine," he insisted. He limped across the clearing, sniffing the ground, his tail twitching as he picked up Reena's scent. Algernon's and Sparrow's mingled with it, and he could smell Bess and Mole, too. He followed the trail through a hawthorn bush and past a gorse thicket, stumbling as leaves slid beneath his paws. Jake darted to his side, pressing against him.

"Lean on me," he ordered.

"I'm okay," Talltail meowed, but he let some of his weight rest against Jake's soft shoulder. They padded on through the forest, Talltail sniffing for scent, Jake watching the ground for twigs and ruts. Talltail slowed as he saw the forest lighten ahead. They must be near the edge.

Jake stiffened beside him. "Can you hear that?"

Talltail pricked his ears. A buzzing, like swarming bees, hummed in the distance. "What is it?" A Thunderpath stench touched his nose, but the noise was too whiny to be monsters.

"It sounds like a grass-cutter," Jake told him.

Talltail blinked at him. "A what?"

"The Twolegs use them to shave the grass."

Twolegs are rabbit-brains. Talltail strained to see past the trees. "Why would they be using one here?"

Jake sniffed. "Perhaps there's a den beyond the trees."

"Let's find out."

They crept through the trunks, slowing as they neared the edge of the woods. Talltail flattened his ears as the buzzing pierced his pelt, much louder now. The ground trembled beneath his paws. As they broke from the trees, Talltail halted.

A hillside sloped past them. The grass had been churned into wide circles of mud as though huge claws had reached down and raked it. The Thunderpath stench was so strong, Jake coughed. "That's not a grass-cutter," he choked. "What is it?"

The buzzing had grown to a roar—to *countless* roars, which were rolling toward them over the crest of the slope.

"We should stick to the side of the woods," Jake suggested hoarsely. "It might be quieter at the bottom of the valley."

Talltail could feel him trembling. The ground trembled even more. "Perhaps we should head back into the forest," he growled over the noise. "We can pick up the trail farther down—" He stopped as a deafening roar exploded around them, so loud that it blasted them to the spot.

Three huge shapes were speeding over the rise, bouncing over the churned grass toward them. Each ran on two black spinning paws that threw up mud in a wave behind them. Twolegs sat astride, hunkered down over the monsters' dirt-spattered bodies. Talltail froze, choking as Thunderpath stench rolled over him. Heat pulsed toward him.

StarClan, help us! Talltail closed his eyes as a heavy lump of mud hit his flank. More sprayed his cheek. He flinched away, pressing himself against Jake, and braced for searing pain and darkness to swamp him.

The roaring eased. Talltail peered through slitted eyes as mud rained down around them. The monsters were lurching away, heading downslope until they disappeared around the corner of the trees. Talltail struggled to get his breath, his flank throbbing where earth had battered it. "Jake?" He lifted his head. "Jake, are you hurt?" He could feel the kittypet pressing stiffly against him.

"You crow-brains!"

That's not Jake. Talltail looked up. On the slope above, a tom glared down at them. With a gasp, Talltail recognized the creamy, brown pelt of Algernon.

Reena stood beside him, her eyes round with shock. "Why didn't you run? You could have been killed!"

Algernon swished his tail. "You just stood there like lumps of wood!" He paused, his eyes widening. "Tallpaw?"

Reena pushed past him. "Tallpaw!" She pricked her ears. "Is that *you*?"

CHAPTER 35

❧

The roar of the monsters hung in the air, still thick with their stench.

"Tallpaw!" Reena thrust her muzzle closer. "What are you doing here? Is WindClan okay?"

He blinked at her. The *rogues*? He'd found them! He could hardly believe it. As he searched for words, Reena sniffed him, her ginger-and-white pelt pricking. "Why are you here?" she asked.

Jake lifted his muzzle shakily. "We've been looking for you."

Talltail flashed him a warning look. *Don't say any more!*

"Do you need help?" Reena's eyes sparked with worry. "Did Heatherstar send you?"

The buzzing of the monsters was growing louder again. Algernon glanced over his shoulder. "We'd better get out of here." He began to nudge Jake and Talltail into the forest. "Our camp's at the bottom of the slope."

Talltail turned and limped toward the cover of the trees.

"You're hurt!" Reena pressed beside him.

"Just bruised," Talltail told her. The shower of mud had battered him hard and his hind leg ached from the run-in

379

with the fox. At least the scratch on his foreleg was numb from the dock leaf. "I'm fine."

"Good." Reena guided him through a swathe of bracken, which was limp and wilting in the cold, damp air.

Algernon hurried Jake after them. "Didn't you realize you were walking into a herd of monsters?"

"I thought it was a grass-cutter," Jake told him.

"Out here?" Algernon stared at him as though he was crazy.

Reena paused and sniffed. "You're a kittypet!" Her gaze jerked toward Talltail. "What are you doing with a *kittypet*?"

Talltail swallowed. "He helped me find my way through Twolegplace."

Reena frowned. "We'd better keep moving. You can explain everything when we're safe."

"I'll lead." Algernon pushed past her, nosing through the bracken and heading downslope.

Brambles clustered between the trees, fighting hawthorn bushes for the light at the edge of the forest. Talltail kept his eyes on Algernon, trying to follow his paw steps through the tangle of branches.

"Oomph!" Jake gasped as he stumbled behind.

"Are you okay?" Talltail called.

"He's fine." Reena was helping Jake to his paws. "Follow me." She nosed her way between Talltail and Jake and they walked single file, following Algernon.

A stream cut through the trees like a tiny gorge, its banks steep. Algernon sprang across it easily. Talltail teetered on the brink, gazing down at the thin trickle of water below.

"Just jump!' Algernon urged.

Talltail launched himself off the edge, his paws slithering on the mud. He reached out and dug his claws into the far bank and hauled himself up.

"A WindClan cat shouldn't be out here." Algernon shook his head. "You belong on the moor."

Reena landed lightly beside him. "Why *did* you come?"

A thump sounded behind, followed by a small splash. Talltail glanced back. Jake had disappeared. He rushed to the edge of the stream and peered down the steep bank. Jake was writhing at the bottom, trying to find a paw hold in the mud. Talltail curled his hind claws deep into the earth and leaned down, snatching at Jake's scruff and holding him while the kittypet regained his footing.

"Thanks," Jake grunted. Talltail leaned back as Jake scrambled up beside him.

Reena was looking confused. "Why are you helping a kittypet?" She wrinkled her nose as she looked at Jake.

"He helped me," Talltail told her simply.

"Come on." Algernon nodded them onward. The monsters were still roaring at the edge of the trees. "We can talk about it when we reach camp."

"Is this where you live now?" Talltail asked.

"It's just temporary," Algernon told him, padding away.

Bracken scraped Talltail's nose as Algernon led them through another clump. He narrowed his eyes against the fronds, blinking as he emerged into a small, leaf-strewn clearing. Mole lay between the roots of an elm, a gray bundle of fur in a heap of dark green moss. He lifted his head as Talltail followed Algernon from the bracken. "What's he doing here?"

"Who?" Bess stuck her head out from beneath a holly bush. Her eyes widened and she slid out, her black-and-white pelt sleek. Talltail figured they must have lived well since they left the Clan.

"Tallpaw?" Bess blinked. "Is that you?"

"I'm Talltail now."

"You have your warrior name!" Reena mewed in surprise. "Congratulations!"

Bess's gaze flicked to Reena. "Where did you find them?"

"I think they found us, by the sound of it," Reena told her.

Jake stopped beside Talltail and breathed softly in his ear. "What do we do now?"

"Act normal," Talltail murmured. Lifting his muzzle, he stared at Bess. "I'm glad I managed to find you." His explanation would sound more convincing if he offered it before they asked. His thoughts raced. What reason could he give for tracking them here?

"Is there trouble in WindClan?" Bess asked.

"No." Talltail shifted his paws. "Everything's fine. But . . . but when I watched you leave at the end of greenleaf, I realized there was more to see than just WindClan territory." He felt his fur smooth as he eased into his story. "I was hoping you'd let me travel with you."

Algernon looked at Jake, eyes narrow. "What about the kittypet?"

"His name is Jake," Talltail meowed.

The bushes swished on the far side of the small clearing

and Sparrow slid out. "Tallpaw?"

Talltail swung around, meeting the brown tom's impassive gaze. "Hi, Sparrow. It's Talltail now." He swallowed his rage as it tightened his throat. A vision flooded his mind: He was pinning Sparrow to the ground, claws deep in the murderer's throat, blood bubbling at the tom's mouth.

"You're trembling." Sparrow's cool mew snapped him from his thoughts. "Are you all right?"

Talltail shifted his paws, thinking fast. "We were nearly squashed by two-pawed monsters."

Bess faced Sparrow. "He says he wants to travel with us."

"What about WindClan?"

"I was tired of all the duties and rules," Talltail mewed. "I wanted to see what it was like to live free, like you."

"And the kittypet?" Sparrow's gaze didn't give away anything. He simply flicked it from Talltail to Jake.

"He's been helping me track you down," Talltail explained. "He'll be going home now that I've found you." Talltail felt Jake stiffen beside him.

"Not yet." Bess sniffed Jake's muddy pelt. "You look like you need a rest and a meal. You must both stay for the night." She flicked her tail. "Reena, will you find them some moss to make nests?"

Talltail stepped forward. "Thanks, but we can find our own moss," he told her. "I didn't come here to be a burden." Before any of the rogues could argue he padded across the clearing and pushed into the bracken, relieved to hear Jake trotting after him.

"What are we doing?" Jake mewed as soon as they were far

enough away from the clearing to speak privately.

"*You're* going home," Talltail told him.

Jake's eyes flashed with hurt. "And you're going to live here with the rogue who killed your father?"

"Of course not," Talltail snapped. "I just need to wait for my chance."

"Then what?" Jake leaned closer, lowering his voice. "Sparrow looks tough. What are you planning to do to him?"

Kill him. Dread hollowed Talltail's belly. He'd never killed a cat before. He forced himself to picture his father yowling in terror as mud showered around him, sealing him in darkness forever. He growled.

"Talltail?" Jake's eyes were like twin moons, huge and pale. "What's your plan?"

"I want him to admit that he killed my father."

"And then?" Jake's ear twitched.

"You said you wouldn't poke your whiskers where they didn't belong." Talltail padded toward the roots of a tree and began scraping moss from the crevices in the bark.

Jake paced behind him. "That cat looks dangerous, Talltail."

"He's just a rogue." Talltail stripped away a long piece of moss.

"Come back with me," Jake pleaded. "You're not safe here."

"This is why I left my Clan." Talltail hooked out another wad of moss and dropped it onto the pile beside him.

"But you can go back to them, can't you?"

"I'm never going back," Talltail growled.

"Never?" Jake leaned closer. Talltail felt the kittypet's breath on his cheek. "But you're a warrior."

"You don't have to belong to a Clan to be a warrior." The words felt empty as Talltail spoke them. Was that true?

"But what are you going to do once Sparrow is dead?" Jake demanded.

"That doesn't matter." Talltail hadn't thought beyond the moment of his revenge so far. He wasn't going to start now. "Help me gather moss." The sun was sliding behind the distant hills. Talltail shivered as shadows thickened among the trees.

Jake crouched beside him and started picking at the next root. "If you're staying," Jake muttered, "so am I. You're going to need help."

Talltail paused and stared at the kittypet. "This is my mission, remember?"

Jake pulled a fat wad of moss from the bark with his claws. "Now it's *our* mission."

Talltail didn't argue. An odd sense of relief loosened his muscles. He'd grown used to having Jake around. "Come on." He scraped the gathered moss into a bundle. "We'd better get back." He didn't want to give the rogues too long to discuss his sudden appearance. They might start asking questions. He felt sure that Sparrow already had. The cold gleam in the tom's eyes hadn't been welcoming.

Talltail clamped his jaws around the soggy mass and began to carry it back toward the camp. Jake grabbed the rest and followed. Talltail slowed as they reached the bracken and padded though it softly, careful not to stir the stems.

"I don't like it." Algernon's mew made Talltail stop in his tracks.

Jake halted beside him. "What's wrong?"

"They're talking about me." Unease wormed in Talltail's belly.

"We can't turn them away." Bess sounded firm. "They're worn out."

Talltail pricked his ears.

"But these woods are prey-poor," Mole growled.

"There's enough for now," Reena argued.

Algernon snorted. "I knew we should have kept moving before we made camp."

"There are fish in the river, downslope," Reena pointed out.

"Can you swim?" Algernon muttered.

"It's not so prey-poor around here as you think." Sparrow's mew was confident. "That pigeon I caught today is the first of many."

"Really?" Mole's voice rose with interest.

"I've found a place where the Twolegs scatter grain," Sparrow told him. "There'll be pigeons coming for as long as it's there."

Bess purred. "If that's true, two extra mouths will be easy to feed."

Talltail padded out of the bracken and dropped his moss. "We can help you hunt," he mewed.

Algernon gazed past him, his gaze resting doubtfully on Jake. "Really?"

"Jake's a quick learner," Talltail told them. "He caught a mouse the other day."

Jake caught his gaze. "I helped," he corrected.

"We can manage without *kittypet* help," Mole grunted.

Reena padded toward the corner sheltered by the holly bush. "I've piled some leaves here for you to make nests on," she meowed.

"Thanks." Talltail held her gaze in the half light, trying to read whether she was genuinely willing to have them stay.

She tipped her head. "You seem different, Talltail."

"Do I?" Unnerved, Talltail picked up his moss and carried it to the heap of leaves Reena had scraped together.

"Less angry," Reena meowed. "You . . . you didn't seem to want us anywhere near WindClan by the time we left." She sounded hurt and puzzled.

Talltail winced. His rage was still there, burning just below his skin, but he needed these cats to accept him, trust him—at least until he had a chance to avenge his father's death. And deep down, he didn't blame Reena for anything, or Bess, or Algernon, or Mole. "I . . . I guess it took me a while to get over Sandgorse's death," he mewed, trying to sound as if the memories were long gone. "I'm sorry if I offended you."

Reena twitched her ears. "Not offended, exactly." She sounded sympathetic. "I guess it was a lot for you to deal with: Sandgorse dying like that, and Sparrow surviving."

Talltail shot her a sharp look. Reena was dangerously close to discovering the truth. He had to convince her he didn't hold Sparrow responsible. "Oh, it wasn't Sparrow's fault," he forced out through gritted teeth. "He was lucky to get out. Sandgorse wasn't." He stopped speaking as if he needed to concentrate on spreading his moss over the fallen leaves, shifting as Jake slid in beside him and began to shape the rest into a nest.

Bess crossed the clearing, a pigeon in her jaws. She dropped it at Talltail's paws. "I caught this earlier," she told him. "You and Jake can share it."

Talltail shook his head. "We can't take your prey."

"Yes, you can," Sparrow called from the darkness on the far side of the clearing. "WindClan fed us through greenleaf."

Algernon nodded. "It's only fair we feed one of theirs."

"I'm not one of theirs anymore," Talltail told him.

Algernon flicked his tail. "Nonsense," he snorted. "You are Clanborn. You'll be a Clan cat all your life."

Reena reached beneath a low branch at the edge of the clearing and hauled out a damp-looking shrew and a half-eaten squirrel. She tossed the shrew to Sparrow and carried the squirrel to Bess. "Mole. Algernon. Will you join us?"

Talltail leaned down and tore the wing from the pigeon with his jaws. He nosed it toward Mole and Algernon as they crouched beside Reena's squirrel. "Take this," he offered. "We don't need all of it."

"Give them the other one, too," Jake whispered in his ear.

Talltail ripped it off and dropped it at Algernon's paws. He was aware of Sparrow's gaze. *He knows why I'm here.* The thought flashed like fire in his mind. Fear sparked beneath his fur. He swallowed and padded back to Jake's side. Jake was already chewing on the pigeon. Talltail's belly tightened. How could he eat? *Act normal.* His own words echoed in his mind and he forced himself to take a mouthful of pigeon.

"How's Palebird?" Bess's question took him by surprise. She was looking up from the squirrel carcass, her eyes bright with interest.

"Palebird?" Talltail echoed dumbly. Up till now, he'd managed to block thoughts of WindClan from his mind.

"And Whiteberry," Reena purred.

"Are the tunnelers getting used to not tunneling?" Mole asked.

Talltail blinked at them, mind whirling. He never imagined he'd speak his Clanmates' names again. "Palebird had Woollytail's kits," he told Bess.

"That's wonderful!" Bess's eyes flashed with joy.

Talltail spat out a feather. "It's great," he lied.

Reena swallowed a mouthful. "How old are they?"

"A quarter moon when I left." He pictured Wrenkit, Rabbitkit, Flykit, and Bristlekit crowding around his legs, tails high, squeaking with excitement. Their voices echoed in his mind.

Give us a badger ride!

Can we come?

Can I decide my own warrior name?

He closed his eyes, surprised by the sharp pang that stabbed his heart.

"How could you bear to leave them?" Reena's mew cut into his thoughts.

"They're happier without me," he growled, burying his muzzle into the soft flesh of the pigeon.

"Leave him be, Reena." Algernon's mew was gentle. "He's had a long journey. We can ask all our questions tomorrow, when he's rested."

The moon was glowing through the branches. Night wrapped the forest in silence. Far away, beyond the trees, a fox barked shrilly.

Jake licked his lips. "I'm exhausted." He stretched and climbed into his nest.

Talltail nosed the remains of the pigeon toward Algernon. "Thanks for the prey." He climbed into the nest beside Jake's, their fur touching. Jake's warmth eased the racing of his heart as he watched Algernon and Mole gather the prey-scraps and hide them under the holly bush. Reena and Bess settled in their nests beside the bracken. Algernon curled up beside Mole between the roots of the oak. Sparrow circled down into a thick pile of leaves in a shadowy corner of the camp.

Talltail watched through narrowed eyes as Sparrow stirred in his nest, no more than a shape in the darkness. Flexing his claws, he let his lip curl as he stared at Sparrow. *You killed my father.* His thoughts hardened, like stone shaped in fire. *Now, I will kill you.*

CHAPTER 36

❧

"Aren't you used to forest hunting yet?" Reena called over her shoulder as she streaked ahead, zigzagging between the trees. She was chasing a squirrel.

Talltail stumbled on a stone that rocked beneath his paw. He blinked with surprise as Jake overtook him, leaping a frosty log and gaining on Reena. "How'd you get so good at this?" Talltail puffed, dodging a branch a moment before it hit his muzzle.

"It's a bit like alley running." Jake disappeared through a wall of bracken.

Talltail pelted after him, the stems crunching as he dived through them. Milky sunshine seeped through gray cloud. An icy wind whipped flecks of snow through the trees. He had lost sight of Reena through the bracken. As he plunged after her, he heard her angry mew ahead.

"Dog dirt!"

He broke from the stems to see her staring up the trunk of an ash tree. Above, a fluffy tail flicked away between the branches.

Jake circled beside her. "Can you climb up after it?"

"Not *that* high," Reena mewed sulkily.

Talltail stopped beside them, his flanks heaving. "Why don't we try the field?"

Jake stared at him. "The one with the monsters?"

Reena dragged her gaze away from the disappearing squirrel. "They won't be there today," she meowed. "They only come sometimes."

"Great." Talltail tasted the air, picking up the scent of grass, and headed past the tree. He was sick of struggling through woodland. A run across the field would help stretch his muscles. Sleeping so close to Sparrow had knotted them until it ached to stand still. *The wind might blow my thoughts clear, too.* He'd spent most of the night wondering how to take his revenge on Sparrow. One plan replaced another until his head hurt. None of them seemed right. The only thing he was sure of was that he had to gain Sparrow's trust enough to get him alone.

Does he trust me already? It was hard to tell what the brown rogue was thinking. His pale stare gave nothing away. *I don't even know if he realizes he caused Sandgorse's death.*

Anger flared in Talltail's belly and he broke into a run. "I see the field!" he called to Reena and Jake.

The pale dawn brightened the trees ahead. Talltail scrambled around a clump of ferns, paws skidding on the icy leaves. Digging in with his claws, he raced for the light, excitement surging through him as he broke onto frost-whitened grass. The slope stretched ahead. Looking up the hillside, he could see the scars the monsters had left behind. Thunderpath stench pricked his nose as he headed across the slope.

"Wait for us!" Reena caught up first, Jake reaching them a moment later.

"Are you really going to catch a rabbit?" Jake panted.

"If I can find one." Talltail opened his mouth and let the snow-flecked wind spray his tongue. He tasted the familiar musk of rabbit. "Come on." He led the way across the grass.

Reena purred. "It's great having young cats to hunt with." Her eye caught Talltail's. "And I'm glad you've stopped being such a grumpy old badger."

Jake fell in beside her. "Talltail's not grumpy."

Talltail glanced at his friend. Should he remind Jake how bad-tempered he'd been when the Twoleg had locked him in Jake's den?

"When I was staying with WindClan," Reena recalled, "I hardly dared talk to him. I was scared of getting my head bitten off!"

"We're here to chase rabbit, remember?" Talltail muttered, memories of his grief flooding back.

"See?" Reena flicked her ears at Jake. "Grumpy old badger."

"He's not grumpy with me." Jake wound past Talltail, lifting his tail.

Reena shrugged and sat down. "Any sign of rabbit?" she asked Talltail.

"They must still be asleep." The sun was lifting above the horizon. The wind whisked the frosty grass, scattering tiny dots of snow.

"I wish they'd wake up." Jake sighed. "I'm hungry."

"You're probably missing kittypet food." Reena licked her paw.

"Maybe," Jake conceded. "Catching your food is hard work."

It's even harder when you've elders and kits to hunt for, too. Talltail's pelt pricked as he wondered how WindClan was surviving leaf-bare. Had they stocked enough prey? Colder weather was on the way and without the tunnels to hunt in, prey might be scarcer than Heatherstar had predicted.

It's their problem now. I just have to look after myself. And Jake. He looked at his friend, wondering how long they had together before the kittypet returned to his Twoleg. A sharp pain stabbed his heart.

"Aren't you embarrassed?" Reena asked Jake suddenly.

Jake blinked at her. "Embarrassed?"

"About being a kittypet."

"Why?" He sounded confused.

"Taking food from a Twoleg." Reena's wide gaze was curious. "It's undignified for a cat."

"Is it?" Jake tipped his head on one side.

"A cat should rely on itself, not the kindness of Twolegs," Reena argued.

"I was born a kittypet," Jake pointed out. "I'm not doing any harm." He stared across the field. "And if I'm eating kittypet food, it means there's more prey for rogues like you." He nodded toward a distant tussock. "Did something move over there?"

Talltail followed his gaze. "Yes!" His paws pricked as he saw rabbit ears twitch in the grass downslope. He flicked his tail at Reena. "See?" he challenged. "Even a kittypet has the same instincts as we do."

Reena's eyes sparkled. "I bet he can't catch it, though." She padded past Talltail, her tail brushing his flank. "Not like you."

Talltail's fur rippled. He glanced self-consciously at Jake, but Jake was staring across the field at the twitching ears.

"What now?" Jake asked.

Talltail waved his tail upslope. "You two head up there and circle around it."

"Like we caught the thrush!" Jake's eyes glowed.

Talltail nodded. "I'll stalk it from here. Then we'll see which way it runs."

As Reena and Jake headed uphill, Talltail dropped into a crouch and ran low, as fast as a swooping hawk. The wind streamed past his ears and filled them with snow till he could only hear his own heartbeat. As he neared the rabbit he stopped and watched. It was munching the tips of the grass, lifting its head from time to time to peer nervously around. Talltail glanced upslope. Reena was nudging Jake into a crouch until they were both stalking low, circling wide around their prey and halting a little way past it.

Talltail lifted his head just high enough to catch Jake's eye. Jake stared at him, questioning. Talltail nodded. Jake and Reena stalked forward. Talltail closed in. The rabbit was halfway between them, head down, ears flattened now against its spine. The warm smell of it bathed Talltail's tongue. His belly rumbled. He padded closer, gaze fixed on its brown pelt.

He glimpsed the ginger and orange pelts of Reena and Jake beyond. Another few paces and he'd be within pouncing distance. He quickened his step, eager to reach it before Reena. He wanted to carry this catch home to the rogues. It would help earn Sparrow's trust.

If only the brown rogue would choke on it.

Rage stirred as Talltail realized he was hunting for the cat who'd killed his father. A growl rumbled in his throat. The rabbit lifted its head, eyes sparking with panic. *It heard me!* Furious, Talltail leaped for it. The rabbit shot away, eyes widening in terror as it spotted Jake and Reena lunging from the other side. It headed downhill, pelting through the thickening snowfall.

Talltail hared after it, his paws thrumming, wind howling in his ears. The field sloped steeper. He narrowed his eyes against the snow, his gaze focused on the brown pelt of the rabbit.

"Talltail!" A panicked yowl sounded from behind.

Reena? He could hardly hear for the wind and the roaring of the blood in his ears. It felt great to be tearing over the grass again, the scent of prey in his nose, no branches to trip on, no trees to swerve around. He was gaining on the rabbit easily. Just so long as it didn't have a burrow to dive down. And even if it did, he could chase it inside. *I'm a tunneler's son.* With a rush of triumph Talltail sprang and landed squarely on the rabbit.

"Talltail!" Reena's terrified shriek sounded through the wind as he skidded down the slope, snow spraying from beneath his paws. He grabbed the rabbit in his jaws and, swinging it up, crunched through its spine. It stopped struggling and hung limply in Talltail's mouth.

Reena was racing toward him. Jake's orange pelt flashed behind. "Don't move!" Reena screeched.

"Why?" Talltail dropped the rabbit and stared as Reena scrambled to a halt a tail-length ahead of him.

"Just walk toward me," Reena ordered.

Bewildered by the terror in her eyes, Talltail picked up the rabbit and padded toward her. She weaved around him, herding him farther up the slope, her pelt bristling.

"What's wrong?" Talltail asked.

"You nearly went over the edge," Reena croaked.

"What edge?" Talltail glanced back through the blizzarding snow.

"That's a cliff."

"Like the gorge?" Talltail stiffened, remembering his first day as an apprentice, when he nearly fell into the river.

"Worse." Swallowing, Reena padded warily forward.

Talltail followed her, stopping when she stopped and peering over the edge of a steep, sandy cliff. Through the snow, he saw monsters hurtling below them along a huge Thunderpath. It cut through the gorge like a wide, angry river. He flinched as wind from the monsters' backs ruffled his whiskers.

"You stopped just in time." Jake halted beside him and stared down. His ears flattened when he saw the monsters streaming along the gorge, teeming like fish in a river. "You would have been killed if you'd fallen down there."

Talltail swallowed. He'd nearly died! The snow had hidden

the Thunderpath's sound and scent. He was lucky he'd caught up with the rabbit when he did. Another tail-length . . . He pictured plunging down, down, down, a monster hurtling toward him. He closed his eyes. *I could have been killed.*

An idea flared inside his mind. He trembled, not with fear but excitement. *That's how I'll do it!* All he had to do was lure Sparrow here. One push and the murdering rogue would plunge down beneath the paws of a monster.

Talltail's heart pounded in his chest. *Sandgorse! I promised you I'd avenge your death. Sparrow will never harm another cat again.*

CHAPTER 37

❧

Talltail twitched in his nest as a dream wound its way into his sleep. With his fur lifted by the wind, he stepped onto a broad, sloping moor. Heather trembled in the distance and grass streamed around his paws. A hole yawned in the ground beside him. Talltail trembled as he peered inside. Darkness sucked him in, drawing him down through the tunnel before he could stop himself. He struggled to find his paws, scrabbling against the muddy walls, the scent of water and earth filling his mouth.

"Talltail!" Sandgorse's agonized yowl echoed from the shadows.

Through the darkness, Talltail could see the anguished face of his father, half-buried in mud. Lunging forward, he reached for Sandgorse's scruff and dragged him backward, hauling him, heavy as stone, up toward sky and wind. Bursting out onto the moor-top, he laid his father on the streaming grass. "Sandgorse!"

Mud bubbled at Sandgorse's lips. His flanks quivered weakly. Eyes closed, he twitched and fell still.

"Don't die." Talltail crouched down and pressed his nose against Sandgorse's cheek.

Sandgorse's eyes blinked open.

Talltail jerked back, pelt bushing up. "You're alive?"

Sandgorse stared at him blankly, his eyes black as night.

"Sandgorse?" Talltail thrust his muzzle against his father's fur. "It's me, Talltail. I'm going to avenge you. Your death won't go unpunished. Sparrow will pay for what he did!"

Sandgorse's head lolled, his eyes gazing back emptily for a moment before they closed. Talltail felt his father's body slump against him. *I'm alone now.* Talltail yowled to the starless sky while grief scorched through him, as pitiless as fire.

"Talltail?" A muzzle poked his shudder. Talltail blinked open his eyes, dazed. "Talltail!" Jake's face loomed above him.

Talltail jerked his head up. "Is it dawn?" He stared blearily around the rogues' camp. Shadow swallowed the clearing.

"Not yet," Jake soothed. "You were twitching in your sleep. I was worried."

"It was a bad dream." Talltail looked into Jake's steady gaze, comforted by his friend's soft, sleep-hazy scent.

Jake curled down beside him. "Go back to sleep."

Talltail pressed closer, grateful for Jake's warmth, and closed his eyes. His dream flashed in his mind. Over and over, he watched Sandgorse die, his belly tightening each time. As Jake relaxed beside him and drifted into sleep, Talltail's tail-tip twitched.

A nest rustled across the clearing. Talltail snapped open his eyes. He saw a shadow move from Sparrow's nest. Where was the rogue going? Holding his breath, Talltail strained to see through the darkness. He could just make out Sparrow as he slid into the bracken. Was he going hunting?

This is my chance. Talltail leaped to his paws, leaves rustling beneath him. *I'll ask to join him.* He hopped out of his nest. *I'll lead him to the cliff.* The fur rippled excitedly along his spine.

"Talltail?" Reena was blinking at him from her nest, her eyes shining in the darkness. "Where are you going?"

Talltail froze. "I saw Sparrow head into the woods," he whispered. "I wanted to see if he was hunting so I could join him."

"Sparrow doesn't like company when he goes out early," Reena warned him.

Talltail's pelt pricked with frustration. "He might like mine."

"I wouldn't risk it." Reena stood up and stretched. "You can hunt with me, if you want."

Talltail shook his head. "I'll get some more sleep, thanks." He left her staring at him, round-eyed, and climbed back into his nest. Jake didn't stir as he curled down beside him. Talltail's paws itched. How much longer would he have to wait?

It was dawn by the time the rogue padded back into camp. Weak daylight was filtering though the branches. Thick clouds hid the sun, and snow was flecking the forest, settling lightly on top of yesterday's thin coating. Talltail stretched in his nest and pretended to yawn, then trotted into the clearing.

Sparrow was carrying a fat pigeon in his jaws. He dropped it and met Talltail's gaze. "Have you just woken up?"

"Yes," Talltail lied. He glanced at Sparrow's catch. "Another pigeon?" He remembered what the rogue had told them. *I've found a place where the Twolegs scatter grain. There'll be pigeons coming for as long as it's there.*

"The Twolegs leave food for them in the field," Sparrow reminded him.

Talltail's ears pricked. "In the *field?*"

"Near the Thunderpath." Sparrow padded to a pool of snowmelt caught in the crook of a twisted root and began to drink.

Talltail's thoughts quickened. *Can I persuade him to take me hunting there?*

"Pigeon!" Bess's delighted mew interrupted his plans. She hopped out of her nest and sniffed the fresh-kill. Still warm, it was melting the thin snow beneath it. Reena hurried to join her, licking her lips while Mole stretched in his nest. Jake was still sleeping, a light coat of snowflakes dappling his fur.

"Will you take me there?" Talltail called to Sparrow.

"Where?" Sparrow glanced around.

"Where the pigeons come." Talltail pressed back excitement.

Sparrow shrugged. "Okay."

Talltail felt the need to explain. "I want to hunt for you. To thank you for letting us stay."

Jake stirred in his nest, lifting his head. "Who's letting us stay?"

Sparrow gazed impassively at Jake. "No one's letting anyone stay." He licked water from his lips. "You're just sharing the camp for now."

Talltail dipped his head. "Of course."

Reena rolled the pigeon over. "They can stay, though, can't they?"

Bess's gaze darkened. "Warriors and kittypets don't belong with rogues," she murmured.

"I'm *not* a warrior. I'm a—" Talltail hesitated. The words had come before he'd had chance to think.

Jake hopped out of his nest. "You'll always be a warrior, Talltail." He shook the snow from his fur. "Just like I'll always be a kittypet."

Algernon padded from his nest. "And we'll always be rogues." He stretched, nose twitching. "Who caught the pigeon?"

"Sparrow." Bess looked fondly at the brown tom.

Talltail's pelt pricked. "Come on, Jake." He padded toward the bracken. "Let's practice your stalking."

"Stalking?" Jake blinked at him. "Aren't we eating first?" He glanced at the pigeon.

"Later." Talltail stared at Jake. *I want to talk to you. In private!* He willed Jake to understand, relieved when Jake padded toward him. "We might catch something while we're practicing," Talltail went on. He led the way into the woods, nosing through the bracken. Snow fluttered onto his spine as he pushed between the stems.

"What should we stalk?" Jake asked when they emerged into a narrow clearing.

Talltail paced the leaf-strewn forest floor. "Did you hear?" he demanded.

"Hear what?" Jake was looking distractedly around the woodland.

"Sparrow!" Had Jake forgotten why they'd come here?

"What?"

"He's taking me hunting beside the cliff."

Jake stiffened. "You're not thinking of—"

"Of course!" Talltail cut in. "That's why we're here. It's the perfect place. No fighting. No explanations. I just need to time it right and I can give him a push."

"Onto the Thunderpath?" Jake's eyes widened in horror.

"It's perfect!" Talltail insisted. "He'll pay for my father's death beneath the paws of a monster."

"Don't do it, Talltail."

Talltail narrowed his eyes. "You said you would help me."

"Do you really want to kill a cat?"

"If I'd stayed in WindClan, I'd have probably killed a cat in battle by now!"

"In battle," Jake pointed out. "That's different. Killing in the heat of battle, to defend your Clanmates—that makes sense. But to kill a cat moons later—"

"He never understood the damage he did." Talltail curled his lip. "That's why he must be punished. To make him sorry."

"Just *tell* him!" Jake's fur rose along his spine. "*Make* him understand. How Sandgorse's death hurt you, and how you feel he's responsible."

Talltail glared at Jake. "Don't you think I tried that when Sandgorse died? He wouldn't admit it. Even when I told him to his whiskers that he killed Sandgorse, he just shrugged it off, like he shrugs everything off. He doesn't care about anything.

So I'm going to make him care about this."

"By killing him?" Jake shook his head. "I know you, Tall-tail. You're not a killer. You'd die to defend those you love. But kill a cat you hardly know?" He shook his head. "I don't think so."

"He has to pay!" Talltail hissed. Why was Jake arguing? Was that why he'd come? To stop Talltail from doing the one thing he'd sworn he would do—the one thing that would make sense of his life? "If no one pays for Sandgorse's death, then it's not fair!"

"Life isn't fair!"

"It's not fair to *me*!" Talltail realized that he was shaking with fury.

Jake gazed at him. "Don't do this, Talltail," he begged softly. "Please."

"I *have* to!" Talltail snarled. "If you don't agree, then go home. You're no use to me." Raging, he stamped away, push-ing through brambles and barging past hawthorns, too angry to feel their thorns scrape his muzzle. Even Jake had betrayed him! Why had Talltail trusted him? Why had he trusted *any-one*? Hadn't he learned that he could only rely on himself? *I came here for revenge and I'm going to get it!*

Snow flurries came and went. The wind grew colder. Shiv-ering and hungry, Talltail headed back to camp. "Can we hunt now?" he asked Sparrow as he padded into the clearing.

Sparrow looked up from his nest. "There's fresh-kill under the holly bush."

"What about the pigeons?" Talltail pressed.

"They'll be wary after this morning," Sparrow warned. "Let's wait until tomorrow. We don't want to scare them off for good."

Frustrated, Talltail paced the camp.

"I'll hunt with you." Reena's offer came as a relief. But woodland hunting only made Talltail more restless, even though he and Reena caught a squirrel and a fat blackbird. Back in camp, Talltail avoided Jake's gaze, though he could feel the kittypet watching him in silence. As dusk darkened into night, they shared fresh-kill with the rogues. Then Talltail climbed into his nest.

"Are you tired already?" Reena called. "I thought we could go for a walk."

"It's a bit cold for a nighttime walk," he grunted, resting his muzzle on his paws.

"I'll go with you, Reena," Jake offered.

Reena blinked. "No, thanks." She sighed. "Talltail's right. It's too cold."

Jake's fur twitched. He glanced around at the rogues, then climbed into the nest, curling up a muzzle-length away from Talltail.

Talltail swallowed back a growl and stared at Sparrow. The rogue was calmly washing in his nest. *Tomorrow.* Talltail's heart was racing too fast to sleep. Fury throbbed beneath his pelt. His claws ached as he curled and uncurled them, picturing Sparrow hurtling into the gorge, a monster racing toward him as he landed on the hard stone.

Above the trees, the sky cleared slowly, the moon showing

just as dawn began to push back the night. As soon as milky light showed over the horizon, Talltail hopped out of his nest. He crossed the camp and thrust his nose close to Sparrow's ear. "Let's hunt!" he meowed.

Sparrow lifted his head, blinking. "Now?" He glanced at the dark blue sky. "The sun's not even up."

"I thought you liked early hunting." Talltail stepped back, whisking his tail. "The pigeons will hardly be awake. If we get there before them, we can choose a good hiding spot."

"You sound like a warrior planning a patrol." Sparrow narrowed his eyes. "I thought you'd left the Clan to get away from rules and duties."

"Hunting isn't a duty," Talltail muttered. "It's fun."

Sparrow yawned and climbed out of his nest. "Come on, then." He headed into the forest.

Talltail stalked him through the silent dawn, keeping a muzzle-length behind. Blood roared in his ears. Sparrow was prey to him now, more deserving of his death than any mouse or pigeon. Talltail's heart pounded harder until his whole body seemed to ring with its beat. Images flashed in his mind. He saw Sandgorse struggling to escape from the collapsing tunnel, pinned by the earth, mud blocking his yowls as he fought desperately to escape. Ahead, Sparrow's tail disappeared as he threaded through a dense laurel bush. Was Sparrow's tail-tip the last thing Sandgorse had ever seen? Talltail pushed after him through the waxy leaves, clenching his teeth to stop himself from growling.

As they reached the field, Sparrow slowed. "The grain is

over there." He nodded downslope toward a smooth stretch of grass. It rippled in the light breeze, gray in the pale dawn light.

Talltail headed toward the cliff. "Let's check the Thunderpath first."

"What for?" Sparrow called, trotting after him.

"Crows would pick fresh-kill from the Thunderpath back home." *Home?* He corrected himself quickly. "Back in WindClan territory."

"What good is that to us?" Sparrow fell in beside him. "Who eats crow-food? Or crows? The cliff's too steep to climb down anyway."

"Is it?" Talltail asked innocently.

"Come on." Sparrow veered toward the patch of smooth grass. "Let's wait for a pigeon."

"Let's look at the Thunderpath." Talltail struggled not to growl. Was Sparrow going to make this impossible? He uncurled his claws, ready to fight the rogue if he had to.

"Okay." Sparrow shrugged. "If that's what you want."

Talltail glanced over his shoulder, relieved to see Sparrow following him toward the cliff. He could smell the tang of stone and monsters, and as he neared the edge, he slowed.

"Any sign of crow-food?" Sparrow grunted, padding past him and peering over the edge.

Elation thrilled through Talltail.

Sparrow leaned forward. "I can't see anything."

Talltail lifted his paws, ready to slam them into Sparrow's flank. Heat pulsed through his pelt. This was it. He was finally avenging Sandgorse's death. *Are you watching, Sandgorse?*

I'm punishing this cat for you! Can you see?

"Talltail?" Sparrow turned, his paws crumbling earth over the cliff edge. "What's the matter? You look odd."

Talltail stretched his claws. "Take a good look at me, Sparrow. I'm the last cat you're ever going to see. I brought you here to kill you," he hissed.

"Kill me?" Sparrow's pelt rippled. "Why?"

Talltail felt cold air pierce his fur. "Don't you *know*?" He dropped onto all fours. Couldn't this heartless rogue even *guess*?

For the first time, emotion sparked in Sparrow's gaze. "Tell me."

"You killed my father." The words caught in Talltail's throat.

"Sandgorse?"

"You *made* him go into that tunnel!" Talltail found he was shaking. "You left him there to die."

Sparrow blinked. "That's not how it happened."

Talltail hissed. "I saw you run from the tunnel like a frightened rabbit! You left my father behind!"

"I didn't know what to do. I'm no warrior." Sparrow glanced over the edge. "I had no training. Your father *knew* that. He gave his life so that I could escape. That's why he died. He held back the earth long enough for me to run."

He held back the earth. Talltail's head began to spin. A monster sounded in the distance, its roar echoing through the still dawn air.

Sparrow edged closer. "He died a hero, Talltail."

"Why should I believe you?" Rage swept through Talltail. Why wait till now to tell him? *The rogue must be lying.*

"Don't you believe that Sandgorse would give his life to save me?" Sparrow turned his head toward the monster as it rumbled beyond the gorge.

He's playing with me like I'm *the prey!* Talltail curled his claws into the grass. He'd waited too long for this moment. Sparrow wasn't going to take it away from him. His ear fur trembled as the monster thundered closer. Its yellow eye beams showed faintly on the cliff face.

Just push him!

"So you're going to *kill* me?" Sparrow breathed. "A life for a life? Is that part of the warrior code?"

"You know nothing of the warrior code," Talltail snarled.

"I know courage. Your father showed it when he helped me escape."

Talltail's breath caught in his throat. Sandgorse *was* brave. He would have given his life for another cat.

"This isn't courage, Talltail," Sparrow pressed. "Killing me won't bring Sandgorse back."

Jake's words flashed in Talltail's mind. *I know you, Talltail. You're not a killer.* Sandgorse's voice joined Jake's. *Another cat's life is as precious as your own.* Talltail's thoughts whirled. *What if he's telling the truth?* Alarm ripped though his chest. *I can't kill him, Sandgorse. I'm sorry!*

As he backed away from Sparrow, the ground trembled. Talltail glanced along the Thunderpath. The monster was coming, shaking the earth. "Let's get away from here."

Sparrow's eyes widened. "Help!" He jerked clumsily backward as the cliff started to give way beneath his paws. "I'm falling!"

Talltail flung out a paw, reaching for the rogue's pelt. He felt fur brush his claw-tips as they curled around thin air.

Then Sparrow disappeared.

CHAPTER 38

♣

Talltail flung himself onto the grass and wriggled forward to peer over the edge. Sparrow was slithering down the cliff face, showering grit as he fought to get a grip. "Talltail!" he wailed, a moment before he landed with a thump on the Thunderpath.

There was a heartbeat of ominous silence; then the gorge echoed with the roar of a monster as it howled closer. Sparrow scrambled to his paws and darted back and forth, pressing close to the cliff. Talltail stared down at him in horror. The smooth, black stone reached right to the edge of the Thunderpath. There was nowhere for Sparrow to hide.

The eyes of the monster lit up the curve.

"Help me!" Sparrow reached up with his front paws, trying to get a clawhold. "Help me up!" His mew was sharp with terror. He jumped, clinging to the sandy stone, but it crumbled in his claws and he tumbled back onto the hard, gray Thunderpath. "Talltail! Help!"

I have to save him! Talltail stared around desperately. *How?* A thought struck him. *There must be ditches somewhere along the Thunderpath, like the ones near WindClan land.* Without them, the gorge would become a river when it rained. If there was a ditch close by, they could hide inside while the monster went past. If they reached the ditch ahead of the monster. And if the ditch was big enough for two cats. If, if, if . . .

Talltail scrambled over the edge. He half skidded, half fell down the steep, sandy cliff, landing heavily beside Sparrow.

Sparrow blinked. "What are you doing?"

"Follow me!" Talltail hared along the Thunderpath. He glanced behind him. Sparrow was on his heels, his eyes huge with fear. Behind him, the vast head of a gleaming black monster loomed around the curve. "Run!" Paws burning, Talltail raced over the hard black stone. The gorge thrummed with the monster's roar. Talltail flattened his ears, pushing harder, stretching further with every paw step.

He scanned the edges of the Thunderpath, straining to see a hiding place carved somewhere in the rock. Ahead, a shadow darkened the stone where the Thunderpath touched the rugged rock of the gorge. Talltail's heart leaped. As he raced nearer, he could a see channel dug into the ground, just wide enough for a cat. Talltail sprang into it and looked back at Sparrow.

The terrified rogue was several tail-lengths behind. The monster thundered after him, so huge it blocked the sky.

"Hurry!" Talltail shrieked.

As Sparrow neared, Talltail reached up and grabbed the rogue's pelt. Sinking his claws into the dense fur, Talltail hauled him into the narrow ditch. Stones battered his flanks and the earth shook beneath him. Foul wind tugged his fur.

He shuddered with terror, his flesh shrinking beneath his pelt as the monster hurtled past.

"Sparrow?" Talltail scrambled backward and looked at the cat squashed beneath him.

Sparrow lifted his head. "We're alive!"

Talltail tried to stop himself from trembling. Dawn was lighting the sky. More monsters would be coming soon. "We have to get out of here." Could they make it to the end of the gorge without meeting another?

Sparrow seemed to guess what he was thinking. The rogue's gaze flicked past Talltail. "What about that way?" he suggested.

Talltail wriggled around in the narrow space. Sparrow had spotted a small tunnel that opened into the ditch. That must have been where the rainwater flowed out. Talltail padded toward it and sniffed the darkness. Fresh air washed over his muzzle. "Good idea." He beckoned Sparrow with a nod and started to duck inside.

He paused when there was no sound of paw steps following. Looking back, he saw Sparrow staring wide-eyed at the mouth of the tunnel, fur bristling and claws unsheathed. Talltail looked at the tunnel, then at Sparrow again. A pang of sharp emotion—pity, sorrow, even guilt—stabbed his belly. The last time Sparrow had entered a tunnel, he had barely escaped—and the other cat had died.

"Come on," Talltail mewed. "It's perfectly safe, I promise."

Sparrow took a step forward. His fur still stood on end.

"Stay close to me," Talltail told him. "You'll be fine." He

ducked his head and walked into the tunnel. The sides were round and smooth, made of hard, gray stone rather than hewn from wet earth. Talltail's claws skittered on the surface. Sheathing them, he padded cautiously on. He could hear Sparrow's pelt brushing the walls behind him. Darkness swallowed them and Talltail quickened his pace. He told himself that this tunnel would not collapse, that they would be out soon because he could feel air being funneled toward them, rich with the scent of grass. For a moment, he imagined how terrifying it must have been for Sparrow when the gorge tunnel collapsed around him. Talltail knew what it was like to feel mud and earth raining down on him, but when he had been in a tunnel accident, every other cat had made it out alive.

"You're doing great," he called over his shoulder.

"Thank you." Sparrow's mew echoed close behind, his breath warm on Talltail's hindquarters.

Talltail felt numb. Because of him, Sparrow had nearly died falling off the cliff. And now, because of him, Sparrow was alive. This wasn't what he had planned. He felt like he was walking in another cat's body.

Sparrow's muzzle touched his tail-tip. "I'm sorry your father died." The rogue's words were hardly more than a breath, but they rang around Talltail like spiraling wind. "It was an accident. Sandgorse saved my life. And I'll never forget him."

Of course Sandgorse saved him. Talltail's throat tightened.

"When we don't know the truth, we invent stories to fill the gaps," Sparrow went on quietly. "Sometimes it's the only way we have to make sense of our lives."

"Why didn't you tell me what really happened?" Talltail asked. "At the time?"

"I didn't think you'd believe me," Sparrow confessed. "You were so angry—so determined that someone must be to blame."

Talltail didn't argue. It was true.

The end of the tunnel glowed ahead, small at first but growing with each paw step until they emerged into dazzling, cold daylight. Talltail blinked as his eyes adjusted after the gloom. They were close to the Thunderpath, but the gorge was gone and meadows stretched away on either side. Sparrow stood still, taking deep breaths of the sparkling air.

"Where are we?" Talltail mewed.

Sparrow flicked his tail. In the distance, woodland nestled between two gently rolling hills. "The camp's up there." He jumped a swathe of long grass and pushed through a hedge. Talltail bounded after him.

They walked in silence across frosty fields until they reached the trees. Sparrow seemed to know his way and Talltail was happy to let him lead, scrambling over logs and sliding into dips as he tried to keep up. He scented the camp as they neared a patch of silvery bracken. Orange fur flashed in front of it.

Talltail broke into a run. "Jake? Is that you?"

Jake was pacing back and forth, his eyes like huge moons. He stopped when Talltail reached him. "What happened?" he demanded.

Talltail glanced at Sparrow as the rogue caught up with him. Jake blinked in surprise.

"You didn't do it!" Jake breathed after Sparrow had padded past and pushed through the bracken.

Talltail sat down wearily. "No."

"Why not?"

"Sandgorse saved him."

Jake's eyes clouded with confusion. "He *saved* him?"

"It's what Sandgorse would do." Now that the rage had gone, Talltail wondered how he could ever have thought of killing Sparrow. Had grief taken away all his faith in the warrior code?

"I knew it!" Jake paced around him. "I knew you couldn't do it!"

Talltail's pelt pricked. *What if Sparrow hadn't had time to explain? What if I'd pushed him over as a monster came into the gorge? What if he'd—?* He shifted his paws. With cold, crushing certainty, he knew that killing Sparrow wouldn't have changed anything. "I let anger change who I am." He gazed helplessly at Jake.

"No, you didn't!" Jake argued. "In the end, you let Sparrow live. That was being true to yourself, far more than you were when you wanted to kill him." His gaze softened. "I know you, Talltail. Your thirst for Sparrow's blood, your belief that only his death would change the way you felt—that was never really you."

Talltail blinked up at his friend. "You're right. But that's all I've thought about for so long. What do I do now?" He felt shaky, as if the path ahead had vanished into mist.

Jake glanced toward the camp. "Does Sparrow know you planned to kill him?"

Talltail's whiskers twitched. "Oh yes," he meowed grimly. "He knows."

"Then we'd better leave," Jake murmured. "We can't expect him to share food and shelter with us now, even if you did change your mind."

Talltail nodded, feeling numb. "I have to say good-bye first," he meowed.

"Really?" Jake's fur rippled along his spine. "After what you did?"

"Yes." Talltail knew he couldn't vanish without telling the other rogues he was leaving. That wouldn't be fair, to let them think they had done something to offend him or Jake. "You wait here." He wove through the crisp bracken into the center of the camp. Sparrow sat on the far side, washing his paws.

"Talltail!" Bess trotted over to him. "Sparrow told us you were both nearly killed by a monster!"

Reena bounded across the clearing. "Are you hurt?"

Algernon sat up, his ears pricked. "Sparrow said it was pretty close."

Mole sniffed Talltail's pelt. "You've still got the monster's stench on you."

"I'm fine." Talltail looked at Sparrow.

Sparrow stared back, his impassive gaze as unreadable as ever.

Talltail dipped his head. "Jake and I must leave now."

"Now?" Bess sounded surprised.

"You can't go yet!" Hurt flashed in Reena's eyes.

Sparrow stopped licking for a moment. "They must, actually," he meowed.

Algernon looked over his shoulder at the brown tom.

Talltail shifted his paws. "Jake needs to go home," he explained.

"What about you?" Reena's muzzle was a whisker away from his. "Are you going back to WindClan?"

"I'll see Jake home," Talltail meowed. *After that, who knows?*

"I can show you the way," Reena offered. "I know the Twolegplace." She began to circle him. "If we start now we can be there by—"

Talltail cut her off. "We can find our own way," he told her. Reena flinched as though he'd raked her nose with claws.

Bess pressed against her. "You heard him, Reena." There was sympathy in the she-cat's mew, and Talltail suddenly wondered if Reena had been hoping that Talltail would be her mate: that they'd have kits and travel together. Had she started to imagine a whole new life ahead of them?

Guilt rippled through his pelt. "I'm sorry, Reena." Part of him wished that he could make her happy. Their kits would be brave and strong. Talltail shook the thought away. Reena's path wasn't his. He was destined to travel alone. "I'll miss you," he meowed a little awkwardly.

She touched her muzzle to his cheek. "And I'll miss you."

Sparrow got to his paws. "We won't be visiting WindClan next greenleaf."

"Really?" *Because of me?* Guilt jabbed Talltail's belly.

"Times have changed," Sparrow meowed. "We need new

paths to roam. Old tracks grow stale."

Algernon's eyes were wide with shock. "You've decided this just now, have you?"

Sparrow shook his head. "Not right now, no. But I think it's the right decision. We have our lives; WindClan has theirs. Rogues like us don't belong in Clans. The warrior code wasn't made for us. Right, Talltail?"

Stunned, Talltail nodded.

Sparrow went back to washing his paws. "Give our regards to Heatherstar and Hawkheart," he mewed. "Tell them we wish them well."

"I'm sure they would do the same for you," Talltail croaked. He dipped his head to Mole. "Take care." He wondered if the elderly tom would make it through many more leaf-bares.

"Travel well, Talltail," Mole rasped.

"I will." Turning, Talltail padded from the camp.

"Good-bye! Good-bye!" Bess and Reena called behind him.

"Watch out for dogs!" warned Algernon.

"I will," Talltail muttered.

What will the Clan think when the rogues don't appear next greenleaf? Will they think something terrible has happened? Or will they remember Sandgorse's death, and think that the rogues are too ashamed to return? Talltail shook himself. He had left WindClan. What they felt about something far in the future was not his concern.

Jake hurried to meet him as he emerged from the bracken. "Is everything okay?"

Talltail nodded, heading between the trees.

Jake fell in beside him. "Did Sandgorse really save Sparrow?"

Fresh grief welled in Talltail's throat. "Yes," he meowed thickly.

Jake pressed against him. "Then your father died a hero," he murmured.

Talltail couldn't answer, his eyes clouding.

They padded through the woods, heading upslope until they reached the clearing where they'd first made camp. The hollow between the oak roots was still lined with wool and Talltail climbed in gratefully, too weary to hunt.

"I'll catch something," Jake offered. He headed away, returning as the sun touched the tops of the trees. He was carrying a tattered, old blackbird.

Talltail wrinkled his nose. "Couldn't you find one that was even older?" he teased, climbing out to sniff the ancient bird.

Jake lifted his muzzle. "I caught it, didn't I?" He took a bite, screwing up his face as he chewed the tough flesh.

Talltail bit into the bird. The blackbird was more sinew than meat, but he swallowed it anyway, grateful for Jake's new hunting skills.

"Will you go home now?" Jake's mew was muffled by feathers.

"I don't know if I have a home." Talltail took another bite.

"Of course you do!" Jake struggled to swallow. "You have WindClan!"

"I *left* WindClan."

"They'd let you back."

"I thought I'd keep traveling for a while," Talltail muttered. "Would you like that?"

Jake took another bite of blackbird and chewed. "I think you should go home."

"Home?" Talltail blinked at him. "I have no home. I don't even know who I am anymore."

Jake leaned forward and rested his muzzle on the top of Talltail's head. His chin felt warm and soft. "I know who you are. You're my best friend, and you always will be."

CHAPTER 39

Talltail was dreaming. Stars whirled around him, twirling him
through blackness. Then he plummeted down until the wind
pulled at his fur and his eyes watered. Exhilaration surged
through him as he fell, until soft peat touched his pads and
Talltail realized he was standing on the ground. He blinked,
and the darkness cleared. Light spilled around him, flooding
the landscape. Above, a wide, blue sky stretched to the horizon. Heather as purple as dusk rippled over the soft curve of
a hill. Grass, greener than Jake's eyes, lay in swathes between
the bushes, its scent so rich it made Talltail dizzy. A tawny pelt
was slinking through the heather.

Brackenwing!

Talltail's heart leaped. He bounded toward the she-cat,
but she was moving too swiftly. Other pelts showed around
her—black, gray, tortoiseshell—pelts he didn't recognize. But
he knew their scent as well as his own. *WindClan.* He was in
StarClan's hunting grounds.

"Brackenwing!" he called across the heather, but Brackenwing didn't stop. Talltail hurried after her, trying to catch the
eye of the other cats as he passed. But no cat seemed to notice

him. A tabby looked straight through him as though he didn't exist. A striped tom didn't flinch as Talltail raced by.

I must catch Brackenwing! She'll know me.

He burst from the heather onto a grassy summit. Brackenwing was looking down into a valley.

Talltail raced to her side. "It's me, Talltail!" he cried.

Brackenwing didn't move. She just kept staring down the slope. Talltail followed her gaze. Cats were moving over the grass below. *Palebird. Dawnstripe. Hareflight. Hickorynose.* Talltail's heart lurched as he recognized their pelts. Brackenwing was watching what was happening in WindClan territory. Talltail's paws ached with pain that felt like longing. Slowly at first, then faster, his feet carried him forward until Talltail found himself racing down the slope toward his Clanmates.

"Palebird!" He yowled his mother's name, the sight of her tugging deep in his belly as though she'd hooked her claws in and was pulling him closer. Talltail's mother didn't look around.

"Dawnstripe!" Surely she would speak to him? But his mentor kept padding across the grass, her tail down.

Talltail ran faster. He had to make them see him! But his paws grew heavier with each step. The harder he pushed, the slower he ran, as though the air around him had turned to water and was holding him back.

"Dawnstripe!" The longing in his paws deepened; the claws hooking his belly tugged him harder. But he couldn't get close enough to make the other cats notice him. "Dawnstripe!"

A paw poked his shoulder. "Wake up!"

Talltail jerked up his head. Jake was nudging him with a paw. "Another bad dream?" he meowed.

Talltail frowned. "Not exactly." He could still see his Clanmates as clearly as if they were in front of him. The claws in his belly tugged again. He flinched.

Jake leaned closer. "Are you okay?"

Talltail lifted his muzzle and gazed at Jake. "My belly hurts. And my paws. As though they're being pulled by something I cannot see."

Jake sat back, nodding. "Your home is calling you."

"What do you mean?" Talltail pushed himself up.

A purr rumbled in Jake's throat. "Don't you know?"

Talltail tipped his head on one side. "No."

"I guess Clan cats aren't used to leaving home." Jake sounded amused. "I know the feeling you're having. The nagging pain, the tug in my pelt and paws? I get that whenever I'm away from my home too long."

"Really?" Talltail blinked. "Why?"

"Every creature needs to belong somewhere," Jake told him. "Your paws know where that is, even if you don't."

Suddenly anxious, Talltail hopped out the nest. "But I don't belong anywhere."

"Are you sure?" Jake mewed. "What about your Clan?"

"I *left* my Clan." Why did everyone act like he had just strayed for a while? Talltail glared at Jake. "My paws must be calling me somewhere else."

Jake shrugged. "Wherever it is, let them guide you. The pain won't go away otherwise."

Talltail circled restlessly. "Will you come with me?"

"For a while." Jake watched him, his expression guarded.

Talltail stopped. "This feeling I have—do you have it too?" Jake nodded, and Talltail felt a tiny, cold stone inside his belly. "You want to go back to your Twoleg, don't you?"

Jake was quiet for a long time. Then he ran one front paw lightly over the ground. "That's where I belong," he mewed. "I can't stay away forever."

"I won't stop you," Talltail whispered. But he wondered if that was true. He didn't like the ache in his paws, or the claws tugging at his belly. The future suddenly stretched into shadow. And he hadn't even done what he'd set out to do—he hadn't killed Sparrow. He knew he'd made the right decision when he let the rogue live, but where was the satisfaction? It felt like returning from a hunting patrol with no fresh-kill for his Clan. He felt lost and empty, and his dumb paws were tugging him who knew where. Would he really be able to let Jake go?

"Come on." Jake headed toward the field. "Let's catch a rabbit first. Last one to that tussock is a fox-breath!"

Jake caught the rabbit. Talltail was impressed. He'd chased it, but Jake was the one who veered around to cut off its escape and killed it with a single bite. The kittypet looked thrilled, his eyes gleaming as he carried it back to Talltail.

"I could teach you warriors a thing or two about hunting!" Jake teased as they ate.

After burying the remains of the rabbit, they climbed the craggy summit they'd crossed on their way into the valley.

Clouds covered the sky, blocking the weak, leaf-bare sun. The breeze had lost its icy chill, but it was blustery, cold, and damp as it lifted Talltail's fur. He felt better now that his belly was full, the rich flavor of fresh-kill distracting him from the invisible tugging claws.

As they reached the top, Jake sat down and gazed at the landscape ahead. "What can you see?"

Talltail squinted through the wind that was battering his whiskers. He felt as though he were being assessed on Outlook Rock. "Fields." He recognized the first meadow he'd crossed with Jake. More meadows stretched around it, surrounding a dark mass of walls and dens. "And Twolegplace." It sprouted in the middle of the valley like an ugly forest.

"What about beyond?" Jake prompted.

Talltail peered at the smudge of leaf-bare forest on the far side. "ThunderClan territory, I guess."

"And beyond that?"

Talltail narrowed his eyes. Where the distant horizon met the sky, he could see swathes of brown heather. In a few more moons, they'd be greener than grass, burgeoning with fresh growth. *The moor.* His paws itched to pull him forward at the sight of his old home. He forced himself to stand still, but the effort made his heart ache.

"If we follow the path of a bird"—Jake pointed his nose directly toward the moor— "we only need to cut through the edge of Twolegplace before we reach Clan territory."

"Why do we need to go to Clan territory?" Talltail nodded toward the fields sweeping on every side. "There are so many other places we could go."

"But I've always wanted to see where the Clans live," Jake reminded him. "I've looked in from my fence so often. Now that I'm with you, I can see the territories close up."

"I don't think ThunderClan would be pleased to find me showing their home to a kittypet."

"Go on," Jake coaxed. "We won't get caught. I just want to take a look." He blinked at Talltail.

Talltail felt a prickle of unease. He couldn't refuse his friend after everything they'd been through. "We'll just look," he muttered. "Then go somewhere else."

Jake didn't reply, but followed Talltail around the rocks to the smooth grass beyond. They skirted the hedge, staying outside Twolegplace until a row of dens jutted into their path.

Talltail halted at the bottom of a wooden fence. "You lead." He flicked the tip of his tail. "This is your territory, not mine."

Jake hopped easily onto the fence, balancing as Talltail scrambled up behind him. A maze of fence-tops zigzagged ahead. Jake began to pad along them, turning one way, then another, as they bypassed row after row of gardens. Talltail followed, concentrating as he tried to keep his balance on the narrow strip of wood despite the buffeting wind.

His paws ached with the effort by the time they'd crossed Twolegplace. As he spotted trees crowding beyond the fences, he hurried forward, sliding past Jake and taking the lead. There were faint ThunderClan scents as he neared.

Talltail dropped onto the forest floor and began sniffing the roots of an elm. No ThunderClan warrior had brushed past this bark. He padded on, heading deeper into the forest.

Leaves crunched behind him as Jake caught up. "I can smell Thunderpath!"

Talltail stiffened. They must be near the Thunderpath that cut between ThunderClan territory and ShadowClan's forest as it headed close to Fourtrees. The claws that had been sunk into his belly ever since his dream suddenly tugged harder.

Jake paced around him, tail flicking excitedly. "The moor's close?"

"Close enough." Above, the branches clattered as wind stirred the forest.

"Let's take a look," Jake suggested.

"It's dangerous," Talltail told him. "We'd have to follow the Thunderpath along the ThunderClan border."

"We've done dangerous things before." Jake began to head toward the rumble of the Thunderpath. "Let's go a little farther. I want to see WindClan territory."

Talltail wondered if he should argue. But the tugging in his belly silenced him. Perhaps a glimpse of his old home would remind him why he'd left. Perhaps he could keep going: past WindClan territory, past Highstones. He could finally see the mountains for himself.

He followed Jake. His thoughts were as jumbled as the familiar scents that wreathed around him as he headed closer to Clan territory. Memories crowded at the edges of his mind: chasing rabbits across the moor; sitting vigil on Outlook Rock; plunging through the heather with Doespring; the first time he'd outrun Stagpaw. Then he pictured Wrenkit and Hopkit scrambling clumsily over the tussocks to beg him for a badger ride. His heart twisted with a sudden and terrible ache.

"Which way now?" Jake's call jolted him from his thoughts.

Talltail tasted the air. They were close to the Thunderpath. He glanced along the line of thick bushes at the forest's edge, which crowded for light where it cut through the trees. "Let's head along there." The bushes would give them shelter from the Thunderpath, and somewhere to hide if a ThunderClan patrol passed.

He led Jake over the leaf-strewn forest floor, pushing through frost-withered bracken until he reached a long swathe of brambles. Ears straining for the sound of ThunderClan warriors, mouth open for scents, Talltail pushed on. The clouds began to clear, driven toward the horizon by the brisk wind. Before long, the sun was shining weakly through the branches. As it slid behind them, Talltail detected more familiar scents. Above the tang of ThunderClan and the stink of ShadowClan, he could smell the sweet scent of heather. Even in leaf-bare it seemed to drench the air. And the earthy musk of peat and rabbit rolled toward him. Without thinking, Talltail quickened his pace. Suddenly the Thunderpath veered away, leaving the cats trekking through thick forest. The ground steepened beneath Talltail's paws and he was soon out of breath, climbing blindly through bracken until light showed between the trees at the top of the slope.

He wrinkled his nose as he picked up ThunderClan's border scent. "We're nearly there." At last they broke from the trees. A deep hollow yawned ahead of them and Talltail stared at the four tall oaks growing at the center.

"Fourtrees!" His heart soared. "Come on!" Talltail streaked down the slope. "This territory belongs to all the Clans!" He suddenly felt more at ease than he had for moons, the ground familiar beneath his paws as he raced into the clearing between the oaks. He circled it, staring in delight at the towering trees. The claws in his belly seemed to uncurl and release him. His paws felt light.

"Those trees are gigantic!" Jake stood in the center of the hollow, staring wide-eyed into the branches. Then he looked around. "Which way is WindClan's territory?" Talltail nodded at the far slope. Jake bounded toward it. "Come on."

Talltail raced after him, leaping up past shriveled clumps of fern.

Jake stopped at the top and gazed across the moor. "Why did you ever want to leave?" he whispered. The heather rocked in the blustery wind, the wide swathes of grass streaming around it.

Talltail couldn't reply. The border was only tail-lengths away. The scent of it seemed to reach deep into his chest. *I left because I don't belong here.* But the words rang hollow in his ears. As the scents of wind and heather filled his nose, he felt a sense of belonging stronger than he'd ever felt. Cloudrunner had passed this way recently. And Dawnstripe. He could smell their trail. Larksplash, too. Talltail's heart began to race. "I can't go home!" He stared in panic at Jake. "They won't want me! I broke the warrior code when I left my Clan. They'll drive me away again!"

"Are you sure?" Jake padded around him, pelt ruffled by the wind. "You won't know unless you go back."

Talltail closed his eyes. Was the wind tugging him onto the moor, or was it the pull of home? His heart ached to see the camp again. And Palebird. Had the kits grown? They must have. They'd be eating fresh-kill by now. Perhaps he wouldn't be too late to give them their first taste of lapwing.

"This is your home, Talltail." Jake's breath touched his ear fur. His green eyes glistened. "This is where you belong. Listen to your heart."

WindClan. Longing seared through his chest. "I know," Talltail whispered.

Jake touched Talltail's cheek with his muzzle. "I'll miss you."

Talltail gasped. "Don't go! Come with me! Come and meet my Clan!"

Jake stepped back. "This is where *you* belong, not me." His mew was hardly more than a whisper. "My home is with my housefolk. He'll be wondering where I am."

Talltail's throat tightened. "Will I ever see you again?"

Jake glanced over his shoulder toward the far horizon. "Who knows? Maybe."

Hope flared in Talltail's chest. "Become a warrior!" he blurted. "You'd be great! You learned how to hunt so quickly. And you can fight foxes!"

Jake dropped his gaze. "No, Talltail. I wouldn't be happy."

"You wouldn't be happy with me?" Pain stabbed Talltail's heart.

Jake lifted his eyes. "I can't live as a warrior." He looked away, his mew cracking. "But I'll always remember you. You've shown me a life that I've always dreamed about. But now I know where I truly belong."

"Then I'll come with you and live in Twolegplace!" Talltail wanted to do anything to stop the pain in his heart.

"Don't be rabbit-brained!" Jake's eyes flashed. "You hate it there! You'd be so unhappy." He paused, his tone softening. "I'd hate for you to be unhappy."

"Then why are you leaving?" Talltail pleaded. "You're the best friend I ever had."

"I'll always be your friend, Talltail," Jake meowed. "But I'm a kittypet, and you're a warrior." He stepped forward and rested his muzzle on Talltail's head. "You'll always be a warrior."

CHAPTER 40

You'll always be a warrior. Jake's words echoed in Talltail's mind as he headed up the hill toward the WindClan camp. The kittypet had assured him he'd be okay going back through the woods.

"I'll follow our trail through the brambles," Jake had promised. "I'll be fine."

Talltail trusted him. Jake wasn't a rabbit-brain. He'd learned enough to travel silently and keep his ears and nose open for signs of warrior patrols. *Will I be fine, too?* The idea of walking into his old home suddenly seemed far scarier than retracing his steps through enemy territory. *Will they take me back?*

Talltail forced his fur to smooth along his spine. He could smell his Clanmates all around him. Every tuft of heather carried familiar scents. Redclaw, Aspenfall, Mistmouse, and Appledawn had passed along this grassy track not long ago. Talltail imagined their paw prints still warm on the grass. He gazed across the swathe of dusky heather. Darker clumps of gorse grew up ahead, marking one end of the WindClan camp.

His heart pounded like rabbit paws on hollow ground. He pricked his ears. The wind blustered over the moor-top; far away a buzzard's wings beat the air, and closer, the tiny, excited squeal of a kit shrilled through the air. *Wrenkit!*

Happiness flashed through Talltail's paws. The brown she-kit had been less than a moon when he'd left. She must be over two moons old by now. He could hear her calling to her littermate.

"Flykit! Come and look!"

"I'm coming!"

Talltail paused. It sounded like the kits were out of camp, their mews as clear as birdcalls beyond the heather. He slid between the branches and crept forward, peering through the stems.

Wrenkit was sniffing at the entrance to a rabbit burrow. "Should we go in?"

Flykit blinked, huge-eyed. "It's very dark down there."

"We can use our noses and whiskers to find our way."

"What if we meet a rabbit?" Talltail could see Flykit's pelt spiking. He was no bigger than a half-grown rabbit himself. But it wasn't rabbits he should be afraid of. Talltail's fur rippled along his spine. They knew nothing about tunneling. They might get lost. And the tunnels had been neglected for moons. No one had checked their roofs or walls, or shored up the stretches weakened by rain or frost. Talltail began to nose his way out of the heather. He had to stop the kits before they disappeared inside.

A shadow flitted across the grass. Wings beat the air

overhead. Talltail looked up. A hawk circled low just above him. He could see by the tilt of its head that it was watching the kits. They'd make a tasty treat for a bird of prey and its young. As Talltail opened his mouth to warn them, the hawk folded its wings and plummeted straight down.

"Wrenkit!" Talltail lunged forward. "Watch out!"

Wrenkit jerked up her head, eyes wide in shock. Flykit jumped back, hissing. The air whistled above as the hawk dived.

Talltail thrust out his forepaws, landing squarely across the two frozen kits. Pulling them to him, he bundled them down the rabbit hole before leaping high into the air. He unsheathed his claws and swiped at the hawk as it flapped at his head. Its broad, brown wings stuttered and stalled, sending feathers spiraling down.

Talltail hooked the bird from the sky and pinned it to the ground. Faster than a snake, he bit down on its thick neck, crunching through muscle and bone. The hawk fell still beneath him.

Wrenkit's tiny face stared out of the hole. "You caught it!" she squeaked.

Flykit crept from the shadows, pelt thick with soil. "Talltail?" He blinked, confusion clouding his gaze. "What are you doing here?"

"He's come home!" Wrenkit's eyes lit up. "I knew he would!" She bounced toward Talltail, clambering onto his shoulders as he crouched over the body of the hawk. "And he saved us!"

"No one's ever caught a hawk before!" Flykit stared at the golden feathers of the dead bird.

"Whiteberry might disagree with you," Talltail purred. It felt good to feel kit paws on his shoulders again. He glanced at Flykit. "Do you want a badger ride home?"

Flykit looked crestfallen. "We were going to sneak back through the dirtplace tunnel," he mewed. "We're not supposed to be out of the camp."

"No! You're not!" Larksplash's stern mew sounded from upslope. She was marching toward them, tail flicking angrily.

Talltail watched, his breath catching in his throat. The she-cat's eyes were fixed on the kits.

"Palebird was worried sick—" Larksplash halted. "Talltail?" She blinked at him in disbelief. "You're back?" Her gaze dropped to the hawk at his paws.

"Yes, I'm back." Talltail leaned down and nosed the hawk. "I've brought prey."

Wrenkit clung to his shoulders, her sharp claws digging in. "He *saved* us!" she squealed. "That hawk was diving at us and Talltail jumped up and plucked it out of the air like it was a swallow."

Larksplash stopped. Uncertainty showed in her eyes.

"It's okay," Talltail told her. "You don't have to welcome me. I chose to leave the Clan."

Wrenkit fidgeted on his shoulders. "You went on an adventure!"

Flykit scrambled over the hawk's carcass and tried to jump up beside his sister. Talltail crouched down to let him on.

"You should speak with Heatherstar," Larksplash murmured.

"I know." Talltail padded forward, stepping carefully so the kits could keep their balance. He felt the warmth of their bellies as they pressed close against this back. They were heavier than the last time he'd given them a badger ride.

"Do *big* paw steps!" Wrenkit begged.

"We won't fall; we promise!" Flykit mewed.

Talltail lifted his paws high, thumping them down to jolt the kits as they clung on, squealing with delight. When Talltail reached the clearing outside camp, a black-and-white pelt slid through the heather and halted on the grass.

"There you are!" Palebird stared angrily over Talltail's head. "Heatherstar was about to order a search party."

"Talltail's home!" Wrenkit scrabbled from Talltail's shoulders and hurried to meet her mother.

"He saved us from a hawk!" Flykit jumped down after her and weaved through Palebird's legs.

"Talltail?" Palebird stared at her son.

He stared back. Had she forgotten him already?

Palebird snatched her gaze away. "You know they weren't supposed to be out of camp." She gave Wrenkit's head a brisk lick. "Why in the name of StarClan were you playing with them, Talltail?" she snapped. "You should have brought them straight home."

Talltail blinked at her. Palebird was acting like he'd never left. *But I did leave.* He lifted his chin. "I was bringing them home," he meowed. "You shouldn't have let them out of the camp. They were nearly taken by a hawk."

Larksplash stopped beside him. "He's right, Palebird," she meowed. "If Talltail hadn't come back when he did, you'd have lost them."

Wrenkit gazed up at her mother with round eyes. "He put us down a rabbit hole and caught the hawk."

"You caught it?" Palebird mewed in surprise.

Talltail glanced over his shoulder. "You might want to send some warriors to fetch it. It'll provide food for the Clan." He padded past his mother, dipping his head. "It's good to see you again, Palebird," he muttered. Ducking through the heather, he headed into camp.

"Talltail?" Barkface was carrying a bundle of dripping moss to the elders' den. He dropped it and bounded over the tussocks. "You came back!" A loud purr rumbled in his throat.

Talltail nosed his old friend's cheek. "Yes." His gaze flicked around the camp.

In the cold leaf-bare light, the heather looked dull. The grass had wilted in the frost. The bracken patch where the tunnelers made their nests was bent and shriveled. Only Tall-rock seemed the same, looming above the Meeting Hollow.

The bracken stirred as Hickorynose got to his paws. "Plum-claw, come see who's here." He nudged his denmate, keeping his eyes fixed on Talltail.

Whiteberry peered out of the elders' den. "Where's that moss, Bark . . ." His mew trailed away as he spotted Talltail.

Lilywhisker pushed past him. "I smell Talltail's scent!" Her eyes lit up. "You're back!"

"*Who's* back?" Shrewclaw padded sleepily from the long grass.

Ryestalk followed him out. "Is that Talltail?"

"Talltail?" Stagleap scrambled out of the Meeting Hollow and raced past Aspenfall and Cloudrunner as they emerged from the shadows at the edge of the clearing.

"Did you find him?" Barkface's urgent whisper sounded in Talltail's ear. "Did you kill Sparrow?" His eyes were dark with concern.

"I found him," Talltail told him. "But I let him live."

Barkface closed his eyes. "Thank StarClan."

"Sandgorse died saving him when the tunnel collapsed," Talltail went on. "How could I kill him, knowing that?"

"Talltail!" Stagleap nudged Barkface aside. "You look well!"

Shrewclaw caught up to him. "The wormcat's back?" He looked Talltail up and down. "I thought you'd left for good." There was a taunt in his mew.

"No, I've come back." Talltail glanced around the camp. "If Heatherstar will let me." Where was she? He strained to see into the gloom of her den beyond Tallrock.

"She's leading a hunting patrol," Stagleap meowed.

Ryestalk stopped beside Shrewclaw. "It's good to see you, Talltail."

"And you, Ryestalk." Talltail tipped his head. Ryestalk's pelt was touching Shrewclaw's. Their whiskers brushed casually. Were they mates now? It was strange to think that life had carried on in the Clan while he'd been away.

"Talltail!" Dawnstripe leaped from the Meeting Hollow. "You came back!" Delight lit up her eyes.

Talltail stood still as she raced to meet him. "I couldn't stay away."

She stopped in front of him and gazed warmly into his eyes. "Then my training wasn't wasted."

"It was *never* wasted," he meowed softly. "Not once."

Behind him, Palebird was shooing Wrenkit and Flykit crossly through the heather. "I can't take my eyes off you for a moment!"

Bristlekit and Rabbitkit came haring from the nursery. "Where did you go?" Rabbitkit demanded, glaring at Wrenkit. "Why didn't you let us come?"

Bristlekit nudged his brother, his gaze fixed on Talltail. "Who cares? He's back!"

Larksplash padded into camp. "You would have lost Wrenkit and Flykit if he weren't." She flashed another stern look at Palebird.

Ryestalk pricked her ears. "What happened?"

"Talltail saved them from a hawk," Larksplash explained.

"Impressive!" Stagleap nudged Talltail with his shoulder.

Larksplash nodded toward the entrance. "Why don't you and Cloudrunner go get it? There'll be fresh-kill for everyone tonight."

"Don't bother." Heatherstar's mew took Talltail by surprise. He spun around as the WindClan leader padded through the entrance with Reedfeather at her heels. "Redclaw and Hareflight are carrying it back." She narrowed her eyes. "I thought I smelled your scent on it, Talltail. It seems you've learned new skills while you've been away."

Reedfeather stopped beside his leader. "Let's hope he's learned more than *skills*," he muttered.

Talltail kept his gaze on Heatherstar, his heart quickening. Would she let him rejoin the Clan?

Shrewclaw stepped closer. "What are you doing here, Talltail? Was the land beyond the Clans too scary for you?" But there was curiosity and affection in his mew, underneath the teasing.

"My heart wanted to be home." Talltail dipped his head. "And my paws carried me back."

Heatherstar blinked slowly. Branches rustled behind her. Grunting with effort, Hareflight emerged, dragging the hawk carcass through. Redclaw followed, a taloned foot in his teeth as he helped Hareflight heave the bird into camp.

Whiteberry padded around the body as they laid it on a tussock. "You caught this by yourself?"

"I surprised it," Talltail confessed. "The hawk thought it was the hunter, not the hunted. It was easy to knock it out of the sky."

Whiteberry sniffed its bloody neck. "You must have been quick to kill it before it escaped. These wings could crack a warrior's spine."

Talltail hadn't thought about the danger, only saving the kits. He swallowed, relieved that StarClan had been kind to him. Was it a sign that he was welcome home? He glanced at Heatherstar.

She flicked her tail toward the entrance. "Walk with me, Talltail." She turned, pausing beside Reedfeather. "Organize the dusk patrol while we're gone, please."

Heatherstar didn't speak as she led the way upslope. She weaved through the bushes, following an old rabbit trail. Talltail trotted after her, relishing the feel of familiar stems brushing his pelt, his tongue steeped in scents he'd known since he was a kit. As he emerged onto the moor-top, the wind buffeted his face. It promised rain. He opened his mouth and tasted the distant tang of Highstones. Gray clouds dragged along their peaks, hiding the mountains beyond. Heatherstar kept moving, head high, pelt smooth. *She's heading for Outlook Rock.*

The familiar crop of stones jutted from the moor, pale gray against the dark gray sky. Talltail padded onto the ledge and felt the smooth stone underneath his paws. He'd spent so many moments here, dreaming of traveling farther than he could see. Now he'd been beyond the horizon that had once made him feel trapped and suffocated. And still he'd come back.

Heatherstar sat at the edge of the rock and stared across the valley. "Are you glad to be home?"

Talltail stopped a muzzle-length behind her. He opened his mouth and let the wind wash his tongue. He'd traveled far, far away, where every paw step was strange and new. Now he was walking on WindClan land once more. His kin had walked this moor since the dawn of the Clans. Sandgorse and countless others had tunneled beneath it. This was home. He belonged here. His Clan needed him. Even if they didn't know it, *he* knew it, as surely as he knew that daylight would bathe the Highstones every sunrise.

"Yes, I'm glad to be back," he murmured.

"Good." She kept her eyes on the distant peaks. "You always loved it here."

"I did." Talltail had never felt more free than when he was sitting on the rock, the sky high above, the land far below.

"Did you find what you were looking for?" Heatherstar's question sounded casual, but Talltail guessed from the stiffness in her shoulders that she knew exactly what she was asking.

"No."

"So Sparrow is alive."

Talltail swallowed. "Yes."

"Couldn't you find him?" Heatherstar's mew was soft.

"I found him," Talltail replied. "But he told me that Sandgorse had given his life to save him in the tunnels. I couldn't kill him then. Sandgorse would have died for nothing."

"So you didn't need to leave the Clan after all?" Heatherstar probed.

"That's not true," Talltail growled. "I didn't leave just for revenge. I didn't feel like I belonged here."

"Sometimes we have to leave to find out where our heart truly lies," Heatherstar whispered.

Talltail's pelt pricked. Heatherstar had said the same thing when he'd left. *Does she know something she's not telling me?* Right now, he didn't care. She understood that he had needed to leave, and that was what mattered. Relief swamped him. "I learned a lot," he told her. "Friendship and kinship matter more than adventure. Boundaries only exist in our minds. A heart can travel to the horizon without moving a paw step. And I made the best friend any cat ever had."

Heatherstar glanced over her shoulder. "But your loyalty

is with the Clan now, right?"

Talltail's pelt pricked with irritation. "I came back, didn't I?"

"For good?"

Talltail winced. She was right to question his loyalty. "Yes," he meowed.

Heatherstar turned her muzzle toward the horizon once more. "I always knew you would leave."

Talltail stiffened. "What do you mean?" He padded forward and stopped at her side.

"When I received my nine lives, Mothflight warned me a warrior would leave my Clan." A purr edged Heatherstar's mew. "I was headstrong then. I told Mothflight that no warrior of mine would dare abandon his Clan." She dipped her head. "But Mothflight was right. Sometimes a cat needs to go a long way to find that his true home is right where he started."

Talltail's ear twitched. "How did you know that cat was me?"

"You were restless even as a kit. You were a tunneler's kit who hated tunnels, and a moor runner who couldn't grasp the importance of boundaries. I let you go, as Mothflight had told me I should, so that you'd come to understand that it's not boundaries that tie us down. We are held by much deeper bonds."

Grief stabbed Talltail's chest. *Jake.* That was the deepest bond he'd ever known, and yet Talltail had left him to return to his Clan. He shifted his paws. "This friend that I made, he's the one who told me to come back."

Heatherstar nodded. "He sounds like a wise cat," she

murmured. "He knows you better than you know yourself."

Talltail turned away, his heart aching.

Heatherstar called to him as he padded from the rock. "You'll still have to earn the trust of your Clanmates."

Talltail hesitated. "I know."

"You must prove that you're willing to lay down your life for any of them," Heatherstar meowed. "Even Shrewclaw." There was a hint of amusement in her voice.

"I'll try," Talltail promised. As he headed onto the grass, relishing its softness beneath his pads, Heatherstar called after him.

"I'm glad you came back."

The claws that had been sunk for so long into Talltail's belly seemed to give one final squeeze before letting go. "So am I," he answered.

CHAPTER 41

Steadily falling water turned the hills gray. It had rained every day since Talltail had returned, and the familiar trails ran like streams through the heather. Out in the open, sand washed around Talltail's paws as he trekked toward the gorge.

Reedfeather trudged beside him. "A hard frost now would burn away the youngest heather," he commented as they skirted a swathe of dripping bushes, their roots exposed where rain had washed away the soil.

Talltail glanced at the heavy sky. "There won't be frost for a while."

Reedfeather shook out his pelt. "I prefer snow," he grumbled. "It stays out of my fur." The WindClan deputy was limping. A sprain in his shoulder that he'd suffered half a moon earlier was refusing to heal.

Talltail noticed him wince with every step. "Do you want to find shelter and rest?" he offered. "I can hunt alone."

"I can still hunt for my Clan." Reedfeather shot him a look. "Even on three legs."

"You're not on three legs yet." Talltail eyed the stretch of grass ahead. A thrush, impervious to the rain, was pecking for worms. "See that?" He nodded toward the bird.

Reedfeather paused. "Your eyesight's as good as ever."

"Go around and come up behind it," Talltail whispered. "Send it toward me. I'll do the rest."

Reedfeather hesitated.

"Hurry," Talltail urged. "I can't catch it alone."

Reedfeather headed away, keeping low, rain dripping from his whiskers as he veered wide around the thrush. Talltail waited. The bird had gripped a worm in its beak and was tugging it determinedly from the ground. As Reedfeather closed in, Talltail stalked forward. He kept one eye on the deputy. The old warrior would know when to make his move.

Talltail's paw steps were hidden by the thrumming rain. The thrush only realized what was happening when Reedfeather darted at it. With a shriek, it fluttered away from the WindClan deputy. Talltail sprang as it flew toward him. Stretching up his forepaws, he knocked the bird from the sky. It dropped to the ground, dazed, and he nipped its spine.

Reedfeather hobbled to meet him. "That's a useful technique," he grunted. "Even an elder could make a catch like that."

"Or a kittypet." Talltail fought to keep the wistfulness from his mew as he remembered Jake's startled face when he caught his first mouse.

The rain was easing by the time they reached camp. Reedfeather led the way through the heather, nodding to Talltail before he carried their catch to the prey heap. Talltail scanned the camp. Water dripped into a puddle in the apprentices' den. With no apprentices, the gorse had not been patched and the nests were wilting and soggy. Meadowslip was resting outside the nursery, Palebird sitting beside her. Lilywhisker was dragging old bedding from the elders' den. Heatherstar sheltered below Tallrock with Aspenfall and Doespring. On the Hunting Stones, Wrenkit, Flykit, Bristlekit, and Rabbit-kit were bickering about who got to sit on the highest rock.

"It's my turn!" Rabbitkit sounded indignant.

"You sat there last time," Wrenkit argued.

"I *never* get to sit on the highest one," Bristlekit complained.

Talltail headed away before they spotted him and begged him to decide. As he padded toward the long grass, hoping to find enough shelter to wash some of the rain from his fur, Hopkit scrambled out of the nursery. One moon from becoming an apprentice, he looked too big for the old gorse den. Perhaps it was time to start clearing the old nests from the apprentice den and repairing the roof.

"Talltail!" Hopkit raced around the edge of the Meeting Hollow. He ran nimbly, compensating so well with his three strong legs that sometimes Talltail forgot about his useless, twisted forepaw. "Will you help me practice my attack crouch like you promised?" Worried that he wouldn't be given a mentor because his paw made the moves more difficult, Hopkit wanted to learn everything before he left the nursery.

Talltail glanced at the sky. The clouds were beginning to tear apart, showing patches of blue. It was the first sign of good weather in days. "Okay."

The black kit flicked his tail excitedly.

"Let's use the Meeting Hollow." Talltail jumped into the dip, feeling the wet earth slide beneath his paws. Days of rain had washed the hollow clean, and stones hidden for moons beneath the soil flashed and sparkled on the surface as the sun peeked through a gap in the clouds.

Hopkit scrambled down and crouched into an attack stance, his flanks quivering as he tried to balance.

"Spread your hind legs farther apart," Talltail advised him. "It'll give more power to your leap." He pressed Hopkit's shoulders lower with his muzzle. "Keep your chin close to the ground. That way you'll be ready to duck under your enemy if he leaps first. And remember to use your *hind* legs to push you forward." He padded around the young tom, stooping to inspect his twisted paw. "Your forepaws are for balance, remember?"

Hopkit was leaning to one side where his twisted paw couldn't quite hold his weight steadily. The young tom snorted and sat up. "I knew it." He stared angrily at his odd paw.

"Don't worry," Talltail soothed. "Your forepaws need to match each other. You'll only fall off balance if one is stronger than the other."

Hopkit frowned. "But one *is* stronger than the other."

Talltail shrugged. "Then use the stronger one more lightly."

Hopkit brightened. "Okay." He crouched again, adjusting his paws one at a time until he was steady as a rock.

"Perfect." Talltail was impressed. It was impossible to see the weakness in Hopkit's twisted paw. "Now try leaping. Don't forget: Keep your ears flat. And your eyes must be narrowed.

In battle there'll be claws flying at you from all directions."

Hopkit screwed his eyes to slits and drew his ears close to his head. His haunches quivered for a moment; then he sprang forward. He darted neatly through the air, perfectly balanced.

"Very good!" Talltail praised him as he landed.

"Ow!" Hopkit stumbled, then drew himself up sharply, holding his forepaw high.

"What's happened?" Talltail rushed to his side. "Did you land badly?" Talltail saw beads of scarlet liquid dripping onto the earth. The strong tang of blood bathed his tongue.

"I landed on a s-stone," Hopkit whimpered.

Talltail saw a sharp edge of flint sticking up from the ground where the rain had washed away the soil. "Quick, let's get you to the medicine den."

Blood was welling fast on Hopkit's pad, soaking the fur around his claws. Talltail didn't dare look to see how deeply the flint had torn the young tom's flesh. He grabbed Hopkit's scruff between his teeth and hauled him up out of the hollow, ignoring his yowls of protest as he hurried to the medicine den. "Stop struggling, for StarClan's sake," he growled through his teeth. He let go at the entrance and nosed Hopkit into the gorse cave.

Barkface looked up from a pile of herbs. "I smell blood." He trotted over and sniffed Hopkit's paw.

"Is it bad?" Talltail asked.

"It's deep." Barkface darted back across the den and reached through a gap in the branches, hauling out a wad of cobweb and a pawful of leaves. "But I'll soon get him fixed up."

"Good." Hopkit held out his paw. "I want to get back to my training. I'd just worked out a really good attack crouch."

"No more training for you until this has healed." Barkface began to fill the wound with herbs. "How did it happen?"

"There are sharp stones in the Meeting Hollow." Talltail glanced through the den entrance and caught sight of Shrewclaw. He ducked outside. "Shrewclaw!"

The warrior was padding toward the long grass with Ryestalk at his side. He stopped when Talltail called out. "What?"

"There are stones sticking up all across the Meeting Hollow." Talltail nodded toward the dip.

Shrewclaw followed his gaze. "How did they get there?"

"The rain's washed the soil away," Talltail explained. "Hopkit just cut himself on one."

Ryestalk frowned. "That's dangerous."

Talltail nodded to Shrewclaw. "Can you organize a patrol to dig them out?"

Shrewclaw narrowed his eyes. "Why don't you do it?"

"I want to keep an eye on Hopkit."

Ryestalk nudged Shrewclaw. "Come on. Talltail's right. We need to clear the hollow before another cat gets hurt." She hurried across the tussocks to where Stagleap and Appledawn were sharing prey in the shelter of the heather wall.

Shrewclaw padded after her. "We should ask Hickorynose and Mistmouse to help," he muttered. "They're used to digging."

As Talltail turned back to the medicine den, the ground trembled. Paws were thrumming beyond the camp wall. The heather shivered as Plumclaw burst into the camp. Woollytail, Larksplash, and Cloudrunner thundered after her, skidding to a halt on the wet grass.

"ShadowClan!" Plumclaw gasped. Her flanks were heaving.

Heatherstar raced around the rim of the Hollow and stopped beside Talltail. "What's happened?"

Reedfeather limped from the long grass, pelt bristling. "Have they crossed the border?"

"As good as," Cloudrunner growled. "They've left scent marks on the brambles at Fourtrees."

Heatherstar's gaze sharpened. "What's wrong with that?"

Woollytail lifted his chin. "They've *drenched* it in scent markers, right on the boundary."

"It's deliberate provocation," Larksplash added.

Heatherstar narrowed her eyes. "But they haven't crossed the border."

"They didn't need to," Plumclaw snarled. "Their scent's done it for them. Our land smells like ShadowClan territory."

Shrewclaw's pelt spiked. "We should send a patrol to scent *their* borders!"

Ryestalk twitched her tail. "I'll go!"

"No." Heatherstar stared at her warriors. "No one will cross the border," she ordered. "They're just trying to provoke us. We won't fall for their tricks."

"It's no trick." Cloudrunner lashed his tail. "It's a warning. We need to show them we're not afraid."

"We can do that by carrying on as normal," Heatherstar

told him. "Same patrols, same scent markers. Let them waste their scent stinking up the border. So long as they don't cross it, we won't react."

Talltail glanced at her uneasily. ShadowClan warriors didn't make empty threats. His paws pricked with worry. They'd crossed the border before. Last time, they'd attacked the camp. What would stop them this time? But Talltail hadn't been back long enough to question his leader's wisdom. Besides, she might be right. Why rush into a battle that didn't need to happen?

He turned and headed for the medicine den. "Hopkit?" He peered in.

Hopkit blinked from the shadows. "What's happening?" His tail flicked restlessly as Barkface wound cobweb around his paw.

"Sit still," Barkface ordered.

Hopkit growled. "But I heard Plumclaw say ShadowClan had crossed the border!"

"They've left scents on the brambles by Fourtrees," Talltail told him.

"Is Heatherstar organizing a battle patrol?" Hopkit shuffled his hind paws beneath him.

"I said keep still!" Barkface grunted, frowning as he wound the web tighter.

Talltail nosed his way in. "No patrol. Not yet."

Hopkit's shoulders slumped. "I wish I were an apprentice," he grumbled. "I'd teach ShadowClan to keep away from our borders!"

Barkface looked up at him, his eyes gleaming with amusement. "You won't have four paws to attack them with if you don't let me finish this dressing," he warned.

Talltail nodded. "He's right, Hopkit. Hold still. Your Clanmates need you fit and ready to fight." He caught Barkface's eye and held back a purr.

Hopkit sat up straight, quivering with effort. "Still as a stone, right you are!" he mewed. "Barkface, carry on!"

Talltail stretched across the width of his nest, then hopped out. He padded over the frosty grass, screwing up his eyes against the early beams of sunlight that flashed over the camp wall. Pigeonkit and Sorrelkit were already awake and chasing Palebird's kits around Hunting Stones.

"Help!" Wrenkit squealed happily as Pigeonkit lunged for her. She scrambled through the crack between the rocks and escaped to the far side.

Palebird was curled beside a tussock, watching fondly, her pelt glowing in the early sunshine.

Where's Hopkit? Talltail looked for the black pelt of the young tom, relieved to see he wasn't playing with his denmates. *He must be resting at last.* Hopkit had insisted on practicing his battle moves every day since his injury, despite Barkface's warnings. Only when Hawkheart had ordered him sternly to his nest on the threat of not being made an apprentice, ever, had the kit given up.

Doespring was standing at the entrance beside Hareflight. "Are you coming, Talltail?"

"Yes." He began to cross the clearing.

In the sunrises since ShadowClan had drenched the bramble in their scent, Heatherstar had ordered extra border patrols. Reedfeather had already led Mistmouse, Appledawn, and Stagleap out before sunrise. Now Shrewclaw, Ryestalk, and Doespring were preparing to leave.

"Hopkit!"

Talltail halted as Meadowslip's anxious mew drifted from the nursery.

"Hopkit! Can you hear me?" Heather crunched inside the gorse den. "You're too hot. Can you make it outside? You need to cool down."

There was no answer.

Talltail stiffened. "Go without me!" he called to Doespring. "I'll join the next patrol."

Doespring frowned. "Is something wrong?"

"I want to check on Hopkit."

Shrewclaw scowled. "Reedfeather told us Talltail was joining this patrol."

Hareflight snorted. "Talltail makes his own rules." There was bitterness in the warrior's mew.

"Yes, the warrior code doesn't apply to Talltail." Shrewclaw barged through the entrance.

Talltail ignored him and headed for the nursery. "Meadowslip?" he called through the entrance.

"Come in!" Meadowslip's mew was taut with fear.

Talltail pushed his way through the gorse. His nose wrinkled. The den stank of sickness. "Fetch Hawkheart," he ordered. Meadowslip hesitated. *"Now."*

She slid from the den. Talltail leaned into Hopkit's nest. Heat pulsed from the young tom's pelt. His eyes were half-open but glazed. "Hopkit?" Talltail thrust his muzzle closer, gagging as the putrid stink of pus bathed his tongue. He grabbed Hopkit's scruff and hauled him from his nest. *He's burning up!* He carried Hopkit out into the frosty air.

Hawkheart was hurrying past the Meeting Hollow, Meadowslip at his tail. He stopped as he caught sight of Hopkit. "Bring him to the medicine den."

"He needs to cool down," Talltail growled through clenched jaws.

"I can give him something for the fever." Hawkheart led the way into his den, clearing away drying herbs to let Talltail lay the kit down on the smooth, sandy floor.

Meadowslip pushed in beside him. "What's wrong?"

"The infection's spreading." The medicine cat sniffed Hopkit's paw. "I'll make a poultice." Muttering under his breath, he turned away.

"Where's Barkface?" Talltail's pelt twitched. He wanted the reassurance of his friend. Hopkit was going to be all right, wasn't he?

"He's gathering herbs," Hawkheart meowed over his shoulder.

"Should I go get him?" Talltail offered.

"He'll be back soon."

As Hawkheart spoke, the den entrance rustled. Barkface nosed his way in, eyes widening as he saw Talltail, Hopkit, and

Meadowslip. He dropped the wad of herbs clamped between his jaws. "What's wrong?"

Hawkheart didn't look up from the poultice he was mixing. "Did you get any marigold?"

"There wasn't any." Barkface bent down and sniffed Hopkit's paw. "The infection's spreading, isn't it?"

"We need to treat it fast." Hawkheart glanced at Meadowslip. "Talltail," he grunted, "take Meadowslip outside. It's too crowded in here."

"But I want to be near my kit," Meadowslip protested.

"You'll be more use to him if you stay out of the way," Hawkheart meowed.

Barkface padded around Hopkit and began chewing Hawkheart's herbs into a pulp. Talltail tried to catch his eye, but the young medicine cat's gaze was fixed on Hopkit. He turned and nudged Meadowslip toward the entrance. "It's too hot in here with all of us," he murmured, coaxing her into the sharp, fresh air.

He paced the frosty grass outside while Meadowslip crouched beside the heather wall. The sun rose above the horizon, shimmering in the pale leaf-bare sky. *If only there were snow to pack around the burning kit,* Talltail thought. *Hawkheart knows what he's doing.* His heart seemed to echo in his chest, hollowed by worry. *Barkface is with him too. Hopkit will be okay.*

"Talltail?" Barkface slid from the medicine den.

Meadowslip leaped to her paws. "How is he?"

"You can go and see him now." Barkface nodded her inside. His eyes darkened as he turned toward Talltail. He waited until the she-cat had disappeared into the gorse, then crossed the grass. "The infection's in his blood," he whispered to Talltail.

"That's bad, isn't it?"

Barkface looked grim. "He could die."

"Is there anything you can give him?"

"We've given him everything we can." Barkface's eyes were round with worry. "But it's leaf-bare. We're working with wilted herbs, and dried ones. They don't have the same power as newleaf herbs."

A groan sounded from the medicine den.

"He's in pain!" Talltail's memory flashed back to the rainy night he'd writhed in agony as poison seared in his belly. "Can't you stop it?"

"Hawkheart's giving him poppy seeds, but they can only ease it a little."

"I was really ill when I was in Twolegplace."

Barkface jerked up his head. "You were?"

"I was saved by a Twoleg."

"A *Twoleg*?" Barkface moved closer. "How?"

"I don't know," Talltail confessed. "I can hardly remember what happened. But Jake told me that there are medicine Twolegs who cure cats." Hope flashed in his chest. "Perhaps we could take Hopkit to one."

Barkface backed away. "No!"

"Why not?" Talltail swished his tail. "I could carry him to Twolegplace and leave him somewhere he'd be found. He'd be cured like I was."

Barkface stiffened. "You were *very* lucky," he growled. "Who knows what would happen to Hopkit? How would he even survive the journey?" His pelt lifted along his spine.

Talltail flinched. "I just want to help."

"I know." Barkface's gaze softened. "But that isn't the way."

Talltail glanced balefully toward the medicine den, then turned away. Whiteberry and Lilywhisker were hauling dusty heather from their den.

Whiteberry halted, sitting down to catch his breath. "I can't wait until we have apprentices again."

Lilywhisker dragged a bundle of heather stalks across the grass and turned back for more. "We only have one more moon to wait," she panted.

Flailfoot pushed his way out of the den, struggling with a trailing piece of sheepswool. "I just hope Stagleap remembers to bring fresh wool back from patrol or we'll be sleeping on bare heather tonight."

"I can fetch some." Talltail trotted toward them. He hooked the lump of wool from the Flailfoot's paw and tossed it away. A flea leaped from it and bit his leg. Grunting, Talltail jerked his head down and cracked the flea between his teeth.

Lilywhisker shook her head. "We try to keep the bedding clean." She glanced at the older cats and lowered her voice. "Their eyesight isn't what it used to be. They find fleas hard to spot."

Flamepelt padded from the den, his orange fur glowing in the sunshine. "I pulled a tick from your tail yesterday."

"But you missed the fleas." Lilywhisker's fur rippled. "They kept me awake all night biting."

Whiteberry scratched his ear. "Fleas are faster than ticks."

"Let me look." Talltail began to snuffle through the fur on Lilywhisker's flank.

"What's all the fuss in the medicine den?" Flailfoot asked, craning her neck to see across the clearing.

Talltail burst a flea in his teeth and straightened up. "Hop-kit's very ill. The infection in his paw has spread."

Lilywhisker flattened her ears. "Does he have a fever?"

Talltail nodded. "Barkface doesn't know if his herbs will help—"

"Talltail!"

Brown fur flashed on the edge of Talltail's vision. Barkface was racing toward him. The young medicine cat skidded to a halt. "I have an idea!"

Talltail pricked his ears. "What?"

"I remember Brambleberry mentioned sedge at the Moon-stone once." He looked at Heatherstar. "It grows all through leaf-bare, doesn't it?"

"Yes, you can see it around the RiverClan camp from the gorge," Heatherstar agreed.

"Brambleberry said there was one type of sedge that cured infection." Barkface's eyes shone. "Sweet-sedge, I think she called it. She uses the roots. She might have some in her store."

"How can we get our paws on it?" Heatherstar's pelt pricked. "We can't send a patrol; RiverClan might take it as a sign of attack."

"Well, we're not going to steal it." Barkface paced around

her. "If I went by myself and asked, RiverClan might listen. I'm a medicine cat, not a warrior, and it's part of our code that we have to save the life of a kit, whatever Clan they are from."

Heatherstar stared. "You want to walk into RiverClan territory *alone*?"

Talltail stepped forward. "I'll go with him."

Heatherstar lifted her chin. "WindClan cats don't cross borders and we don't beg other Clans for help."

"But what about Hopkit?" Talltail pleaded. "He might die if we don't do something."

"He has StarClan to protect him."

"Sometimes StarClan isn't enough." Talltail flexed his claws. "They didn't save Sandgorse."

"Or Brackenwing," Barkface put in.

Heatherstar stared at the young medicine cat. "Are you doubting StarClan?"

"I believe that they trust us to help ourselves," Barkface mewed softly. "If there is some way of saving Hopkit, I'm going to find it."

Talltail's heart quickened. "We can't let boundaries get in our way!" Why were the Clans so obsessed with scent lines? They were great for deciding who hunted where, but when a kit's life was at stake how could anyone believe that invisible boundaries were more important?

Heatherstar looked at the elders. They returned her gaze in silence.

Then Flailfoot spoke. "Talltail is right."

Lilywhisker nodded. "There are no boundaries in StarClan."

"If Barkface and Talltail are willing to ask RiverClan for help on behalf of their Clanmate, we should honor them." Whiteberry dipped his head.

"Very well." Heatherstar nodded briskly. "If it must be done, then do it now. There's no time to lose." She turned toward the medicine den and ordered over her shoulder, "Go!"

Talltail turned and dashed toward the camp entrance. He felt Barkface's breath on his tail as he raced through the tunnel.

"Not so fast!" Barkface panted when Talltail hared down the slope.

He glanced over his shoulder. Barkface was trailing behind as they streaked toward the border. Talltail slowed. "How are we going to cross the river?" he asked as Barkface caught up.

Barkface frowned. "We might be able to signal a RiverClan patrol from this side."

"Good plan." Talltail wasn't looking forward to getting his fur wet. He wasn't even sure he could swim. *Please let a River-Clan patrol be passing.*

Talltail didn't pause as they crossed the border markers, ignoring the RiverClan scent as it touched his tongue. They scrambled down the steep path at the end of the gorge, and met the river where it widened and slowed after tumbling between the cliffs. Downstream, thick sedge hid the far bank.

"The RiverClan camp must be somewhere over there." Barkface pointed with his tail toward the dark green rushes.

Talltail tasted the air. Damp, lush scent rolled over his tongue. Then he scanned the flat meadowland beyond the river, hoping to catch sight of a pelt moving through the long grass. "No sign of a patrol. We're going to have to swim across."

"Can you swim?" Barkface asked.

"Let's find out." Talltail padded over the pebbly shore and waded into the water. He was surprised by the weight of the current. It pushed against his legs and dragged at his belly fur, cold as ice. He shivered. "Do you want to wait here?" Was there any sense in risking both their lives?

Barkface splashed into the water beside him. "They're less likely to attack if I'm with you," he meowed. He pushed determinedly into the river.

Talltail watched the water swallow Barkface's shoulders. "Are you swimming?"

"My paws are still on the bottom."

Talltail's heart pricked with hope. Perhaps it was so shallow they'd be able to wade across.

"I'm swimming now!" Barkface's call was cut short as he disappeared beneath the surface. He appeared a moment later, splashing and coughing.

"Barkface!" Talltail dived after his friend. The icy water soaked through his fur, its chill piercing his bones in a heartbeat. As the bottom disappeared from beneath his paws, he fought panic. Flailing, he tried to haul himself forward, stretching his neck to keep his muzzle in the air. "Barkface!"

"I'm okay!" The medicine cat's dark pelt moved ahead of him. Barkface wasn't splashing now; instead he was moving steadily through the water.

Talltail churned his paws, struggling to keep up. The river seemed to be trying to drag him downstream, pulling harder at his haunches than his shoulders so that Talltail felt himself spinning slowly around. He pushed harder with his forepaws, trying to keep straight, his gaze fixed on Barkface. Gulping air, he moved forward jerkily. *Imagine that you're running. Push against the water the same as you would against the earth.* He forced his paws into a steady rhythm and braced himself against the current.

He suddenly realized that the far bank was getting closer. A moment later, Barkface was wading out of the water, his pelt dripping, and Talltail felt pebbles roll beneath his pads. He scrabbled to find his paws, weak with relief to be walking on solid ground. He felt as light as air as he staggered from the river.

"We made it!" Barkface stood on the bank and shook the water from his pelt.

Talltail ducked away before the drops showered his face. He'd never felt so cold! A shiver ran through him and he sneezed. "Let's find a patrol and get out of here," he growled through chattering teeth.

Barkface stared past him, eyes widening in fear. "Tall—"

A menacing snarl cut him off. "If you're looking for a patrol, *trespassers*, you just found one."

CHAPTER 42

Talltail stepped backward, shielding Barkface. "We need to speak with Brambleberry."

Three RiverClan cats glared at him. He recognized the sleek pelts of Ottersplash, Rippleclaw, and Owlfur from Gatherings.

Rippleclaw, a black-and-silver tom, tilted his head. His eyes glittered threateningly. "Did Heatherstar send you?"

"Yes." Barkface ducked out from behind Talltail. "I'm Barkface of WindClan. I must speak with your medicine cat."

"I know who you are." Ottersplash curled her lip. "I'd get back in the river, if I were you."

"Unless you want to be shredded." Owlfur stepped forward, his brown-and-white pelt twitching.

"There's no time for fighting," Barkface hissed. "One of our kits is dying. I need Brambleberry's help."

"A kit?" Ottersplash glanced at Rippleclaw.

Rippleclaw's tail stilled. "Dying?"

Owlfur showed his teeth. "Why'd you bring a warrior with you?" He padded forward and stopped a whisker from Talltail's muzzle. Fishy breath clouded from his mouth.

"I'm here to protect him." Talltail dug his claws among the pebbles. "Would *you* let your Clanmate travel into enemy territory alone?"

The brown-and-white tom's eyes gleamed. "Then you admit you're on enemy territory?"

"Do you think we swam the river without noticing?" Talltail looked at the RiverClan warrior's sleek pelt. "Not all warriors are half fish."

"Talltail!" Barkface's sharp mew cut through the freezing air. "We need their help!"

Talltail dipped his head, suddenly remembering Jake's gentle respect toward Jay, the old she-cat in Twolegplace. His approach had gotten them the information they wanted. "I'm sorry." He rounded his eyes. "Please let us see Brambleberry. Hopkit's life may rest in her paws."

"Let them see her." A gruff mew sounded from the reeds and Piketooth slid out. He caught Talltail's eye, wary and tense. Talltail suddenly wondered if Piketooth's Clanmates knew about his catch on WindClan territory.

Barkface leaned forward. "If Brambleberry says no, we'll leave."

"It's Hailstar who will decide." Rippleclaw barged past and slid into the reeds.

"This way." Piketooth beckoned Talltail forward with a flick of his tail and followed Rippleclaw.

Talltail padded after him. "Stay close to me," he hissed to Barkface. The reeds were stiff as he pushed his way through. Piketooth's tail disappeared a few paw steps ahead. Behind him, the stalks rattled as Barkface, Ottersplash, and Owlfur followed. After walking along the river for several long moments, during which Talltail felt as if he was being lashed on both flanks by the springy reeds, they emerged into a clearing. The river lapped at one side, seeping through a thick wall of reeds and silvering the marshy earth. Dens dotted the camp, woven from sticks.

"They look like more like birds' nests than dens," Talltail whispered in Barkface's ear.

"They float if it floods," Barkface whispered.

Talltail blinked, surprised at the ingenuity of the RiverClan cats. Were they as smart as WindClan?

"Wait." Rippleclaw nodded to Barkface, then ducked into one of the tangled dens.

RiverClan cats blinked from the edges of the clearing, staring in surprise at their visitors.

"Rainflower! Look!" a russet kit squeaked to a gray she-cat.

"What is it, Oakkit?"

"Intruders!" The kit fluffed out its fur, hissing.

Ottersplash padded across the clearing. "They've come for our help."

Rainflower sniffed. "Why should we help WindClan cats?"

"They say they have a sick kit." Owlfur prowled beside the reed wall, hackles up.

Rippleclaw reappeared, Hailstar following. The RiverClan leader was round-eyed, his gaze anxious. "You need medicine."

Barkface hurried forward. "It's leaf-bare. Our herbs aren't

strong enough. We were hoping Brambleberry would share some sweet-sedge. It's powerful even in the hardest season."

Brambleberry's white face appeared from one of the stick dens. "What's going on?" She slid out, the black spots on her fur like smudges in snow.

"Brambleberry!" A weak cry sounded from inside the den.

Barkface craned his head, trying to see in. "You sound like you have a sick kit of your own.

"Stormkit." Brambleberry's eyes clouded. "He fell."

"Can I help?" Barkface offered.

"There's nothing more to be done." Brambleberry glanced back into the shadows. "Time and care will see him through." She turned back to Barkface. "Why have you come?"

"Hopkit has an infected paw. The infection's spreading fast."

Brambleberry cut him off. "You want sweet-sedge."

Barkface's eyes lit. "Can you spare some?"

Brambleberry glanced at her leader. Hailstar dipped his head. "I have some," Brambleberry mewed, turning back to her den. "Come."

Talltail watched Barkface disappear into the shadows after the RiverClan medicine cat. He could feel the probing eyes of the RiverClan warriors, hot on his pelt. Shellheart, the dappled-gray deputy, sat on the arching root of a willow, watching through narrowed eyes. Nightsky appeared beside Piketooth. She whispered into her clanmate's ear, then dipped her head to Talltail. He nodded back. He'd been right to let them cross the border to feed their Clan. Now

RiverClan was returning the favor. *StarClan willing.*

Hailstar lifted his chin. "WindClan has never asked for help before."

Talltail met his gaze. "WindClan has never needed help before."

Owlfur's growl hardened. "But now you do. Has leaf-bare weakened you?"

Talltail's hackles lifted. Was the RiverClan warrior goading him? He dug his claws deep into the marshy ground. *You're outnumbered, Talltail.* Jake's voice echoed in his mind. *Are you really going to start a fight?* Warmth stirred in his chest and his fur smoothed. "WindClan is grateful for your kindness." He bowed his head low to Hailstar.

"No warrior would let a kit die, no matter the Clan." As Hailstar spoke, Barkface padded from Brambleberry's den with a thick, white root between his jaws.

"He must swallow the sap!" Brambleberry called after him.

Barkface flicked his tail, his mouth too full to answer.

Hailstar stepped forward. "Ottersplash and Rippleclaw will help you cross the river."

"We managed to get here alone," Talltail pointed out.

"You were lucky," Hailstar meowed grimly. "There are dangerous currents when rain has swollen the waters."

Talltail pushed back a growl. He hated being treated like a kit. And he suspected that the RiverClan leader was more interested in making sure they left his territory than in keeping them from drowning. But they had been given what they'd come for. That was enough. He paused as Rippleclaw pushed in front of him and led him along a winding trail through the reeds. Barkface trotted after him with Ottersplash at his heels.

At the shore, Rippleclaw stayed close to Barkface as the medicine cat waded into the water. The RiverClan warrior guided Barkface across, boosting him forward with her shoulder.

"I can swim by myself," Talltail told Ottersplash.

Ottersplash stared at him coldly. "Would you let me run through rabbit tunnels by myself?"

Talltail stiffened. Did RiverClan know about the maze of tunnels beneath WindClan? *Of course not. She's just guessing that we chase rabbits into their burrows.*

"Come on, then!" Ottersplash was already padding into the water.

Talltail braced himself as the freezing water lapped over his shoulders. He churned his paws clumsily while beside him, Ottersplash moved through the water like a snake. As he struggled to stay afloat, she glided at his side, hardly ruffling the surface. An eddy tugged him suddenly, spinning him off course. Water dragged at his paws down. The river was trying to swallow him! He thrashed in panic, jerking his head around. Where was Ottersplash? Had the river swallowed her too?

Suddenly something hard pushed against his belly. Beneath the water, a strong back steadied him while he regained his balance, then disappeared. A moment later, Ottersplash broke the surface. She blew water from her nose.

"Hailstar warned you about the currents," she murmured,

and swam close beside Talltail until they reached the shore where Barkface and Rippleclaw were shaking out their pelts.

Talltail stretched his feet down to the pebbles, relieved as he felt them underpaw, and staggered out after Ottersplash. "Thanks," he grunted.

Ottersplash shrugged. "I'm impressed a WindClan cat can swim at all."

Rippleclaw nodded along the trail toward the gorge. "We'll watch you go," he meowed. "To make sure you don't have trouble on the path. It's steep beside the gorge."

He wants to make sure we cross the border. Talltail prickled with irritation. Why was an invisible scent line so important?

"Thanks." Barkface shook the water from his fur. He dipped his head to the RiverClan warriors, the precious plant in his jaws.

Talltail swished his tail, stirring the pebbles behind. "Thanks," he grunted, and headed toward the gorge.

At the top, Barkface dropped the root at Talltail's paws. "Take this to Hawkheart as quickly as you can. You're faster than me and he'll know what to do with it."

"Okay." Talltail grabbed the root and pelted up the slope toward camp. The wind streamed through his ears, freezing the tips.

As he burst into camp and raced across the clearing, Hawkheart stuck his head out of the medicine den. "You got it!" He snatched the root from Talltail's mouth and disappeared inside. Talltail paced in a tight circle outside.

Meadowslip hurried over with her mate, Hickorynose.

Hickorynose glanced at Talltail's wet pelt. "Did you swim the river?" His eyes widened.

"It was the only way across."

Hickorynose dipped his head. "Thank you, Talltail. Your courage may have saved our kit's life." He looked past Talltail toward the medicine den.

Talltail followed his gaze. "Let's hope it works."

"I smell grouse." Dawnstripe jerked her head toward the heather. It shimmered, frost-tipped, in the early morning sunshine. Beside her, the bramble that marked the Fourtrees border still reeked with the stench of ShadowClan.

Aspenfall tasted the air, nodding. "Definitely grouse."

Plumclaw lifted her tail. "It'll make a good meal for the elders."

Talltail was impressed with how willingly the tunnelers had slipped into the role of moor runners now that all the tunnels had been blocked off. Their underground duties had given them agility and strength, traits easily turned to hunting on the moor.

Dawnstripe headed across the grass. "Perhaps Hopkit will be well enough to eat some today."

In the sunrises since Talltail and Barkface had returned from RiverClan, Hopkit had rarely been conscious. The sedge root hadn't cured him overnight, but it seemed to have slowed the infection and given the young tom a chance to fight for his life. Barkface had even reported that the swelling in his paw had begun to ease. Hopkit might yet recover.

"Talltail?" Dawnstripe's mew jolted Talltail from his thoughts. Plumclaw and Aspenfall were already nosing their way into the wide swathe of heather. "Are you coming?"

Talltail's nose twitched as he scented rabbit. "You can catch grouse without me," he told her. "I smell prey here."

"You'd rather hunt alone?" Dawnstripe narrowed her eyes, then followed her Clanmates without waiting for an answer.

Why waste four warriors on one catch? Talltail watched her tail disappear into the heather, then sniffed the grass. The ShadowClan stink from the bramble was distracting, but as he followed the faint rabbit scent along the slope to where it dipped toward the Thunderpath, it grew stronger. His mouth began to water. He'd never caught rabbit here before. Rabbits rarely strayed this far from their burrows. Halfway down the slope, he paused. Unease pricked in his pelt.

Lifting his head, he tasted the air. There was more than one rabbit scent here. There were many. Had they dug new burrows on the slope? He scanned the grass, looking for tunnel openings, but it was smooth and unbroken. Why had so many rabbits passed this way? Deep in his belly, worry churned harder.

The Thunderpath ran along the bottom of the slope. Monsters hurtled past, their roars ringing through the stone-cold air. Talltail blocked out their stench and tried to focus on the scent of rabbit. He suddenly realized it was tinged with blood. He wasn't smelling live prey; he was smelling *fresh-kill*! He padded farther down the slope, flattening his ears. His time in Twolegplace had taught him that the monsters were more noise than danger so long as he stayed clear of their path.

The blood stench sharpened as he drew closer. Perhaps rabbits were killed by monsters here. Talltail scanned the glittering, black stone of the Thunderpath. There was no sign of crow-food. Sniffing, he followed the blood scent along its edge. He slowed. He was nearing the tunnel that passed underneath the Thunderpath and joined WindClan territory to ShadowClan's border, echoing with the howls of the monsters hurtling over it. He hadn't been here in a long time. Dawnstripe had shown him the opening when he was an apprentice, but WindClan warriors rarely patrolled in this corner. There was little to hunt here, and ShadowClan scent markers didn't begin until the other side of the Thunderpath.

Curiosity pulled Talltail on. The blood scent tainted the air, stronger as he neared. He scrambled down the ditch at the edge of the Thunderpath and pushed through the long grass choking the tunnel entrance. Blood streaked the stems, and as he slid into the dank, stinking tunnel, he saw more blood frozen into the muddy water pooled at the bottom. How many rabbits had been killed and dragged through here? Talltail swallowed. ShadowClan scents hung fresh in the air.

Pelt bushing, he turned and raced up the slope. Pushing hard against the rough grass, he pelted toward the heather. "Dawnstripe!" At his call, a grouse fluttered up from the bushes. He shouldered his way in, the stems scraping his muzzle as he raced along a rabbit trail.

"What in the name of StarClan are you doing?" Dawnstripe burst out of the heather and blocked his path.

Talltail skidded to a halt. "ShadowClan has been stealing prey and taking it through the tunnel!"

Dawnstripe's pelt spiked. "Have you seen them?"

"I saw blood trails and ShadowClan scent was everywhere."

Plumclaw stormed out behind Dawnstripe. "You scared off the grouse!" Her eyes blazed.

Aspenfall barged past her. "I was about to attack."

Talltail squared his shoulders. "ShadowClan is using the tunnel under the Thunderpath to steal prey from the moor." He glared at Aspenfall. "Go and tell Heatherstar. Bring warriors. We need to re-mark the border. They have to know that if they cross it again they face a fight."

Aspenfall turned and pushed away through the heather.

"Come and see." Talltail beckoned Dawnstripe to follow as he turned and headed back toward the tunnel.

He led her down the slope, Plumclaw close behind. "Ignore the monsters," Talltail muttered as they neared the Thunderpath. "They'll stick to their path." He padded to the tunnel, pushing back the grass with a paw so that Dawnstripe could lean in and sniff the rabbit blood.

"It reeks of ShadowClan," she growled, flinching away.

Plumclaw sniffed, frowning. "How long have they been doing this?"

Dawnstripe lashed her tail. "Quite a while, by the smell of it," she hissed.

Talltail ripped the grass with his claws. "Heatherstar should keep a patrol here day and night." Rage pulsed in his paws. "ShadowClan needs to learn that WindClan doesn't give up prey without a fight."

Dawnstripe eyed him. "Wasn't it you who gave WindClan prey to RiverClan?"

Talltail bristled. "It was RiverClan's prey to begin with," he reminded her. "And they took it with *my* permission. They didn't steal while our tails were turned." He glared across the Thunderpath, blind to the monsters flashing past. "There's a difference between a starving Clan and a thieving Clan."

Plumclaw circled Dawnstripe, pelt ruffled. "How dare they—"

"Hush!" Talltail silenced her. Paw steps were thrumming through the tunnel, echoing against the stone walls.

"Attack!" A shriek ripped through the air. ShadowClan warriors streamed from the tunnel, eyes blazing with hate.

Talltail unsheathed his claws. "Invasion!"

CHAPTER 43

✿

"ShadowClan, attack!" Cedarstar yowled as he charged up the slope. Ears flat, teeth showing, he raced at Dawnstripe. Talltail hurled himself in front of her.

"I don't need your help!" she hissed, dodging around him to meet the ShadowClan leader head-on.

Paws slammed into Talltail's side. White fur blinded him as Blizzardwing knocked him off his paws and lunged for his throat. Talltail rolled. Teeth snapped at his cheek, catching his whiskers and plucking them out. Talltail scrambled to his paws, reared up, and brought his claws down on Blizzardwing's ears. Plumclaw was wrestling in the mud downslope, locked in combat with a ginger tabby. Did the tunneler have enough battle skills to fight him off? Dawnstripe shrieked with pain. Talltail whipped around. Newtspeck had joined Cedarstar. The black-and-ginger she-cat was battering Dawnstripe's muzzle while Cedarstar raked her flank with vicious claws.

"You can't save her, rabbit heart!" Blizzardwing snarled.

Talltail boiled with rage. "I'm no rabbit heart!" He dived forward, butting Blizzardwing's shoulder with such force that the ShadowClan warrior staggered backward. Talltail ducked and nipped his forepaw and the tom fell to the ground, rolling onto his back. Leaping onto him, Talltail clung to his shoulders and churned his claws against Blizzardwing's belly. He tipped his head away as Blizzardwing snapped at it, springing off before the tom could tear out more whiskers.

Plumclaw screeched with fury as a ShadowClan apprentice, Raggedpaw, joined the ginger tabby's attack. The tunneler was beating them off with a flurry of blows, but they were driving her farther down the slope, closer to the monsters thundering past. Less than a tail-length from Talltail, Cedarstar wrestled Dawnstripe onto her spine. Newtspeck nipped at her thrashing hind legs. Blood stained her muzzle.

Dawnstripe! Talltail tried to jump toward her but claws pierced his flanks and Blizzardwing dragged him back. He glanced desperately up the slope. Had Aspenfall persuaded Heatherstar to send warriors? Dawnstripe shrieked. If help didn't come soon, they'd have to retreat. Talltail turned and swiped Blizzardwing's throat, rage surging through him.

Blizzardwing staggered back, his eyes lighting with surprise as blood splashed from his white scruff. "Not bad for a WindClan cat," he hissed.

Snarling, Talltail lunged at the tom. Blizzardwing reared up on his hind paws. Talltail saw him totter, unbalanced by the slope. Twisting in the air, he aimed for the tom's unsteady hind leg and sank in his teeth. Blizzardwing yowled with rage, and curling around, bit deep into Talltail's shoulder. Pain scorched through him.

"Talltail!" Dawnstripe's panicked screech ripped through the air.

Talltail twisted away from Blizzardwing. Cedarstar loomed over Dawnstripe as she writhed on the grass. Newtspeck leaned back, her lip curling in delight. Talltail braced himself to watch the ShadowClan leader deliver the death blow. Then he felt the ground tremble beneath him. Paws were thrumming toward them across the moor. *Help is coming!* If they could just hold the ShadowClan patrol for a few moments more. Energy surged beneath Talltail's pelt. He ripped free of Blizzardwing's grip, ignoring the burning sensation of losing fur.

Familiar pelts were streaking down the slope toward them. Reedfeather hared across the grass, his limp vanishing now that his blood was up. Hareflight, Cloudrunner, Redclaw, and Shrewclaw raced at his heels. Beside Talltail, Blizzardwing's eyes stretched wide as Redclaw smashed into him, hissing. With a hefty blow, Cloudrunner sent Newtspeck staggering away from Dawnstripe while Reedfeather and Hareflight raced to help Plumclaw.

Shrewclaw glared at Cedarstar as the ShadowClan leader pinned Dawnstripe to the ground. Talltail saw hate gleam in his denmate's gaze as Shrewclaw sprang onto Cedarstar's back and dragged him off Dawnstripe. His claws sank deep. "This is for my mother! Remember Brackenwing?" Shrewclaw snarled. Jerking Cedarstar around, he slammed a hefty paw against the leader's cheek. Blood spattered the grass as Cedarstar fell. Eyes blazing, Shrewclaw lunged at him again.

Talltail stared, shocked by the savagery of Shrewclaw's

attack. *That's what revenge is.* There was nothing cold or planned about Shrewclaw's rage. In the heat of battle, it drove him like fire through bracken. This was a true warrior's battle.

Heart pounding, Talltail jumped in beside Shrewclaw, pummeling Cedarstar down as the ShadowClan leader tried to struggled free. Shrewclaw glanced in surprise at Talltail.

"I'll help you kill him," Talltail hissed.

Shrewclaw lifted his forepaws and together they swiped at the blood-spattered tom, driving him toward the Thunderpath.

"Cedarstar!" Newtspeck's yowl split the air as the tabby warrior rushed to help her leader. She dived for Shrewclaw, ears flat, lips drawn back. She sank her yellow teeth into Shrewclaw's shoulder, thrusting her paws around the WindClan warrior and hauling him off Cedarstar. Shrewclaw snarled and thrashed with his paws as he tried to reach for Cedarstar. But Redclaw had grabbed Cedarstar and was pinning him to the ground.

"Retreat!" Cedarstar fought free of Redclaw and fled for the tunnel.

At his cry, his warriors followed. As the last tail disappeared into the tunnel, Talltail heard a groan. He turned. "Shrewclaw!"

Hareflight was crouching over the WindClan warrior. Talltail raced to his side, slipping on the wet grass. He glanced down and saw his paws turn red. The wetness was blood. It pumped from Shrewclaw's belly like water from the spring. "Fetch Barkface!" he shrieked to Dawnstripe. She met his gaze, her eyes glittering with horror, then dashed up the slope.

"Hang on, Shrewclaw." Talltail leaned over his denmate, his heart twisting.

Hareflight crouched stiffly beside him. "He'll die like his mother." The warrior's mew cracked. "Killed defending the moor against ShadowClan."

"He won't die!" Talltail growled. "He can't! Not like this. It wouldn't be fair."

Life isn't fair. Jake's words rang in his ears.

Shrewclaw shuddered, another groan escaping his lips. Talltail pressed his paws against Shrewclaw's wounds. Blood ran over his fur. "It won't stop!"

"Wormcat?" Shrewclaw rasped weakly. "Avenge Bracken-wing for me."

"You can avenge her yourself!" Talltail gasped. "Don't die, Shrewclaw. There are too many battles to fight."

Shrewclaw twitched, his eyes rolling, then fell still.

Hareflight's shoulders drooped. "Shrewclaw." The word came out as a sob. Trembling, the brown warrior leaned forward and closed Shrewclaw's eyes with a soft lap of his tongue. "You were a good apprentice," he murmured. "And a great warrior. WindClan honors you."

Talltail turned away, his gaze blurring. This battle had been fought over rabbits—and now Shrewclaw was dead. Were ShadowClan's warriors so hungry they were willing to kill for stolen prey, or did their hatred for WindClan run deeper than he'd ever imagined?

CHAPTER 44

Talltail stretched, enjoying the warmth of the newleaf sun on his pelt. Beside him the heather was bright with green bud. Overhead, a blue sky stretched, cloudless, across the moor. In another half moon, the gorse would be aflame with yellow flowers.

He could hear Hopkit purring outside the medicine den as Hawkheart picked fleas from the young tom's spine. Hopkit was well enough to groom his own pelt and should have moved back to the nursery by now. His fever had healed in the moon since the battle with ShadowClan, but the nursery was overcrowded. Pigeonkit and Sorrelkit were too big to share a nest, Meadowslip was restless, and Ryestalk had just moved in, her belly swelling with the promise of new kits.

"Sit still," Hawkheart growled, cracking a flea between his teeth and spitting it onto the grass.

"Hawkheart?" Hopkit rolled lazily over. "If Heatherstar says I can't become a warrior, do you think I could be a medicine cat?"

"No." Hawkheart sat up. "You're too fidgety." He gazed across the clearing to where Barkface was making sure that Dawnstripe's battle wounds had properly healed. "Besides,

WindClan doesn't need another medicine cat."

Hopkit held up his paw. Although the infection had gone, his foot was limp and flat, and he had no feeling in it. "But how can I be a warrior with this?"

"You can walk on it, can't you?" Hawkheart wasn't giving a drop of sympathy.

"I can *limp*."

Hawkheart snorted. "If you can limp, you can walk. If you can walk, you can hunt."

"What about fighting?" Hopkit persisted. "What if I can't fight?"

"Then you'll just have to argue your enemies to death." Hawkheart settled onto his side and half closed his eyes. "You're great at arguing."

"No, I'm not."

Talltail's whiskers twitched. He wondered if Hawkheart was mellowing now that gray whiskers were showing on his muzzle. But he suspected it was Hopkit's warmth that had thawed the stern, old medicine cat.

Barkface headed across the clearing. Talltail sat up as he neared. "Is Dawnstripe okay?"

"She's fine. An extra scar on her muzzle, but it's healed cleanly." Barkface settled down beside Talltail, narrowing his eyes against the bright sun. "I'm worried about Reedfeather's shoulder, though," he mewed. "The battle made it worse and he's not getting any younger. If he strains it again, he could be lame for life."

Talltail gazed across the Meeting Hollow to where the

WindClan deputy lay beside Heatherstar, sharing a plover. Reedfeather's pale tabby pelt looked as ragged as an elder's. Talltail felt a pang of sorrow for the old warrior. He'd served his Clan loyally for moons. He deserved to be leader one day, but he'd never survive for another eight lifetimes.

The heather shivered as Palebird padded into the camp. A mouse hung from her jaws. Wrenkit looked up from where she was stalking Flykit behind the Hunting Stones. She bounded toward her mother. "Is that for us?"

Flykit chased after her, Bristlekit and Rabbitkit popping up from the grass and scrambling over the tussocks. Palebird dropped the mouse at Wrenkit's paws. Wrenkit hooked it toward her with a claw. "Don't worry, Palebird," she told her mother earnestly. "I'll make sure everyone gets a fair share."

"You're a good little warrior," Palebird purred, before heading toward Talltail.

Talltail lifted his chin. "Hello, Palebird," he meowed. "Good hunting?"

Palebird licked her lips. "Very good."

Talltail was pleased to see Palebird catching her own prey again. She seemed a lot more cheerful now that she had begun to leave the camp to hunt.

Woollytail called to her from the bracken patch. "Did you bring something back for me?"

Palebird looked at him fondly. "Catch your own prey, you old badger! I'm already feeding four mouths."

Woollytail flicked his tail happily but didn't move from his nest.

"Do you think he misses the tunnels?" Talltail asked his mother.

"Of course," Palebird meowed. "We all do. But at least I don't have to worry about cave-ins anymore."

Talltail shifted his paws. Cave-ins weren't the only danger to warriors. Life aboveground held just as many risks. Once more, Shrewclaw's death flashed in his mind. Talltail had managed to wash the young tom's blood from his paws, but he couldn't wash away the terrible memory. He tried to distract himself. "How's Ryestalk settling in?" He nodded toward the nursery.

"Fine, but it's crowded. She'll be more comfortable once Heatherstar's made Pigeonkit and Sorrelkit apprentices. They must be six moons by now. They're as big as hares."

"Is Ryestalk still grieving for Shrewclaw?" Talltail meowed.

"Of course," Palebird told him, looking surprised. "But her grief will ease once she sees his kits."

Knowing that Ryestalk carried the dead warrior's kits had given comfort to the whole Clan, and they fussed over Ryestalk like she was a precious egg waiting to hatch. The young queen had more wool in her nest than an elder, and was never alone. Lilywhisker made sure there was always someone to watch her, bringing her food whenever her belly rumbled and fetching water-soaked moss if she mentioned thirst.

Guilt flickered through Talltail. "I wish I'd fought harder," he mewed. "Shrewclaw might still be alive."

Palebird's gaze softened. "You can't save everyone, Talltail."

Outside the medicine den, Hopkit pounced lopsidedly as Hawkheart tossed a clump of moss for him to catch. Talltail straightened up, an idea flashing in his mind. "I might not succeed," he murmured. "But I can try." He trotted across the grass to the Meeting Hollow. "Heatherstar." He stopped by her side. "May I speak with you?"

Reedfeather struggled to his paws. "Should I go?"

"No," Talltail told him. Why shouldn't the WindClan deputy know what he was planning?

"What is it?" Heatherstar sat up, licking a feather from her lips.

"I'd like to be Hopkit's mentor," Talltail announced.

Heatherstar blinked. "You think he's fit enough to train?" She glanced past Talltail to the medicine den. Hopkit was chasing Hawkheart's moss bundle in spirals, springing up to bat it down with his lame paw as it flew into the air.

Talltail followed her gaze. "Don't you?"

Reedfeather shifted his paws. "He looks agile."

"He can play," Heatherstar conceded. "But can he hunt or fight? Would he be any use in battle?"

"You might as well wonder if Pigeonkit can fight," Talltail pointed out. "His legs are short. And Sorrelkit will never have the speed of Stagleap."

"Or you." Reedfeather dipped his head to Talltail.

"We all have our flaws," Talltail pressed. "But we overcome them." He suddenly thought of Jake. His friend's kittypet softness hadn't stopped him from leaping into battle with a fox. "And sometimes, it's our flaws that make us who we are."

Hopkit bounced again and again for the moss, undeterred even when he missed.

Reedfeather nodded toward the young tom. "He's Clan-born," he meowed. "What else can he be but a warrior? Would you confine him to the elders' den for life?"

Heatherstar met her deputy's gaze, then turned to Talltail. "Very well." She stretched. "Let's do it." Leaping onto Tall-rock, she called to her Clan. "Let all cats old enough to catch prey gather beneath Tallrock."

Hickorynose sat up in the bracken patch beside Woollytail. "What's going on?"

Woollytail lifted his head. "Let's find out."

"I think I know!" Hickorynose jumped out of the bracken and hurried toward the nursery, where Meadowslip was already squeezing out.

She met Hickorynose's gaze hopefully. "Is it what I think it is?"

He glanced past her. "I think so. Where are they?" As he spoke, Pigeonkit and Sorrelkit scrambled through the gorse.

"Is it time?" Pigeonkit blinked up at Heatherstar.

Hickorynose smoothed the fur tufting on his shoulder. "Yes, it is."

Sorrelkit looked at the medicine den. "What about Hop-kit?" she asked quietly. Hopkit had stopped playing and was staring wistfully up at Heatherstar on top of Tallrock.

"Your brother understands that he can't be an apprentice like you," Meadowslip told her briskly.

"I'll teach him a few hunting tricks," Hickorynose

promised. "Just because he's not an apprentice doesn't mean he'll be stuck in camp."

Talltail flicked his tail with irritation as he overheard. Why had everyone given up on Hopkit so easily? He jumped into the Meeting Hollow and sat down, ears pricked as his Clan-mates gathered around him. He'd show everyone that Hopkit would make a great warrior.

Heatherstar leaped down from Tallrock and padded to the middle of the hollow. "Sorrelkit, Pigeonkit!" she called.

Sorrelkit and Pigeonkit scrambled into the hollow and trotted over to the Clan leader.

"It's been a hard leaf-bare, with too many losses." Heath-erstar dipped her head to Ryestalk, watching hollow-eyed from the nursery. "But today WindClan has new apprentices. Pigeonpaw." She flicked her tail along the gray tom's spine. "Your mentor will be Doespring."

Doespring stepped forward looking proud and touched her nose to Pigeonpaw's head. Pigeonpaw plucked excitedly at the ground.

"This is your first apprentice, but I have no doubt you will train him well. Share your spirit and speed with him," Heath-erstar instructed Doespring. The pale brown she-cat purred with delight.

The WindClan leader turned to Sorrelkit. "Sorrelpaw, your mentor will be Stagleap."

Sorrelpaw's eyes widened as the broad-shouldered tom padded forward to greet her. Her tail twitched nervously as he touched her head.

"Don't worry, Sorrelpaw," Stagleap whispered. "You'll be a great apprentice. And I promise not to eat you."

"May you learn boldness and loyalty from him." Heatherstar's eyes shone.

"I will!" Sorrelpaw promised.

Heatherstar lifted her head and looked at the medicine den. "Hopkit, come here."

Hopkit stared back, eyes stretched wide. "Me?"

Heatherstar nodded. She caught Talltail's eye and gave a tiny flick of her tail-tip, inviting him to join her. Talltail stepped onto the sand, his heart quickening with excitement. Hopkit limped down into the hollow and hobbled toward Heatherstar.

"Welcome. Your apprentice name will be Deadpaw," Heatherstar announced.

"Deadpaw?" Meadowslip's gasp rang over the hollow. "Heatherstar, no! You can't name him because of what's wrong with him!"

Deadpaw raised his chin. "It's okay; I don't mind! I'm going to be a warrior. My paw may be dead, but the rest of me is still alive!"

"Well done, Deadpaw!" Whiteberry rasped.

Hickorynose looked thoughtful. "A name like that could trick our enemies into thinking he can't fight. You'll show them, won't you, Deadpaw?"

The little black tom nodded earnestly, and purrs of approval rippled around the Clan.

Heatherstar went on. "Your mentor will be Talltail." She

beckoned Talltail forward with a nod, but he was already hurrying across the sandy earth. "Share your sense of adventure and courage with him, Talltail."

Deadpaw pushed up his head to meet Talltail's muzzle. "I'm so glad it's you!"

"Deadpaw!"

"Sorrelpaw!"

"Pigeonpaw!"

The Clan lifted their voices, calling the names of the new apprentices.

"I'll teach you to be a great warrior," Talltail whispered in Deadpaw's ear. *I'm a mentor!* Only a few moons ago he'd been living a rogue's life far beyond the borders of the Clan. Now he was helping to make WindClan strong. Deadpaw depended on him to learn how to hunt and fight. *We'll show them. Even on three paws, you'll be able to outfight a ShadowClan warrior!* Deadpaw's purr rumbled beside him.

Talltail looked up, across the top of the heather and beyond the rolling green moor. *I wish you could see this, Jake.* His old friend would be proud to see how much he had changed. *You always said I was a warrior.* His heart swelled. *Now I truly am.*

CHAPTER 45

"Are you ready?" Barkface's eyes glowed in starlight as he paused at the entrance to the tunnel. Mothermouth loomed ahead, gaping black in the silver cliff.

Talltail nodded. "I'm ready."

The journey across the valley had been filled with memories. As he walked the same fields he'd walked so many moons before, Talltail had been swept back to the troubled curiosity of his youth. But now the boundaries that had once made him feel trapped and restless were his to protect and honor. If StarClan accepted him, he would be WindClan's leader by dawn.

Grief wrenched at his heart with sharp claws. Heatherstar's last moments had been cruel. Greencough had wracked her body, choking her savagely into an agonizing death.

"Talltail." She had beckoned him closer as she lay in her nest, heat pulsing from her flanks, her pelt clumped and stinking. Swallowing back sorrow, Talltail had crouched over her.

"Have courage, Talltail," Heatherstar had croaked. "You followed your heart once and it made you stronger. It forged a bond between you and WindClan that nothing can ever break." A cough shook her body. She didn't fight it, too weak to do anything but submit. As it released her, she dragged in a shuddering breath. "Always follow your heart, Talltail, as you did then. Let it guide you in everything you do." Her chest rattled as she struggled to breathe. "WindClan is yours now." With a rasp, she stiffened and fell still.

Barkface squeezed past Talltail and nudged Heatherstar gently with his muzzle, straightening her twisted body and curling her tail around her paws so that she looked as though she were comfortably asleep. "Mudclaw!" he called through the entrance. "Tell the Clan it's time for them to sit in vigil for their leader." He nosed Talltail to his paws and guided him from the den.

Outside, the dying sun streaked the grass red. A cold wind whistled across the heather. "We should go to the Moonstone so you can receive your lives," Barkface told him.

Talltail nodded. He could feel strength seeping back into him as he watched his Clanmates padding slowly toward Heatherstar's den. He was responsible for them now.

Onekit scampered behind Wrenflight. "Is she really dead?"

"Hush," his mother scolded. "Show some respect."

"But she'll be in StarClan!" Onekit squeaked. He gazed up at the sky as stars began to show. "Do you think she's watching us yet?"

"Come on, Talltail." Barkface flicked his tail toward the camp entrance. "If we leave now, we'll be back in time to join the vigil."

Now, at Highstones, Talltail shivered—half with cold, half

with fear—as Mothermouth yawned before him. All his life, it had seemed as if tunnels shaped his destiny. Now this one would guide him to becoming WindClan's leader. He glanced at the sky, wondering if Sandgorse was watching. Or Palebird, who'd died moons before. Squaring his shoulders, he padded into the darkness. Barkface followed, his breath billowing in the cold before the shadows swallowed it. Talltail's paws seemed to guide him without thinking, leading him along the twists and turns, as though the Moonstone drew him on.

Light glowed ahead. The moon was already shining on the Great Rock. As Talltail turned the corner, the light blinded him. Fear flashed through him. Last time he'd been here, StarClan hadn't shared anything with him. He'd been an apprentice, confused about where his path would lead, doubtful that he truly belonged in WindClan. What would his ancestors say to him now?

As he hesitated, Barkface padded past, no more than a dark shape against the dazzling rock. "It's time," he meowed, and his voice echoed around the unseen walls of the cave.

Talltail padded forward and settled beside the sparkling stone. Closing his eyes, he stretched his muzzle forward and touched the Moonstone. He twitched as the stone floor lurched beneath him, then blinked open his eyes. He was on the moor. Stars spiraled down until they sparked among the heather like silver flames becoming cats. Talltail stared, openmouthed, as countless starry pelts lined the hillside.

Mole stepped forward from the glittering ranks. "Welcome, Talltail."

Talltail gaped at him in disbelief. "You're in StarClan! But . . . but you weren't a warrior."

"I believed in StarClan." Mole looked over his shoulder at the rows of glittering cats. "And they believed in me."

"You never said anything while you were alive." Talltail didn't understand. "Why didn't you join WindClan if you believed the same as us?"

"How could I abandon my companions?" Mole asked him. "They were like kin to me." He leaned forward and touched his nose to Talltail's.

Energy surged through Talltail at once, more powerful than a gust of wind. He rocked on his paws like heather.

"With this life, I give you courage, Talltail." Mole's mew sounded through the fury. "The courage to do what you believe to be right."

Stillness enfolded him like the shadow from a bird's wings. Talltail opened his eyes. Mole was gone. "Where is he?" Talltail cried.

"He is where he belongs."

Talltail recognized his mother's voice as Palebird stepped from among her starry Clanmates. Her pelt glowed with a warm light that made Talltail's eyes ache. He narrowed them as she leaned close and touched his muzzle.

"I give you the love of a mother for her kits," she whispered.

Talltail's heart swelled, warmth surging through it. Suddenly he felt Palebird's love for him more strongly than he'd ever known before—a burning certainty that he'd never doubt again. He felt weak as she stepped away, swaying on his paws.

Palebird began to fade in front of him. *Don't go!* He felt like a kit again.

"Talltail?" A young cat padded forward, her pelt shining brighter than any star.

"Who are you?" Talltail stared at her, wondering how any kit so small could be in StarClan. Then he realized. "Finchkit!" It was his sister, as young as the day she died.

"I have watched you," she mewed. "And envied you so much for having the chance to live in WindClan."

Shame washed over Talltail. Had he really wished he had died in her place, believing that Palebird would have loved her more than she loved him? How foolish he'd been. And how wrong to be so ungrateful for the life he'd been given. "I am lucky," he agreed. "I will never waste another moment." He gazed at her. "I'm sorry that I never had a chance to know you."

"You will know me one day," she purred softly. She reached up and Talltail had to stoop to touch her nose. "I give you this life so that you may seize every opportunity that comes before you, like a rabbit waiting to be hunted. I give you the strength to act without fear or hesitation."

Excitement thrilled through every hair on Talltail's pelt, shocking in its intensity. When Finchkit pulled away, he gasped. "Thank you!" The words caught in his throat as he watched Finchkit pad away and take her place beside Palebird.

A she-cat appeared in front of him next, her sparkling pelt no more than a shimmer on the grass. Talltail blinked in surprise. Why was she so faded? A breath of wind might blow her away.

"I am Mothflight."

Talltail shifted his paws. He'd heard stories about this ancient WindClan medicine cat. "I am honored to meet you," he meowed.

Mothflight's eyes flashed. "I was once a cat just like you. I still am, even though I walk with StarClan. The only difference is that I have watched over all the generations that followed me, as you will one day."

"Did you watch me?" Talltail felt the words sharp on his tongue. There had been so many times when he felt StarClan didn't care. "You weren't there when I first came to the Moonstone."

"We were always there," Mothflight replied gently. "But you weren't ready to see us. You had to find your own path before you could walk ours." Her eyes shone even brighter than her pelt. "You did well, Talltail, and we are proud of you. And you have only just begun your journey."

Talltail blinked at her. What did she mean?

"You will discover something that will bring great change, not just for WindClan, but for all the Clans," Mothflight warned. "You must have faith in your destiny, for only then can you lead your Clan to where it truly belongs. Never forget the time you spent beyond the boundaries of your Clan. You alone know that a Clan cat can survive anywhere." She leaned forward and touched his muzzle.

Talltail's body was wracked with spasms as power jolted though him like lightning. Gritting his teeth against the pain, he barely heard Mothflight's final words. "With your fourth

life I give you a sense of adventure so that you may embrace
even the greatest challenge with determination."

He struggled to stay on his paws as the starlit cat moved
away and the surge of energy released him. Heatherstar
stepped forward. Talltail's heart leaped. She looked young
and strong, her pelt glittering and sleek, with no sign of the
illness that had taken her ninth life. She touched her muzzle
to his.

"I'm proud of you and I know you will lead WindClan well.
With this life I give you the power to judge wisely. You above
all know how to see through the clouds that trouble our Clan,
and you will always choose the best path forward." A feeling
of great joy and confidence surged through Talltail, his mind
clearing until it seemed to sparkle with the crystal purity of
the Moonstone itself.

"Woollytail!" As Heatherstar vanished, Talltail greeted
the old tunneler with a purr. How had he not seen him glittering in the shadows?

"It is good to see you again, Talltail," Woollytail meowed.
"You know how the tunnelers have shaped WindClan's his-
tory. We may not tunnel anymore, but you must never let the
skills that once protected and fed your Clan be forgotten." His
gaze pierced Talltail like sunlight. "WindClan must never be
afraid to seek out new places to shelter and to hunt. I give you
this life for honoring old traditions on behalf of the future."
His nose touched Talltail's with a spark. Talltail felt heaviness
pull him down until wisdom seemed to sit like stones in his
paws. He might struggle to carry this weight at first, but he

knew it would give him strength and clear-sightedness for all the moons to come.

As Woollytail pulled away, Talltail relished the lightness returning, which turned to joy as Dawnstripe stepped forward. He leaned forward to greet her.

"I'm so proud of you, Talltail," she meowed. "I always knew you'd be a great warrior. You were right to train as a moor runner and turn your tail on tunneling." She glanced over her shoulder. Was she flashing a triumphant look at Woollytail? Talltail's whiskers twitched. Even in StarClan, they bickered over who was best.

Dawnstripe turned back and touched his nose with her wind-cold muzzle. "With this life I give you patience. Training the young takes kindness, compassion, and forgiveness. They are small gifts, but they will be rewarded many times." Talltail felt a sense of calm wash over him with the softness of her breath on his muzzle.

"Thank you," he murmured. "For your kindness and patience and for everything you taught me. It meant a lot."

Dawnstripe's eyes sparkled as she turned away. Shrewclaw took her place.

Talltail stepped back in surprise. "Are you here to give me a life?" His old rival was the last cat he expected to see on this night. He searched Shrewclaw's dark brown pelt, looking for signs of the wounds that had killed him. But the tom's glittering fur showed no scars, only starlight.

Shrewclaw lifted his muzzle. "I know we were never friends, Wormcat."

"I'll be Worm*star* soon," Talltail corrected him with a purr.

Shrewclaw's ear twitched. "But loyalty isn't rooted in friendship. It is much stronger than that. It comes from being born and raised under the same sky, from walking the same path as our ancestors, and from sharing the warrior code." He pressed his nose to Talltail's. "With this life I commit you to upholding the warrior code, whatever challenges you might face. This is the wisdom of our ancestors, all our traditions distilled. Trust the code to lead you along the right path." Stars swirled through Talltail's mind as the life pulsed through him. He and Shrewclaw were one. Not friends. But they would fight side by side in any battle.

Shrewclaw drew away, dipping his head. Talltail took a deep breath. His paws ached from the effort of staying upright with so many lives flowing into him, and his mind was full of dizzying images. But there was one more life to come.

A broad-shouldered tom appeared, his amber gaze glowing with reflected stars. *Sandgorse!* Talltail felt his eyes glisten as he recognized his father.

"I knew you would be a great warrior, Talltail." Sandgorse's mew was thick with emotion.

"Really?" Talltail whispered.

"Really." Sandgorse's eyes shone even brighter. "You never needed to kill Sparrow to prove it."

"Didn't you want me to avenge your death?"

Sandgorse shook his head. "There was no reason for vengeance."

"So you really *did* give your life to save Sparrow?" There had always been a shadow of doubt at the back of Talltail's mind that the rogue might just have lied in a desperate effort to save his own life.

"What if I hadn't?" Sandgorse didn't move. "Would you still have killed him?"

Talltail's thoughts whirled. "I don't know." He remembered his rage so clearly it took his breath away. But he also remembered the relief when it faded, and he had saved Sparrow from the Thunderpath. He dipped his head. "I guess that whatever happened to you in the tunnel, I'm glad I didn't kill him."

"I *did* save his life, Talltail," Sandgorse told him. "Sparrow was telling the truth."

Talltail's heart seemed to shift and lighten in his chest, as though an ancient wrong had been righted. Sandgorse took a pace forward and touched his nose to Talltail's. At once stars swept down and swirled him through the night-black sky. Dizzy, he heard Sandgorse's words over the rushing of the silver wind.

"I give you this life for forgiveness. No death need ever be avenged. Forgiveness brings peace far more surely than vengeance."

Talltail felt his ruffled fur smooth, his claws retract into his pads, his breath come steadily. Mercy was his, and always would be.

"I'm sorry you had to learn the hard way, *Tallstar*," Sandgorse meowed.

Tallstar opened his eyes. Behind his father, the ranks of starry cats glowed and shimmered against the wind-stirred heather. Tallstar let his gaze rest on each cat. "I promise you all that I will lead WindClan with the fierce devotion of a father and the pure love of a mother. Nothing matters more to me than making WindClan strong so that future generations may live with dignity and peace. Every cat I have known—" He paused as Jake filled his thoughts. He pictured his old friend's green eyes glowing with pride. "Every cat I have *loved* has taught me the meaning of friendship and the unbending power of the warrior code."

Sandgorse leaned forward and lapped Tallstar's cheek with his rough, warm tongue. "I couldn't be more proud of you, Tallstar," he whispered. "Go well, lead strongly, and protect WindClan from the storms that lie ahead. For they will come, no matter what StarClan does." He took a pace back and fixed Tallstar with his gaze, brimming with love. "And there will be a kit, kin of your dearest friend, who will need your help more than he knows. Watch over him, guide his paws, for he is important to all the Clans."

Tallstar gaped at his father. *My dearest friend?* Would Jake father kits? He lifted his chin, certain in the knowledge that he would watch over any kit of Jake's as though it were his own.

Sandgorse's eyes clouded. "I can say no more, but you will know this cat when you see him. Just remember, there is no need to be afraid of every flame. Fire can bring life, warmth, new growth, as well as death."

Tallstar blinked. The vision of cats was fading in front of him, and he could see the dazzling light of the Moonstone piercing the shadows. "I will remember," he vowed. "I will always remember."

Turn the page to see what happens next
in an exclusive manga adventure...

CREATED BY
ERIN HUNTER

WRITTEN BY
DAN JOLLEY

ART BY
JAMES L. BARRY

ABOVE ALL ELSE, ONEWHISKER, WE MUST LET TALLSTAR REST AFTER THE JOURNEY.

BARKFACE. WINDCLAN'S MEDICINE CAT. EVER THE WATCHFUL EYE. HE MEANS WELL, OF COURSE, BUT...HE MAKES ME FEEL MY AGE.

ARE YOU IN PAIN, TALLSTAR? IS THERE ANYTHING I CAN GET FOR YOU?

I'M FINE, BARKFACE. JUST TIRED.

I WATCH AS BLACKSTAR, THE SHADOWCLAN LEADER, PREPARES TO ADDRESS ALL THE CLAN CATS.

FOR NOW, I AM HAPPY TO LET HIM SPEAK FOR ALL THE LEADERS...AND NOT JUST BECAUSE I NO LONGER THINK I COULD HAVE MADE THAT JUMP.

CATS OF ALL THE CLANS!

WE HAVE REACHED THE PLACE STARCLAN MEANT FOR US TO FIND, BUT WE ARE ALL TIRED AND HUNGRY.

WE WILL MAKE CAMP HERE UNTIL WE HAVE RESTED.

COME ON, TALLSTAR...

LET'S FIND YOU A COMFORTABLE PLACE TO REST.

HERE...LIE DOWN.

TRY TO GET SOME SLEEP.

YOU'RE JUST AS EXHAUSTED AS THE REST OF US, BARKFACE.

YOU SHOULD GET SOME REST TOO.

I'LL SIT WITH TALLSTAR.

"SIT WITH TALLSTAR." AM I THAT FEEBLE?

DON'T WORRY, TALLSTAR.

I'LL DEAL WITH ANY LEADERSHIP ISSUES WHILE YOU'RE RESTING.

I'M NOT DEAD YET!

FIRESTAR. ONEWHISKER. LISTEN. MUDCLAW IS A BRAVE WARRIOR...

BUT HE IS NOT THE RIGHT CAT TO LEAD WINDCLAN.

IN THESE LAST MOONS WE HAVE LEARNED THAT THE FUTURE OF OUR CLANS LIES IN FRIENDSHIP.

I WANT NO RIVALRY BETWEEN WINDCLAN AND THUNDERCLAN AFTER I AM GONE. WE MUST HAVE NO ENEMIES.

THIS WILL NOT HAPPEN IF MUDCLAW RULES THE CLAN.

I CAN STILL CHOOSE THE CAT WHO WILL LEAD WINDCLAN AFTER ME.

AND FROM THIS MOMENT... MUDCLAW IS NO LONGER DEPUTY OF WINDCLAN.

I SAY THESE WORDS... BEFORE STARCLAN. WINDCLAN MUST HAVE...A NEW DEPUTY.

ONEWHISKER.

YOU MUST LEAD THE CLAN WHEN I AM GONE.

WHAT?

TALLSTAR, NO.

I AM GLAD TO HAVE BROUGHT THE CLAN THIS FAR...

...AND TO HAVE SEEN OUR NEW HOME.

ONEWHISKER, TREAT OUR FRIENDS WELL WHEN YOU LEAD OUR CLAN.

REMEMBER EVERYTHING THUNDERCLAN HAS DONE FOR US.

TALLSTAR, I'LL DO MY BEST, BUT--

TALLSTAR...

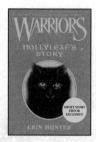

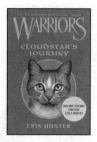

Warrior Cats Come to Life in Manga!

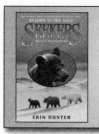